CAGE OF FIRE

PARALLEL MAGIC: BOOK ONE

EMMA L. ADAMS

To be notified when Emma L. Adams's next novel is released and get a free prequel short story, sign up to her author newsletter.

The moment when I saw the crate contained vampire chickens was when I started to question whether taking this job had been a good idea.

Tay, my best friend, wore a mirror of my own incredulity on her face when she looked at the red-eyed feathery contents of the crate that our boss, Starker, had left in the basement for us to pick up.

"He has *got* to be kidding." I moved the cloth over the cage back into place and surveyed the scrawled note on top from the boss, telling us to deliver the crate to his ally, Sketch. Not his real name, obviously, but if I were picking a badass code name, I'd have picked something more impressive. Most of Elysium's criminals were lacking in the imagination department.

"He wants us to take this thing two miles across the city?" said Tay. "Why not hire a cab instead?"

"He's a cheapskate," I responded.

Here in the Parallel, transportation was far spottier

than in the non-magical world on the other side of the nodes, with cars being a rarity and public transport non-existent. Carrier services were more of the horse-and-cart variety, and with a crate of disgruntled livestock, the odds of drawing unwanted attention were too high.

We picked up the crate between us—which emitted a loud squawk of protest—and lifted it into the air. I was the more coordinated of the two of us, so I volunteered to walk backwards while Tay steered us towards the stairs.

"Why did he hide the damn thing in the basement?" I remarked.

"Because he didn't want to be arrested for trading in illegal magical animals," she responded. "You okay to climb, Bria? I'll go slow."

"Sure."

I had a decent enough sense of balance, but climbing up a staircase backwards with a box of cargo who were *not* thrilled at their abrupt transportation took more finesse than I'd been prepared for. *Why did I sign up to this again?* Oh, right, because we were broke, and it seemed vampire chickens were in high demand. Personally, I thought the chickens had the better deal. Tay was good with animals. Our boss wasn't even good with people. The dickhead hadn't even shown up to give us a hand, instead shoving a message under the door of our shared hovel. Yet another downside to living in the Parallel: the only way to complain to the boss was to use handwritten notes or wait for him to come back from wherever he'd skived off to. It was quicker just to take the damn chickens with us, collect our payment, and be done with it.

"How did Starker even get these?" I said through

gritted teeth, sweat trickling down my spine underneath my threadbare coat.

"Don't ask me," said Tay. "He'd better have the payment ready when we get back. Did the note say where he was?"

"No, but it said, 'don't get bitten,'" I said. "Helpful. Wait, how do the chickens pass on the vampire virus, then? They don't even have teeth."

Her nose scrunched up. "I have no idea. Watch out, it's slipping."

"That's because it's heavy." Not only that, the box kept shaking and it sounded like a flock of pigeons stuck in a washing machine.

Sometimes I seriously questioned my life choices, but when life offers you nothing but a bag of crap, you could either deal with it or bury yourself alive in it. Or get pecked half to death by it, as the case may be. As we stepped over the threshold and out into the street, I halted to make sure the cloth covering the cage was firmly in place so we wouldn't end up exposing our cargo to the public. The movement jostled the pendant around my neck, a fist-sized round stone tucked into the neckline of my jacket.

"Okay, step back and to the right," said Tay. "There's a corner up ahead."

"Right." I took a careful step back then right, and we continued on our way down the street.

My arms protested at the cage's weight, while Tay's forehead furrowed in concentration as we navigated the winding streets and back alleys. At this hour of the morning, there were few people out, but the sun was high enough that the monsters stayed put. Vampire chickens aside, that is. The cage's weight pulled at our arms while its contents screamed their discontent.

It was then that I noticed the man watching me. Tall and lean, he stood at the side of the alleyway, a knowing expression on his face that made it clear he knew I knew he was watching. Which was kind of distracting, to say the least. I did my best to ignore him as we walked down the street and around a corner... to find the exact same stranger standing across from us.

Had he walked through the wall? No, he must have taken another shortcut like we had. It wasn't like I could put the cage down and check, and besides, Tay didn't seem to have noticed him. I had bigger problems than being watched by an odd stranger. It wasn't like he could possibly know what was in the crate, surely.

I continued to follow Tay's instructions and walked on, rounding another corner until the stranger vanished from sight—yet there he was, waiting at the street's end, again. This time, I knew I hadn't seen him overtake us. He caught my eye and shot me a knowing grin, as though he knew exactly what I was thinking.

"Tay," I said. "Don't panic, but I think we're being followed."

She swore under her breath. "By who?"

"This random guy. He's behind you."

"Thanks a bunch." Her steps faltered. "Does he know what's in the crate?"

"I doubt it. Also, I'm the one who has to look at him and walk backwards at the same time." I spoke in a low voice, quickening my pace until he was out of hearing distance.

She snorted. "Why, is he good-looking?"

"Who even cares?" It wasn't like I could see his face from this far off, but that knowing smirk reached me even at a distance. "I'm pretty sure he just walked through that wall, unless there's a shortcut here I don't know about."

We rounded another turning—and there he was *again*, right behind Tay. There was no mistaking it: he definitely knew he had my attention. The weird part was how he was utterly ignoring Tay, even though her vibrant red hair stood out more than my tangle of muddy brown curls. I also wore a coat which swamped my five-six form, since it had belonged to a man of at least six feet tall before I'd stolen it. My eyes were dark brown, too, and the cantrip concealed in the pendant around my neck ensured anything less than ordinary about me remained hidden.

There was no reason for someone to single me out... unless they recognised me from my previous life. And nobody who knew me from that life was any ally of mine.

I kept walking, trying to keep my breathing steady, though my hammering heart urged me to drop the damn crate and run before it was too late.

"Walked through a wall?" echoed Tay. "What, do you think he's a mage?"

"Even mages can't walk through solid objects." Elves and vampires could move at speeds which left ordinary humans in the dust, but I hadn't seen any pointed ears or fangs on him. Vampires didn't come out during the day, while elves didn't share their propensity for toying with humans and mostly wanted to be left alone. "You know, maybe we ought to—"

The man reappeared again, directly beside us. No pointed ears, no fangs, and... I could see right through him. Literally. I came to an abrupt halt.

Tay's foot caught on a raised section of pavement, and the cage's weight hit my arms all at once. Then it slid from my grasp. *Shit!*

Curses exploded from Tay as the cage hit the ground, the cloth falling aside and the door opening with a cracking sound. At once, the chickens surged to the exit in a chorus of loud squawking noises, tripping over one another in an effort to get out.

Tay dove to the ground and tipped the cage upright, trying to calm the chickens down. "What the hell was that?"

"Did you see him?" I pointed wildly, but the man had vanished, as though the chickens had finally scared him off. "The guy was right there."

"No, because I was watching the bloody cage. *Ow.*" She recoiled as one of the chickens pecked her finger viciously as it struggled out and waddled away to freedom. "I bloody *hope* the virus can't be passed on that way."

"Me too." I ran in pursuit of the chicken and caught it in both hands, careful to avoid putting my fingers near its beak. Unfortunately, by the time I got back to the cage, three more had escaped. The cage door hung from its hinges, and while Tay was attempting to tie a knot of rope to hold it together, every chicken that escaped was a stack of money we'd never see again.

Tay took the chicken from me and returned it to the cage. "I swear I didn't see anyone. What did he look like, really?"

"He looked…" *Transparent.* Which brought up a whole lot of other issues, most of which called my sanity into question. "Definitely human, but I think he was a ghost."

"A ghost." Her tone dripped with scepticism. "Not that

I don't believe you, but the dead… they don't usually look like you or me."

"Believe me, he wasn't a lich, either." Liches—shadowy ghoul-like creatures who'd once been mages—were the closest to the ghosts of actual people here in the Parallel, but as far as I knew, all of them lived in the Court of the Dead. They also left their human faces behind along with their mortality. "How many chickens escaped?"

Tay braced her arm on the cage door to close it. "Three others."

"I'll get them. You hold the cage."

I ran, putting on a burst of speed when I was sure nobody was watching, and caught up to one of the chickens at the street's end. Unfortunately, the others had run in opposite directions, and I didn't know this part of Elysium's warren of tangled streets.

I returned with the chicken in a firm grip to find Tay struggling to re-tie the makeshift knot and restrain the other residents of the cage. "Striker is going to kill us. What am I supposed to say, a creepy man appeared and then vanished in front of us? He'll think we're bullshitting."

"I'll back you up." I held out the squirming chicken, only to get pecked on my wrist for my trouble. Blood gushed out, and I dropped the chicken. "Ow!"

Shit. Would I turn into a vampire the way I would if it'd been a regular vamp who'd bitten me? I hadn't a clue, and I'd bet Striker didn't either. Cursing, I grabbed the chicken around the middle and handed it to Tay.

"Bloody menaces." Tay pushed the squirming chicken into the crate. "I think we're too late to catch the other two runaways. Look."

I followed her gaze, and my heart sank. A node gleamed in an alley nearby, a current of energy surging from the ground to the heavens. The nodes were the only possible way to travel from the Parallel to the world on the other side. A world in which most people had zero idea about anything magical, and where they wouldn't have a clue what would happen if they picked up one of the strange birds. Granted, I didn't know either, but I had to put a stop to this before London had a sudden outbreak of vampiric chickens terrorising the public.

"Wait by the cage!" I urged Tay, then ran around the corner towards the node. I *might* be able to chase them down, but if there were ordinary people out on the streets on the other side, we'd be in even deeper shit than if we stayed put.

As I stepped towards the current of energy, its brightness grew, and a scream came from Tay's direction. I wheeled on the spot, my eyes widening. The cage had burst open entirely, and the chickens fled in all directions.

"What was that?" I ran over to help her, but dodging the chickens was like trying to navigate a minefield. Worse, half of them were heading right for the node. Oh, *shit.*

"Where are you going?" she yelped.

"The node," I returned. "If we can't salvage them all, we can at least stop them flooding London."

"Who cares about that? If we get caught, we'll get arrested."

"We can't just abandon ship." We had nowhere safe to put the chickens now the cage had broken, true, but who even knew what kind of chaos they might unleash on the other side of the nodes? If they interbred with regular chickens… that was the start of a horror story there. We had to deal with them first. "Tay, can you stand here and stop any more of them from escaping through the node? I've got this."

I veered around the corner and straight into the node's path. The current of energy flooded me, blurred my surroundings, and spat me out into a dirty street drenched in rainwater. The overcast sky and grey buildings didn't look familiar, but I hadn't spent long enough on the other side to learn my way around.

Unfortunately, Tay was right. The vampire chickens had made a bid for freedom down the rainy streets of London, scattering in all directions. Nodes were the only sources of magic in this world, and to ordinary people, they were invisible… but we weren't, and neither were the vampire chickens.

"For the Elements' sakes," I muttered, unable to believe our shitty luck. Whoever that ghost guy was, I hoped he stepped on a cactus.

Tay appeared behind me. "We're too late, Bria. We should go."

"We're in trouble," I murmured. "What if someone gets infected with the vampire virus?"

"Chickens don't carry the regular vampire virus," she said. "Now, I can't say they don't carry any other potentially fatal diseases…"

"Not helping," I said. "We can't let them run loose without at least telling…"

Tay backed up a step. "Telling the Order? No need—they're already here."

Sure enough, I spotted a group of people dressed in dark clothing which looked more like it belonged to the

Parallel than the regular world. They crowded around the roadside, one of them holding a struggling chicken in his grasp.

"Guess someone was quick on the uptake." Whoever had called in the Order of the Elements—the ordinary world's go-to organisation for dealing with all magic-related drama, from megalomaniacal mages to runaway vampire chickens—surely hadn't known we'd be coming, but if we stayed here, we'd end up taking the blame for their escape.

Tay had the same idea. "C'mon. We just lost an entire payment, but it's better than getting locked up by the Order."

No kidding. As mages who didn't fit into the usual mould, we ranked high on the Order's list of potential troublemakers just by existing. Their punishments for mages who broke the laws weren't worth sticking around for. "Then it's their problem, not ours."

I stepped through the node and back into the Parallel. At once, the rain vanished, to be replaced by overcast skies and dark alleys. This realm had been created as a mirror of the world on the other side of the nodes, a long time ago, but it'd grown and developed into its own entity and it was easy to forget that everything here was a creation of the mages who'd founded the place.

Tay swore bitterly when she caught sight of the wrecked cage. "I swear someone blasted the cage open while I was holding it."

"What, the ghost?" I didn't see him anywhere. If his intention had been for us to wind up in trouble with the authorities, then he'd bloody well succeeded. "I'm not sure we should head back home yet. He might be waiting for us there."

"Screw that," she said. "If we don't go back, that shithead Striker will repossess everything we own."

She had a point there. "All right, but we're not sticking around. We'll pick up our stuff and go."

This would be the fifth hideout we'd have to abandon in as many years. One of the dubious perks of living in a city ravaged by a magical war was the number of empty houses vacated by ordinary folk fleeing the carnage, most of whom had never come back to the city or even into the Parallel at all. The previous three decades had brought little improvement, which left almost all of us worse off than the people in the world on the other side.

For some of us, though, living in the ordinary world wasn't even an option.

I walked home with Tay, trailed by guilt. Not only had we lost a major payment, I'd potentially put us on the Order's wanted list, too, though it was highly unlikely they'd ever catch either of us. In the Parallel, the regular forms of identification were non-existent, and all semblance of infrastructure had pretty much crumbled after the war.

By necessity, that also meant most of us were out for ourselves alone. Yet Tay and I had found our way to one another anyway, and we weren't about to let a shitty boss and a weird ghost cost us our friendship on top of our jobs. At least the ghost seemed to have quit tailing us, though he likely wouldn't have risked following us through the node to Earth. Without the Parallel's magic to sustain them, spirits simply disappeared. Pity I couldn't say the same for the vampire chickens.

When we rounded the corner into our street, the stranger waited for us. Silent, transparent, and hovering above the ground not five metres from our house. A faint glow surrounded his form which hadn't been obvious before. *Of course.* Now I understood. Assuming he wasn't a lich—and given the absence of a creepy dark cloak and mask, I'd guess he wasn't—he could only be a spirit mage. It'd been the spirit mages who'd started the war which had led to the Parallel's collapse. No wonder he hadn't followed us through the node. The Order would have arrested him on the spot.

Wouldn't that be a pity.

I halted. "Tay, go ahead."

"Why?" Her gaze found the transparent guy, and her eyes widened. "That's him?"

The stranger tilted his head at me, then gave a little wave. Anger surged within me. *All right. I'll handle this.* "Yeah. Stick with the plan. You go into the house and grab our stuff, and I'll deal with him."

"You can't confront him alone. He's a spirit mage."

"He's not here in person," I reminded her. "He's astral projecting. I'll send him on his way."

"All right, but you'd better not take long." She went to the house, while I kept one eye on the stranger and beckoned him to follow me. We might be on the brink of abandoning our hideout, but that didn't mean we needed to advertise it to a stranger.

A stranger... and a spirit mage. Who even was he? I'd left no traces of my former life behind when I'd arrived here in Elysium, and I hadn't known my family had had any links with the spirit mages. It made little sense for him to astral project rather than coming here in person, unless he wanted to make sure I didn't punch him in the nose or set him on fire. Which I might have done, had he been solid. I'd just have to use my words instead.

I came to a halt when we hit a dead end. "What will it take to make you go away? You cost me my job and my home, arsehole, and I have no idea who you even are."

"Vampire chickens?" he said. "You know they're highly illegal, right?"

"Yes, I do," I said. "What, did you work for the authorities when you were still alive?"

"I *am* alive." He sounded insulted. "The name's Miles."

I stepped around him. "Goodbye, Miles. Don't let the door hit you on the way out."

"I want to talk to you," Miles said. "I have a job for you, Bria."

He has a what *for me?*

"How do you know my name?" I said. "If you spoke to my boss, you'd better be ready to tell him it was your fault those damn chickens escaped."

"I assume you mean that low-life calling himself Striker," he said. "Forget him. I have something better on offer. Have you ever heard of the Spirit Agents?"

"Spirit Agents?" The name rang a bell, but it made no sense for a spirit mage to offer me employment. "I'm not a spirit mage. Besides, I have a job."

Or I had, before it'd gone up in a cloud of vampire chicken feathers.

"I know," he said. "You're a fire mage. A very good one, I'm told, though you're wasting your talents running around carrying illegally bred hybrid monsters."

I gave a shrug. "Thanks for the unwanted critique, dickhead. Now, if you don't mind—"

Footsteps sounded nearby, followed by squawking. *Oh, hell.* The authorities, it seemed, had found some of the runaway chickens… and if they came here, Miles could easily vanish and leave me to take the fall. I wouldn't be so lucky.

I backed out of the street and broke into a jog, hoping he'd get the hint this time around. Unfortunately, he floated alongside me as I ran. "Don't you dare laugh at me. It's your damn fault."

"I'm not laughing," he said. "Besides, I didn't think you'd be stupid enough to have something as illegal as vampire chickens in that crate."

"Do you think insulting me is going to convince me to take you up on your offer?" I put on a burst of speed, knowing I was moving faster than most regular people and that it wasn't wise to do so in front of him. I didn't know how much he knew of my history. Maybe nothing at all. But I would *not* end the night in a prison cell.

I couldn't run forever. Once I was sure I'd shaken off any possible tails, I backtracked and went on a winding route home. By the time I returned to the ramshackle hideout where Tay and I had made our home, I was breathless and in dire need of a nap. Instead, though, I'd have to spend the rest of the day finding a new hideout while shaking off a spirit mage who didn't know when to quit.

"Hey, Tay," I said, opening the door. "Ready to leave?"

The house was deserted. No sign of Tay, nor anyone else.

"Tay?" I left the door partially open and advanced through the hallway. "You okay?"

Cold hands brushed my neck from behind. "Hello, sweetheart. I heard you fucked up the job."

Hell. It was one of Striker's notorious vampire bodyguards. Tall and slender, he bore the pointed fangs and chilled skin of the reanimated dead.

"Striker is a lying bastard." I jerked away from his icy hands, my heart thundering against my ribcage. "He fucked up as much as I did by giving us a broken cage and then leaving us to take the heat."

"Speaking of heat," he purred, "I wonder if the House of Fire's jail still has a place for you?"

Flames sparked from my hands, causing him to step out of the way. Vampires were highly flammable, as we both knew well.

"Don't threaten me," I warned. "Where is Tay?"

I wanted to ask how he knew I'd once been an inmate of the House of Fire, but I could guess. That bastard of a spirit mage had ratted me out so that I'd have no choice but to take whatever job he wanted me to do. Unless it was Striker who'd wagged his tongue to the wrong person. It wouldn't surprise me if he had.

The vampire hissed in fury, his pale skin reflecting the flames dancing in each palm of my hand. "Put those away and I won't throw you back in the dirt like the gutter rat you are."

"You can try to hand me over to the House if you like." Flames swirled, higher, forming a barrier between me and him. "I wonder what they'll do when they find out about Striker's trade in illegally bred magical creatures?"

The vampire's eyes were flinty. "Go on. Run, and hope they don't find you."

I didn't move. "Tell me where Tay is. I'm not leaving without her."

He laughed. "That friend of yours already ran."

A likely story. My hands clenched, the fire raging higher, threatening to break from my control. "Where. Is. She?"

From behind, another cold hand reached for me, and I recoiled instinctively, my flames lurching in that direction. The second vampire dropped his hand, but the damage was done. Flames licked up his arm, and he screamed as they ate through skin and bone.

The first vamp lunged at me with inhuman speed, but my fire burned brighter than ever, catching him in its orbit, too. In seconds, the flames devoured the pair of them until nothing remained but ashes.

Oh, damn. My cover was blown, Tay was gone... and I'd just turned two of Striker's prized vampire bodyguards to ashes.

Yet Tay wouldn't have taken off on me with no warning. *They took her. Someone took her.*

"Word of advice?" Miles appeared in the doorway as though he'd been watching the whole performance from a safe distance. "Get out of here before reinforcements show up."

"You're still here?" I whirled on him. "I told you, I'm not interested in working for you. Especially if you're the one who handed Tay into the authorities."

"Who, your friend?" he said. "I was next to you while you were running away, remember? I couldn't have told tales. But if I had to guess, it was one of the people connected to the vampires you just turned to ashes."

My gaze skimmed the hallway. Tay's bag lay discarded

on the floor, as though she'd been ready to run when someone had come in here and taken her. No blood, no signs of a struggle.

Who took her? Not Striker, surely. No, he'd sent the vampires to get the both of us and bring us back so he could read us the riot act, unless he'd already had someone hand her in to the authorities.

In other words, the House of Fire.

Unfortunately, Miles was right. I needed a hiding place, desperately, or I wouldn't last out the week. And I needed allies. Because if Tay was where I thought she was, I'd never get her out of there alone.

2

I started out by grabbing what I needed from the
house. There wasn't much left, but I still filled a
backpack with the essentials, like spare clothes and
weapons.

Rule One for living in the Parallel: always be ready to
run. It wouldn't be safe to remain outside for long, but
Miles tailed me down the road as I left the hideout
behind. "You haven't asked me about my job offer."

"I declined when you cost me the job I already had."
The guy just couldn't take a hint. "And I put you on my
'never work with' list when you tipped off my boss and
got my best friend kidnapped."

"I wasn't responsible for that, but it sounds like you're
in need of a place to lie low," he said. "Come and hear me
out, and we'll figure out how to get to your friend."

"No, thanks."

My words went unheard, because he vanished into
thin air.

"Good riddance." I kept walking, more disconcerted

than relieved. Without my job and with Tay missing, I was short on allies, to say the least. The spirit mage might claim not to be responsible for her disappearance, but his sudden intrusion in my life couldn't be coincidental.

The sound of hammering footsteps sounded, then shouts rang through the streets followed by a loud series of squawks. A small feathered creature ran around the corner ahead of me, and the footsteps grew louder. Oh, hell.

I veered sideways into an alley, gripping my rucksack tight. The squawks grew quieter, and the footsteps passed me by, vanishing into another side street.

I came to a halt at the end of the street, my heart swooping downward. Three individuals waited for me, and one of them was Miles. No longer transparent, he had ashy blond hair and brown eyes, and would have been decently good-looking if he hadn't caused me so much trouble that I never wanted to set eyes on him again. His companions were a dark-haired white guy of around the same age, and a black woman with a streak of pink in her curly hair.

I turned to Miles first. "You left your body standing around in the middle of the city while you were stalking me?"

"Hardly stalking," he said. "You're welcome, by the way. I just distracted that runaway chicken so the authorities didn't catch up to you."

"You did that?" Astral projection must be a hell of a useful power. Too bad his persistence had been the reason for their escape in the first place. "Look, who even are you?"

"I thought you'd take more convincing, so I brought

some friends to wait for you," he responded. "This is Shawn, and this is Shelley. It's nice to meet you. For real, this time."

"The feeling isn't mutual," I responded. "Fuck off."

"What did you do to deserve that?" asked Shawn.

"There was a mishap with a crate full of vampire chickens," Miles told him.

"Aren't vampire chickens illegal?" asked his other companion, who must be Shelley.

"Oh, for crying out loud," I said. "What's with you people? As if you don't belong to the group of mages who started the last elemental war."

"Okay, that's unfair," Miles said. "I wasn't even born when the war started. Also, I'm not the one who was stupid enough to stick those vampire chickens in a cage."

"But it *is* your fault they escaped," I said. "Tay said someone knocked the cage open using magic."

His brows rose. "Magic? Not me. If anything, I reckon the person who put them in there was counting on them escaping so he wouldn't have to pay you."

He might have a point, given what I knew about Striker, but that didn't absolve him of his responsibility in this. "You still haven't apologised for getting my best friend kidnapped."

"Who got kidnapped?" asked Shelley.

"My best friend is missing." I gave Miles a glare. "She left her bag behind. She wouldn't have done that if she'd run away of her own free will. I swear, if any of you knows where she is—"

"We don't," said Miles. "I was hoping to speak to you alone. I didn't expect to find you with company."

"Including the vampire chickens." Shawn gave a smile that wilted when I shot him a warning look.

"You haven't even told me who you work for," I said to them. "Even if I took your word for it that you didn't cause Tay's disappearance—which I'm not inclined to—I don't have anything you're looking for."

"I beg to differ," said Miles. "As for who I work for, I'm the leader of the local Spirit Agents, and trust me, we had nothing to do with your friend's disappearance."

A likely story. Yet the three of them had me surrounded, and while I was reasonably sure I could fight my way out, what if one of them knew who'd taken Tay? If it *was* someone from my past who was responsible, the odds of these Spirit Agents being involved were slim.

"Am I supposed to know who the Spirit Agents are?" The name rang a bell somewhere in the recesses of my mind. There was no official House of Spirit like there was for the other four Elements, so they must be vigilantes, living off the grid—like me. Except that didn't explain why they could possibly want to hire me.

"Probably not," said Miles. "I'll explain later, but this job we're offering… it's kinda time-sensitive. And risky. Fair warning."

"You got me into a lot of trouble already," I told him. "I'm not here for you to throw into whatever illegal shit you're doing."

"You were already into illegal and dangerous shit, by my observation," he remarked.

"Vampire chickens usually don't *kill* people."

He looked insulted. "I don't kill people. I'm not one of the spirit mages who started the war. On account of the fact that they're all dead. Anyway, it's a fire mage whose help we need."

"And why is that?" I might be better than the average mage at wielding fire magic, but spirit mages could run circles around the rest of us and they knew it. No other type of magic compared to the ability to wield power over life and death. All I could do was set things ablaze. And people, if necessary.

"The King of the Dead is having a contest," said Shawn. "To hire a new Fire Element. We need someone to infiltrate the contest on our behalf and spy on the Court of the Dead."

My mouth parted. The Death King was hiring, was he? It was well known across the Parallel that he employed one mage from each elemental class of water, fire, air and earth, and he was rumoured to reward them handsomely for the dangerous job of guarding his extensive territory.

On the other hand, the espionage angle was not my thing. "Why do you need a spy inside the Court of the Dead?"

"The contest is one of the few times where the Court of the Dead is open to outsiders," said Miles. "The Death King himself believes an outside threat will come from among the contenders, and while he has his own security in place, there needs to be someone on the lookout for trouble who can blend in among the others."

"I'm sorry, who am I spying for?" I looked between them. "Do you work for the Death King or not?"

"We've helped him in the past," responded Miles. "And vice versa. That said, there are rumours of some kind of coup brewing in the Court of the Dead. We have reason to believe they're going to use the trials to attack the Death King—which would spell bad news for all of us."

Huh. Now I thought about it, the Court of the Dead was rumoured to be nigh impossible to break into, and it was beyond me to figure out why anyone would want to. It was nice to imagine living in a castle, but not one that sat in the middle of a stretch of swampy wasteland inhabited only by the dead. On the other hand, the Death King was also rumoured to keep more secrets inside his castle than an earth mage's treasure trove.

"We need to ensure we can back the Death King up if things get ugly in there," added Shawn. "Whether you win the trials or not, the contest only lasts for a week, and that's more than enough time for you to shake off anyone who might be chasing you. The Court of the Dead is probably the best hiding place there is."

He had a point. In the Court of the Dead, I'd officially be out of the House of Fire's reach. Nobody would be able to touch me—or Tay, once I found her. But waiting a week might be leaving it too late. I might be in desperate need of a place to stay, but she was in a worse situation than I was.

"A nice thought," I said, "but the King of the Dead will be on the lookout for spies. He rarely opens his Court, so I'm pretty sure he'll see right through my act. Besides, how am I supposed to get from here all the way to the Court of the Dead in time for these trials?"

"Slight problem," Miles said. "The trials already started this morning. You're late."

I swore. "Then why bother mentioning it?"

"Latecomers aren't disqualified," he said. "As for getting to the Court of the Dead, that's the tricky part. His castle is designed to keep out everyone, even spirit mages. There's a single node inside the castle for the Death King's own personal use. All other nodes are out of range."

"So?" Nodes covered the whole Parallel. It made sense that the Death King would have one for his own use, though rumour had it the guy could appear out of thin air without needing any external magic source. Didn't change the fact that most of us couldn't astral project miles away, let alone travel through the magic-proofed fences surrounding his territory. "How do you plan to get around that, then?"

"Because I have this." Shawn held up a gleaming disc engraved with runes. A cantrip. "Custom-made. This transporter will allow you to bypass the node's defences and get into the Death King's territory."

"Without ripping any of my limbs off?" As a rogue fire mage, caution was ranked low on my list of priorities, but that didn't mean this was a smart idea. I didn't even know who these guys were, much less trusted them with my safety. I'd never used a custom magical transporter, either. In my experience, experimental magic was a great way to lose an arm.

"If it bothers you, I'll go with you," Miles said in what sounded like it was supposed to be a soothing tone. "The transporter won't hurt you."

I bristled. "Yeah, no thanks. I'm going to find Tay, and I'll thank you not to get in my way this time."

I sidestepped Miles and the others, heading through the alley. Hell if I knew where I'd be able to lie low, but anything had to be better than risking my life on behalf of those mages.

The image of the transporter appeared in my mind's

eye. The thing must have cost a fortune. Anyone with those resources at their disposal must have others. Including, perhaps, spells for finding a missing person.

Shawn sighed behind my back. "Told you she wouldn't go for it."

"What did you expect?" said Shelley. "She worked for Striker."

I spun around. "And just what is that supposed to mean?"

"People like Striker are known for hiring the desperate," she went on. "People who wouldn't take a hand offered to them if they were hanging from a cliff."

Miles cleared his throat. "Not helping, Shelley."

"You aren't offering me a hand, you're offering me a cage of velociraptors," I said.

Miles grinned. "Or vampire chickens."

"I might be inclined to take you up on your offer if you can sort out the shitfest you left behind," I said. "Besides, you don't know anything about me."

"I know you served time in the House of Fire," said Miles. "Your friend has a similar history... and there's only one outcome if they catch you."

Two, actually. Spending the rest of my life in the House of Fire's jail was the least unpleasant of the two possible options. The second was much worse. It involved my family, and if *they* had Tay... both of us were utterly screwed.

"There's only one outcome if the Death King catches me, too," I said. "Doesn't he rip out the souls of anyone who pisses him off and conscript them into his undead lich army?"

"Well... yes," Miles admitted. "But you won't get

caught. If you've gone this long without anyone figuring out who you are, you must have some serious stealth skills."

Not really. It wasn't hard to burn bridges if you were a fire mage. "Not sure I'd say that."

The sound of raised voices came from a neighbouring street. The police were back.

"Bugger." I ran around the corner, pursued by the three spirit mages. "You know, I could turn the three of you in if you don't agree to fix this mess."

"Shit, she has a point," said Shawn. "Go on, give her the transporter. It's up to her whether to use it to get to the Court of the Dead or not."

"Does it even work?" I swore under my breath, hearing the thunder of footsteps drawing closer.

Miles pressed the disc-shaped transporter into my hand. "It does, but you need to be standing on top of a node in order to use it."

A node gleamed around the corner—at this point, my only way out. Maybe seeking refuge with the King of the Dead wasn't such a bad idea after all. I was already on the run, and I didn't *have* to commit to participating in this contest of his. All I had to do was gather allies, keep an eye out for Tay, and lie low in a place where my family would never find me. And if I actually did get the position of the Death King's official Fire Element, I'd have an army of liches at my back.

If Tay survived that long.

My hands clenched. If the enemy hadn't taken her for her own sake—and I doubted they had, because I was the real prize—they wanted to lure me in.

I'd give them what they wanted… and come with an army.

I met Miles's eyes. "If you're up for bargaining with me, then I don't come cheap."

Relief flared in his expression. "My side of the bargain? Go and compete in the trials. You can win, or you can deliberately lose at the last minute, it's all the same to me. Just keep an eye out and report back to me. What did you want in return?"

"Tay," I said. "If you know where she is and how to get her out, I want to know as soon as you do. If not, then help me find her. That's my condition."

"I don't know where she is," he said. "I would have told you if I did. I'll do my best to track her down."

"Miles," warned Shawn. "They're close."

"Another thing," I added. "I also want a guarantee that if anyone—Striker, the House of Fire, or anyone else—wants to know where I am, you won't give me away to them."

"Done." Miles stepped in behind me. "Shawn, Shelley, can you cause a diversion somewhere? I'll get her to the node."

I opened my mouth to argue, but the footsteps grew louder by the second. As the other two spirit mages hurried off, Miles and I approached the unbroken current of streaming energy, like sunlight spilling from an open door. I held out the transporter spell, eyeing the gleaming switch on the side. "And you're sure this won't blow my head off?"

"Ninety-nine percent."

Hmm.

Rule Two for living in the Parallel: do whatever is necessary to survive.

I stepped into the node's path. Then I flicked the switch on the transporter and pictured the Death King's castle in my mind's eye. I'd only seen it once before, but it was enough.

The world faded in a flash of blinding whiteness.

Pain splintered my limbs, ripples of agony spreading up my arms and legs and all over my body as though I'd trodden on an open plug socket. Light bloomed around me, then faded, and I landed in a muddy field.

"Ow!" I dropped to my knees, reeling. "Elements, that hurt."

"Nice going." Miles hovered behind me. He'd left his body behind, sparing himself the pain of the transporter. "You're in."

Water soaked my knees. I looked up through the node's glowing light to see swampland extending around me. A blocky building a few metres away hid me from sight, while the towering shape of the Death King's castle overlooked the swamplands, dark bricks standing out against the overcast sky. Bleak as hell, but less so than my future if I didn't get to the other contenders without anyone spotting me... living or dead.

A chill breeze swept through the swamp, bringing the

sound of dozens of voices interspersed with the faint crackle of flames. Or rather, fire magic. I might have made it in, but my next task would be to compete against dozens of highly trained fire mages for a position at the side of the King of the Dead's side—aka the most feared entity in the Parallel by a long mile.

Definitely having second thoughts, I crept from one bush to the next, following the sound of shouting. Earthen walls enclosed an arena at the foot of a set of stone stairs leading to the castle itself. Around the arena, the ground was totally exposed aside from a few bushes which had seen better days and scrawny trees which wouldn't hide my presence from any onlookers.

The other three Elemental Soldiers stood at intervals around the arena. *So that's them.* Each wore armoured clothing along with a cloak embossed with the Death King's symbol—a skull surrounded by the symbols of fire, earth, water and air. Not the fifth element, spirit. Even here, it seemed the other mages had hard feelings about old events.

The Air Element in particular looked quite capable of tossing someone through a window without the use of air magic, with broad shoulders and hair shaved to stubble. The Water Element, tall and dark-skinned with long curly hair and a blue-lined cape, looked almost as impressive. The Earth Element, skinny and Asian, looked the weakest of the three, but only earth magic could have created the arena itself.

That's when I noticed the other guards, dark shapes drifting around the swampland. Liches. Undead, invincible and faceless, they were as tall as humans but less substantial than an astral projecting spirit mage. Chills raced down my spine at the proximity of their lethal magic, capable of severing someone's soul with a touch. They'd definitely see me if I appeared now. I remained absolutely still, waiting for my moment and seriously regretting hiding myself in the bushes. The transporter was still clenched in my hand. After a moment's pause, I carefully slid open the stone attached to my pendant and slipped the disc inside it. Better to keep it hidden and safe in case I needed it again in the future.

I prepared to straighten upright as the liches passed out of sight, but a fourth person stepped in and joined the other three. Human, not a lich, with shoulder-length brown hair, pale skin, and a similar uniform to the Elemental Soldiers. One of the Death King's soldiers, perhaps, but not a contender. She must be a mage, to be allowed in here, but she wore no obvious signs which indicated her magic type.

Her gaze passed over my hiding spot and landed on the node. Was Miles still there? I couldn't see, and I didn't dare move in case she spotted me. Worse, she was walking this way. Fast. She reached the node, and a torrent of energy erupted into her face. I ducked my head as she flew backwards, skidding through the swampy mud. A second hit knocked her onto her back. Serve her right for sticking her nose where it didn't belong, if you asked me.

Unfortunately, the blast of light had drawn the liches' attention. They swarmed closer, a mass of shadows shaped like people, and the one at the centre turned my blood to ice.

The Death King.

He couldn't be anyone else. Despite wearing the same shadowy guise as the other liches, armoured clothing covered his body, a black cloak across his shoulders. An equally dark mask filled the gap where his face should be. More than his forbidding appearance, though, was the pure hostility which radiated from him as he surveyed the node in search of the intruder.

The woman climbed to her feet. "Hang on. Don't you want to find out who it is before you kill them?"

"There's no need. The attacker has gone."

Well, that's something. Miles had scarpered, and I was stuck in the bushes in hostile territory, trying hard not to breathe. My legs cramped, my back ached, and my feet and legs were soaked with swamp water. I hoped the arena was water-free, or else I'd be hard-pressed to access my fire magic. That would put a dampener on my plan. Ha, ha.

"Who was that?" asked the woman. "Was it a lich?"

"No," said the Death King. "It was a spirit mage."

Miles was nowhere to be seen. Worse, it seemed that the Spirit Agents had not asked the Death King's permission before sending me to spy on their behalf.

My one consolation? Dying here would be marginally better than being beaten to death by Striker's bodyguards or handed back over to the House of Fire.

A cold breeze ruffled the bushes, and a new group of transparent creatures appeared nearby. Phantoms. The liches' less intelligent cousins. *Bloody hell.*

The phantoms drifted past my hiding spot, approaching the arena. Behind the earthen wall, someone screamed. *Go on,* I thought at the woman. *Move away from the bushes so I can get out of here.*

As bursts of flame rose from behind the arena's low earthen walls, the woman and the Death King walked in that direction. The knot in my chest loosened a fraction. Not that I was particularly keen to walk into the arena while everyone was being attacked by phantoms, but they provided a handy distraction to hide my entrance. The Death King swept up the stairs towards the castle, approached the oak doors, and then vanished within.

As I prepared to leave my hiding spot, the woman turned, her eyes narrowed. Then, as the wind rustled in the leaves, she raised a palm, blasting energy into the bush that sent me flying a good five feet backwards. I skidded into a crouch in the mud. *She's a spirit mage?*

I met her gaze with as much defiance as I could muster, my heart sinking in my chest.

"Who are you?" she demanded.

"Whoa," I said. "I just got here. What's the problem?"

"Someone tried to assassinate the Death King," said the woman. "You don't happen to know anything about that, do you?"

"No, I told you." Did she mean Miles? Was that really what she thought was going on? "I'm here for the contest."

"Is that why you're avoiding the arena?" she said. "Paying a visit to someone in jail, were you?"

"No, I overslept and I was running late." She had nothing on me whatsoever. We were miles from Elysium, and nobody would know about the vampire chickens here. It seemed the large blocky building which hid the node from view must be the Death King's jail, which might be useful to remember later. "I'm not breaking any rules."

"We'll see what the Elemental Soldiers have to say to that," she said. "Are you even a fire mage?"

In answer, I conjured up a flame between my palms. At least I didn't have to lie about that part.

"Broken rules or not, you clearly have a death wish," she told me.

"I wouldn't be applying to work here if I was afraid of death." I followed her gaze to the arena as I climbed to my feet. "That's where the action is, right?"

"Yes, but you're too late," she said. "You can't just walk into the middle of—"

I did exactly that, cutting her off mid-sentence and heading to the arena. Nobody had mentioned the Death King hired spirit mages, but I wasn't about to let her hand me over to the guards. Not when I'd been through so much trouble to get myself in here. If I didn't play along with the contest, I was dead.

The woman spoke to the Air Element, who then addressed the other Elemental Soldiers. "Claims she's here for the contest, but she was hiding over there."

"Hiding, was she?" said the Earth Element. "Kick her out."

"There's no rule against latecomers being allowed in," responded the Water Element. "She's a fire mage, and we've already expelled more contenders than we'd expected to at this stage."

"How'd you get in?" asked the Air Element.

"I walked."

The Earth Element scowled. "Thinks she's funny, this one does."

"She has a name," I said. "It's Bria. I was running late. Can you give me the chance to prove myself? If I don't get through the first day, I'll be going home anyway."

"She has a point," said the Water Element. "Let her give it a try. She's not the first to show up late."

"But she'll be the last," said the Air Element in decisive tones.

A phantom drifted past, bearing down on a younger contender who looked barely out of his teens. Fire licked my palms and I shot a handful of flames at the phantom. It recoiled, hissing, its scrawny form flailing in mid-air.

"Good shot," said the Water Element. "Go on, Ryan, let her in. If she makes it to the end of the day, we can have a vote on it then."

I grinned. I was in. "Where do I leave my bag?"

"Right here." The Water Element indicated the ground beside her, and I dropped the bag there. "Also, take off that pendant. It might get damaged."

Damn. I casually looped the pendant around my neck, trying not to show my unease at the idea of leaving it behind. While its effects would remain active on me even if I wasn't touching it, it also held the transporter spell, my only way out of here.

I tucked the pendant into the inner pocket of my rucksack and entered the arena through the gap in the earthen walls. Inside, phantoms surrounded the terrified contenders. Wisps of smoke formed semi-transparent creatures with grasping, shadowy hands, and several drifted my way when they noticed my presence.

I conjured a flame to each hand. "Come on, then."

The phantoms hissed and recoiled from the flames, allowing me to make my way forward. I'd dealt with phantoms on a regular basis back home, but some of the contenders had plainly never seen them before. One girl curled up in a ball in the arena's corner, whimpering. A heavyset guy with a mullet shoved another contender into the nearest phantom's path.

"Hey, cut that out!" I headed his way, flames leaping from my palms. "Use your fire. It's not rocket science."

Flames flickered among the contenders, and gradually, the phantoms retreated, leaving us singed and bedraggled. At least the heat had dried the swamp water off my clothes.

The heavyset guy from earlier eyed me suspiciously. "You're new."

"As of about five minutes ago," I said. "I was running late. I'm Bria."

He grunted. "Sledge."

That sounded like an alias. Like the ones the House of Fire used. Was anyone from *there* here? I should have known there'd be a catch to the contest being open to everyone, but I shouldn't jump to conclusions based on a nickname.

"Nice to meet you, then." Given how quick he'd been to shove another contender into the line of fire, I doubted the feeling was mutual, but it couldn't hurt to give a decent first impression.

The contenders who'd been hiding from the phantoms climbed to their feet, while others faced the Elemental Soldiers gathering outside the arena.

"Is the goal for us to just... survive?" asked a dark-haired woman with a faint pattern of scars on her pale forehead and neck. "I mean, we aren't supposed to fight each other or anything?"

"The combat rounds will be later in the week," the Air Element called over the side of the arena. "Today, the goal is to weed out the unqualified."

"It still looks too crowded in there," added the Earth Element. "Let's see what you make of this."

The ground erupted beneath our feet. Everyone grabbed onto the arena walls or the nearest person as a series of spiky worm-like protrusions rose from the earth, jabbing at anyone who got too close.

"What the hell is that?" bellowed Sledge.

"Giant worms?" And I'd thought the vampire chickens were bad enough. I braced a hand against the nearest wall as the ground continued to buckle. "Guys, I don't think they're deadly. Just spiky."

The others didn't seem to agree. Several people had fainted. Others climbed on each other's heads to get out of the spiky worms' paths. I backed up a few steps, and a pair of jagged teeth sank into my ankle. *Okay. I take it back.* Swearing, I kicked out, conjuring fire to my hand in an attempt to drive the worm to let go. Another firm kick dislodged it.

"They won't burn!" Sledge stood surrounded by a circle of flames, but the worms kept burrowing their way inside the barrier.

"They're fireproof," said one of the others. "What crap is this?"

"They wouldn't make it easy for us, would they?" I kept both eyes on my feet as I backed up to make sure I didn't get bitten again. "They're not deadly. I think the point of this is to scare off anyone who can't handle it."

"Then why is the floor moving?" said the scarred woman.

Oh, boy. As the worms moved beneath the surface, the ground rippled as though something larger stirred beneath. A contender fell into a sizeable hole with a cry of alarm.

"Hold onto something!" I grabbed the arena wall and climbed up the side. As I clung on for dear life, several other contenders vaulted over the walls and fled. Liches drifted towards the arena to escort the quitters out.

I expected the young woman to be one of them, but instead she backed up to the wall and whipped out a pair of blades. Then, as everyone gaped at her, two worms fell, cleaved in two.

A bell rang out, and the Earth Element approached the arena, a smirk on his face. At a sharp gesture, the worms sank into the ground again, leaving the bedraggled survivors half-buried in mountains of soil.

"Give those here," said the Water Element, indicating the blades in the contender's hands. "No weapons allowed."

"All right." The girl handed over the two blades.

The Water Element tilted her head. "*All* your weapons. Go on."

With a sigh and an eye-roll, the contender retrieved no fewer than five weapons from her clothing. I arched a brow. That was impressive, given that they must have searched everyone on their way in. I liked her already.

The Air Element eyed my position perched on top of the wall. "All participants who leave the arena are disqualified."

"I haven't left the arena," I pointed to the wall beneath me. "See?"

The Air Element couldn't argue with that. The woman with the excessive knife collection shot me a grin as I hopped off the wall back into the arena, which was more of a pile of mud than anything by now. At least the worms had vanished. I picked a handful of dirt out of my hair and turned to listen to the Water Element as she addressed us.

"You have an hour-long break," she said. "There are showers next to the dorm, should you want to use them."

I didn't see much point if we were going to get buried in mud again this afternoon, but I wasn't about to complain about a reprieve—and a chance to have a proper look around the castle and talk to the other contenders.

My third rule for surviving in the Parallel: adapt to your surroundings wherever possible.

The Water Element beckoned me aside as I left the arena. "You haven't seen the dorms yet, but I took your bags there after we searched them."

"That was… generous." I translated that to mean the Elemental Soldiers had taken out anything valuable or dangerous. That's what I'd have done, anyway. Unfortunately, I had the sinking feeling that meant my pendant, too. "Anything else I should know?"

"Yes." She glanced over at the Air Element. "The others don't agree with you being given another shot, so please try not to break any more rules."

"Good to know." I was less than certain on what the rules were, but at least nobody here seemed any the wiser about the vampire chickens or the Spirit Agents.

I followed the rest of the contenders through a side door in the castle, where a long corridor lined with wooden doors awaited.

"One of these rooms will belong to the new Fire Element." Sledge gave the door on the right a shove with his hand. "It's locked."

"Move along," called the Earth Element. "That way.

And if any of you set foot in my room, you'll be fed to the worms."

At that, everyone moved down the corridor, forming a line of bedraggled, muddy contenders.

"There's only one bathroom per dorm," someone grumbled. "How are we supposed to have time to shower?"

"We aren't," said the young woman who'd brought the half-dozen knives in her clothing. "I'm starving, anyway."

I shouldered my way through to the dorms and went looking for my bag. Sharing a single row of showers between dozens of people would be a nuisance, while the dormitories were mixed and it seemed they expected us to change in front of one another. I guessed the liches didn't need to worry about modesty, being dead, while the Elemental Soldiers had their own quarters.

I found my bag beside a vacant bed where a uniform had been laid out. The dark trousers and shirt were plain but more well-made than most of the clothes I'd picked up during my time working for Striker. I lifted the bag and dug inside the pocket, my heart swooping down to my shoes. *Dammit, they took my pendant.* And with it, they'd swiped my only way out of here. They'd even emptied the pockets of my coat, and I had the sinking suspicion they'd removed anything magical the contenders had brought into the castle.

I'd need to improvise, then. I grabbed my clean clothes and then went to check out the shower. All of them were taken, so I had a quick wash in the sink and changed into the uniform, resolving to take a proper shower when the mud-wrestling portion of the contest was over and done with.

Decked out in my new uniform and feeling a little cleaner, I went looking for the cafeteria, a room filled with long tables covered in plates of sandwiches which looked like they'd been bought from a supermarket on the other side of the nodes.

"I wondered how they were going to feed us," said one of the contenders. "I mean, everyone here is dead."

"Not the Elemental Soldiers," said the woman with the scars from earlier, piling sandwiches onto her plate. "They're alive."

"Gotta be some perks to the job," said a guy with dreadlocks. "I saw the room that'll belong to the new Fire Element. Their quarters are seriously swanky, yet they expect us to sleep in these shitty little dorms?"

"It could be worse," said the woman. "At least we're not being kept in the dungeon."

"There isn't a dungeon."

"It's a big motherfucking castle, of course there's a dungeon," said Sledge. "I heard that Air Element talking about it. He—"

"They," corrected the woman. "They use gender-neutral pronouns. Anyway, the Air Element can knock your head off with one blast of magic if you're not careful. I've seen them use that power."

Sledge made a sceptical noise. "Are we expected to be that good at magic? I thought the Elemental Soldiers learned on the job."

"Who'd give them magic lessons here in the arse-end of nowhere?" She rolled her eyes.

I picked up a plate and moved into the line behind her. Given the obvious newbie nature of some of the contenders, I inferred that a fair few of them had been born on Earth and were new to the Parallel. That would explain their reaction to the phantoms. Even living in the Parallel didn't make one qualified to work for the King of the Dead, though. Admittedly, competing in the contest meant we all had a roof over our heads and decent meals lined up for the next week, which most Parallel-dwelling folk wouldn't sniff at. Pity Tay couldn't say the same. Guilt rose within me, killing my appetite, though if she were here now, she'd tell me to lie low and survive long enough to set her free. As soon as I had a spare moment, I'd go and ask the Elemental Soldiers for my pendant back—preferably without them finding out what was inside it.

I walked after the young woman to a vacant table and joined her with my meal. Might as well gain some allies before I started rocking the boat.

"Hey," I said. "I'm Bria."

"Harper," she replied. "Did anyone tell you half the contenders would be amateurs?"

"Nah, but it thins down the competition a little." I held a hand over my sandwich and used my fire magic to toast the edges. Several of the contenders gaped at me, as though they'd never considered using their magic for that purpose.

"I wouldn't give them ideas," she said in an undertone. "Someone might set the table on fire next. My brother and I have a bet on that more than half the contenders will be gone by the end of the first day, so I reckon he'll owe me."

"Probably." I dug into my sandwich, feeling a little better. At least I'd met one friendly face, though I couldn't say the same for the Elemental Soldiers. Which one of them had taken my pendant? The Air Element... or that spirit mage. That one was trouble.

Then again, I suspected she thought the same of me.

Harper and I finished our meal, at which point I excused myself and went looking for the Elemental Soldiers. When I got outside, though, I spotted a transparent figure who was definitely *not* a lich. Miles was back, and it seemed he hadn't let our close call with the liches dissuade him from coming back in. I walked towards him, casting a quick glance at the castle to make sure nobody was watching from the windows.

"What," I said, "are you doing here?"

"Just came to make sure you didn't get kicked out."

"No thanks to the stunt you pulled in the node," I said accusingly. "You hit the Death King's spirit mage in the face."

"Oops," he said. "I assumed it was one of his liches."

"I doubt he'd be thrilled if you hit one of them, either." I glanced around to make sure none of said liches were nearby. "What's going on back in Elysium?"

"Do you want the good news or the bad news?"

"Give me the bad news first." Just to get it over with.

"The authorities ransacked your house," he said. "Turns out they ambushed Striker, and he started babbling about being innocent and blaming you and your friend."

"That bastard!" I said heatedly. "He sold us out."

"The good news is, he's not off the hook," he said. "He ran, straight after they left, and was last seen fleeing through a node. Shawn told me."

"Hope they catch him," I said. "But if he didn't take Tay, someone else did. You promised to help."

"I know I did," he said. "Shawn says he thinks the House of Fire has started rounding people up without trial again, but he has this hang-up about the Houses and tends to blame them for everything."

My heart lurched. "Did Striker rat us out to the House of Fire?"

"Unless he did it before those chickens of yours escaped, it's unlikely."

"Dammit." At least Striker was an obvious target to aim at. Even the House of Fire were an enemy I could put a name to. Without anyone to point fingers at, I was left with the guy hovering in front of me... who, despite everything, had saved me from arrest. If I'd been tearing up the house looking for Tay when the authorities showed up, I'd have wound up behind bars myself. "I never asked... how'd you even know who I was?"

The question raised a series of screaming red flags. I didn't exactly hide that I was a fire mage, but as for why he'd picked me of all people to recruit as a spy? Either he'd been watching all Striker's employees, or he knew me from somewhere else.

Sure enough, he said, "Striker, of course. We figured no official members of the House of Fire would want to take time away from their posts to play spy, so we had to find someone..."

"With nothing to lose." I folded my arms across my chest. "Don't deny it. That's pretty much what your friend Shelley implied. You found out Striker employs the desperate and downtrodden and decided to 'rescue' me by costing me my job."

"I wouldn't call it a rescue, but it didn't play out the way I planned," he said. "I assumed you'd drop the job with Striker as soon as something better came along, and we had to find someone fast, before the trials kicked off. Shawn found out Striker's best fire mage was out on a job, and then we had to find a way to get your attention without your friend getting involved. It wasn't supposed to blow up the way it did."

I arched a brow. "You didn't think that enticing me away might cause the backlash to fall on Tay instead?"

He grimaced. "That's why I followed you home. I didn't count on you taking off alone."

"So it's *my* fault?" I lowered my voice in case the others overheard me in the castle. "You're not winning yourself any friends here. You claim to have asked Striker to point you in my direction and then expected him to ignore the fact that my best friend was likely to get into trouble?"

He swore under his breath. "Striker didn't know we planned to recruit you. Shawn said it wasn't even Striker he spoke to when he asked the name of the best fire mage to recruit."

"Is that supposed to make me feel any better?" I said. "You might have noticed Striker's bodyguards are vampires who can cross the city in four seconds flat. They could have tracked us down within seconds of the question being asked."

"Shawn told me he wasn't followed, and the guy is sharp," he said. "Anyway, you're pretty fast yourself."

My shoulders tensed. "I really wouldn't push me. I know you're transparent, but I can still inflict some serious pain on you when I get out of here."

Miles dug his hands in his pockets. "If I was your friend, I'd have run. All the evidence suggests that's what she did."

"She wouldn't have," I insisted. "Not without telling me first."

If she'd been taken, she might have gone through any node, fleeing to any corner of the Parallel. If she'd run, though? For all I knew, she'd been planning to return to our hideout later, when the coast was clear.

He looked over my shoulder. "You have company."

I turned around and spotted Harper heading my way. My head whipped back to Miles. "Find Tay, or I'll send a lich after you."

Harper drew closer. Her gaze wasn't on Miles, so I already knew he'd vanished. Handy, and bloody annoying, for that matter.

"Who were you talking to?" asked Harper.

"Myself," I said.

"Uh-huh." Her tone made it clear she didn't believe me, but she didn't push me for answers. "I thought you met the sprite."

"Sprite?" A nature spirit? The Death King apparently attracted all sorts. I'd already seen a few wights—reanimated skeletons riding equally skeletal horses—as well as the liches and phantoms. And then there were the mages, of course.

"Yeah," she said. "I heard a sprite works for the Death King's security team."

"That's news to me." Sprites didn't usually take sides and were often overlooked by most people, so perhaps I might be able to sway them to my side. Or at the very least, figure out how to get out of here without risking having my soul stripped out by a lich.

The other contenders had begun to come out of the castle, so I'd have to wait until later to speak to Miles again. Time to head back to the trials. The arena had been a churned-up mess when we'd left it, and the earthen walls were still flattened, while the swampy water had turned into a bog that rose up to my ankles when I walked in.

"We've already had phantoms and spiky worm monsters," I said to Harper. "What will they dream up next?"

"Don't forget the towering inferno stage," said Harper. "Wait, you weren't here at the start, were you?"

"No," I said. "What towering inferno?"

"At the start of the trials, the Elemental Soldiers set the whole arena on fire to scare off the non-fire mages."

"I did wonder how they'd ensure the contenders were fire mages and not impostors." Lucky I'd missed that part.

When all the contenders were back in the arena, the Air Element took central stage. "The second round of today's trials will now begin," they said. "A number of tokens have been hidden throughout the grounds of the castle. Your goal is to find one and bring it back to the arena. Stepping out of bounds will result in immediate disqualification."

That sounded pretty straightforward... which meant there must be a catch somewhere.

"If you ask me," said Harper, "it's so they can fix the arena after the mess those worms made of it earlier. We can't fight in a swamp."

"Fair point." I kicked mud off my shoes and waited for the signal.

At a bell's ring, I was off, and so were the others. The Air Element hadn't specified what the tokens actually looked like, which was probably deliberate. Everyone scattered through the area, digging into bushes and picking up rocks.

I went slower, figuring this was a handy way to learn my way around. The castle grounds consisted mostly of unbroken swampland, surrounding the castle on all sides. Aside from the arena, the only two landmarks were the gleaming node—currently guarded by two shadowy liches—and the smaller building I'd seen near the node earlier. Another pair of liches guarded the door around the back of the building.

"That's the jail, right?" I muttered to Harper.

"Yep," she whispered back. "They say nobody stays in there long."

"Because they get executed and turned into liches," I said. "I've heard the rumours."

I hadn't seen the Death King himself since his return to the castle following our near-miss by the node, which to be honest, was something of a relief. Once he showed his face, I'd be hard-pressed to figure out a way to escape without the transporter spell. Not that I had many ideas. Cloaked liches guarded every inch of the gate near the arena, while the fences surrounding the castle were too smooth and tall to climb.

Spotting a glint of light near the bushes, I crouched down and unearthed a small silver coin. *Hello, a token.* As I picked it up, I heard a commotion nearby. Sledge and another contender wrestled one another over another coin.

"Hey, I got it first!" Flames sparked from his hands, and the other guy's shoes caught fire.

"Ow!" The young man hopped up and down, cursing in agony, and Sledge took the opportunity to grab the coin from him. I glanced towards the Elemental Soldiers, but none of them had moved an inch. Wasn't that against the rules?

"Hey!" said the guy with dreadlocks, clearly agreeing. "You cheated."

"Shut the hell up." Sledge lumbered over, but the contender he'd set on fire blocked his way. Punches flew left and right, and within seconds, the Elemental Soldiers ran over, the Air Element taking the lead and raising their hands. A bolt of air shot from their hands, and Sledge and the others flew backwards as though knocked aside by a speeding cart.

"Damn," I said to the Air Element. "Nice one."

They grunted. Not prepared to meet on friendly terms, then. Still, nobody ever said I didn't try. If I wanted to be in with a shot of surviving this, I could do worse than try to befriend the people in charge.

4

My plan didn't exactly go as intended. Not only did the Elemental Soldiers remain distant and unfriendly, but when I tried to engage any of the liches in conversation, they ignored me, too. I knew for a fact that liches weren't incapable of speech, despite their faceless mask-like appearance, so presumably they'd been ordered not to talk to the contenders.

So much for sending one to beat the shit out of Miles.

At the end of the day, we returned to the dorms, where the Air Element called everyone to attention. "There are spare uniforms for you on the beds. If you have any problems, ask one of us."

"I have a problem," said Sledge, picking up the grey outfit nearest to him. "This looks like a prison uniform."

The Air Element shrugged. "If you want to find someone who gives a crap, you're going to be looking for a long time. Alternatively, you can try directing your complaints to the Death King and see how that goes for you."

The uniform wasn't exactly as fancy as the Elemental Soldiers' gear, but at least no more of my clothes would fall victim to the swamp. Lucky, because all I had was my single bag of possessions. After double-checking the pendant wasn't in there, I waylaid the Air Element by the door. "Did you confiscate anything from my bag?"

"Anything magical will have been taken," they responded. "We don't want anyone having an unfair advantage. You'll get it back when you leave the trials… or if you win."

If you asked me, my magical skills would be more of an advantage than any device I brought in, but I wasn't about to start an argument in front of an audience. If the Elemental Soldiers found out how I'd sneaked in, then I'd be booted out of the contest and they'd probably keep the transporter spell for their own.

"Okay, as long as I get it back later," I said. "I don't have much more with me than the clothes on my back."

The Air Element made a noise that sounded more disdainful than sympathetic, and walked away, leaving me alone in the entryway. I walked back into the dorm, shaking my head, and sat down on my bed.

"You okay?" asked Harper, two beds over. "Did they take your weapons as well?"

I grunted. "Bloody Elements. They live in luxury and they still had to swipe all our stuff."

"They took my cantrips as well as my weapons," she said. "Dick move, but I can understand why. That Sledge cheated a dozen times without any magic being involved."

"Unless you count lighting people's shoes on fire."

The guy was trouble, yet he'd been allowed to stay, and so had I. For now, at least. The Elemental Soldiers didn't seem to suspect I'd sneaked in with the aid of a group of spirit mages who'd claimed to be the Death King's allies and yet sent me to spy on his potential future Fire Elements.

You'd think his own security team would be enough to deter any potential mischief-makers, but the Death King didn't exactly seem to be keeping an eye on us. Unless he had security cameras here, Earth-style. He might. As someone who was possibly the richest person in the Parallel, living or dead, he could afford it.

After the Elemental Soldiers called us to dinner, I waited for the dorm to empty before searching under the beds and in every corner, but I found no traces of any cameras. No hidden magical traps, either. That they'd taken everyone's cantrips as well as mine was a massive nuisance, because I could have 'borrowed' one from, say, Sledge, and used it to explore the castle overnight without getting caught.

The Elemental Soldiers must have put our confiscated contraband somewhere, right? Assuming one of them hadn't taken it for themselves, anyway. Breaking into their rooms was pretty much a non-starter, but tonight, I'd have a look around the castle and see if I could find another way out of this place.

The Elemental Soldiers patrolled the corridor until after most of the dorm had dozed off, but I couldn't sleep. Not because of Sledge's snoring on the other side of the room, but the sense of guilt over Tay's absence hammered at the inside of my mind and made it impossible to relax. I kept my clothes on, too, but my chances at escape during full darkness were not high. With all the lights off in the castle and no artificial lighting outside at all, how was I supposed to spot an oncoming lich when I couldn't even see my own hand in front of my face?

Dammit, I need that transporter spell back.

When I was sure the footsteps had faded from the corridor outside, I slipped out of bed and tiptoed to the door, easing it open as quietly as I could before exiting into the dark corridor. The right-hand path led to the Elemental Soldiers' rooms and then to the grounds, but to the left lay the rest of the castle, which was mostly a mystery to me. The other liches presumably lived somewhere in there, but it wasn't like they needed to sleep. It was time to familiarise myself with the rest of the castle, so I turned left, finding myself in a draughty corridor, and spotted the Air Element walking through a wooden door. Holding my breath, I remained out of sight until the door closed behind them. Then I trod closer, listening out.

A familiar cold voice spoke, turning my blood to water. "What is it?"

"I wanted to talk to you about a contender who showed up late," the Air Element responded. "We found her hiding in the bushes after we already fished out everyone who sneaked in with the first group. Liv thinks she should be disqualified."

Dammit. If this Liv was who I thought it was, it seemed the spirit mage hadn't given up her vendetta after all, and now the Elemental Soldiers had decided to take the matter straight to the Death King. If he'd found out that

I'd sneaked in through the node as a spy, I'd be lucky if he didn't rip out my soul on the spot.

"Is this candidate the one who started the brawl earlier?" asked the Death King.

"No," they responded. "That was Sledge."

"Tell Olivia that unless this candidate has done something else to warrant being disqualified, then she is to leave it alone."

Thanks, Death King. Plainly, the guy didn't want to get involved in any disputes among the contenders, which worked in my favour.

"I will, Sir," said the Air Element. "It's unlikely that someone with little discipline will survive until the final round, regardless."

Hey! Bloody cheek. Not that I planned to stick around, but there was something odd about the Spirit Agents' stealth mission which went beyond the half-cocked way they'd gone about it. What did they want me to find in here?

"Do as you like," said the Death King. "And please do not disturb me again."

The door creaked, warning me of the Air Element's return. Grabbing the nearest door handle, I pushed it inwards and instead felt a vigorous shock jolt through my nerve endings. Every hair on my body stood on end, and I let go with a hiss of pain.

"What," said the Air Element, "are you doing out here?"

Oh, hell. I forced my chattering teeth apart. "Got lost. What in hell was that?"

They eyed the door. "Trying to break into the storeroom, were you?"

"I didn't know what was in there," I protested. "I heard footsteps and I panicked."

The storeroom, huh? Was this the room where the Elemental Soldiers had stashed my pendant? If so, they'd taken great pains to ensure nobody would break in. My gaze went back to the smooth wood, and I spotted the gleam of a cantrip wedged into the door frame. An improvised piece of security, but it worked. My skin was still tingling all over.

The Air Element's eyes narrowed. "What were you looking for?"

"The bathroom," I lied. "Then I heard you say my name and got curious. Are you going to kick me out?"

"My boss has decided to give you another chance," they responded. "It's not up to me. And if you were thinking of stealing anything from the storeroom, you can forget it."

Busted. "It's not the cantrips I want. That pendant I was wearing is valuable to me. I don't want it to get stolen."

"It's less likely to get stolen here than in the dormitory." They pointed over my shoulder. "Go back, before I change my mind about giving you another chance."

I hesitated for a moment. "Why does that spirit mage work for the Death King? I didn't know he employed other mages aside from the Elemental Soldiers."

The Air Element's frown didn't budge. "That's between the two of them. Go on."

I backed around the corner to the dorm, caution telling me that getting booted out of the contest in the middle of the night would not be a smart idea. Phantoms and other beasts lurked in the swampland, and the only safe place in the area was, ironically, behind the walls of this very castle. The liches guarded all the ways in and out of the grounds, night and day, so there was no chance of making a quick trip outside. Once I was out, I was out.

The Air Element left me outside the dorm and walked back through the doors into the main part of the castle. I heard their footsteps retreat, and a rush of recklessness seized me. Once I was alone, I walked swiftly past the dorm in the other direction, past the Elemental Soldiers' quarters, and tried the door to the quarters of the future Fire Element.

I didn't expect the door to be unlocked, but it swung inwards, revealing a dark sitting room. *Hey, this is pretty swanky.* Certainly by the Parallel's standards, anyway. I closed the door behind me, admiring the leather sofa and polished wooden furniture... and the transparent figure on the other side of the room.

I jumped violently, fire leaping to my palms and revealing the figure wasn't a lich, but one of the three spirit mages I'd met earlier. Shawn, the third member of Miles's contingent.

"What the hell are you doing in here?" I gasped.

"I could ask you the same question," he responded.

"Excuse me? You asked me to spy on the Death King." I let the fire die down a little, glad I'd closed the door behind me first. "Now his Elemental Soldiers have confiscated my only way out."

His brows rose. "They took the transporter?"

"I hid it inside a pendant," I explained. "They don't know it's in there, but they confiscated every cantrip or other magical object the candidates were carrying and stuck them in a booby-trapped room."

"Shit," he said. "That throws a wrench in things."

"You're telling me," I said. "What're you doing in the Fire Element's quarters?"

"Having a look around," he responded. "Astral projecting here is a pain, but it's my only way in."

"Why here, though?" I asked. "What do you expect to find?"

"There are rumours the Death King covered up the real reason his last Fire Element got kicked out," he said. "I wanted to find out the truth."

"First I've heard." I switched on the light and gave the room another scan. I spotted a bathroom through a side door and a kitchen at the far end. Nothing appeared out of place, but I'd assumed the former Fire Element had taken his possessions with him when he'd left the castle. "I thought you wanted me to spy on the contest so you and your mates could back the Death King up against a potential incursion."

"That's what Miles says," he said, "but I think there's something more than an impending coup going on. Can you open that drawer there?"

I moved over to the desk he indicated and pulled open the top drawer. Nothing was inside it. "What're you looking for?"

"I don't know." Frustration underlaid his voice. "The last guy—Davies—vanished off the face of the earth after he lost the job as Fire Element. I think the Death King wants someone else to take his place to stop people talking about why he really kicked him out."

"So?" I tried the next drawer, spotting a scrap of paper wedged down the side. On it were several inexplicable scribbles. "Can you read this? It's worse than trying to decipher one of Striker's notes."

The reminder of Tay made a fist of guilt clench around my chest. My gaze panned over the scrawled words on the paper. I picked out the word 'cantrip', the word 'mage', and the word 'Arcadia'.

Shawn peered at the page. "Looks like an address, I think."

"In Arcadia." The text had smudged and faded, so I conjured a flame to my hand to illuminate the last part. The note was signed, *Flare*. A code name, I'd guess.

"Damn," he muttered. "If that's his handwriting, it means the last Fire Element was meeting with a vigilante behind the Death King's back."

"He's not here anymore," I reminded him. "If the Fire Element *was* conspiring with someone from outside, the Death King already caught him at it."

"And hid it from everyone else," added Shawn. "Including his potential replacements."

"I don't get it." I lowered my hand. "I'm not keeping this note, though. The Elemental Soldiers will think it implies that *I'm* involved with whoever that Flare person is."

"Sounds like a fire mage."

"You think?"

He shot me a sideways look. "I don't want to be here either, you know. I'm just convinced there's something more going on."

"Yeah, good luck with it," I said. "I'm going to get the transporter back and then get the hell out. Also, thanks a bunch for getting me on Striker's hit list."

His mouth parted. "Miles told you that?"

"He said you're the one who got me on Striker's radar as a troublemaker by asking about me," I said. "And it's clear you didn't think through the potential implications either."

"Wait," he said. "Bria, I know we didn't tell you everything, but we weren't counting on you being on the run from the authorities before you got in here."

"Or them taking my friend captive," I added. "Which wouldn't have happened if you hadn't drawn their attention to me."

"I don't think it was the authorities," he said.

"What makes you say that?"

His gaze was steady. "Bria, I know you're mad at me, but think about it. Was your bolt hole ransacked when you got back?"

"Well… no." Actually, Tay had left her bag behind. Which, now I thought about it, indicated the person who'd took her hadn't been inside the house when they'd grabbed her. "But I haven't been back since."

"I have," he said. "Her bag was gone, but everything else was still in the same place."

"Her bag was gone?" Dammit, I should have brought it with me, though she needed it more than I did, and plenty of Tay's possessions wouldn't have survived the Elemental Soldiers' purge either. "Did you see who took it?"

"Maybe one of Striker's people, maybe the authorities, maybe Tay herself." His gaze shadowed. "I swear none of us intended this to happen—"

"Spare me," I interjected. "I'm getting out of here. I don't care if I have to live on the run, but there are places I can hide which aren't stuck behind a wall of liches."

Problem was, I was pretty much out of allies and short

on resources. I'd walked out of the House of Fire's prison once before, but not with another person in tow. Assuming that's where Tay was, and not… somewhere else.

"What kind of defences are on the room where they put the transporter spell?" he asked. "I'd help you get in, only I can't open regular doors, let alone booby-trapped ones."

"Which is why you need me, I know," I said. "I was under the impression you had a whole stash of magical weapons. Like that transporter."

"That was one of a kind," he said. "We're lucky the authorities didn't catch us after you ran."

"Miles gave me the only one you had?" Nice of him. Part of me kind of regretted getting mad at him earlier. Ultimately, I was the one who'd chosen to leap headfirst into this crap. "Where'd you get it, anyway?"

"Ask Miles," he said. "I bet the Death King has more resources than we do, but he doesn't like sharing."

That, I could believe. "What resources?"

"I wouldn't consider stealing from him if I were you," he said. "He's been an ally to the Spirit Agents in the past, but word says he's losing his grip on his territory and that makes him dangerous. And his loyal Elemental Soldiers, of course. They likely know everything he says and does and would do anything to protect him."

I thought back to his interactions with the Air Element. I hadn't got that impression from their brief conversation, but it was hard to draw any conclusions when I knew so little about any of them.

"I doubt it would endear me to him if I admitted you sent me in here as a spy," I said. "Clearly, you and your fellow spirit mages *can* get into the castle yourselves, which made this farce completely unnecessary."

"There are some places that are out of bounds even for spirit mages," he said.

"Like where?" I asked.

"The hall of souls."

I frowned at him. "You mean the place the Death King's liches keep their soul amulets? Why would you want to get in there?"

In order to become immortal warriors, liches took part in a ritual which involved binding their own soul to a magical amulet. As long as their soul remained bound to another vessel, they could be killed a million times and never truly die. If a soul amulet was destroyed, it was the one sure-fire way to kill a lich, but I couldn't think of another practical use for one of them. Certainly nothing worth risking the Death King's wrath over.

He glanced over his shoulder. "There's a rumour going around... a rumour that someone tried to break in there recently."

I made a sceptical noise. "I doubt that would end well."

"The thing is, I think it's true," he pressed on. "The Death King—hell, the entire Court of the Dead is committed to a cover-up, and I think that contest of his is hiding some shady crap that has the potential to make trouble for the lot of us."

I turned this over in my mind. "You mean I'm not the only spy."

"Unlikely," he said. "I mean, you might have gathered that it's usually impossible to get inside the castle."

"To do what, though?" The Death King was pretty much invincible. "I thought the Death King stayed out of most conflicts in the Parallel. Who'd have a grudge against him?"

"A lot of people," he said. "Did you know he's a supporter of the Houses of the Elements? A lot of people aren't happy about that."

That was news to me. "But he's *your* ally."

"Supposedly." He pulled a face. "According to Miles, but the two of them were friends before he decided to turn himself into a lich."

"What?" That couldn't be right. The Death King stood apart from the rest of the magical world. He might have been a mage while he was still alive—spirit mages made the strongest liches—but that didn't mean he, or Miles for that matter, supported the shitheads who'd captured Tay. Right?

"Look, it's dangerous for me to be telling you this, but I want you to know the truth," he said. "The Death King left the Spirit Agents behind a long time ago. He doesn't give a shit about any of us. He won his position by slaughtering mages and conscripting them into his army. He's well aware of the Houses' habit of incarcerating mages, but he doesn't care."

"You know, you're not doing a great job of convincing me to stay here," I said. "I'd walk out right now if the swamp wasn't crawling with monsters."

"Don't you want to know what fate the last Fire Element ended up facing?" he asked. "It shouldn't be hard for you to get that information. The Elemental Soldiers would expect you to be curious about your predecessor."

Fair point, though the other rumours worried me. The magical community at large had come down heavily on mages over the elemental war, even here in the Parallel.

That the Death King didn't give a crap wasn't a huge surprise. To most people, the Houses were a necessary evil. And compared to my previous life, the House of Fire's jail cell had been like a nice holiday at a luxury hotel.

"I can ask, but Tay might be in serious trouble," I said. "Also, everyone here is so hellbent on cheating that the odds of me making it through to the next round of the contest are debatable even if I try to stay in."

"Cheating, huh?" he said. "Maybe one of them will be up for helping you break into that storeroom and steal back the transporter. I'm sure you can think of a way to get past the security if you put your minds together."

Good point. I *could* recruit someone else to help out. Maybe Sledge would be up for it, though I didn't see that guy as being much use in the stealth department. Harper, though? I might be able to convince her.

"All right, but I expect a decent update on Tay's location tomorrow."

"Look for me in the morning," he said. "I'll try to get Miles to come along, too, but he has a habit of taking matters into his own hands lately."

"Sure." I might not have entirely made my mind up on where I stood with the Spirit Agents' plan, but I was stuck here for now. The least I could do was figure out if any of the other contenders were spies, too.

5

———

Unsurprisingly, I didn't sleep much for the remainder of the night. Shawn's words circled my thoughts like a vulture hovering over a carcass. Was the Death King seriously in league with the House of Fire? Had he really been Miles's friend? Well, that part would be easy enough to check, but it didn't change the fact that the castle had more secrets than a thief's treasure trove. Nor that I'd wandered into something that might link straight back to the past I'd tried to escape.

Somehow, no matter where I went, I always ended up running for my life even when standing still.

I woke at the first sound of movement from the other contenders. I dragged myself to the shower before they got too busy, then dressed in my new uniform, wishing I had my pendant back. The dorm was too crowded to approach Harper yet, so I waited until we both headed to breakfast and claimed an empty table.

"I saw you sneak out last night," she said in a low voice. "What for?"

"My cantrips," I muttered back. "I know where they hid the stuff they confiscated from us, but the door is rigged with a security cantrip and I couldn't get in without being electrocuted."

I figured I'd start with her, and then if two of couldn't figure out a way in between us, we could recruit some of the others. The more people who knew our plan, the higher the risk of being caught, though. If all else failed, I could plead guilty and hope they didn't lock me up for it. Sledge and the others had done far more egregious shit yesterday and hadn't been arrested or conscripted into the liches' army.

"Hmm." She was silent for a moment. "I know a way to disable a security spell, but it needs a steady hand. And I need to know what type."

"I can check."

"What do you have in there, anyway?" she queried.

"Something I'd rather didn't get stolen," I whispered. "They didn't just confiscate cantrips, they swiped our valuables, too. You don't have to get involved, but I figured two heads were better than one."

"You aren't wrong," she said. "Okay, I'm in."

Sorted. Once I had the transporter back, I'd be free to leave here on my own terms. It wouldn't hurt to have a look at the other confiscated cantrips, too. If the Spirit Agents didn't have as big a hoard to share as I'd initially assumed, I'd get my hands on as many spells as possible that would allow me to go after whichever scumbag had taken Tay.

Firstly, I needed to see if the door was rigged with any other traps, and plan accordingly.

I took my chance to head down the corridor to the storeroom when the others were on their way to the arena. With a casual stride, I found my way to the door and gave it a nudge with my foot. Locked, of course. I knew how to pick a lock, but I'd need to disable that cantrip first.

I peered through the gap in the door at the cantrip wedged there. Definitely a handmade job. Not something you could disable without magic, but I had a few ideas.

The murmur of voices caught my ear. With careful steps, I followed the noise around a corner, and halted out of sight when I spotted the Earth and Water Elements talking to one another.

"I realise he thinks we have it under control, but what happens if one of Davies's allies comes back?" said the Water Element. "Why did he decide now was the perfect time to go swanning off and leave us to run the show?"

Who did they mean? Surely not the Death King?

"Because we do have it under control," responded the Earth Element. "It's only a group of fire mages who can't hold a candle to any of us. Stop nit-picking."

"I'm not," the Water Element replied. "You know perfectly well that half those contenders are out to make trouble for us. I don't care if the boss planned it that way—we can't be in five places at once."

"Let it go," said the Earth Element in a bored voice. "Look at what happened with Davies. The boss had it under control."

"Please don't say that in front of Ryan. They nearly died."

I backed up, my mind whirling. Had they implied the Death King had left them to handle the contenders alone —and that he was perfectly aware that some of them weren't who they seemed to be? Did they include me in that number? Maybe. It seemed the Elemental Soldiers were less than thrilled at being left in charge of the trials, but it did leave me wondering whether this whole setup was an elaborate trap on behalf of the King of the Dead.

As the voices became louder, I headed back to the dorms, almost colliding with someone coming the other way—a certain spirit mage. *Dammit.* Of all the people to run into. Worse, the Air Element was with her, too.

"He actually let you stay?" Liv asked. I assumed she meant the Death King.

"Oh, it's you," I said, attempting a casual tone. "Turns out I performed well enough in the rest of the tasks yesterday to be worthy of a place in the trials."

Liv wore an expression which suggested she thought I was talking utter crap.

The Air Element shifted towards the doors. "I'll go and catch up to the others. Don't forget you have to be outside in ten minutes… that includes you, Bria."

"That's your name?" Liv said. "Bria?"

"Yeah, why?" I gave her a challenging stare, wondering who'd shoved a stake up her arse. Maybe working for the Death King wasn't all fun and games. Or maybe she was still pissed off at me about how I'd got int the contest after sneaking in behind her back.

"Some mages use aliases." Her gaze followed Ryan as they left the corridor, and then the two of us were alone together. I tensed. She wasn't about to attack me, was she?

"C'mon. You have to join the others. What're you doing alone in here, anyway?"

"Forgot my coat," I lied. "Then I got lost. This place should come with a map."

"The Death King doesn't normally have visitors," said Liv. "As you may have gathered."

Was that an invitation to ask questions? Hey, it was worth a shot.

"What's it like?" I asked. "Working for him?"

I didn't expect a response, but she paused for an instant before saying, "A trial. Don't tell him I said that."

Huh. Maybe she was trying to undo the mistrust she'd evoked herself when she'd been so damn rude to me. Then again, she might be trying to probe me for information instead.

Two could play at that game. "I can see why it would be. I haven't met the man himself yet. What's he like?"

No need to let on that I'd seen him talking to his Elemental Soldiers the previous day. She must know I'd witnessed their tussle with Miles through the node from the bushes, but that didn't really count.

"Dangerous," came her response. "I mean, he's an immortal lich lord who's been in power longer than I've been alive, and then some."

That, I knew not to be true. The guy had come to power a decade ago... which would make his former alliance with Miles and the Spirit Agents plausible.

I told her so, and she reacted with genuine surprise she tried her best to conceal. Weird, but maybe she hadn't grown up here in the Parallel, despite her clothing and her obvious knowledge of the castle. How, then, had she earned this job?

"I guess if you don't live here in the Parallel, you might have missed it," I said to her.

I'd hoped to give her an opening, but she didn't take the bait. I told her I wanted the job for the pay, to see her reaction, but she didn't seem surprised.

"Pay isn't everything," she said. "There are risks, too. But I guess you knew that."

"Meaning, the risk of getting killed by a phantom?" I said. "Oh, that's old school. We get them everywhere back home."

"Do you get liches, too?"

An interesting question. "Nah, they're all conscripted into the Death King's army, aren't they? They can't turn on us."

She hesitated. "Actually, there have been a few incidents recently. It's why I'm here."

That, I hadn't expected. Some of the liches had turned on their master, had they? "Really?"

"Just giving you a head's up," she said. "In case you end up getting the job without anyone telling you."

"Thanks for the reminder, then." I turned to the door Ryan had gone through. "Is that the way out?"

"Yeah, we should head outside before we're late."

She was definitely probing me for information, but she'd inadvertently given me a major clue about the Death King's reasons for holding a contest for a new Fire Element. After all, if the liches had turned on their master, perhaps the Fire Element had, too.

The question was, where had he ended up? Locked up in jail, or turned into a lich himself?

Liv and I walked out of the exit and towards the arena, where I found Harper and the other contenders. I couldn't tell her what I'd found out while we were surrounded, but I could at least confirm one suspicion.

"Hey," I said to her. "I have a question… what was the last Fire Element's name?"

"The last Fire Element?" said Harper. "Davies, I heard. Why?"

I thought so. So that's who the Elemental Soldiers were talking about. They were worried the last Fire Element was going to come back here, along with his allies, and… and do what? Attack the castle? Take us all hostage? Kill his former master? Shawn was right to be suspicious about the situation in here, but the Elemental Soldiers must know they couldn't keep the truth under wraps forever.

My gaze panned across the grounds and pinpointed Miles hovering a safe distance away with his hands in his pockets. He gave me a wave, and I narrowed my eyes right back. Now was not the time for me to get distracted.

I had a trial to win… and a castle full of secrets to unearth.

6

―――――

"The goals of today's trials," Ryan told us, "are to test your ability to improvise and act on your quick thinking to solve problems. Everyone who isn't in the contest, I'd advise you to get out of range."

That didn't sound promising. The other Elemental Soldiers, along with Liv, climbed the castle steps until they stood at a safe distance away. The Air Element, meanwhile, approached the arena, hands raised.

A sudden whirlwind whipped over our heads, knocking most of the contenders off their feet. I hit the ground beside Harper and rolled upright only to be knocked down again. The others weren't having much luck, either, except for Sledge, but it would take a steamroller to knock that guy down.

I looked up, dazed, seeing a number of baskets floating towards the arena courtesy of the Air Element's magic. The baskets halted in the air above our heads.

"Your task is to catch as many discs as possible," they

said. "Everyone takes one basket. *One* basket, Sledge, not five."

Sledge dropped a handful of baskets with a scowl. Meanwhile, everyone leapt to their feet, grabbing for the baskets before the Air Element's magic swept them away. My fingers closed on the edge of a basket and I held it protectively to my chest as the wind kicked up again.

"What're those?" someone asked.

I looked up, squinting at the disc-like objects soaring towards us. Cantrips? Sledge was the first to catch one in his meaty fist.

"It's blank," he announced.

Not cantrips, then. Wouldn't want us to use magic, would they?

In seconds, the air was thick with flying discs. Everyone jumped into the air, grabbing as many discs as possible. The shorter among us were at a disadvantage, in theory, but Harper compensated by climbing up someone's back to grab discs while he struggled to dislodge her. Ryan, seeing, directed a current of energy at her, knocking her flat on her back. The Air Element looked positively thrilled to be able to use their power to its full extent. *Nice to see someone's getting some amusement out of our misfortune.*

Before long, things got ugly. Sledge took every opportunity to swipe a disc from anyone who stood still for too long, while he resisted the wind's attempts to knock him over better than any of the rest of us. I moved among the others, basket in hand, but someone always seemed to be in my way every time I got within reach of a disc. Harper's new method was to hide behind the other contenders to protect her stash. That might work out for her, assuming Sledge didn't knock her flat on her face first.

As for me? I decided to go with another approach. I found a corner of the arena as far from Sledge as possible, and I waited, watching the air. The swirling currents of the whirlwind must follow a certain pattern, because even a mage as powerful as the Air Element needed a certain level of control to keep the wind from inadvertently tearing up half the Death King's territory.

As a disc flew overhead, I watched, counting seconds until the next one came along. Twenty seconds passed between each disc. Perfect.

Every twenty seconds, I jumped and caught a disc, and soon enough, my basket was full to overflowing. When the wind came to a halt, a bell rang out. I remained still with my basket piled high behind my back, until the others stopped grabbing for the remaining discs.

Liv stood on the bottom step near the castle. I caught her eye and shot her a grin. She looked suspiciously back, but it wasn't like I'd broken the rules.

"That's enough," said the Air Element, lowering their hands. The wind died down and the remaining discs bounced into the mud. "Who has the most discs?"

Sledge elbowed his way to the front and dropped the basket, revealing his treasure trove. "Did I win?"

"Nope." Stifling a grin, I stepped aside and revealed my own haul. "I did."

Now Liv definitely looked suspicious, but it was Sledge who looked the most disgruntled when he saw the number of cantrips I'd collected. The other contenders showed off their spoils, most of which they'd hung onto by hiding in their clothing or in their shoes. I, meanwhile, wedged my basket between my feet to be sure nobody tried to swipe them before they'd even been counted.

It was at that point that I realised the coins *were* cantrips, but unmarked ones, like spares from the market. They might not be capable of magic on their own, but if someone applied the right tools, they could be. I casually slipped a couple of the discs into my pockets and then handed the others to the Elemental Soldiers.

"The next trial will take place in the dungeon," said the Water Element. "Come with me."

So there was a dungeon, after all. Maybe this was where the Death King would finally make a public appearance. It was about time he did, though perhaps he'd planned to save it for the final day. Just to lull us into a false sense of security. Who the hell knew?

While the other Elemental Soldiers retreated into the castle via the oak doors at the top of the stone staircase, the Water Element led us around the back, past the dormitories and through the corridor I'd been in earlier today. Then we headed down a winding staircase which led into a vast hall, presumably the dungeon. It contained nothing but a layer of sand covering the stone floor and was as cold as a refrigerator.

The sand clearly hadn't always been there, but nobody offered an explanation as we filed into the room and assembled below a stone balcony. Liv and the Elemental Soldiers gathered on the balcony, and the Water Element moved to the front of their group.

Once we were all inside, a loud grating noise filled the dungeon, echoing off the high ceilings as a slab of stone moved into place, blocking the staircase we'd come in through. *That... doesn't look good.*

"Your test is to find a way out of here," said the Water Element. "Don't bother trying the stairs over here. They're barred. And so is the way you came in."

No shit. But how were we supposed to get out? Sledge, genius that he was, walked over to the wall and punched it, then bellowed with pain.

I rolled my eyes and turned to Harper. "Do you think he'll try climbing it next?"

A gasp rose from among the others as the Water Element raised her hands, sending a current of water sweeping across the floor. At once, the fire inside me shrank to a spark. *That's not good at all.*

The sand vanished below our feet as the water kept on coming, sweeping higher and higher. First to ankle-height, then up to my knees, then my waist. Shock and alarm rippled through the crowd, and more than a few people made for the doors and attempted to shove the block of stone aside. It didn't budge an inch.

I tilted my head to the balcony, and anger flared inside me to see the smirk on the Earth Element's face. He thought it was funny that we'd had our magic snuffed out, did he? Within a few seconds, I had to tread water to keep from being submerged. Sledge was okay, being six-and-a-half feet tall, but the shorter among us found ourselves treading water, not very well. Some of us hadn't even learned to swim.

The water finally stopped at my neck, and the panic gradually died down among the contenders as the ones with their heads still comfortably above the surface started looking around for a way out. The odds of us using our magic to get out were less than zero, but they couldn't have given us an impossible challenge, so there must be a way through.

Someone jabbed a finger into the air, pointing at a section of the wall opposite us which glimmered around the edges, hiding a magically concealed door. *Thanks for helping us all out, mate.*

The first contender to reach the door grabbed the edge, but nothing happened. She pushed the brick as though hoping it would reveal a hidden passageway, but that didn't work either. Others caught her up, surrounded her, and tried climbing the wall. Sledge gave it a punch, with predictable results.

Harper, who'd dived under the water, resurfaced with a gasp. "There's something hidden under the sand!"

"There's a keyhole!" someone shouted.

Aha. So that's how they expected us to get out. Problem was, the key was out of my reach already as the crowd converged on the spot Harper had pointed out.

Sledge grabbed the girl who'd found the door and shoved her under the water. "Go on, grab the damn thing."

"Hey, stop that!" I shouted at him.

The Air Element had already spotted him. With a blast of air, they knocked Sledge flat on his back into the water. The others backed off as a wave crashed over their heads, then he stuck his head out and clambered to his feet. "Spoilsport."

One of the contenders surfaced and their fist rose into the air, holding up the gleaming key. At once, everyone swam for the doors, only to be knocked aside by the Air Element's magic. These people had no survival instincts, that was their problem. I waited for the inevitable rush to die down and saw the girl with the key manage to get it into the lock. The doorway opened, revealing a small corridor. She sprang through the gap, but when someone tried to follow, the door closed, knocking everyone back into the water.

Damn. Surely there couldn't be only one way out. This was only the second day of the trials. There must be more keys hidden in here. Which probably meant we all had to dive under the water and get one.

Rule two for living in the Parallel... do whatever is necessary to survive. I drew in a deep breath and plunged beneath the surface of the water, scanning the floor for any signs of another hidden key but seeing nothing but people's legs and murky sand. I surfaced, noting that I wasn't the only one who'd figured out that they might have hidden more than one key. Hands stirred the sand, and more gleaming lights appeared as other keys were unearthed. Sledge shoved the others aside and did his best to wrestle any key that the others got from their hands, but the combined efforts of the rest of the crowd kept him from getting his paws on one. Punches flew left and right, blood streamed through the water, and each time someone escaped, everyone lost their shit.

"There can't be enough keys for all of us down here," said Harper, sounding panicked. "I bet this is how they eliminate a bunch of us from the contest."

There aren't enough keys. Bastards. I shot Liv and the others a glare from below. I couldn't be kicked out at this stage. No way in hell.

As a shorter dude dove through the exit, Sledge grabbed him from behind, and once again, the Air Element's magic forced him to let go. He fell back in the water with a splash that took half of us along with it.

Coughing and spluttering, I surfaced, no longer able to feel the sand beneath my feet. That wasn't a good sign.

The water was rising again.

I kicked out, treading water, but I could count on one hand the number of times I'd been swimming and none of those times had been by choice. If I wasn't careful, I'd be in real trouble. *Where's that bloody key?*

I dove down to look as panic brewed within the crowd. After several frantic seconds, I kicked my way to the surface and sucked in a painful breath, and my heart jump-started when I realised my feet were no longer within reach of the bottom.

"We're all going to die!" someone yelled.

"I'm gonna kill those Elements!" bellowed Sledge.

"It isn't them." None of them had used magic, and even the Water Element looked shocked as the currents surged higher, higher. People panicked, screamed, kicked one another, and generally hastened their own demise. I held my breath and dove down once again to search the sand, but no key appeared. Worse, the next time I surfaced, the door was totally submerged.

Oh, hell.

A loud splash and a scream prompted me to look up—no, across—to the balcony, where a wave had swept the Elemental Soldiers into the water. Liv, too. I might have laughed at the irony, but at this rate, all of us would drown before we got out.

I dove again, and under the water, I spotted a transparent figure hovering nearby. A Spirit Agent? Had someone come to give me a hand? It was about damn time. Wait. They were too small to be a person.

A... sprite?

My lungs screamed for air, but a sudden blast rocked the water around me. The doors burst open, and the current escaped in a flood that propelled me out of the dungeon. I landed in a heap halfway up the stairs, coughing up water, shivering uncontrollably. *That was a close one.*

I climbed to my feet, but the tide surged from the dungeon at my feet, carrying me up the stairs and into the corridor above. I half-swam, half-scrambled across the bare stone, drenched to the skin and still coughing as though I had half an ocean lodged in my lungs.

If we were expected to use our fire magic in the day's trials, mine would be out of commission for a while. It also looked as though the whole castle had flooded. Which would have concerned me if I didn't know most of the staff didn't need to breathe. *It's all right for some people.*

The question was, did the person who'd flooded the place know that? Had they been trying to kill off the competition… or had the Death King been the intended target?

I climbed to my feet, coughing, and staggered through puddles of water. Now would be the perfect time to break into the storeroom, assuming that hadn't flooded, too. But I saw no signs of Harper among the other contenders, most of whom lay sprawled in the corridor, stunned and soaking wet. Judging by the Elemental Soldiers' evident surprise, they hadn't seen this coming either.

I trod down the corridor towards the storeroom, then halted when a glinting light caught my eye. A transparent figure, hovering out of sight.

I approached it. "Hey. Who are you?"

"Bria?" Harper stuck her head out of an alcove. Her

wet hair was plastered to her face, and the brief flicker in her gaze towards the sprite told me everything I needed to know.

Shock rooted me to the spot. "That's a water sprite. Was the flood *your* fault?"

The sprite recoiled, and Harper shot me a pleading look. "I can explain."

"People might have died."

She flinched. "I wasn't trying to kill anyone."

"Uh-huh." I arched a brow. "Going to tell the Death King?"

"No!" she said. "He'll kill me, and then… and then I'll lose everything. It's not just me whose life depends on me staying in the game."

Her words hit me in the core. She was trying to protect someone, just like I was.

"If you wanted to win the contest, you might have tried something a little more subtle."

She shook her head. "It wasn't supposed to go that way. I have… I have a cantrip that boosts my magic. I didn't know it'd affect hers, too."

"You told me you didn't have any cantrips, though," I said. "They were confiscated."

She fidgeted. "I used it before I came in here. I figured they'd probably take my weapons off me, and I wanted to guarantee my victory."

"Right." Dammit. While part of me wanted to leave her to deal with the consequences of her ill-conceived plan, her words had hit on a sore point, and I had the sneaking suspicion it wasn't the Death King whose retribution she feared. "Why do you want to win so badly?"

"I just need to get the job, that's all," she whispered.

"I'm indebted to someone dangerous, and I'm still safer here than out there even if they find out it was me."

"Indebted to whom?" Suspicion gripped me like a vice. "You're not from Arcadia, are you?"

She shook her head. "No. As for who… you've probably heard the name."

The House of Fire. They owned her, somehow, and she'd come here to escape them.

Ah, crap. Why had I picked her as my confidant? I'd wanted to *avoid* the House. *If they have Tay, you're involved no matter what.* I might have managed to cut all ties with my background, but not everyone else would have. Even in here.

"Look," I said in a low voice. "I think I might know who you're indebted to, but trust me, it's not worth doing shit they ask in the hopes that they might spare your life."

"It's not just me who's involved in this," she muttered.

"Family?" I guessed. "Do you really think this job will guarantee their safety? Why are you here, then?"

"Because it's my only way out."

Didn't that sound familiar. We'd already made an arrangement, but if I were sensible, I'd back out now. I'd get the transporter back, with or without her help.

"Please," said Harper. "I didn't mean to harm anyone. I'll help you get into the storeroom, and I won't do anything else like that again."

Dammit. "Look, I'm trying to protect someone, too. I get it. I want to help you, but I'm in deep enough crap already."

Now I sounded like a complete arsehole. Okay, she'd flooded the entire castle and risked bringing the wrath of the Death King down on the pair of us if the Elemental

Soldiers had caught on to our friendship, but I'd be a hypocrite to call her out for bending the rules, considering she at least wanted to be here.

She blinked, hard. "I understand."

"Wait." The word came out before I could quite consider my plan. "I'm still planning to get into that storeroom. But I think you should run your next scheme past me first before you start screwing around with magical cantrips. Deal?"

She shot me a faint smile. "Okay."

I might be ready to leave, but I could at least give her a shot at winning in my place. She might have cheated, but who hadn't?

"We'd better go back before they catch us alone here and draw their own conclusions."

She nodded, walking alongside me until we found ourselves in another damp corridor where the Air Element was helping revive some of the contenders. An equally damp Liv looked directly at me, as though she thought... no, she knew, I had something to hide.

She didn't know how right she was.

Harper and I joined the others, as nonchalant as we could possibly be, considering the circumstances. I couldn't help thinking I'd made a mistake in not turning her in, because she could easily drag me down with her.

Then again, wasn't that what I wanted? To get the hell out of here and back to Tay?

The Air Element, still soaking wet, addressed all of us. "Everyone, get into the main hall. Cal, can you get some heating cantrips to dry them off?"

The Earth Element muttered something unfavourable under his breath. *God forbid he help us stay alive.* Everyone was soaked through and miserable, but we all dutifully trailed into the main hall. I watched the Earth Element walk across to an oak door and push it open, presumably fetching the cantrips to dry us off. So the Death King did have his own private collection. *Hmm.* I'd bet they wouldn't be watching that room as closely for thieves as the place where they'd stashed our confiscated belongings.

Liv reached the front of the hall, climbing onto the dais which I assumed belonged to the Death King.

"Hey!" she said. "Excuse me. I want to talk to you."

The murmurs among the crowd faded to silence.

"One of the people in this room is responsible for this recent act of sabotage," said Liv. "If anyone would like to make a confession, now is the time to do it."

Shockingly, nobody stepped forward.

"Your choice, then," said Liv. "All of you are going to be questioned by myself or one of the Death King's Elemental Soldiers. If any of you saw anything that might point to who did this, then you can tell us that information in confidence and it won't be held against you."

"Wait, who are you?" said Harper. "You're not an Elemental Soldier."

"I'm head of security," Liv told her. "And I think you're up first. None of you is to leave this hall until everyone has been questioned."

I could only assume the Death King had given her permission to question all of us, unless she was acting behind his back. I mean, he hadn't come in here to yell at us in person, so perhaps he wasn't even in the castle at all. Which made this the perfect time to break into the storeroom.

Liv climbed down from the dais to speak to the Air Element, who then beckoned someone to follow them into one of the side rooms. I, meanwhile, sat down on the damp stone floor with the others and tried to stop shivering. My gaze travelled around the hall, from one closed door to the next, until my attention came to a halt at a door of dark metal, sitting at the right-hand side of the entrance.

Is that the hall of souls? The metal door, engraved with symbols and radiating power, must lead somewhere important. A faint shape hovered in front of it, vaguely humanoid. A sprite. Not Harper's, judging by the orange glow around his shadowy form. *A fire sprite.*

A sprite was the guard? If anything, I'd have thought the Death King would have given the job to his liches, but Liv's warning about the liches possibly betraying their master came back to me. Maybe he didn't trust them after all. Sprites were strange beings, made of pure magic and rumoured to be as intelligent as humans were, but that was about as much as I knew about them.

The Earth Element emerged from the storeroom and started handing cantrips out among the crowd. I took one and the dampness vanished from my clothes, while I finally stopped shivering. I made a mental note of the room's location for later. It wasn't even locked.

"Bria," said Harper. "You're in next."

Liv stood in the doorway and beckoned me to follow her into the room. I drew in a breath, put on a smile, and did so.

The room she'd picked out resembled a small library or perhaps a rich person's living room. Bookshelves lined one wall, while several plush armchairs filled the space within. I sank into one of them, trying my best to keep my expression neutral. Bored, even, and confident in not being caught. After all, she had nothing on me. I hadn't started the flood, though if she'd seen me talking to Harper, that might cause her to assume we'd been working together. But I didn't think she had. She was just naturally suspicious of me.

She asked me the questions I'd expected, like if I'd seen anything out of place during the trial or if I knew someone else who might be involved. Lying was easy enough, as long as I mixed in enough truths to round out my answers. She also seemed to think it'd been a deliberate act of sabotage aimed at the Death King.

"I assume whoever did it doesn't know liches can't drown, in that case," I commented.

"Perhaps," she said. "Or maybe they were trying to cover up another crime."

"A conspiracy theory." I gave a smile. "I like it. Is your job always this exciting?"

"I'm just here as head of security for the week, so I can't speak to how it usually is. You might find it dull."

I sincerely doubted so. Also, it surprised me that someone who clearly had little experience with the castle had been given a position of authority the way she had. I hadn't seen any other spirit mages on the Death King's staff. She wasn't one of the Spirit Agents, I was sure, which implied she was either a rogue or new to magic entirely. *Even more interesting.*

"Steady work is hard to find," I said. "Guess you probably know that, being a spirit mage. Work is hard to come by when people think you'll set their place of business on fire. I imagine the threat of ripping someone's soul out is a similar deterrent."

A brief flash of panic tightened her face. Her tone, however, was calm. "You might say that. Do you know many other spirit mages, then?"

"Not personally," I replied. "Ever heard of the Spirit

Agents?"

"No…" She paused. "Who are they?"

So she doesn't know. "They're, like, vigilantes."

"They are?" she said. "Whereabouts are they based?"

It was my turn to blink in surprise. "Well, if I knew, I wouldn't broadcast it."

If she wasn't with the Spirit Agents, then who had sent her here? Unless she'd come in search of other spirit mages, but this didn't strike me as the place to look. For living ones, not dead ones, anyway.

She wasn't from *Earth,* was she? In most places on the other side of the nodes, spirit magic was punishable by death or at the very least a long jail sentence. In the UK, it was, anyway. Kind of odd, given that it'd been the Parallel which had suffered the most damage from the war, but the Order of the Elements hadn't wanted to take any chances. A blanket ban had been unanimously agreed on, and that was that. Though it did explain why Liv had wanted to come here of all places, if she'd had to pick between here or death at the hands of the Order. Not much of a choice, really.

Whatever the case, if Liv didn't know anything, I was wasting my time when I could be figuring out my next move. "Should I send the next person in?"

She barred my way when I tried to leave the room. "If I wanted to learn more about the Spirit Agents, who would I ask? I'm here working as the Death King's security, and I need to know if there is any possibility these people might be a threat to the contest."

Damn, she must be desperate. As much trouble as the Spirit Agents had caused me, however, I didn't think they'd intended to harm anyone in the castle.

"Nah, they're not here in Arcadia," I told her. "I haven't heard any mention of them since I arrived here. I reckon the vampires keep them away."

"So you don't know anyone I can talk to about rogue spirit mages who might target the contest?" she pressed on. "I don't know how much you know about recent events…"

"Nothing, probably. I've been off the grid." I should never have brought up the Spirit Agents to begin with, though it surprised me how little the Death King seemed to have told her. Maybe it shouldn't have, considering what I'd heard from his Elemental Soldiers about him leaving them to hold the fort alone.

"A spirit mage attacked the contest yesterday but escaped through the node," she explained "It's why I reacted as I did when I found you."

She means Miles. I stifled a laugh. Miles had been trying to divert her attention from me, not attack her, and she'd apparently invented a whole conspiracy theory from that. "That explains a lot. I don't know about any spirit mages who might have reason to target the contest. It wasn't one of them who flooded the place, I wouldn't think."

She gave a nod. "All right. That does help. I'm asking these questions because this is going to be a major issue for the person who wins the trials and becomes the next Fire Element, and they're going to have to work with all of us to keep the Court of the Dead safe from outside attackers. Anything you can tell me, I'd be grateful."

Hmm. She seemed sincere enough, but she'd willingly signed up to work with the King of the Dead. She must have some idea about what threats were likeliest to stand in our way.

"The Spirit Agents aren't local, but if you want to know more about the local mage groups, I'd start out with the Houses of the Elements. There'll be a branch in Arcadia, no doubt."

She must know the Houses… though if she didn't live here in the Parallel, maybe she didn't. at least it'd take her attention off me.

Liv didn't ask any more questions, so I left the room, hoping I hadn't made a huge mistake in telling her anything at all. If the Death King had gone walkabout, that meant the only living people in the castle were right here in the hall, and unless the liches roamed the place without their master, most of the castle must be deserted. Including the storeroom. As I walked back to join the other contenders, I let my gaze drift in the direction of the room the Earth Element had vacated. Not only had he left the door unlocked, nobody else seemed to have noticed the place existed at all.

I returned to Harper's side. "Hey. Can you make sure nobody looks in my direction for two minutes?"

"Sure. What's the plan?"

"Someone left a door open," I muttered. "I want to make sure nobody sees me go in."

Harper rose to her feet and walked across the hall to the door leading into the main corridor. Then she opened it. Water surged into the hall, soaking everyone nearby.

"Idiot!" someone yelled.

"Sorry!" Harper said. "I thought we could leave."

As the others looked in her direction, I darted into the storeroom and closed the door behind me.

Row after row of gleaming golden cantrips greeted me, so many that I could have sold the lot and bought myself a manor house. Half of them I didn't even know the use for, while others would have cost me six months of hauling vampire chickens around for Striker to pay for.

I stared for a moment, taking it all in, then selected a few cantrips I might need. Invisibility would make getting into the other storeroom easier. There were unlocking spells, but nothing to disable an already active spell like the one wedged in the doorway of the other room, so I'd need to improvise. I didn't know every cantrip—each one was marked with different symbols depending on its use —but some tools for carving spells lay on a separate shelf, and I picked up a couple of them, too. They'd come in handy if I found someone with the skills to use it on one of the blank cantrips I'd sneaked into my pocket.

I picked up my stolen contraband, stashing the cantrips carefully into my pockets so that they didn't fall out and give the game away. Then I took out the invisibility spell first. When I flicked the switch on the side of the coin, my body vanished from sight. I returned to the hall, still invisible. The clamour of the other contenders ensured nobody heard my footsteps, so I risked a wander closer to the hall of souls. The room appeared to be locked and bolted thoroughly, while despite the ruckus from among the contenders, the sprite hadn't moved from his spot guarding the door. He floated in mid-air, a bored expression on his pointy little face.

He must have some secret skills if he'd been hired as a security guard, but I wouldn't be getting through that door in a hurry. Instead, I went to hide my contraband and to prepare for my next move.

I trod quietly down the corridor, where the Water Element was using her magic to drive the floodwater away from the dorms. She was too close to the storeroom for me to risk sneaking over for a look, so I headed outside to find a quiet corner in which to check my stolen cantrips. After finding a spot out of sight of the windows, I withdrew each cantrip individually to examine them. I'd grabbed a handful at random near the end, and now I looked closer, some of them bore other markings aside from the runes which gave them their power. On the back, a familiar insignia marked the corner which made a chill race down my back.

It can't be theirs. My family was nowhere near here. But why would the Death King have a cantrip with their mark carved into it? Maybe he'd taken them into his possession without knowing who'd created them. Or maybe… maybe he wasn't who I thought he was.

My gaze travelled towards the node, where I spotted a transparent figure hovering there. Shawn.

I made sure to turn off the invisibility cantrip before going to speak to him. He gave me a nod, and we circled the castle to the back, out of sight of the windows—not that anyone was looking out of them. Even the liches had sensibly left the castle to avoid being caught in the flood.

"Did something happen in there?" he said.

"Another contender accidentally flooded the place," I said. "Not me, but I did get the chance to have a look around and steal some cantrips from the Death King's personal collection while they were distracted. Now I just need to wait for the Elemental Soldiers to clear out of the corridor and I'll be able to get to the transporter from the storeroom."

"Oh, good," he said. "Have you learned anything useful so far?"

"The last Fire Element betrayed the Death King," I said. "His people tried to cover it up, and they think he might come back and attack them."

"Interesting."

"You knew," I surmised. "Right?"

"I figured as much," he said. "From the note we found in his room, it sounds like he was communicating with someone outside of the castle. Most of the time, the Elemental Soldiers keep to themselves."

"Well, now they're having to dry out the place instead of watching the trials," I said.

He laughed. "If someone wanted to get you the day off, then they succeeded."

"Yeah, they did." I doubted that was Harper's intention, but I'd bet I wasn't the only person out to take advantage. "Where's Miles, anyway?"

"Why, did you want to talk to him?" His voice held a faint edge of annoyance.

"He promised to help me find Tay, that's all," I said. "Then again, so did you. Any news?"

"No," he said. "It sounds like your ex-boss has run out of town, but when we eavesdropped on the authorities to figure out who they might have hauled in recently, we found no mention of a lone mage."

"She's a practitioner, not a mage." Not officially, anyway.

Unless they'd found out about her gift.

He frowned. "Then why would you think the House of Fire had her?"

"They have… a history." But it wasn't my secret to share. "Striker's a cowardly shit. When I have the transporter, I'll go back and wring his neck. I'm sure he knows where she went."

"Tell you what, once you have that thing back, you can come into Arcadia and meet us there," he said. "We'll figure out how to find your friend. The other Spirit Agents and I have made a temporary base inside the Citadel of the Elements."

"Seriously?" I couldn't think of a less likely place to meet up than one of the Parallel's haunted towers, abandoned after the war three decades prior. "Weird choice of hideout."

"You'd be surprised," he said.

Hiding in plain sight. My kind of strategy. With the transporter in hand, I'd be able to leave the castle anytime I wanted to. Technically, I could use the cantrips I'd stolen to turn invisible and slip through the gates right now, but I wasn't a hundred percent certain the liches wouldn't be able to sense me anyway. Besides, I'd offered to help Harper, and even with my new cantrips at the ready, I needed backup if it turned out the House of Fire or worse had taken Tay captive.

"I've never been to Arcadia," I told him. "Would I have to walk on foot? Because this swamp goes on for miles."

"I'll take you on a shortcut through the nodes," he said. "I'll meet you outside the gate at eleven tonight."

Later than I'd like, but I'd have time to prepare and to help Harper so I could leave the castle with a clear conscience. "Sure."

He nodded. "Just… be careful you don't get caught."

"Wasn't planning to." Not now I was so close to getting out.

This time, I'd leave on my own terms.

8

With the Elemental Soldiers prowling the corridors of the castle, it took me longer than intended to return to the hall. I made sure nobody was looking in my general direction before I turned off the invisibility cantrip and sat behind Harper.

She jumped. "Where'd you disappear to?"

"I'll tell you later." I casually slid the invisibility cantrip deeper into my pocket. "Did they mention what's happening with the trials?"

"We have the rest of the day off." She fidgeted. "But we have to stay here until the questioning is over."

"That figures." I dropped my voice. "The Elemental Soldiers are cleaning up near the storeroom anyway."

The castle would be shut down for the rest of the day as they tried to get rid of the floodwater, so once they cleared out of the way, I wouldn't have a better chance to get to the storeroom.

When the questioning finally ended, Harper and I went out into the grounds. We'd been given free run of the castle, with a promise of dire punishment if we went anywhere we weren't supposed to. I led Harper to the distant corner behind the castle where I'd spoken to Shawn earlier.

"Go on." Harper put on an expectant look. "Tell me where you went when you sneaked off."

"I'll tell you," I said, "if you let me know how on earth you managed to smuggle a sprite in here without him being caught."

"Through the node," she responded. "Easy enough. Mav doesn't have a body, so she can get through without setting off the security alarms or drawing attention the way she would if she flew through the gates. None of us can do the same."

Unless you use a transporter. Too bad mine was still in the storeroom... for now. "Thought so. As for where I disappeared to, I may have taken a look in the Death King's cantrip stores."

Her eyes rounded. "Oh, so you don't need to get into the storeroom, then?"

"I do, but I have this." I revealed the carving tool I'd slipped into my pocket. "You don't happen to know someone with any skill at carving cantrips, do you? Among the other contenders, you mean?"

"You have blank cantrips?"

"From the trial this morning." I grinned. "If I can get someone to carve me a quick spell neutraliser, we can get into that storeroom."

And then? I'd be on my way to freedom. Relatively speaking, anyway.

"Sledge might know someone who can do it."

I pulled a face. "The guy can't keep his mouth shut.

He'd tell the other Elemental Soldiers if he thought it meant getting rid of the competition, besides."

"Fair point." Her brow wrinkled. "I can try asking Muller. He's not Sledge's favourite person. He'll be in the dorm. He might freak out if we both corner him at once, though."

"Then I'll wait here." I stood within sight of the node behind the jail, which would enable me to see if Miles showed his face here. I wouldn't have minded asking him to back up Shawn's claims, but I'd doubtless be able to speak to both of them tonight.

Five minutes later, Muller accompanied Harper back to our meeting point, looking bemused.

"What d'you need a neutralising charm for?" he asked.

"Breaking into the storeroom where they put everything they confiscated from us when we came to the castle," I said, deciding for an honest approach. "If you help us out, I can bring you anything you like that they put in there."

His sceptical expression vanished. "If you get in, can you bring me my cantrips? They're in a bag with my name on them."

"Done." I handed him the tool and one of the spare blank cantrips, and he got to work. Harper and I took it in turns keeping a lookout for any curious onlookers, but we'd chosen our spot well, around the back of the castle with nothing but an unbroken stretch of fence on the other side. Beyond, the swampland stretched out as far as the eye could see. The Death King's domain. Not much of a Court, really, but the liches seemed to like it.

Within a couple of hours, the cantrip was done. A fair few of the other contenders had come into the grounds by now, but even if they figured out we were sneakily carving cantrips, they couldn't possibly know my plan.

Cantrip in hand, Harper and I made our way to the castle and through the door at the back. I handed her an invisibility cantrip and switched on my own before peering into the corridor to check the coast was clear. The Elemental Soldiers had finally cleared out of the way, and while the corridor was still slightly damp, the path to the storeroom was wide open. *Here we go.*

Harper hovered behind as I approached the door to the storeroom. Lifting the nullifying cantrip carefully, I slid it through the gap in the door towards the cantrip which had been wedged there. At once, the faint electric current humming around the door went dead.

Next, I pulled the carving tool from my pocket and used it to pick the lock on the door. A clicking sound came from within, and I pushed the door inward, closing it behind me.

Inside the room, several boxes contained heaps of cantrips and other confiscated items. I examined the box full of jewellery in search of my pendant and spotted another box filled with chocolate bars and crisps. They'd confiscated everyone's snacks, too? That was unnecessary.

I found the pendant and clicked it open to check the transporter was still inside before looping it around my neck, relieved to feel the cool touch of the inbuilt spell spreading across my skin. I then moved the box back into place and peered into the box of cantrips beneath it. I sifted out the bag of cantrips that Muller had asked me to bring him, examined the others in the box, and spotted a large, round coin marked with crude engravings.

In the corner was the insignia I knew too well. It

matched one of the cantrips I'd taken from the store-room… and the only place I'd ever seen that insignia before had been on cantrips custom-made by a certain sect who *definitely* shouldn't be making cantrips anymore.

Once might be a coincidence, but this… this was different. On impulse, I picked it up and hid it among the others in my pocket. Then I left the room and carefully closed the door behind me. A locking charm re-sealed the door, after which I retrieved the neutralising spell. At once, electricity leapt to life on the door's surface as the defensive spell kicked into gear again.

I crossed the corridor to the spot where Harper waited. "Mission accomplished."

"Awesome." She bounded down the corridor, turning off her own invisibility cantrip when we were within a safe distance from the storeroom.

I followed more slowly, unable to get the image of the insignia on that cantrip out of my head. Who among the contenders could possibly have access to cantrips decorated with a mark which ought to have disappeared five years prior? How could the Death King, for that matter?

I ran my finger over the pendant's edge, tensing when two liches swept past the dorms. Soul amulets were the one kind of spell I hadn't seen, which meant every single one in the castle must be in the hall of souls. It would take more than a deactivation cantrip to get through those doors, that was for sure… and yet Shawn had implied someone *had* recently tried to break in there. That thought unnerved the hell out of me, I wouldn't lie.

If the threat was real, it was a safe bet that the contenders didn't know. Including Harper. Liv had told me, in a bid to get me to confess my own secrets, but I had zero intention of ending up being the last one standing. With the pendant back, I should leave as soon as possible.

Not before warning Harper.

Once we'd reached our meeting spot, I turned off the invisibility cantrip and handed Harper the cantrips she'd asked me to fetch for her.

"Don't worry," she said. "Nobody saw you go in there. I think the Elemental Soldiers went to blow off steam in the training rooms."

"They deserve hazard pay from that dickhead boss of theirs for this."

Her brows rose. "You mean *your* potential future boss?"

I hesitated, then said, "Not really. I have no intention of actually winning this thing. I'm just here to escape from someone. Like you."

Her surprise turned to shock. "You're leaving? Now?"

"Tonight." An inexplicable feeling of guilt tightened around my chest. "If you like, you can run your plan past me before I go, and I'll try to give you advice. I'm not trying to desert you or anything, but I have someone else I need to help."

Her expression softened. "Oh. I get it."

I didn't doubt she did. Too bad I had to leave, one way or another. "Your plan?"

"Win," she said. "With these cantrips, I reckon I'm in with a shot. My power is boosted, so I shouldn't have a problem with the combat rounds. All I have to do is watch out for Sledge's cheating."

"And the Elemental Soldiers," I added. "Liv, too. They're sharp as hell, and between you and me, they're less than happy about being left here while the Death King does… whatever the king of the liches does."

"He's not here?"

"It was implied, but I don't know if it's true," I said. "Don't go looking for proof. Focus on the contest."

She fidgeted. "All right. You have some kind of spell on you, too, don't you? I saw how fast you moved during the first challenge."

"Something like that," I said. "I'm trained in combat, but you probably saw I'm useless in the water."

"Pretty sure no fire mage isn't." She smiled. "Thanks for having my back out there."

"You're welcome," I said. "Please don't get caught."

"You too," she said. "If you do decide to come back, I won't hold it against you."

"Hmm." The sky had already begun to darken, and when night fell in the Parallel, monsters came out. I'd be hard-pressed to make my way from here to Elysium and not run into anything nasty.

Shawn, on the other hand, had promised to show me the way to the spirit mages' hideout in the citadel… and I had to admit I was curious as hell as to what they wanted to do inside one of the out-of-bounds magical monoliths which had survived the war even when the spirit mages who'd built them had perished.

Harper gave me a curious look. "You never told me what you took from the storeroom for yourself."

I fingered the pendant. "Something that might save my neck."

That night, I walked out to the node, invisible, my rucksack slung over my shoulder. Shawn wasn't around, but there were so many liches hidden in the night that it was probably better if I met him as far from the castle as possible.

I stepped into the node's path, turned on the transporter, and pain ripped up my limbs, dragging a gasp from my mouth. I landed hard, on my knees, and lifted my head. I'd come out through the node on the other side of the fence circling the Death King's territory, but the castle still loomed overhead, even spookier than usual at night. My gaze skimmed the swampland in search of liches, but it looked as though they only guarded the front of the gates, and they hadn't noticed my appearance outside.

Now all I had to do was find my way to the Citadel of the Elements in Arcadia—assuming I found my way out of the swamp first. My knees were soaked through after my trip through the nodes, while the swampland had darkened so thoroughly that I couldn't see more than a few feet in front of me. When Shawn appeared out of nowhere, I damn near fell flat on my face. "There you are."

"You made it out?" he said. "Excellent. I'm astral projecting because it's easier, but I can still take you with me. C'mon."

I slipped and skidded through the swampland until I came to another node, surrounded by yet more unbroken swampland. Shawn drifted ahead of me, positioning himself in the centre of the current of energy.

"I've got this," he said. "Stay close behind me, and I'll take you to the node closest to our base."

"All right." Anything to get out of the bloody swamp.

I stepped into the node's path, and we vanished into the light. This time didn't hurt, since we didn't use the transporter, and we reappeared in a darkened street with shadowy buildings on either side. The starless sky nearly hid the spired shape of the citadel, which stood across a wide stone square. No streetlamps. *Crap. Don't the vampires come out at night here?* There weren't as many back home in Elysium, so I hadn't thought of the possibility, but they were abundant here in Arcadia.

"Creepy," I muttered.

"Isn't it?" Shawn was barely visible, a transparent shape against the darkness. "But effective. Nobody will find us."

"I'll take your word for it on that." I had to get to the truth… and that meant going into the citadel.

"I'll meet you inside." He vanished. *Too late to turn back now.* I crossed the square towards the towering form of the citadel—which, my brain chose that moment to remind me, was supposed to be haunted by the ghosts of the mages killed in the war—and looked for the side entrance Shawn had mentioned.

Then I glanced behind me, feeling eyes on my back, and spotted Liv, of all people, watching me across the square. *What the hell is she doing out here?*

I quickened my pace and halted beside the hidden entrance, hoping she'd think twice about following me in. Most sane people would, anyway. Liv remained still, so I knocked on the side door, my heart thudding against my chest. To my relief, it opened, Shawn beckoning me inside.

"C'mon," he whispered. "You're safe."

"Someone's following me."

"Don't worry." He closed the door behind me and then pulled a bolt into place. "They won't get in."

A few seconds later, there came a jolt and a yelp from outside. It sounded like Liv had tried to follow me in and shocked herself in the process. Shawn laughed. "Yeah, we put up defences. Who is it, anyway?"

"One of the Death King's security guards," I said. "Don't ask me what she's doing here in the middle of the night, I haven't a clue."

"Well, we have more important things to discuss." He beckoned me ahead, as I heard another crash and a yelp from behind. It seemed Liv was determined to get in. Ah, well. I'd have done the same in her place, and it wasn't like she'd have the faintest idea what we were all doing in here. I'd think of a cover story later, if I needed to. It wasn't like I planned to go back into the castle, after all.

The entire lower floor consisted of a wide room dominated by a staircase which spiralled up to another door above our heads. The sounds of phantom whispers echoed in the air, though I didn't see another living soul within the room.

"Why pick this place as a meeting point?" I whispered to Shawn. "Isn't it supposed to be haunted?"

"Exactly why nobody will think to look for us here," he informed me.

"Aren't you based in Elysium?" I asked.

"We *are* in Elysium," he said, in smug tones. "And several other places at once."

"I don't follow."

"This way." He hopped onto the lowest stair and led me up the spiralling staircase to the door at the peak. The whispers grew louder, as though the souls of the damned were trapped in the very walls. "Glad you could make it, anyway. Any updates from the contest?"

"What if I think there's a spy from the House of Fire among the other candidates?" I kept my voice low, caution urging me to tread carefully.

"Do you know who?"

I shook my head. "I managed to break into the storeroom where the Elemental Soldiers put the cantrips they confiscated from us earlier, and I found a cantrip marked by someone who had links to the House of Fire. But I don't know whose it was."

"Can you try to find out?" he said. "You don't have to hurt them, just get them kicked out the contest."

I said nothing, thinking of Harper and the trouble she might be in. More than me, possibly, because she didn't have a group of vigilante spirit mages at her back.

Yet Tay's plight weighed on me as well. Especially when I thought of the marked cantrips, and the mystery of how they'd ended up in the Death King's hands. Was now really the time to turn my back on the castle, when the key to saving her might still be inside it?

Shawn reached the top of the stairs and opened the door ahead of us, revealing an equally wide room which looked too big to fit inside the building I'd seen on the outside.

"Damn," I murmured.

"Yeah, it's impressive," he said. "The spirit mages created this place before the war. Nobody's ever been able to tear it down, which is saying a lot."

"No kidding." The spirit mages had lost the war with their fellow mages, but not without taking half the Parallel to pieces in the process. This place, though as grand as ever, was clearly abandoned. Pieces of inexplicable machinery littered the floor, and in the very centre, a raised platform gleamed with light around the edges.

"Not only is this a good meeting spot, it's also a way for us to travel between the cities without being detected," Shawn told me. "That platform is like a node which links to the other citadels in the area. It's how we've been getting back and forth between here and Elysium without being caught by our enemies."

"Meaning who?" I could guess. "The Houses, right? Why're they interested in you?"

"Because of this." He indicated the room around us. "Did you know this is where the Order of the Elements executed the survivors from the war?"

I hadn't, but history wasn't my forte. "They did?"

He nodded, his mouth twisting in distaste. "They were unarmed, completely beaten down, but the Order didn't want the spirit mages to rise again, in any form. So they had them line up over there, and…" He mimed cutting his own throat.

My stomach lurched. "Lovely."

He nodded, his eyes glittering. "They think we're all inhuman killers. Nothing we haven't heard before."

He was starting to freak me out, I wouldn't lie, but I'd heard similar things, once. "The person who followed me here is a spirit mage."

"The Death King employs spirit mages?" he said. "That's new."

"I think she's the only spirit mage he has on staff," I said. "Why is it a surprise, though? He hires one person from each other mage class."

"For one thing, a lot of the liches *were* spirit mages," he said. "When they were still alive. Including him."

Right... that's why it made sense that he and Miles had once known one another. Spirit mages were all about life and death magic, so they'd certainly make the strongest liches. That must be why Liv was so concerned when one of them had 'attacked' the Death King at the node. While the lord of the liches must be more than a match for a regular spirit mage, someone as powerful as the ones who'd started the war could give him a run for his money.

"Well, maybe he needed a living one for some reason," I said. "Where are the others?"

"They'll be here in a moment." He indicated the platform. "It took us a while to get the transporter working again, but it hasn't been touched since the war, I think."

Being able to use its magic to hop around between cities must be handy. Nodes had the same purpose, but they were less easy to find if you didn't already know their location. Everyone knew the citadels, but nobody ever set foot inside them. Until now, it seemed.

"Uh-huh." I couldn't restrain my impatience any longer. "Can you use its magic to get into the place where Tay's kidnappers are keeping her?"

"No," he said. "It only links to the citadels, and the others are empty."

I folded my arms. "Have you been looking, though? Or is that what you sent Miles to do?"

"Miles is supposed to be on a mission," he responded. "As for your friend... well, anyone can disappear if they want to."

His words carried an edge that made my chest tighten.

Tay and I had done exactly that once already. Out of necessity.

But she wouldn't take off without telling me. Never.

"It's got to be the House of Fire," I insisted. "Look, I should head off."

"Wait." He stepped forwards as I backed towards the door. "You... I get it, Bria, I really do, but if this week goes the way I think it will, then Tay will be far from the only person to meet that fate."

"I'm not following."

He drew in a breath. "The House of Fire sent people into the contest, Bria, to ensure one of them wins. To ensure they have the Death King's back when they..."

"When they *what?*"

There was a short pause. "We believe the Houses are going to make a new alliance which will see any independent mages forced to serve the Houses or submit to incarceration."

I gaped at him. "They can't take in *all* mages, surely."

"They can try," he said. "And they certainly have the resources to. Not just people with your history, either. Innocents."

I shook my head violently. "That can't be why they took Tay."

She wasn't innocent, though, not by their definition. And nor was I.

He didn't meet my eyes. "I'm not saying it is. I'm just saying it's usually easier to lock up or murder troublesome mages than negotiate with them."

I glanced around the wide, empty chamber. "The spirit mages didn't try to negotiate with the Council of the Elements. They slaughtered them."

He shrugged, uncomfortable. "Not quite what I was getting at. The original spirit mages are dead. The Houses survived, and they'd rather *we* didn't, innocent or not."

"Well, what am I supposed to do about that?" I was starting to regret ever agreeing to this meeting. "I thought I was supposed to be a spy. I didn't hear anything from the Death King that implied any involvement with the Houses."

Unless that what's he did on his mysterious excursions. Who knew? He was equally likely to be off golfing. Whatever the case, I was wasting my time here when Tay needed me.

"I'll level with you, Bria," he said. "Miles didn't want me to tell you any of this. He preferred to keep you in the dark, but I had to tell you the truth. We're safe as long as the Death King remains neutral, but once he has a House of Fire representative on his team…"

"What, you want me to win the trials so nobody else will?"

That was Harper's plan, and *she* wasn't with the House of Fire, but that didn't mean I wanted to provoke the Houses any further.

"More than that," he said. "We need you to ensure that we can get into the castle when we need to and take the Death King's soul amulet. That's the best way—hell, the *only* way to kill the Death King and remove him from his position before he gets us all killed."

"What? You can't be serious." The hall of souls was barred even against spirit mages. Besides, if it hadn't been, breaking in there would mean execution. I wanted no part in it. "People have died for much less. Besides, won't another Death King take his place?"

"Not if it goes as planned," he said. "Whoever holds the soul of the Death King will be able to wield the might of his entire army. Someone came close to succeeding at stealing it recently, but he and his pet spirit mage thwarted them."

"Why not just ask the Death King to help your cause rather than stealing his soul?" Incredulity crept into my voice. "I thought he and Miles knew one another."

"I told you, that was a long time ago." He shook his head. "The Death King is a ruthless killer. Miles remembers him as someone different. He'll come around in the end, I'm sure, but it won't be long before our window of opportunity closes."

What the hell? "Look, I didn't sign up to commit murder. Which is basically what you're doing, even if he *is* an immortal death lord."

"Think of the big picture, Bria," he said. "The Death King is a liar and a murderer, and none of us has ever managed to get as close to him as you are right now. You might save lives if you help us."

"My big picture involves finding Tay and getting the hell away from this." I grabbed the door handle, and this time, he didn't stop me. "Have fun with your new toys."

I yanked open the door and climbed the spiralling staircase down to the bottom. There was no safety rail, and the lack of lighting didn't help the fear that I'd take one wrong step and plummet to my death. Thankfully, I reached solid ground, found the side entrance, and crept out into the night.

Liv wasn't outside, and the node I'd come in by glowed brightly, guiding me across the square. Did anyone else know Shawn was in the citadel? The vampires ruled this city, but they mostly left the mages alone, and even they had the good sense to avoid trespassing in the monoliths the spirit mages had built back when they'd first founded the Parallel. While I understood why Shawn would feel the need to protect his fellow spirit mages, he and the others must have been born into regular mage families. After all, the Order hadn't left any spirit mages walk free.

I trod further down the road, towards the node. If I hopped through to Elysium, I could go home and look for Tay, or verify that Shawn had been telling the truth…

Shit. The node wasn't unoccupied. Several figures gathered around it, their spindly arms reaching into the current of energy. Those weren't humans, but fleshless beings covered in maggoty white skin. Revenants, the vampires' less attractive, less powerful cousins, who fed on the nodes like regular vampires fed on blood.

One by one, they turned in my direction, eyes glowing with the light of the node.

"Don't mind me." I backed up a step. "I'm just leaving."

Three of the revenants lunged at me. Fire sprang to my hands, but I hadn't been prepared for them to move so damn fast. Two landed on me and my back hit the ground under their weight. I gagged on the stench of rotting flesh. Kicking one of them off me, I rolled upright and spotted something glinting in the revenant's hand. The pendant.

"Hey, give that back!"

I ran in pursuit, in the same instant as someone exited a building further down the road.

"Get outta here!" bellowed a deep voice. A blast of air shot down the alley, knocking the revenants in all directions. Unfortunately, the pissed-off local had hit me, too, and I flew back a few feet, out of reach of the pendant.

I caught my balance and sprinted after the fleeing revenant, but the ground abruptly ran out beneath my feet. Flames leapt from my palms as I tumbled down, and then the revenants and I landed in a confused tangle of fire and burning flesh.

Dazed and bruised, I looked up at the rungs of a ladder. *Oh, right.* The revenants lived in the tunnels under the city during the day, so it made sense that there'd be a way downstairs near the node. They were also as flammable as vampires. One of them crawled away from me, half its arm missing, flames licking at its foul skin.

Just where I needed to end the night—stuck at the bottom of a pit with my pendant buried somewhere under a pile of flailing, dying revenants. Holding my breath to stave off the foul stench, I clambered to my feet. I conjured a flame in front of my face in an attempt to see my surroundings and spotted two revenants loping away from their burning brethren. A glint in their hands drew my eyes.

"Get back here!" I broke into a sprint, using the fire in my hands to light my path. The revenants hissed and recoiled away from the flames, as I pursued them through the darkness. My feet caught on something solid—something *alive*—and I landed hard on my knees. "Ow."

The body groaned. "Ow!"

I knew that voice. "Miles? What are you doing down here?"

He lifted his head. "I could ask you the same question."

"Revenants stole my pendant." I rose to my feet. "Shit. I have to catch them up."

"Pendant?" He staggered to his feet, wincing. "What pendant?"

"The one I put the transporter spell in." I headed down the tunnel in pursuit of the fleeing revenants, and Miles followed close behind me.

"They kicked me in the head on the way through. That's why I was lying down there. Until I heard you." He drew spirit energy into his hands, lighting the way. "You used the transporter to leave the castle?"

"Well, yes," I said. "I wasn't about to let a good opportunity go to waste."

"Looks like I had good timing, then."

I arched a brow. "Not sure getting thrown into the dark by a bunch of zombies counts as good timing to most people."

"I've had worse nights."

"Don't speak too soon." I trod forward into the darkness. "Bloody things are like magpies. They have no use for a transporter spell."

"We'll get it back." He advanced at my side, limping a little. "I don't suppose you have a healing cantrip on you?"

"Possibly, but all my cantrips were inside the pendant."

"Bugger." He stumbled, and I saw blood on his face which hadn't been obvious beforehand. Despite all the trouble he'd caused me, I didn't want him to die down here in the darkness.

"Hang onto me." I took his arm, trying to ignore the ashes and grime all over his coat. I was covered in the same crap, after all.

He shot me a smile. "I'm glad you decided to help me. Thought you might leave me behind instead."

"Don't speak too soon." I peered ahead, where the path forked. The revenants had gone down one of those tunnels. "Left or right?"

"Right. They left a trail."

"So they did." Bits of dead skin littered the path. Lovely. I turned, still holding Miles's arm. I wouldn't lie, it felt much steadier than going it alone.

The revenants were only inches away, but they had company. A number of worms filled the space within the tunnel, fleshy shapes covered in scale-like armour. It seemed the remaining beasts from the Death King's territory had mobilised underground. Needle-like teeth filled their mouths, and the ground trembled lightly as they moved.

"Shit." I halted, trying to figure out how in hell to get to the revenants without walking into the nest of worms. Short of learning to fly, that is. "Okay, I'm gonna jump."

Miles's hands lit up with spirit magic. "Or we could do it this way."

The ground rumbled beneath our feet. "Watch out. If we piss them off, the whole tunnel might collapse."

"Fair point." He lowered his hands, treading towards the revenants. The beasts were too stupid to realise they were a few seconds from being eaten alive by giant worms. I'd prefer not to have to dig inside one of those monsters to get my pendant back, either.

A hiss rang through the tunnel, and then, in unison, the worms turned in our direction. Uh-oh.

"I think they're already pissed off." He backed up a step, catching the wall for balance, as the ground gave another almighty heave. "Shit…"

The ground lurched under our feet as the worms moved in a tide of spikes and teeth. I dodged between two of them, blasting fire at their spiky hides, but another grazed my shoulder and a fourth wrapped around my ankle. There must be at least a dozen in here.

Miles caught my arm and yanked me into a side tunnel. I kicked the worm off my ankle, and a pair of teeth snapped on the spot where I'd just been standing. "Whoa."

"The revenants are on the other side of those worms," he said. "We'll have to go through a shortcut."

"Fine by me." I edged down the tunnel and hurried around a corner, only to find another spiked worm blocking my path. The revenants continued to amble along, but the ground heaved beneath their feet, burying their spindly legs to the waist. "Hang on."

I reared back and aimed a burst of fire at the revenants' feet. The momentum sent them spinning into the air, and in another flying leap, I landed atop one of the worms. Its spiked back dug into my legs, but I leaned as far as I could and caught the revenant's scrawny arm in my hand.

The ground gave another tremble, and Miles shouted my name. I snagged the pendant by my fingertips and leapt into the air, just as Miles blasted spirit magic into the nearest worm.

The worm recoiled, causing the tunnel to tremble warningly. I landed beside Miles, and we ran, down the tunnel and away from our pursuers.

Miles halted, breathless, beside a set of stairs leading aboveground. His face was pale and blood-streaked, while both of us were covered in earth.

"Damn worms," he said. "What brought them here? I've never seen them in a city before."

"The Death King's Earth Element," I said. "He set them loose on us in the trial."

"That'd explain why they're targeting you," he said. "You moved damn fast back there."

"Thanks," I said to him. "You saved my neck."

"Anytime," he said. "As long as you got what you came for."

I held up the pendant, breathing a sigh of relief when I found the transporter was still inside it. I then extracted a healing cantrip and tossed it to Miles before looping the string around my neck.

"What would have happened if the revenants had used the transporter on the node?" I said.

"The Death King would have had a worse night than us."

I snorted. "Yeah, right. I bet he doesn't care about revenants. It's the other contenders who'd have to deal with the fallout. Though I reckon some of them would be jealous of the transporter. I didn't even see one in the Death King's private storeroom."

"Those things aren't easy to find," he said. "Pretty sure they stopped making them a long time ago."

"How'd Shawn get one, then?"

"He has a knack for finding rare things."

Like that transporter in the citadel. That was a bigger version of the one he'd given me. Not that I'd seen it in action yet.

"In what way?" I reached the ladder first and began to climb. "He was acting weird tonight. He kept ranting about the plight of spirit mages and the war."

Miles swore. "Tell me later. Someone's up there."

I glanced up the ladder and spotted a figure above our heads. "That's not a revenant."

"Damn right it isn't," said the man who'd hit the revenants with air magic earlier. "What're you?"

"Fire mage," I said.

He grunted. "Not with the House, I assume."

I damn near fell back down the ladder, but Miles caught my leg from behind. "Go on. We'll talk aboveground."

We reached the alley, which was thankfully revenant-free. My clothes were covered in bits of ash and decaying revenant, but at least I hadn't suffered any serious injuries. "Is there a representative of the Houses here? In Arcadia, I mean?"

"You're not from here, huh," the man said. "Not as such. The vamps keep the Houses' wardens out of the city, but they keep sending people in anyway, looking for rogue mages."

Uh-oh. "What kind of rogues?"

"Anyone who fits their description." He beckoned us towards a squat building with narrow windows titled 'the Withered Oak'. "This is a safe house. You shouldn't linger out on the street."

Wait. I knew that name. The Withered Oak... this was the place the former Fire Element had been writing to. "A safe house for whom?"

"Any mages with cash enough to pay for a room. Why?"

Damn. That meant the person Davies had been writing to had probably left a long time ago. We wouldn't find any traces of them in here. "No reason."

The door opened, and our group stepped aside as a tall cloaked figure exited the building. In the brief gap before the door closed, I glimpsed someone else in the corridor within… a very familiar someone. Sledge. What in hell was he doing in there?

"You mean *any* mage?" I asked the man. "Like that big dude over there? You know he's one of the potential Fire Element contenders, right?"

"We protect the confidentiality of our guests." He narrowed his eyes at Miles. "I know what *you* are, spirit mage."

Miles frowned. "Hey, I'm not here to make trouble."

"Is there any way to contact the mages in another city from here?" I interjected. "Because a friend of mine went missing."

He grunted. "Mages go missing all the time. The vamps don't care."

It's not the vampires I'm worried about. "Never mind. I'm off."

"Wait." Miles stepped after me. "Sorry. Other mages aren't exactly our biggest fans."

"Shawn said as much." I scanned the street, but the other mage who'd left the Withered Oak had gone. Must have hopped through the node. "I just saw one of the other contenders in there. Guess I'm not the only one who left the castle tonight."

"Who?"

"You wouldn't know him," I said. "Is it true that the Houses are planning on incarcerating all mages who won't play by their rules."

"Nothing more than rumour at this stage," he said.

"Shawn disagrees."

"Shawn is paranoid." He drew in a breath. "Look, you ought to get off the street at this hour."

"Thanks for giving me a hand back there," I said. "I appreciate it. But I have to get back home."

"Home meaning Elysium?" He eyed my rucksack.

"That's where I was going, but the revenants got in my way at the node," I said. "Do you live in Elysium?"

"I do," he said. "I'll come, but if we see anyone from the House of Fire, you'll have to head back to the castle."

"Relax, I have the transporter." And more importantly, the enemy, whoever it was, would likely have given up searching Elysium for me by now. So would Striker, for that matter.

Miles and I approached the node and stepped through, landing in a dark alleyway. I tensed at the sound of movement on the street, but the footsteps passed by without stopping.

"Nobody's looking for us," he said, in a low voice. "We're okay."

"All right." I released a breath. "Let's do this."

The dim night made it hard to see our surroundings. While the spirit mages who'd created the Parallel had also created a mirror of the night sky to go with it, it was only a pale reflection of the starry backdrop on Earth, and the faint shape of the moon gave little to see by. I conjured the embers of a flame in my hands while Miles conjured spirit magic in his own hands. Since we had to extinguish the lights every time movement stirred nearby, we made slower progress than I'd have liked.

Finally, we reached the street where our old bolt hole was located. From the outside, the place was deserted, but I still approached slowly, the flames in my hands dimmed. Quietly, we entered the house where Tay and I had once made our home. No traces remained of any life inside, as

I'd feared. I scanned the empty rooms, an unpleasant chill racing through my body.

"Shawn said her bag already disappeared…"

"Might've been taken as evidence," he said.

"That's what I said." I entered the living room, which was bare of furniture aside from a collapsed old couch we'd found in a pile of junk in the street one day. A glint caught my eye in the corner of the room. I walked that way, crouching down to see what it was.

A cantrip. I lifted it up, holding it to the light, but it was too dark to make out the markings on it.

Miles trod closer. "What is it?"

"I can't read it in this lighting," I said. "Shawn didn't find this when he came back."

Had it not been there? Or had he simply overlooked it?

A rustling sounded, and the door rattled gently in its frame.

Miles tensed. "Someone's outside."

"Damn." If they were outside the door, they'd definitely heard us by now. I conjured fire to my hand and marched into the hall.

Yanking the door open, I crashed headlong into a… vampire. Oh, *shit*. Another of Striker's people looked down at me, fangs exposed.

"You," he growled.

"Surprise," I said. "Where's Tay?"

"Your friend gave us the slip," he growled. "Care to tell us where she is?"

"I wouldn't if I knew." Flames flickered from my hands. "Care to tell me what *you* know about her disappearance?"

"I think you're lying." His hand shot out, fast—except I

moved faster, blasting him from behind with flaming hands.

Brightness engulfed his body devouring it within a few seconds, and the pile of ashes which had once been a vampire scattered on the breeze.

Miles's eyes widened. "How'd you move that fast?"

"I worked with Striker for years. I know all about dodging around vampires." I stepped over the neat pile of ashes. "We should go before more of them come along."

He shot me a sideways look. "I'm not gonna pry into how you learnt to fight like that, but I have to admit that when I picked you to send in as a spy, I got more than I bargained for."

"I assume that was meant as a compliment."

"Elements, yes." He walked alongside me, his hands glowing with spirit magic. "I mean, you're unpredictable. In a good way."

I opened my mouth to reply, and the faint whisper of fabric on earth was my only warning before a vampire slammed into me. I hit the wall so hard that my head rang with pain. Teeth snapped inches from my ear, then a deafening cry jolted me away from the vampire's touch. A bright flare of spirit magic dazzled my eyes, and when I broke away, Miles held the vampire by its *hair*. It screeched and flailed, and the pause gave me enough time to gather my fire and turn the vampire to ash in Miles's hands.

"Damn," I breathed. "I never would have thought of trying that trick on a vampire."

He brushed vampire ashes off his palms and gave a dimpled grin. "I know how to slow a vamp down if need be."

He was boasting a little, but it was a reminder not to underestimate him, either. Which I had, admittedly, because he hadn't made an ostentatious display of his magical skills before now.

"Noted," I said. "*Now* let's get out of here."

"Hmm." I saw him watching me as though he expected me to speed up again. He knew I was hiding something. And what the hell, I knew he had secrets of his own, too. The Spirit Agents all did. That citadel was proof enough.

"I don't get it," I said to Miles. "If Striker doesn't have Tay and the House of Fire doesn't either, where the hell is she?"

"I don't know, but I'm heading back to the Spirit Agents' base," he said. "Want to come with me?"

For once, his tone held a note of seriousness. I almost said yes, but the weight of the new cantrip in my pocket was a reminder that the Death King might have a bigger role in this than I'd anticipated. Yet despite it all, Miles had proven more reliable tonight than Shawn had, conspiracy theories aside.

"I'm going back to the castle," I said. "I want to talk to the other contenders to find out if any of them are connected to the people who took Tay. It's not like they'll know I was gone."

"As long as you keep hold of the transporter, you should be able to get out again," he said. "Tell you what, meet me at the Withered Oak tomorrow evening after you're done with the day's trials. We'll go and have a closer look around and bang some heads together if need be."

"That sounds…" Better than going ahead with Shawn's questionable plan. "Fine."

"Good." He smiled. "You know, I never said this, but I'm glad we picked you out of all the possible fire mages."

"Because I'm the embodiment of chaos?"

"Your words, not mine." He walked me to the node. I found myself glad he'd been there when I'd been in that house, or else I might have got jumped by the second vamp. It'd taken several years of undoing a lifetime of conditioning to be able to trust Tay, and her disappearance had left a gaping hole I still needed to fill. I still shouldn't trust him, and yet part of me wanted to.

Dangerous idea there, Bria.

The trip back via transporter spell was as painful as ever, and once again, I landed inside the castle grounds in a haze of pain. Wincing, I raised my head to see a heavyset figure crossing the grounds. Sledge, back from his excursion, and coming this way. Towards the node.

I ducked out of sight into the bushes. A moment later, Sledge halted beside the node. Several long seconds passed before a lowered voice spoke. "Did you meet him?"

"Yeah, he gave me the cantrips, as planned," Sledge murmured in reply.

What? I lingered for an instant, but I didn't hear the response. All the same, alarm bells rang in my head.

Sledge is the spy.

9

I decided against confronting Sledge right away. For one thing, I couldn't win in a battle against him with my fire magic alone. Besides, I needed to figure out what to confront him about first. Like who he'd been meeting with… and if they knew about Tay.

I waited for his return in the dormitory, but the excitement of the night finally caught up with me and I drifted off to sleep as soon as I lay down. I then woke early to find Sledge passed out and snoring as usual. I'd rather not ask him about his treachery in front of the others in the dorm, so I got up and went for an early-morning walk, heading down the corridor of the castle with an invisibility cantrip at the ready in case anyone came walking the other way.

At least my adventure last night hadn't ended in complete disaster, but I couldn't help wishing I'd talked to Miles about Shawn's fixation on the Houses of the Elements' supposed plan to lock all of us up. Given my experience with the House of Fire, it wasn't an implausible end goal, but we'd have already noticed if they were close to implementing a scheme like that, surely. Once today's trials were done, I'd go back to meet with Miles, and we'd talk over our options.

Then there was Harper to consider, too. I hadn't dismissed my plan to ensure she won the trials—starting with getting rid of Sledge, if possible. My steps slowed as I reached the lobby, which was deserted. No sign of anyone, living or dead... except for the fire sprite guarding the hall of souls. The sprite looked like a miniature human, surrounded by a cloud of flames, and his beady eyes narrowed in suspicion.

"Who's there?" he said. "I heard footsteps. Show yourself, or I'll call in backup."

Bloody castle. Every sound echoed, even when you were invisible. Only the liches could get around that one. Oh, well. At least it wasn't one of the Elemental Soldiers.

I turned off the invisibility cantrip. "Hey."

The sprite zipped up to my side. "Ooh, someone's out of bounds."

"Do you have a name?" I asked him.

"Dex," he said. "Short for Dexter. Who might you be?"

"The name's Bria," I said. "Are you a security guard? I didn't know sprites could get jobs."

"I'm a special case," he said. "The Death King pays me in dice. Well, he pays Liv, and she buys me collectible dice."

"Dice?" I said, blankly.

"Don't tell me you've never heard of Dungeons & Dragons," he said. "Or rather, don't tell Liv, or else she'll be even less impressed with you than she already is."

"I have, but I didn't grow up on Earth, and there aren't

exactly a ton of opportunities for role-playing over here," I said. "So you and Liv are mates, are you?"

"Of course we are," he said. "She's the one who invited me to join her D&D group. Well, she didn't *invite* me, but I stuck around when everyone said what an amazing NPC I was. I played a fire demon. Typecasting, but I do a good job, if I do say so myself."

"Uh-huh." So my instincts were right, and the two of them were close friends. I'd heard of sprites bonding with people before, and what I'd seen with Harper and her own sprite had confirmed that theory. If I played my cards right, I might get some useful information from him.

Or alternatively, he might talk me to death by rambling about dice all day.

"Was Liv the reason you end up living in the castle, then?" I cut through his anecdote. When he scoffed, I added, "Hey, you can't blame me for being curious. I'd never met a sprite until recently. I thought sprites didn't need to live with roofs over their heads."

"Most humans don't notice us," he said. "I knew one who lived up a chimney for years without ever being found. They just thought they had a magical fireplace that turned on every winter."

I snorted. "I heard sprites bonded with elemental mages sometimes, but it's rare."

"You Elements cause too much trouble," he said. "Starting fires and causing floods, storms and other catastrophes. I prefer a quiet life."

"Which is why you're guarding a room full of soul amulets in a castle owned by an immortal death lord with a magical army."

"I'd rather be on his side than against him."

Good point… and one I'd have to consider myself soon. "You aren't wrong."

"Why all the questions?" He flipped over in mid-air. "Are you a spy?"

"No." *Kind of.* At this point, I was asking mostly for my own curiosity than for the sake of telling tales on him to the Spirit Agents. "But I know someone who might be. Not that I'm a snitch."

"Aren't you?" He flew around my head, his small body flaming around the edges. "You're carrying an illegal cantrip, for one thing. I know the Death King had them all confiscated."

I rolled my eyes at him. "I wouldn't have to use an invisibility cantrip if we were allowed to walk around the castle without being kicked out of the trials. What did the Death King expect? Everyone to just stay put and do as they're told?"

"No, which is the only reason I'm choosing to over-look that cantrip of yours," he said. "If you suspect someone of being a spy, though, I'm not the person to tell."

"Let me guess… Liv is." I sighed. "Why doesn't she like me, anyway?"

"Aside from the illegal cantrip?"

I cut him a glare. "If you tell her, I'll make you sorry."

"If I had to guess, it's because you're a former rogue fire mage," he said. "Liv dated one of those and it didn't end well."

"Really?" I could see how that might have gone badly, if the guy had belonged to the House of Fire in any capac-ity. Not that Dex needed to know I'd been associated with the likes of them, though maybe he'd already guessed. The sprite was sharp—and far less concerned about the potential of a spy being in here than I'd anticipated.

"Yes, really," he said. "It was dramatic, as I'm sure you can guess. She's not a fan of fire mages."

"And yet she's overseeing security at the trials for the next Fire Element." Weird choice of a job, but maybe she had another reason for being here. "Um… it wasn't the last Fire Element she was dating, was it?"

"What would give you that idea?"

I shrugged. "I heard he was kicked out for turning against the Death King."

He scowled. "Bloody gossips. All you need to know is that I'll set his shoes on fire if I ever see him again. And if anyone ever tries to get into this room, I'll do worse."

Wait a minute. Had *Davies* tried to steal the Death King's soul?

"Well, that's me foiled." I hitched on a smile. "See you around, Dexter."

"Dex, please," he called after me, as I left the hall.

Hmm. If I told Liv about Sledge's treachery, I'd draw more attention to myself, which I'd rather avoid. Especially after what Dex had just inadvertently given away… the former Fire Element had been the person who'd tried to steal the Death King's soul. I sure as hell hadn't heard *that* from the Spirit Agents.

I walked down the corridor to the dorms and damn near collided with Sledge coming the other way.

"Watch where you're going," he said.

"Where're *you* off to?" Recklessness seized me. "Off to meet more of your rogue buddies for a rendezvous at the Withered Oak?"

Panic flashed across his face. "What do you mean?"

"You're about as accomplished a spy as I am a professional surfer, Sledge," I responded.

He scowled. "You don't know shit. Going to turn me in?"

"No, I think I'll let you do that yourself," I said. "You aren't going to win these trials. You don't have the patience for it."

"You think I give a crap?" he said. "I'm not here to win. I'm here to knock out as many losers as possible."

And not to steal the Death King's soul? The guy had zero stealth skills, but who knew, maybe someone among the contenders was here for that very purpose.

Sledge shouldered past me before I'd quite figured out what to say next. If he wasn't here to win, then was he not the only person working with the House of Fire?

Whatever the case, the Spirit Agents—Miles included—hadn't told me everything. Not by a long shot.

I went back into the dorms alone, thinking they were empty at first. Then I heard the faint sound of someone sobbing and found Harper sitting alone in the corner, her water sprite hovering over her shoulder.

I approached her. "What is it?"

She jumped. "You're still here? I thought you left."

"Change of plans." I sat down on the nearest bed. "I still don't plan on winning this thing, but I figured you could use a hand. Did Sledge corner you?"

Fear flickered across her face. "What did he say?"

"Nothing about you." I drew in a quick breath. "I know he's a spy for the House of Fire. I just ran into him in the corridor and he implied he isn't the only one either. What did he say to you?"

"He…" she trailed off. "The House threatened my brother. He had to run. If they catch him…"

"He's in *here?*"

"No!" she said, then looked around anxiously. "No, but he's on the run, and if they catch up to him, he's dead. So am I, if I get kicked out of the contest. It's the only way to keep both of us safe."

Well, shit. "If he comes here, the House's people might follow him. You know that, right?"

Her eyes brimmed over. "What choice do I have? He's dead otherwise. Sledge is already threatening to tell the others. What did he say to you?"

"He told me he's only here to stir up trouble and he doesn't care if he gets kicked out," I said. "That implies there's got to be someone else he trusts to win this thing."

She wiped her eyes. "It's got to be Bark. Those two are thick as thieves."

"Hmm." A plan entered my mind. "Don't worry about either of them, Harper. Concentrate on keeping yourself and your brother safe. If you break the rules, you're out, and you can't risk that."

She sniffed. "What about you?"

"I've got the situation in hand." Namely, in the form of one of my stolen cantrips. It was about time I put them to good use. I dug into my pocket and pulled out a couple of spare invisibility cantrips. "Here. You should take these."

"Thanks, Bria," she said. "I owe you one."

"Nah, you don't."

Leaving her behind, I headed out of the dorm and to the grounds, where I spotted Shawn hovering around a corner.

"Hey," he said. "I thought I'd come back to make sure you made it here okay after last night."

"Only six hours late. How thoughtful."

He raised an eyebrow. "Bad day?"

"Try bad *week*," I said. "Revenants attacked me on my way back, you know. I also found out who the spy among the contenders is, but it sounds like there's more than one."

"Hold on a second," he said. "Revenants? Seriously?"

"You might have mentioned they think of all Arcadia's nodes as a tasty snack," I said. "If I hadn't run into Miles, I'd have had a job and a half getting out of there. They took the transporter."

His eyes widened. "But you got it back?"

"Obviously."

"What was Miles doing with the revenants?"

"Skipping your meeting, apparently." I frowned at his unnerved expression. "Aren't you going to ask me about the spy?"

"Which spy?"

"The House of Fire's spy, who else?" I said. "Big guy without any brains. It's him."

"Oh, him?" he said. "I think I know who you mean. He's got 'professional arsehole' written all over his face."

"Yeah, and he said he's here to stir up trouble and not win," I added. "So I inferred that there's someone else he intends to ensure gets through in his place. Maybe more than one someone."

"Figures," he said. "Do you have any allies in there?"

"One." Guilt wedged itself in my chest. "She's in trouble, actually. She and her brother are on the run from the House of Fire. As for the contest, though, I have a plan."

"Good," he said. "Be careful, though. The Elemental Soldiers are bound to be on the lookout for trouble."

"I will," I said. "Also, I talked to the sprite guarding the hall of souls, and he hinted that the last Fire Element tried to steal the Death King's soul amulet. That might be why he got kicked out."

"A lot of people want it," he said. "Who wouldn't want control over the entire army of liches?"

"Not me." I gave him a sideways look. "But a lot of people do, and I bet the Death King knows it, too."

He studied me. "Bria, it was selfish of me to ask you to get involved last night. I've talked with the others, and we've decided to make our move tomorrow. If you want to help—say, by distracting the guards around the castle— I wouldn't say no, but we can do it ourselves if need be."

Unease ran down my spine. Did I *want* to be involved in this? If Tay's life hadn't been on the line... and yet he had given me zero useful information to help me find her. Miles had at least helped me.

But Sledge had been talking to someone who wouldn't show their face... and only spirit mages could astral project through the node.

Was it Shawn... or was it Miles? Did he meet him after our discussion?

Had Miles been lying to me about his presence in the tunnel all along? He hadn't given me any reason to suspect he might have been deceiving me, and besides, he and I had parted not a minute before their conversation. He must have known I'd be going to the castle myself. Right?

"Think about it," Shawn said. "I'd better go. See you later."

I spotted several other contenders leaving the castle. "All right, I'm off. Tell Miles I said hi."

He frowned at that last comment. In truth, I didn't know why I'd said it, and I wondered if I was better off handing myself in after all. Or just leaving, but it didn't feel right leaving Harper. Not without ensuring she had a fighting chance of staying in the contest first, anyway.

One thing was certain: I had to get Sledge kicked out. By any means necessary.

I made my way to the arena, readying my cantrips and selecting a simple charm for drowsiness. Then I moved in behind Sledge and prepared to lay my trap. As the crowd grew, I eased the cantrip into my hand and flicked the switch, directing at him from behind. The effects seeped out before the disc turned into dust and blew away on the breeze.

Now all I had to do was wait for the results.

I casually wove my way among the other contenders and stood at a safe distance from Sledge so he wouldn't guess I'd used a cantrip on him. Once I was beside Harper, I faced the front, where the Elemental Soldiers had gathered.

"Today," said the Air Element, "we'll test your combat skills. This will help us narrow down the list of candidates to those who can stand up to a range of opponents. We'll start by pitting you against one another."

Well, crap. If we weren't allowed to use magic, I'd better hope I didn't end up put against Sledge. He could knock the crap out of me in single combat with ease, and even the drowsiness cantrip might not guarantee my victory.

"How do you decide who fights who?" Harper asked.

"Each of you will select a number," they said. "The person whose number matches yours will be your opponent."

A gust of air swept over the arena. Several people grabbed the walls, expecting it to be like the last time. Instead, a series of paper aeroplanes fluttered into view, propelled by the Air Element's magic.

"One piece of paper, Sledge," the Air Element said in a bored voice. "Not seven."

"I can take anyone on, no problem." He dropped a handful of papers all over the floor, a glazed look in his eyes. *Looks like the cantrip is already in effect.*

I grabbed a scrap of paper with the number 4 scrawled on it. The Earth Element raised his hands next, and the ground began to shift below our feet. In seconds, the arena had divided down the middle, and then again, until earthen walls split it into four evenly sized segments.

"Four matches will take place at once," said the Air Element. "The first will be between those holding numbers one through four."

I'm up, then. I waited for the others to move out the way, looking out for my opponent.

"You're up against Carla, Bria," said the Air Element.

Good. At least it isn't Sledge. Assuming no water showed up, I could handle this one. I walked to the front left section of the arena and waited for my opponent to approach. She was taller than I was, broad-shouldered and muscular, but I was reasonably sure I could take her.

In the arena beside mine, Harper faced off against her

own opponent. Hoping she'd be subtle if she used the cantrips, I scanned my surroundings. While the four arenas were separated from one another, if someone threw a fireball, it might be an issue. In the arena behind mine, Sledge yawned.

"Hello?" said Carla. "Are you even paying attention to me?"

Nope. "Sure." I faced my opponent, cracking my knuckles. Here we go.

She started with a feint, then went on the attack. I dodged a punch and blocked another, then swung my fist into her ribs. Two quick punches and a kick to the chest had her on the ground, her eyes widened in disbelief at the speed with which I'd taken her down. Easier than I'd expected, considering I was sleep deprived and nowhere near as prepared as I might have been. If I wasn't distracted by the possibility of more than one person in here working for the House of Fire.

I glanced at Sledge in time to see him miss an easy hit on his opponent, who dodged his clumsy fists. His adversary got a hit in, and while Sledge still had the advantage, I'd definitely slowed him down. Whether he won or lost, the effects would keep getting worse until he either made a mistake or got knocked out cold. Both were fine with me.

Harper caught my eye and smiled. *Now for his allies.*

10

The matches continued, gradually growing more violent. Liv marched around yelling at people for throwing fireballs and otherwise flaunting the rules. While most fire mages had developed some resilience to burns over time, she didn't have that advantage. Even with the armour she wore, it had to sting.

I wondered briefly about telling her there were several spies among the contenders, but I concluded that I'd be better off not drawing any more attention to myself than I had to. Our encounter at the citadel last night felt like a dream, but if she asked me what I'd been doing there, I hadn't come up with a decent excuse yet.

A yell from Sledge's direction drew my attention. He hammered his fists into his opponent hard enough to knock him out, and even as the guy pleaded for mercy, he continued pummelling away at him until Liv stormed over to the arena and stuck her head over the edge.

"Hey!" she yelled. "Stop. You already won."

Sledge gave his opponent another half-hearted punch. "He didn't surrender."

"He's passed out." Liv entered the arena and grabbed Sledge's wrist. "That's enough. You're disqualified."

Good. It seemed he'd decided to go out on his own terms. That, or our conversation earlier had annoyed him enough that he'd decided to take as many of us down with him as possible. Either worked.

Sledge freed himself and swung his fist at Liv. She ducked the blow and kicked at his legs, knocking him onto his back. Before he could climb to his feet, she blasted him down with spirit magic. This time, he stayed put.

The Air Element summoned two liches to escort Sledge from the premises. Liv tailed behind them as though she expected Sledge to give them the slip. By now, I was starting to regret my hasty actions in getting Sledge kicked out. He wasn't the only agent of the House of Fire, or whoever he worked for. Unless I cornered him on his way out and risked getting caught by the guards, I'd have to rely on guesswork to figure out who the others might be.

Liv had already turned away from the gate, scanning the grounds. She peered past the arena, towards the node, and then approached the bushes near the jail where I'd hidden back when I'd first come here. Had she spotted another intruder?

Liv reached into the bushes and grabbed a teenage boy by the shoulders and dragged him out, causing him to drop his invisibility cantrip. I glanced at Harper, who'd paled.

Oh, no, Harper, you didn't.

"What kind of mage are you?" Liv asked the newcomer.

"I—" He faltered. "Water."

Oh, damn. Harper hadn't mentioned her brother wasn't a fire mage, but it explained why he hadn't come to take part in the trials himself. Unfortunately, the flood from yesterday was still fresh in everyone's minds. If Liv blamed Harper, it was one step from there to her finding the sprite.

I could only watch as Liv led the pair of siblings up the stone staircase and into the castle. At least she hadn't booted them out into the swamp, though perhaps that was because the liches were struggling to extract Sledge from the premises. He dug his heels in and refused to shift, despite the cantrip I'd used on him. I dragged my gaze away and watched the doors close behind Liv and Harper. If both of them wound up taken back to the House of Fire, they were as good as dead.

Dammit.

I walked out of the arena and approached the Air Element. "Harper's not responsible for what her brother did. You don't know—"

"Get back in the arena," they said.

I didn't budge. "She won't get kicked out for this, right? She's not working against anyone, and her brother wasn't the one who flooded the castle."

"That's for her to tell Liv, not me," they said. "I'm not unaware that many of the contenders have family to consider, but we can't have people breaking into the castle grounds using cantrips."

I was starting to suspect she'd given her brother one of the invisibility cantrips I'd stolen from the storeroom.

Why hadn't she run her plan past me? *Right, because she thought I was leaving the contest.*

"I get that, but look at Sledge and some of the others," I said. "They broke the rules worse than she did."

"You're arguing with the wrong person," they said. "Harper will likely be allowed to stay, provided her brother isn't found to have interfered with the contest."

But if he was kicked out, the House of Fire would catch him.

"This is bullshit!" Sledge bellowed. "You can't kick me out."

Fire leapt from his palms, straight at the liches. As they retreated out of range, Liv returned from the castle, marching over to him and conjuring magic to her own hands. I then spotted Harper approaching the arena again. Relief swept through me. She'd been allowed to stay… for now. Yet the devastated expression on her face told me the same couldn't be said for her brother.

I hardly paid attention to my next fight, and when we broke for lunch, I waited for her outside the arena. "Harper."

She shook her head. "Don't, Bria. I won't get you into trouble, too."

"Bit late for that." Despite the distraction of the matches, Shawn's words ricocheted around my mind. He and his fellow spirit mages planned to break in here tomorrow, and I hadn't the faintest idea how to handle it. "Come on, talk to me. Maybe I can help."

"You already gave me the cantrips." She drew in a breath. "I had to send him away, but he's hiding in the swamp, and… I know they'll find him. Sooner or later, the liches will stop him and throw him straight to the wolves."

"Who, the House of Fire?" I said. "They're not around. We'd have seen them. Besides, I doubt the Death King would let them get that close to his territory."

"It's..." She paused, swallowing hard. "It's not the House of Fire. Not the ones you probably know, anyway."

My body stiffened. *Oh, no.* Unfortunately, I did know. If it wasn't the public face of the House of Fire, there was only one entity it could be.

"The..." I could hardly bring myself to say the word. "Family."

She flinched. "The House of Fire was a safe haven by comparison, but they wouldn't take my brother in, since he's a water mage. There are far worse things than being behind bars."

"I know that." I wished I didn't. And the House of Fire had been a safe place of sorts for me, too, after I'd left home. After I'd left the Family.

She blew out a breath. "Worse, Sledge is with *them.* He said he got a tip-off about us being in here."

Oh, hell. Had that tipoff come about because I'd told Shawn about Harper being hunted by the House of Fire? If the worst happened and he wasn't who I thought he was, I'd unintentionally endangered her life, not to mention her brother's.

My throat went dry. "Elements. I'm sorry, Harper. Is your brother still hiding nearby? I might be able to help him."

Hell if I knew how, though, if the Spirit Agents had never been my allies after all.

"He's coming back after the trials are done for the day," she said. "In other words, after Liv goes home. She didn't guess about Mav, but considering she's been watching me like a hawk, I won't risk it."

"We'll wait, then." I gave her a quick hug. "I'm sorry. I'll try to help you."

The rest of the afternoon dragged on, unbearably slow. As the trials finally drew to a close, the losers left in droves, but I wasn't in the mood to celebrate with the others who'd got through to the next round. Harper and I waited impatiently for the losers to leave the castle, one eye on the setting sun. Finally, when the others had all traipsed off back to the dormitories, we pulled out our invisibility cantrips.

"It'll be easier for to go out through the gates," I told Harper. "I have a transporter spell which can get us through the node, but it's painful, and I'm pretty sure only one of us can use it at a time."

"You have a transporter?" Her eyes rounded. "Damn. I've never seen one."

"That was why I needed to get into the storeroom." There was no sense in hiding the truth from her now. "Okay, we'll wait for a gap in the liches at the gate. Try not to touch anyone."

Her brow wrinkled. "Can you touch a lich? I always thought your hand would pass right through them."

"Let's not test that one in practise."

The two of us turned on the invisibility cantrips, then we crossed the grounds towards the gates. The liches on guard duty stood a couple of feet apart, so we'd need to walk in single file and hope they couldn't hear our breathing. I took the lead, arms by my sides, and walked straight through, holding my breath. The murky swamp water hid my footprints, and we crept out of the gates and across the swampy ground, until we reached a safe enough distance from the castle for me to breathe out.

"You still there?" Harper whispered.

"Yeah," I whispered back. "You said your brother was hiding somewhere out here?"

"We'll have to reveal ourselves if we want him to spot us," she said. "Better get away from the castle first."

Once we'd walked out of sight of the gates, we turned off the cantrips. Unbroken swampland extended into the distance on either side, and the only signs of life were a few scraggly bushes and spindly trees.

"Percy?" Harper called out. "It's me."

The teenage boy stepped out from behind a tree. He and Harper shared the same dark hair and eyes, and he flinched at the sight of me.

"Hey," she whispered. "This is Bria. She's safe. Bria, this is my brother, Percy."

"Hi." I reached into my pocket. "I have some cantrips for you to use to keep yourself safe. I figured you had more use for them than I did."

I held out a handful of cantrips, and he took them warily. "How'd you get these?"

"I stole them from the Death King," I said. "You should hide somewhere that isn't in the swampland. There's a place in Arcadia called the Withered Oak which proclaims it's a hideout for mages…"

Harper flinched. "No. That place… it attracts the unscrupulous sort."

I frowned. "The guy who runs the place claimed it has nothing to do with the Houses."

Percy shrugged. "Yeah, but he also doesn't ask his guests questions."

I thought of Sledge. "You're right. I'm sorry. I don't know any local safe houses in Arcadia. I know a few in Elysium, though."

"That's where you're from?" asked Harper.

I nodded. "It's not safe for anyone to stick around here. I heard… I heard a rumour that a group of spirit mages is going to try to break into the castle tomorrow."

"You did?" Harper looked startled. "Since when?"

Ah, crap. How would I even explain how I'd wound up involved with the Spirit Agents? Especially when they'd purported to be the Death King's allies before Shawn had revealed his real motives?

Percy's eyes narrowed. "She met them herself. You did, didn't you?"

"It's not what you think," I protested, but Harper's expression had shuttered.

"So that's how you knew," she said. "You were with them."

"I wasn't," I cut in. "The spirit mages… they tricked me into thinking they wanted a spy in the castle, but some of them went rogue, I think."

"I've heard enough," said Harper. "Leave us alone, Bria."

Oh, hell. I'd really fucked up. Worse, Shawn was nowhere to be seen, and I was at a loss to figure out how to stop his mad crusade to steal the Death King's soul. I was out of allies and out of ideas.

11

Harper didn't say another word to me for the rest of the evening. At the first opportunity, I brought out the transporter and used it to cross from the node into the city of Arcadia again, at which point I walked to the Withered Oak. I'd hoped to find Miles in there, but instead found myself face to face with the unfriendly owner.

"Hey," I said, hitching on a smile. "Sorry to disturb you. I wondered if you'd seen—"

"That spirit mage friend of yours?" he said. "He won't come back here, if he has any sense."

"You claim to be a shelter for all mages," I pointed out. "Does that include people who conspire with the Houses behind your backs?"

"We don't ask questions."

Arsehole. "I guess you don't."

That did it. I left the shelter and made for the Citadel of the Elements. Finding my way to the side door, I knocked.

A painful shock jolted through my knuckles, making the hairs on my arms stand on end.

"Dammit!" Shawn had barred the doors against me. I knocked, hammered my fists on the metal surface, but no luck. Cursing, my hands bruised, I marched back to the node before another pack of revenants came after me. I had a quick check of the tunnels, too, but Miles didn't materialise. I wished I'd at least asked for directions to the Spirit Agents' base back in Elysium. Then I'd be able to go there and check if they were on my side.

Miles can't have betrayed me. Can he?

With no answers forthcoming, I returned to the Death King's castle. I debated telling the Elemental Soldiers about Shawn's plan to steal their master's soul, but if I did, I'd end up worse than dead. They also knew of my friendship with Harper, which might lead to her getting kicked out herself. I couldn't take that risk.

The rest of the evening dragged out, leaving me with entirely too much time to ponder how to stop Shawn and his friends from coming into the castle to steal the Death King's soul. Did the Spirit Agents truly exist at all? I'd even told Liv about them, but I assumed she hadn't pursued that line of questioning.

I slept badly that night, and I was still groggy and out of sorts the following morning when we headed to the arena for the next round of the contest.

"Today will be focused on magical combat," the Air Element told us.

Easy enough, and duelling was a welcome distraction from the way I'd broken Harper's trust in me. Since Shawn hadn't given any details of his plans, I could hope that he and his allies didn't endanger the other contenders' lives. My best option was to keep my distance and let the Elemental Soldiers handle him. If they could.

As I'd expected, it was a lot harder for the Elemental Soldiers to keep the contenders under control with fireballs flying everywhere. Jets of flame shot across the arena, wrecking other people's bouts as their clothing caught fire, while Liv wore an expression which suggested she'd rather be hand-rearing vampire chickens than chasing around unruly fire mages.

I was in the middle of my first match when I heard Harper's loud scream. I glanced up, and damn near took a flaming punch to the nose as a result. Reeling back, I blocked another blast of flame and risked a glance in that direction. Harper didn't look injured, thankfully, but her opponent had her on the defensive. Her hands ignited with flames, but an instant later, the fire sputtered and died.

Flames leapt from my own hands, and my opponent backed up, tripping over his own feet as I swept his ankles out from underneath him. I finished up my match and turned to watch Harper stumble back, her hands sparking with feeble flames. Was her magic acting up out of nerves? Or anger at me for betraying her? I wished I could do something to help her, but before I could head that way, Liv got there first.

Damn her. If she kicked out Harper now, I'd have to intervene. I listened out and heard Harper tell Liv her magic wasn't working. Had her water sprite come back? There was no sign of her—or her brother, thankfully.

Liv gave a glare at the arena as a whole as though we'd

all offended her in some way, then focused her attention on me. *Hey, don't look at me.* I hadn't the faintest clue what her problem was, but in the match behind me, both combatants had resorted to a fistfight, unable to conjure up much more than a spark.

"We can't fight like this!" someone protested to an unsympathetic Earth Element.

"Not my problem," he responded.

Several protests rang out among the others, and everyone forgot all about fighting in lieu of yelling at the Elemental Soldiers.

"Hold on," said the Water Element. "Everyone keep still. We're going to sort this."

The Elemental Soldiers strode around the arena, peering into every shadow in case it held a water mage—or sprite. Liv was as sharp-eyed as ever, but I found it bizarre that only half the contenders or so seemed to have been affected. Maybe they'd trodden in the swamp or fallen in a pond or something. Or Harper had invited her brother in again, despite my warnings. *Please no.* I assumed she knew better, but the question of how he'd survived the night on the run gnawed at me, especially after the Withered Oak had proven a let-down. I hoped my cantrips had helped, at least.

Liv walked around the arena's edge and stopped next to me. *And here's interrogation round two.* "A bunch of people are losing their magic."

"Don't blame me," I said. "Maybe they spent too long in the shower."

She didn't look amused, so I suggested Sledge had been responsible instead. What the hell, maybe he had, if he'd been here. It was as good a guess as any. I kept waiting for her to bring up our encounter at the citadel, but instead, she said, "Are you *sure* you don't know any spirit mages?"

"I know *you*," I responded. "If that counts. Why, did you think you had to become buddies with the Death King to learn spirit magic?"

Oops. I probably shouldn't have said that. Annoyance flared in her eyes, and she said, "I'm in the Death King's employment. That doesn't make us friends."

"No, because he isn't around," I said. "He's skiving off, isn't he? Not even watching his own trials."

Stop talking, Bria. I wanted to warn her about Shawn and his mates' plan, but how could I do that if I didn't know when the spirit mages were going to make their move?

"Are you sure you *want* this job?" she said. "Because you're doing a great job of convincing me to kick you out."

"Thought it was up to the King of the Dead," I responded.

"The final decision is." She didn't sound like she truly believed it, though. "Have you been snooping around the castle when the Elemental Soldiers told you to stay put?"

I told her I'd seen the rest of the castle during the flood, but it was when I said I'd met Dex guarding the hall of souls that her brows shot up.

"He got the job because he's the one person I trust to keep any potential saboteurs out of there," she said. And if you're getting any ideas, then I'll gladly escort you to the jail."

No. I'm not, but someone is. More than one someone. "No need for that. I thought you wanted me to give you information about potential saboteurs, not accuse me of doing the same."

"If you know someone in here who plans to disrupt the contest—"

"I don't." And yet I did. "But I don't think Sledge was working alone. He has friends."

Her gaze went to Bark, Sledge's friend. *Yes. Him.*

"Do you know the location of the House of Fire?" she asked.

"Why?" What in hell did that have to do with anything? "If you want to ask them if one of their members is trying to wreck the contest, they'll throw you out on your arse."

Why the sudden interest? She hadn't even heard of the Houses until I'd brought them up. She wouldn't know who the Family was, nor their link to the House of Fire.

In response to my question, Liv said, "For one thing, a former friend of mine might be hiding with them. For another, I'm about fifty percent sure someone in their number sent assassins after me. Do you know them personally?"

The Air Element interrupted by walking over. "We're resuming the matches. No magic. Bria, you're fighting Clancy over there."

"Put her against that dude instead," Liv said, pointing to Bark.

I wanted to finish our conversation, but I could at least see to it that Sledge's mate got kicked out first. I didn't have to use magic, which meant it'd be the same as yesterday's trials. Easy enough.

Question was, who'd dampened the contenders' magic? Liv didn't know, but she seemed under the mistaken impression that I did. Harper might know, but whenever I looked at her, she averted her gaze. I'd have to wait until the matches were over to have another chance to talk to her.

In the meantime, I walked over to Bark, Sledge's friend, and faced him across the arena. "Is *your* magic working?"

"Sure." Flames licked his palms. "They told us not to use it, unless you're looking to get burned."

Fire leapt to my own hands. "Speak for yourself."

We circled one another, hands blazing, waiting for an opening. He tried to hit me, but I pivoted, dodged, and continued to circle him. He fixed on a scowl. "Quit messing with me."

"If you insist." I darted forward and sank a blazing fist into his ribs. He grunted in pain, then struck back. I blocked, my sleeve smoking at the edges. "Nice try."

"I know you're the one who got Sledge kicked out." He swung his fist. I blocked, but pain ripped up my arm where his blazing hand caught the skin. "I saw what you did."

"I could do the same to you." I aimed another punch, the flames snagging his jaw.

He flinched away. "Kicking Sledge out doesn't mean shit. Not now he has—"

"Has what?" I hit out in a series of aggressive punches to his ribs which sent him staggering back.

"Nothing," he gasped out, doubling over.

"Uh-huh." I kept on the attack, dodging his attempts to

retaliate. "A gift from the Family, is it? Some kind of cantrip?"

He faltered and tripped backwards over his own feet. "How did you know?"

"Caught him talking to some mysterious messenger the other night." I drew back for a moment, then went on the offensive again. "I also know they're planning to come here today. Care to tell me when?"

My next strike sent him sprawling onto his back. He staggered upright an instant later. "You asked for it."

His fist clenched and I spotted the glint of a cantrip before it turned to dust in his hand. Then flames leapt to the sky, not just from his hands but from his whole body at once. I veered away from the searing heat, alarm blaring through me. My own fire looked puny in comparison.

Guess that answered the question of what kind of cantrip the Family had given him. Pity I was the one on the receiving end.

"Hey!" I dodged his flaming fist, the smell of burning hair drifting in its wake. "You're cheating."

"I'm gonna burn you to a crisp!" he bellowed.

Not happening. His hands blazed so bright that I doubted he could see clearly, so I put on a burst of speed to get behind him and then threw a cantrip of my own at his back. His body froze in position as the paralysing spell kicked in. He dropped to his knees, still blazing all over with flickering flames. If he wasn't careful, he'd literally burn himself out.

"Tell me." I crouched down at a safe enough distance to be heard over the crackle of flames. "How are they planning to get in? Through the node?"

I had the only transporter spell… though come to think of it, the spirit mages had given me that themselves, so maybe they did have a backup. That, or they planned to come in through the gates instead.

Bark didn't answer, and a moment later, Liv walked over to us, looking at Bark's sprawling body.

"He cheated using a cantrip," I told her. "Gave himself a boost."

"Can anyone back you up on that?" she asked.

A blazing current of light drew both our eyes, then she turned and ran off, jogging past the arena. I gaped after her, realising the light had come from outside the fence, not inside. *The node.*

Had the Spirit Agents arrived to launch their tack.

Leaving Bark sprawled on the ground, I went in search of Harper and stood in front of her opponent, blocking him from reaching her. "Time out."

"Hey!" Harper said indignantly. "What's your problem?"

"That." I pointed at the current of light blazing from behind the gate. "Liv went to check it out. I'd say it's trouble."

Anger hardened her eyes. "Not my problem."

"Bria, get back to your own opponent," said the Earth Element.

Dammit. "Bark cheated using a cantrip," I told him. "If I were you, I'd kick him out."

At another warning glance from Harper, I moved back to my own match and faced my next opponent. The match didn't last long, and as the Elemental Soldiers called the round to an end, I spotted the Air Element walking through the gate, dragging a struggling Sledge along with them.

Don't bring him in here! What the hell were they doing?

I walked out of the arena, raising my brows as the Air Element approached the block that housed the jail cells. Sledge must have really pissed off the Elemental Soldiers if they were locking him up.

I approached the Air Element and their struggling captive. "What did he do?"

"Attacked Liv and me," grunted the Air Element.

"Where's Liv?" I didn't see her anywhere. Was she still dealing with the trouble at the node?

"Something came up," they said. "Can you give me a hand here?"

"You want me to help carry him?"

"No, but I'd appreciate it if you opened the jail door."

"Can't the liches do that?" We approached the block and I saw what the problem was. "Oh. Liches can't open doors."

The two guards turned my way as I neared the jail, their masked faces radiating disapproval. I shot them a smile and opened the door for the Air Element. I let them go ahead and then entered the jail, suppressing a shiver of unease. Rows of cells greeted me on either side, claustrophobic and almost completely dark. Not to mention cold, too, though the whole castle was. Being a fire mage would make it more bearable, but I wouldn't like to be locked up in a place like this. Not that the House of Fire had been a paradise, but still.

I spotted a glittering light in the corner of my eye, but it vanished when I turned back to it, leaving the jail as dark as ever. *Was that a sprite?*

"Go on, Bria," said the Air Element. "Open the cell on the right. Any funny business and you'll be locked in there yourself."

"No need for that." I opened the barred door, then stepped aside as the Air Element dropped Sledge onto a bench inside the narrow cell. "Did he have a strange cantrip on him, by any chance? When you caught him?"

They slammed the door on him. "Yes, he did. What kind of cantrip?"

"No need to sound so accusing," I said. "Bark used some kind of cantrip to cheat in his match against me. It upped his fire to crazy levels. I figured since they were friends, he might have used the same cantrip."

The Air Element regarded me for a moment. "Bark used a cantrip, did he?"

"I told Liv, but I'm not sure she was listening."

"She has a lot on her mind." The Air Element locked the cell door on Sledge, who lay unmoving on the bench. "Did Bark tell you where he got the cantrip from?"

"No, but I think both Sledge and Bark were working with the same people," I said. "He hinted as much."

Question was, had all the Spirit Agents been allied with them, or just Shawn and his friends? With Sledge jailed and Bark kicked out, the intruders might have trouble getting into the castle... unless they had other allies in here. Which they might well do.

The Air Element frowned. "If it turns out you know more than you've told us, then you're liable to be subject to interrogation at the Death King's hands, innocent or not."

My shoulders tensed. "I can't tell you anything about

where those cantrips came from, but I'd suggest sending someone to question Sledge as soon as he's awake."

"I'll deal with him, then," they said. "Go back to the others. It'll be easier for you if you stay out of this one."

I left the jail, thanking my lucky stars that I'd avoided punishment. I would have liked to speak to Sledge myself, but he wasn't the danger here. Not now he was locked up behind bars.

As I passed the bushes near the node, Harper grabbed me by the leg and yanked me on top of her. Surprise stopped me from fighting back when her fist hit me on the cheekbone. *Ow.*

"What's wrong with you?" I struggled out of her grip. "I don't want to fight you."

"You did this," she said. "You took Mav."

"Who?" I said. "Your sprite? Is she the one who's dampening everyone's powers?"

"Not everyone's." She tried to hit me again, and I blocked her with my forearm. "You sold us out, and even that wasn't enough for you. Was it?"

"I didn't sell you out." I yanked myself out of her grip and stumbled out of the bush. "And I didn't take Mav. I didn't even know she was missing. Look around. Where would I hide a sprite?"

Her expression calmed a little. "I don't know, but she's been missing since this morning."

Since... hang on a second. I rose to my feet. "Did you check the jail?"

"What?" she said. "No. Why?"

"Sledge," I said. "I just saw the Air Element take him there and lock him up, and I thought I saw a sprite in there. I didn't realise it might be Mav."

She scrambled to her feet. "What? Why didn't you get her out?"

"I wasn't sure it was her I saw. It's pitch-black in there." I dug in my pocket. "I only have so many of these cantrips left, but I think I can help her out. I need to talk to Sledge anyway, to find out who his other allies are."

We waited for the Air Element to leave first. When they were out of hearing distance, we approached the jail, and the two liches standing outside it. There was no gap between them, so we'd have to create a diversion. I nudged Harper to get her attention—and one of the liches looked directly at me.

"Who's there?" the lich said, in a low, chilling voice. "Show yourself."

Oh, hell. I was fairly sure our cantrips wouldn't work on immortal death lords, but if they alerted the Elemental Soldiers, we'd lose our chance.

Flames exploded from my right-hand-side, turning the liches to dust in an instant. *Damn, Harper.* I took the opportunity to step over the piles of ashes and into the jail.

The door closed behind us, and Harper appeared at my side. "That's that taken care of. Hey, don't look at me like that, Bria. It's not like they're really dead."

"You mean deader than usual." I frowned at her. "If they figure out that we're the ones responsible, they'll march back over here as soon as their regeneration kicks in."

"Nah, they wouldn't have seen or heard us," she said. "I think there's a time gap of a few hours between when a lich dies and when their soul amulet revives them, too."

"Then we'd better hurry up."

I had to admit it was much easier to get around the jail without any potential witnesses nearby. Just as long as the Air Element didn't come back and find their lich guards reduced to ashes. At least with a whole castle full of fire mages, they wouldn't leap on us as the culprits if we weren't caught near here.

While Harper went to rescue her sprite, I found the jail's other occupant lying on a bench in his cell. Sledge stirred, groaning quietly. "Who's there?"

"Bria." I approached his cell, turning off the invisibility cantrip. "What the hell made you think it was a good idea to attack the Death King's guards after you were already kicked out the contest?"

"I was told that I'd have backup," he said. "What's it to you?"

"Was it a spirit mage called Shawn who told you to break into the castle from the outside, by any chance?" I muttered. "Did he promise to back you up?"

He startled upright. "How'd you know that name?"

A clattering noise came from Harper's corner. She turned and stared at me, her face pale.

"He tried to recruit me, too." For Harper's benefit, I added, "I'm not with him, but I need to know who else is. He's supposed to be coming here. Soon."

"What?" Sledge stood, his eyes widening. "He promised to back me up, then bailed on me. I'll kill him."

"Bit difficult from where you're standing."

The bastard clearly had zero loyalty. Had Shawn and the others made a totally different promise to everyone they spoke to?

"Then get me out," he said. "If they're coming here

through the node, they'll need a living person to take the Death King's soul amulet."

"If anything, that's reason enough *not* to set you free."

He had a point though: the node inside the castle grounds was under close watch. Even the one outside the fence was, if Liv's response to Sledge's arrival had been any indication. That meant the spirit mages would have to astral project to get in… and in that form, they couldn't lay their hands on the Death King's soul. They needed a living person, and thanks to me, Bark was out of the contest as well as Sledge.

Harper approached us, Mav perched on her shoulder.

"Are you okay?" I asked her.

She nodded. "Yeah. Mav was hiding in here. I think something spooked her."

An air of wariness surrounded her, but her tone wasn't openly hostile anymore.

"I'm going to try to stop Shawn and the others, but I need help," I told her. "They need a living person to steal the Death King's soul. That means either they have another insider, or they're planning to find one."

"They also need to get past the security sprite guarding the hall of souls," she said. "But Shawn might have cantrips, too. They… we… all do."

Sledge swore. "You, too?"

My mouth fell open. "Wait, Shawn is the one who's threatening your family?"

Shame flushed her cheeks. "Liv, I'm sorry, but if he's calling himself a Spirit Agent or whatever, it's a total lie."

"I know it is, but that doesn't change the fact that he's coming here today," I said. "Sledge didn't get in without being caught, and Bark got kicked out, but there might be others."

"I'll help turf them out." Her jaw set. "Shawn didn't send me here himself. I came here to avoid him. I didn't know the bastard had so many fire mages at his disposal."

"Nor me," I responded. "We'd better go."

"Hey!" Sledge said indignantly. "You can't leave me here."

I ignored him, my thoughts spinning in circles as the implications of Shawn's treachery sank in. Once Harper and I had the invisibility cantrips turned on again, we made our way to the doors, checked no liches were outside, then left the jail behind. We crossed the grounds, ignoring Sledge's shouts, until we were at a safe enough distance away to turn visible again.

I turned to Harper. "Was Mav the one causing everyone to lose their magic?"

"Not deliberately," she responded. "She was trying to warn me, I think."

"I'm sorry," I said. "I can help fix this, but I won't lie, Shawn and his friends strike me as persistent. As well as pathological liars."

"They're complete scum," she said. "I can't endanger my brother, but I can at least see to it that Shawn doesn't get near the castle again."

"Okay." I drew in a breath and moved closer to Mav. "Can you do me a favour and find Dex? Warn him someone else is coming to the castle to take the Death King's soul amulet? He won't hurt you, don't worry."

"He won't," added Harper. "What about you, Bria?"

"I'll warn the Death King's people to expect an attack from the node, and otherwise get their security in gear," I said. "I already hinted as much to the Air Element, but I was about five seconds from being arrested back there anyway—

A yelp of panic from Mav drew my attention to the node... and the transparent figures emerging from it. It was too late for a warning after all.

The Spirit Agents had arrived.

12

At a nod from me, Harper bolted, turning on her invisibility cantrip again. I didn't blame her for getting out of sight, but all I could think of to do was to stall them until the Death King's forces stepped in.

Keeping my own cantrip concealed in my hand, I walked out in front of the group and met Shawn's eyes. "Really good job there weren't any liches hanging around the node. There usually are."

In fact, there would have been… if Harper and I hadn't set them on fire on the way into the jail. Oops.

Shawn studied me. "Have you decided to help us out, then?"

"There's been a change of plans," I said. "One of the candidates who got knocked out of the contest tried to attack the Elemental Soldiers, so they upped security and shoved him in jail. There's also more than one sprite on guard duty."

"Damn," he said. "The Death King must be getting desperate if he's hiring sprites instead of people."

"I'm told some of his liches are breaking ranks," I added. "And leaving to go with whoever wants to dethrone him."

He paused for a long moment. "I wouldn't know. I don't keep tabs on the liches."

That's not what Sledge said. I held my tongue, knowing I'd be in far more trouble if I contradicted him now. Shawn might not be here in physical form, but he had enough magic at his fingertips that he and his buddies could turn me into an undead puppet if they were so inclined. I never should have trusted a single one of them. They were all in on a shared plan, and they thought I was, too. Worse, Liv was nowhere to be seen. Of all the timing.

"Well, go on," Shawn said to me. "Show us to the hall of souls. We can take on a couple of sprites."

I glanced towards the castle, wishing I'd had time to think my plan through before confronting them. The Elemental Soldiers were nowhere in sight, but even their elemental magic couldn't permanently get rid of a group of astral projecting spirit mages unless they found where their real bodies were hiding. "You should go in through the front door, that's quicker. I'm more conspicuous than you are, so I'll have to go in the other way and meet you on the inside."

Suspicion laced his voice. "What other way?"

"The back entrance," I said. "There shouldn't be anyone in the lobby, but I can't walk through closed doors like you can. The hall of souls is through a door on the righthand side of the lobby. Shouldn't be too hard to spot. It's the one covered in locks, and it's spirit-mage-proofed."

"Figured as much," he said. "Go on, then. We'll meet you on the other side."

Here we go. He floated upwards to the stone steps, accompanied by the others. I, meanwhile, jogged around the castle to the back entrance and through the door.

A commotion came from the direction of the dormitories, and smoke poured out into the corridor. Had someone started a fire as a diversion? I didn't have time to check, so I hurried down the corridor and spotted a tall figure walking towards the lobby. Bark. Sledge's friend must have sneaked back in, and he was on his way to the hall of souls to help the Spirit Agents.

Not happening.

I put on a burst of speed and tackled him from behind. We crashed into a heap, and I pinned his flailing arms to the ground.

"Hey!" His eyes bulged as I caught him in a headlock. "Let go of me!"

The door crashed open behind us, and the three Elemental Soldiers ran into the corridor. About time they showed up. Bark shook me off, his eyes blazing with fury, but he didn't move any further. If he went into the main hall, he'd expose his intent of robbing the Death King in front of witnesses. He knew he was stuck.

"Bria, get off him," the Air Element commanded. "Come with me. Felicity, please escort Bark from the premises."

I climbed off Bark and addressed the Air Element. "He was on his way to rob the Death King. Shouldn't he already be locked up?"

"When Felicity is done with him, he'll wish he was."

The Water Element walked past us, her jaw set,

pushing Bark in front of her. There came another loud exclamation from the direction of the hall. *I think Shawn and his friends got caught.*

"Come with me," the Air Element commanded, heading for the back door out of the castle. I was all too happy not to get caught in the backlash when Shawn realised I'd led him into a trap, so I hurried along behind them.

"One more thing," they said. "Don't tell Liv."

"Why not?"

They shook their head. "I meant it when I said Liv is dealing with a lot, and this isn't something she needs to worry about."

We walked through the back door of the castle and around a corner. Liches swarmed across the grounds, surrounding Shawn and his friends as they tried to flee down the stone steps at the front of the castle. A brief flare of triumph rose within me, extinguished almost immediately when a shadow fell over me from behind.

The Death King glided into view, towering over the other liches. Tall, imposing, and utterly terrifying.

The Air Element stepped back. "You deal with her, Death King."

What? No. There was no use in running, though. Shawn and his friends scattered, pursued by the liches, but the King of the Dead made no move to go after the intruders. Instead, he turned to me, and beckoned several liches to join him until they had me utterly surrounded. Coldness seeped into my bones, and my fire went completely out. I was in trouble now.

The spirit mages had disappeared from sight, leaving me alone with the forces of the dead.

"So you're the one who broke into my former Fire Element's quarters," said the Death King. "Given your background, it didn't surprise me. I have to admit, though, it *did* surprise me that you'd have the nerve to help those intruders access my castle when you must know it's protected against spirit mages."

Oh, damn. He even knew about my meeting with Shawn in Davies's old room?

"I'm not working against you," I whispered. "Shawn and his friends tricked me into thinking they were my allies. They didn't just do it to me, they did it to half the contenders, too. I was too late to stop them from getting in here, but I tried to warn your Elemental Soldiers first."

My excuses sounded fake to my own ears. What choice did I have, though? If I'd told them about the upcoming attack outright, I'd have joined Sledge behind bars.

"Forgive me if I don't take your word for it," said the Death King. "Considering your history. Tell me the name of the people those spirit mages are allied with?"

The words felt leaden on my tongue. "The Family."

"The Family," he repeated. "The same Family who you once lived with."

He knew. He'd known all along. My whole body locked up and fear trickled down my spine. "If I'd had the choice, I wouldn't have. They were my guardians."

I used the past tense, though it wasn't accurate. They'd survived, though they shouldn't be walking free. They certainly shouldn't be recruiting spirit mages.

"You ran away from them as a teenager," he went on. "You even went as far as to get yourself locked up by the House of Fire in order to ensure your own safety. Then you talked your way out, and you've earned a living ever since by working for criminals, relying on anonymity to survive."

I swallowed hard. "I swear I didn't know who Shawn and the others were. They tricked me into thinking they could help me rescue my best friend. The House of Fire has taken her captive."

Except maybe they hadn't. Maybe the Family had instead, whoever was giving orders on their behalf. The only way to know was to survive long enough to ask Shawn himself. If he'd got out in one piece and hadn't been slaughtered by a lich during his escape.

"I see," he said. "You strike me as more intelligent than their usual targets. I expected their spirit mage allies to put up more of a fight, too, but perhaps they didn't foresee their allies' capture."

I frowned. "Are you saying you knew they'd break in?"

"What do you think?"

"I'm guessing you didn't tell the others?" No wonder Liv had taken off, because she'd have stuck around if she'd known spirit mages were going to attack the castle. The Death King was one devious bastard, that was for sure.

"No," he said. "I find it hard to believe that you didn't know who they were."

"They claimed to be with the Spirit Agents," I said. "It's not like I'd ever met one before. Anyway, I think that was a ruse. There's another Spirit Agent I know who isn't involved with them." At least I didn't think he was. Miles had been nowhere to be seen since he'd helped me deal with those vampires at our old hideout.

"Given what I know of the Spirit Agents, those people are more likely defectors," he said. "If it's possible for you to get a message to the real Spirit Agents, however, I may be in need of their help."

"Oh?" I said warily. For the first time, hope that he wouldn't kill me outright began to rise within me. "Want me to find them?"

"If you can," he said. "But there's another more important task I have for you first."

He isn't going to take my soul. He still needs me. "What is it?"

"As it happens," he said, "I find myself in need of a spy. If you can speak to those defecting spirit mages and convince them you're on their side, then I'll let you stay in the contest. If not, then you'll leave the castle, tonight, no matter who may be chasing you."

He turned his back and walked away, leaving me reeling on the spot. *Crap. What in the world am I supposed to do?*

In the end, there was only one answer. I'd lost too many people already. I would not let Tay be one of them.

I just had to hope she wouldn't mind me throwing her on the mercy of the King of the Dead.

13

After the Death King's departure, I went in search of Harper and found her in the dormitory sporting a bloody nose and a grin. "I got two people kicked out when I caught them trying to cause a diversion to lure the Elemental Soldiers away when the spirit mages attacked."

"Bet it was them who let Bark back in," I said. "The Elemental Soldiers took him with them, but the spirit mages got away."

"Figures." She dabbed at her nose with her sleeve. "What now?"

"What now?" I repeated. "I'm going to find them."

"Find…" she trailed off, her eyes widening. "You mean Shawn. *Why?*"

"The… the Death King told me to," I admitted. "On pain of a horrible fate. Don't worry, I didn't mention you were involved."

She slumped back, her face turning pale under the

blood. "I guess he's watching us after all. His sprites are, too."

"There's more than one, aside from Mav?"

"Dex has a girlfriend," she responded. "I saw her with him when the spirit mages got into the entrance hall. They're the ones who chased the mages out of the castle. I was invisible, so they didn't see me, but you... if you go back to Shawn, he'll kill you."

"If I don't, Tay dies."

She lifted her head, noting the name. "Tay. Is that who you're protecting?"

"Yeah." My throat closed up. "I swear I won't be long. I'm going to follow Shawn and give him some bullshit excuse for not backing him up, and then come back here before the Death King sends out a search party."

The odds weren't on my side. Not only had I got Shawn and his allies suspicious that I was working against them, but the King of the Dead himself had Tay's life at the end of a rope. Add in Harper's dilemma and I was starting to understand why the Air Element had told me not to tell Liv any of this. One more problem and I might well lose my mind.

———

I waited until the path to the node was clear before heading that way and using my transporter to travel to the middle of Arcadia. Shaking off the pain of the crossing, I headed towards the citadel. While I hadn't been able to get in there last night, I had an extra incentive to be stubborn enough to stick around this time.

I knocked on the door twice, and Shawn answered. "Thought it was you. What do you want?"

"To talk," I said to him.

To my relief, he backed into the lower room, leaving the door open. I walked in and was greeted by the sight of a huge monster. Ten feet of scaled worm coiled up like a snake, encased in a mesh net-like construction which pressed its leathery wings to its scaly spine. When it spotted me, it growled and snapped its jagged teeth.

My mouth dropped open. "Is that a *wyrm?*"

One of the larger cousins of the beasts the Death King had brought into the arena—with added wings. What were the spirit mages doing with that thing, training it to attack trespassers? I walked up the staircase behind an uncommunicative Shawn, unable to believe he'd got that creature in here without someone losing a limb.

On the other side of the door, several other spirit mages crowded inside the upper room, and every one of them glared at me.

"You," said one of Shawn's friends. "You have some nerve showing your face here after you screwed up our plan."

"You didn't *tell* me I wasn't the only insider in the contest," I retaliated. "Someone started a fire in the dorms, and by the time I got outside, you were already running off to leave me to take the fall."

"We were outnumbered," the spirit mage protested. "You don't know what a lich can do to a person."

"I have a good idea," I said. "And what in hell is with that monster downstairs? Is that your next big idea—set a giant wyrm loose on the Death King's territory?"

"Does it matter?" Shawn's friend said. "I wouldn't

expect you to understand, but we need all the allies we can get."

"Yes, because you keep betraying the ones you have." The words spilled out, regardless of my attempts to reel them in. "I wasn't aware that I'd be up against a dozen other challengers who also had instructions from you. Why didn't you tell me? We could have worked together."

The guy walked closer, paced around me. "Whose side are you really on?"

"Mine," I told him. "Got a problem with that?"

Shawn shot his friend a disgruntled look. "Ignore Garber, Bria. I don't know what lies the Death King told you, but they're not true."

"You're talking bollocks," I informed him. "Miles is the only one who at least tried to be straight with me."

Shawn's expression smoothed out. "Is that what you believe? Miles is more of a traitor than even your friend Harper is."

Damn. So it's true. "What the hell did you do with him?"

Garber's eyes narrowed. "You should have just given up. That would have been easier for you."

His hand shot through me, and pain split my soul down the centre. I bit back a whimper of pain.

"Don't kill her," Shawn commanded. "We have to leave her in one piece."

"Someone else is calling the shots, are they?" I wheezed. "You're pathetic."

"I'd prefer not to watch you die," he said. "I need to find Miles, and the slimy little shit has given us the slip. Did you have anything to do with that, Bria?"

"You pretended he was on a mission for you, didn't

you?" The truth dawned, too late. "You sent him into the tunnels to die."

"And *you* helped him escape," said Shawn. "I should have known."

Garber relaxed his grip on me. "You know we have your precious Tay, don't you? I can torture that little bitch whenever I like."

Fury crashed over me like a wave. "The House of Fire never had her. Everything you said was a lie."

"Almost everything," said Shawn. "I didn't lie when I told you that Tay was doomed unless you helped us."

A red glare filled my vision as flames leapt to my hands, but a warning growl beneath my feet reminded me of their prisoner. The warning look on Shawn's face told me if I hurt any of them, I'd be the first to lose a limb.

"You asked me to do the impossible," I told them. "The Death King is well aware there are a dozen different shit-heads trying to steal his soul every day of the week. His own *Fire Element* tried it, which you really ought to have told me beforehand, considering the Death King expected half his potential new employees to try exactly the same thing. Let me guess, Davies was one of your allies, too."

Shawn was silent for a moment. "You know, I really thought you'd see things our way."

"You kidnapped my best friend," I said. "Did you do the same to the relatives and friends of half the other participants? Didn't you expect us to talk to one another?"

"Enough of this crap," said Shawn. "Tell you what, we'll make a deal. You give us Miles's location. I'm sure you can convince him to tell you. You don't care about him that much, surely. It won't make a difference to you... but to Tay, it might be all the difference in the world."

Chills ran through my bones. "You can't kill an innocent person just to get me to help you. Why do you need me, anyway?"

"Why indeed?" he said. "You'll have to ask Tay. Assuming she survives."

"Tell me where you're keeping her," I warned. "Or I swear to the Elements, I'll kill you."

"You're in no position to be bargaining with us." Garber seized my arm in his painful grip. "And you're never to come back here again."

He gave me a shove. I stumbled back, flames leaping to my palms, but I knew better than to think I could fight against a pack of spirit mages in a place they'd created, which had even outlasted the war.

As for me? I couldn't even save one person.

Tay. If she'd been taken as bait for me, she couldn't be dead. I had that much working in my favour... until Shawn got bored of her, that is. Maybe he already had.

I left the citadel, trying to tell myself that my own survival was enough for now. Who knew, I might be able to convince the other contenders they'd brainwashed that we could overcome the traitorous spirit mages if we worked together, but would the others go for that?

Besides, it wasn't Shawn and his allies who I truly feared. If he was working in the name of the Family, then only one person could be giving him orders.

When I arrived back on the Death King's territory, it was to find Harper waiting near the node. "You're back? I thought you were gone for good."

I rose to my feet, shaking off the pain of the transporter. "I was always going to come back. I wouldn't leave you to suffer the consequences for what Shawn and the others did."

"You spoke to him, didn't you?" she said. "Did you pretend to still be on his side?"

"Not quite," I admitted. "I couldn't restrain myself from telling Shawn he was a piece of shit, so I guess I'm out of here when the Death King finds out."

She bit her lip. "They'll punish all of us for this. And their hostages."

I looked down. "You guessed it was them who had Tay, right?"

"Yeah," she murmured. "Who is she to you, anyway?"

"My best friend," I said. "We worked together, but she disappeared when Shawn and his friends wrecked our last job and then everything went to hell. I thought the House of Fire had her, but I never guessed the Family might have been working *with* the spirit mages."

"She's a fire mage, then?"

"No." I studied my palms. "But the Houses are the authorities in Elysium, so there's always been the risk of them catching us again. Miles suggested coming to the castle to lie low while he and the others looked for Tay, but he didn't realise the betrayers were right next to him."

She was silent for a moment. "My brother... he's still on the run, but there's only so many places you can go for shelter when you have a target on your back."

"I understand," I said. "I should have seen through their act from the start."

"This Miles person isn't involved with them?" she asked.

"No, he's with the real Spirit Agents," I said. "Shawn and the others pretended to be his allies and then tried to bump him off. I accidentally helped Miles escape, so at least I did something right this week."

"I shouldn't have taken it out on you," she said. "It's not your fault they came after my brother. He's the one who caught their attention to begin with. Lost a bet with the wrong person, and then I ended up having to bail him out by coming here in the hopes of gaining the position of Fire Element."

"I'll do my best to make sure you win," I said.

She gave me a faint smile. "It's okay if you don't want to tell me, but… the Death King said this wasn't the first time you've dealt with the Family."

"You might say that." I weighed the odds, then I said, "I grew up with them. The Family, I mean."

"Seriously?" She shot me an awed look. "How'd you get out?"

"I escaped them when I was a teenager," I said. "I've been on the run since I was sixteen. I knew they were crooked long before then, but it wasn't until the Houses caught them that I was able to get away. I thought they were still in jail, but someone from the Family has Tay held hostage. Either I give them Miles, or she dies."

"Are you sure?" she asked. "They're liars, you know they are, and they might not be telling the truth about having your friend hostage. Or they might be lying about setting her free if you hand over Miles."

"I know," I said. "I haven't even seen Miles in ages. Maybe they already have him."

But if they did, they wouldn't have threatened me over him, surely. No, he'd ditched me to do his own thing, and I didn't know whether that was on my side or against me.

I was reasonably confident that Shawn and the others

wouldn't dare come back here with the Death King watching out for trouble, at least, but I doubted I'd get away from the castle today. I'd have to lie low for the night and go back to look for Miles tomorrow. He'd evaded the others thus far, and getting more allies on my side wouldn't be a bad idea. I was sure there must be others among the contenders who needed convincing that Shawn was a conniving dickhead.

On my way back to the dormitory, a tall blond guy approached me. I cast around for his name and drew a blank. We hadn't spoken a word to one another, but the instant we crossed paths, he aimed a punch at me. I blocked instinctively, the movement jarring my arm.

"Let me guess… you're one of Shawn's lot." I deflected another blow. "Look, you realise the guy told a dozen of us a totally different cover story, don't you? He told me I was the only spy."

"He said the same about me." He yanked his arm from my grip. "One of us is full of crap, and it isn't me."

"It's Shawn." Carla stepped out of the shadows behind us, her arms folded. "He told me the same. Except with different details. Herod, stop trying to hit Bria. She's not the enemy."

"He got to you, too?" His deception must have begun long before he'd targeted me.

She inclined her head. "He and his buddies cornered me about a week ago, before the trials were due to start. They said I was the only person they trusted."

"I guess he needed several contenders in case one of us was knocked out of the running," I said. "I should have figured that out from the start. I guess his plan relied on making us all think we were special."

Herod cracked his knuckles. "Fuck the contest. I want to rip his head off. Wherever he's hiding."

"You don't know either?" asked Carla. "He said he lived in a top-secret bunker."

"Said he lived in the tunnels under Arcadia," said Herod.

Don't they know where he is. I knew he and the others were hiding in the citadel… but he was bound to have defences in place, and besides, he might have used the citadel's transporter to travel somewhere else. Not to mention that monster he'd tied up downstairs might well be on the loose, ready to take a bite out of any trespassers.

"Wherever he is, he's holding people hostage." Harper stepped out to join us. "He got to me, too. But collectively, we outnumber his allies."

"You too?" said Carla. "Who else?"

I counted on my fingers. "You two, Harper, Sledge, Bark…"

"Sledge?" said Herod. "Wait, isn't he in jail? I heard them saying."

"Yes, and I think Bark is, too," I said. "He set them up to take the fall. The same might've happened to any of us, if we hadn't seen through him."

"So what now?" said Carla. "How do we find him?"

"Not yet," I said. "He and his buddies can astral project from anywhere, so they can run away easily. We need to get to them in person. Luckily, I have enough cantrips to go around."

I revealed my stash, to general approval from the others.

Herod whistled. "You're giving them to us?"

"If you can refrain from getting caught with them." I

handed the invisibility cantrips out. "They only last an hour each, so only use them when you're backed into a corner. We need someone to talk to Sledge, too. I think Shawn tricked him into attacking the guards, but he got caught."

Carla scowled. "He's a scumbag of the highest order."

"Damn right," I said. "But he also has hostages, including a friend of mine. If he shows up here and tries to give any of you a cover story, send him my way. I'll get him to tell me where the hostages are. Then we can feed him to the liches."

"With pleasure." Herod's fists clenched. "If I see him in person, I want to knock his lights out."

"Do as you like," I said. "The important thing is not to get caught. Any of you. The Death King suspects something is going on, but if Shawn and the others are caught before we can get the hostages back, they might be killed as collateral. He has other spirit mages on his side, at least a dozen of them."

"Yeah, I've seen him with someone different every time," said Carla.

"Same here." That was part of his act, the dickhead, and it'd worked. Except on Miles, who'd seen through his act, and had made himself a target in the process. I had to make it up to him.

But first, we needed a plan.

I addressed the group. "He won't be back here today, but tomorrow is his last shot. Here's what we're going to do."

14

It seemed Shawn had rightly assumed coming back to the castle would be a bad move, because he didn't show his face in front of any of us that evening. We traded watches outside the castle and kept an eye open for Shawn and his friends from sunset onward, though Sledge, being the closest to the node, would be in a better position to alert the rest of us if the spirit mages came in via that route. Some agreed to watch the gates in various places, while others went outside under the guise of invisibility cantrips to keep their eyes open for any signs of Shawn or his friends out in the swampland.

Other than that, all we could do was watch our backs. In the end, I didn't tell the others about the citadel. If any of them went in there alone and got killed by the monster, it would be on me.

I needed to find Miles first. As soon as possible.

After all the Elemental Soldiers had retired to bed, Harper and I headed out into the main part of the castle together.

"You're sure we won't get caught?" she whispered to me as we walked through the silent corridor. "Don't get me wrong, I'm glad the Death King might have our backs after all, but if this goes wrong in any way, it's Percy who'll pay the price."

"I need to warn Miles," I said. "Shawn wants me to hand him over, which suggests he hadn't found his hiding place yet, but what if Miles went looking for Shawn himself? He must suspect the dickhead is working against him, and I don't know how many allies Miles has left."

"You're right," she said, "but I have one invisibility cantrip left."

"Same, but I think now's a good time for another visit to the Death King's storeroom," I said. "Can you keep watch outside? I won't be long."

"Sure." Harper and I parted ways outside the mail hall, and I turned on my last invisibility cantrip. Then I crossed the hall to the door leading into the room which contained the Death King's personal cantrip store. I didn't see Dex anywhere, but perhaps he'd retired for the night, too. With the hall of souls already protected in a million ways, it must be tedious to be stuck there for hours on end with nobody else to talk to.

I eased the door open and slipped into the storeroom, then I set about gathering as many invisibility spells as I could. With my contraband safely secured, I slipped out of the room and closed the door behind me.

"Stolen enough cantrips yet?" asked the fire sprite, hovering in front of me.

I jumped. "What the hell? Can you see me?"

"If I know where to look." Dex flew up to me and

perched on my invisible shoulder. "Also, I heard you talking to Harper outside. I've spoken to her sprite, too."

"Right." I released a breath. "I know the Death King probably won't like me stealing his cantrips, but Harper and I need them. To go—"

"To go and do something ill-advised and dangerous," he finished. "Just so you know, he probably has a perfectly good idea of what you took and when. Little escapes him. I'll say that much."

My shoulders slumped. "Look, there's no need to rub it in. Someone I know is going to be in serious trouble if I don't sneak out of the castle and find them. I don't have time to get caught."

"Ooh, a dangerous quest?" he said. "Excellent. I'm coming with you."

"Aren't you supposed to be guarding the hall of souls?" I reminded him.

"Aria took over from me for the night." He beckoned, and a second sprite fluttered out of the shadows near the door. "She's a little shy."

"Oh," I said. "I'm not here to steal the Death King's soul, by the way. That was a misunderstanding."

"Like I haven't heard that one before," he said. "In fact, you're just one in a long line of wannabe-criminals who think they're worthy of the soul of the Death King."

Dex flew at my shoulder as I walked out of the hall, and Harper froze when she spotted him. "He caught you?"

"I'm not here to turn you in," said Dex. "Provided you let me accompany you on your daring quest."

Harper gave me a sceptical look. "Yeah, I don't think this is going to work. Call me untrusting, but isn't he friends with the Death King's spirit mage?"

"I'm not going to betray you," he said indignantly. "Liv doesn't even have to know. She's at home."

"Good," I said. "Because I doubt she'd understand."

"Liv has her own problems to deal with," he responded. "I won't breathe a word to her. Provided you don't do anything to endanger the afterlife of His Deathly Highness, that is."

I snorted. "Can you ask the liches to let us through the gates? Or distract them? I'd rather not have to burn any more of them to get out without being interrogated."

"That was you?" He snickered. "I heard a couple of them moaning about some upstart fire mage turning them to ashes in the hall earlier. Shouldn't've agreed to host a fire mage contest, should they? All right, I'll distract them."

Dex went to distract the liches at the gate while Harper and I slipped out into the swampland, towards the node outside. Dex caught us up when we stepped into the node's path and reappeared in the city of Arcadia.

"Nicely done," said Dex. "I could get used to this espionage stuff. So, who are we spying on?"

"Nobody," I said. "We're looking for a friend of mine. Some dickhead spirit mages claimed to be on his side and are now looking to kill him, so I want to warn him first."

"Sounds heroic." He flew overhead as Harper looked up and down the street, towards the towering shape of the citadel overlooking the square. Darkness filled every corner, and I found myself fervently hoping the revenants would stay far away this time.

"I haven't been here in forever," Harper muttered. "Not without Percy."

"Her brother," I explained to Dex. "He's on the run

from Shawn and his friends, too. Part of their strategy was to take hostages."

"You're not going to the Withered Oak, are you?" he said, eying the building over my shoulder. "I know this place. Liv and I were here earlier this week."

I stopped walking. "You've gotta be kidding me. Liv came here?"

"She isn't there now," he said. "We suspected it to be a hideout of those House of Fire scum... and their associates."

A chill raced down my back. "They don't ask their guests questions, so anyone can sneak in. But if Miles isn't in Elysium, it's the only place I can think of that he might be."

"If you're sure." Harper's shoulders hunched. "I'm ready."

I pushed open the door, Dex perched on my shoulder. As we entered the bar, several people shot suspicious looks in our direction and then turned away almost immediately. Dex laughed under his breath. "This is much better than last time. They don't like spirit mages here. Or liches."

"Good job I'm not one, then." While Dex caught an odd look or two, Harper and I blended in as we walked to the bar.

"Hey, there," I said to the guy behind the counter. "I wondered if you'd seen a friend of mine. Miles... or he might be using an alias."

He jerked a thumb behind me. "Him?"

I wheeled around, my gaze going to a table under the window. My heart backflipped in my chest. There he was. Miles. *He's here?*

"Is that him?" whispered Harper.

I inclined my head. "I'll speak to him."

I crossed the room and sat down opposite Miles, who lifted his head. "There you are, Bria. I was starting to think you'd never show up."

"You can't have been here all day," I murmured. "Didn't they already throw you out?"

"I talked to the owner," he said. "When I explained I was trying to hunt down some rogue spirit mages, they let me in."

"Some of Shawn's allies stayed here, Miles. It isn't safe. They want you dead."

"Funny thing, that," he said. "I got that impression when they sent me on a bogus mission right into a revenant's nest."

A gasp lodged in my throat. "So it *was* them who sent you down there?"

"So that I couldn't find their hideout, I assume," he said. "I should have worked it out sooner. It wasn't until I got back to the base that I realised they'd given me false directions. They beat the shit out of my friend Tate, too. Shelley is seriously pissed off."

"Why did they want me to spy on the Death King?" I said. "In fact, *you're* the one who first told me you needed a spy."

"It was Shawn's suggestion," he said. "It's true that there's been something wrong on the Death King's territory for a while, but it turned out the trouble was closer to home than I thought. I thought the spy was among the liches. I knew there was at least one spirit mage involved, but I assumed it was a dead one, not a living one."

"Were you and the Death King really friends?" I asked.

"Not sure I'd use that word, but we knew one another before he became Death King," he said. "I should have guessed Shawn would try to poison you against him."

"Yeah, well, I'm here on his account," I admitted. "The Death King wants your help if Shawn and his friends attack the trials tomorrow."

His gaze went to Harper. "Is she trustworthy?"

"She and half the contenders are in the same position as I am," I said. "I've told them Shawn is a crook, but I think we're going to need outside help if we're to stop him and his allies."

"Meaning me." He dropped his gaze. "Yeah, I didn't sign up for this shit. I lost half my Spirit Agents to those fucking traitors."

"I'm sorry," I said to him. "Believe me. Shawn played me for a fool, and he did the same to half the contenders."

"Well, I won't hold it against you." He lifted his head, a smile playing on his mouth, and a warm feeling hit me that I couldn't entirely put down to relief that he hadn't turned out to be the traitor after all.

"C'mon," I said to him. "We should go somewhere else. This is too… public."

"What's with the cage?" asked Harper.

"Long story," said Miles.

I peered underneath the table. Sure enough, a cage sat there, almost concealed from sight. "What's in there?"

The door slammed open, and Harper grabbed my arm. "There's trouble."

Several people walked into the bar, a close-knit group dressed in cloaks and heavy-looking boots. My heart sank as every one of them headed for our table.

"Hey, there," I said brightly. "Can I help you with something?"

"We want the spirit mage," said one of them.

Whispers rippled through the bar. Miles swore under his breath. "Is there a problem?"

The glint of a knife flashed. "Come outside and we won't start trouble."

"No, thanks." Then Miles was on his feet, blasting the intruders with spirit magic. His foot knocked the cage, and the door sprang open, releasing a group of feathered creatures into the bar.

Vampire chickens?

My hands flamed, as did Harper's, and a warning look from the bartender prompted me to put out the flames and grab a cantrip instead. The paralysing cantrip went off, leaving the intruders in a heap on the floor.

The bartender strode out into view, and everyone turned in his direction. "You lot, get back to your drinking and stop gawking."

Everyone obeyed, but I sensed them watching us out of the corner of their eyes. Especially Miles, who was in the process of herding the chickens back into their cage. Where in the name of the Elements had he got those from?

The bartender turned to Miles, Harper and me. "As for you lot, I've had enough of you people wrecking the place. That includes the chickens—which are *illegal,* by the way."

"You're welcome," I said. "Might want to yell at the dickheads who're passed out on the floor instead of us. Just saying."

"C'mon." Miles picked up the cage, carrying it to the doors. "I knew that would happen if I met you in public, but I didn't have another way to reach you. Did anyone follow you?"

"Not that I'm aware of." I shot Harper an uneasy look. "More importantly, where the hell did you get those chickens? Were they the same chickens that escaped in Elysium?"

They couldn't be, surely. I mean, the guy was on the run with people out to kill him. Unless this was his new business venture.

He cleared his throat. "Can I explain later? I think we need to get off the street, if Shawn is sending his allies all the way over here."

"He's based in this city," I told him, in a low voice. "He and his allies are hiding in the citadel, but they booby-trapped the door against me after they found out I wasn't going to be their lackey."

His gaze travelled towards the dark shape of the citadel. "Are you sure you can't get in?"

"Not now I'm on their shit list," I said. "They also have a wyrm in there. A full-grown one. How they caught it, I have no idea."

He swore. "So *that's* what they didn't want me to see."

"Apparently," I said. "Tomorrow is the last day of the trials and Shawn's last shot to get at the Death King, so all his attention is going to be there. What he doesn't know is that all the people he duped into taking his side are now aware that he was talking complete bollocks. We're ready for him."

"I like where this is going." Miles grunted, adjusting his grip on the cage. "Okay, tell me the plan."

"When Shawn shows up, we'll send word to you," I said. "Harper's sprite, Mav, will be waiting next to the node. You wait near another node—any will do—and she'll come through and give you the signal."

"We'll have people watching out for any signs of Shawn's approach," added Harper. "There's half a dozen of us involved now."

Miles nodded. "Okay. I'll wait for your sprite's signal and I'll bring my allies to help. There are enough of us left to give Shawn and his mates some serious grief."

"Good."

We parted ways with Miles, and Harper and I headed back to the Death King's territory. When he'd vanished from sight, I fell into step with her. "I think that went well. Even the part with the vampire chickens."

Harper laughed under her breath.

"What?" I said. "Help me out here."

She broke into full-on giggles. "Didn't you tell me he made you drop those chickens in the middle of the city and cost you your job in the process?"

"Yes," I said, nonplussed. "Why?"

"Because—" she broke off with another laugh—"he clearly felt so bad about that misstep that he went there in person to collect up every single one of them."

"No way." She had to be kidding. "That would be a complete waste of everyone's time. Besides, he just let them go again."

"To save your neck." She stopped laughing. "He's totally sweet on you, Bria."

"A likely story." Okay, he seemed to forgive me for believing Shawn's lies, but that wasn't enough to warrant him risking arrest from the Order of the Elements to recapture a bunch of vampire chickens I'd all but forgotten about already. It was almost weirder than the fact that a bunch of us were about to face off against rogue spirit mages with the help of the King of the Dead of all people.

Whatever happened, if Shawn planned to strike the Death King before the trials were up, we had to be ready for him. And we would be, if my plan went ahead without a hitch.

I was counting on it.

15

Upon our return to the castle, Harper and I split up and went back to the dorms to prepare for the following day. I slept for an unsatisfying couple of hours and rose at dawn, at which point I visited Sledge under the guise of an invisibility cantrip to remind him of the plan. In truth, I didn't trust him not to screw up, but I didn't want to leave him out in case he objected and caused trouble for all of us later on.

"Watch the node, okay?" I said. "That's where the signal will come from. Mav is going to be there."

When Shawn showed up, Mav would go through the node to meet Miles on the other side and give him the signal, too.

Sledge grunted. "When do you let me out of here?"

"When the distraction is in progress," I said. "One of the others will help you escape. The important thing is that you cause as much of a diversion as possible when Mav gives you the signal, so the liches will swarm over to the node."

"And the liches will surround Shawn and his friends, right?" he said.

"Better hope they do," I said. "If you don't see any signs of him, then don't cause a ruckus.

There's no guarantee they'll come through the node. It's the closest route to the castle, but it's also the riskiest."

For that reason, I suspected they'd try to break through the front gates instead, but that didn't mean they wouldn't try something none of us had thought of yet. I could think of a hundred possible ways this might go wrong, and at the very least, we could expect an ugly conflict between the liches and the spirit mages. If the Death King shut down the contest, we'd lose our chance to snag Shawn in our trap, so our best bet was to act as though nothing was wrong.

Easier said than done.

I left the jail, checked there were no liches within sight, and met Harper near the node. "All set?"

"Not exactly," she said. "Carla disappeared overnight. Herod thinks she went back to join Shawn."

"Shit." I'd expected at least one person to clear off, but not this close to the end of the trials. "He'd better not have come here and threatened her."

"I doubt he'd have taken the risk," she said. "Mav, you ready?"

"You bet." Mav gave a wave from within the node.

"She'll give Miles the signal when Sledge tells her to," I said. "Is Dex ready?"

"Yeah, I asked him to keep an eye out from the castle," she said. "Aria, too."

"That's it, I think." Everyone in on our plan was on

high alert, and yet a sense of unease remained hanging over me like a dark cloud.

"They're calling us in," said Harper, indicating the arena. "Better go."

"All right." I walked with her to join the other contenders, wondering if anyone else had run off overnight like Carla had. What would we do if Shawn showed up and nobody gave the signal?

Did we screw it up by getting the others involved at all?

Unsurprisingly, my focus levels on the actual contest that morning were pretty much non-existent. The remaining contenders were divided up into groups to make jigsaw puzzles out of magical pieces of stone and then light them up using our fire magic. Harper and I were put in different groups, which was an annoyance, but even Liv hardly seemed to have any attention span left, instead pacing around peering into bushes as though expecting to find Percy or someone else lurking out of sight. If she hadn't gone walkabout yesterday, I might have told her my plan, but now wasn't the time to drag anyone else into it. Besides, for all I knew, she might be in league with Shawn and the other spirit mages.

When the Elemental Soldiers stopped near the arena wall to converse, I caught a whisper from the Water Element—"Did you know the contenders' magic is still acting up?"

Seriously? Is it Mav? Surely not—she was waiting all the way over by the node to give the signal and wasn't paying any attention to the contest—but I couldn't think of an obvious reason as to why anyone's magic would be glitching out now. Unless it was part of the Death King's final test. Not that I'd seen *him* today, either. Maybe that was the reason for the bone-deep sense of unease thrumming in my nerve endings.

A short while later, a shout came from the direction of the jail. *Sledge's signal.* He'd spotted Shawn or one of the other spirit mages. Go time. I caught Harper's gaze across the arena and was on my feet an instant later.

Liv had clearly been waiting for an attack, too, because she was the first to run towards the jail. I waited, tensed, for Shawn's appearance, but it never came. Instead, Liv returned to view, carrying Mav in a firm grip. *Crap.* She must have spotted the sprite hiding inside the node. If Mav couldn't give the signal to Miles, he and the others wouldn't know when to show up and help against Shawn. Yet I didn't see him either, or any of the other rogue spirit mages.

Had Sledge given the wrong signal? Or was the enemy mage already hiding somewhere in the grounds?

Liv approached the arena and waylaid Harper. The sheer panic in her expression made it impossible to hide that Mav was her responsibility. I tried to catch her gaze, but Harper left the arena and followed Liv, her gaze fixed on the struggling water sprite. Liv's grip on the sprite didn't relinquish, and I cursed her under my breath as I looked for someone who could tell me why Sledge's signal had come at the wrong time.

Another howl from the jail made the hairs on my arms stand on end. Something else was going on over there. I wouldn't get another chance to warn Miles, so I left the arena and headed that way at a jog. If Mav hadn't been able to get the signal through, I'd do it myself.

In front of the jail, the liches who guarded the doors were nothing more than twin piles of ashes. Someone had taken them down… but no spirit mages were in sight, and none of the other fire mages had left the arena.

Sledge. The bastard must have turned on us.

As I ran towards the jail, Liv appeared behind me, some kind of cantrip gleaming in her hand. On instinct, I grabbed a cantrip of my own, but she didn't aim at me. Instead, the disc flew from her hand and slammed into the gleaming node. At once, the current of light died to a flicker.

What in the world?

Spirit magic blasted from her hands, this time aimed at me. I staggered back, panic rising. Did she think I was the villain, or had she been a traitor all along? Whatever the case, she'd done something to turn off the node—and with it, she'd taken away my chance to warn Miles.

If the enemy was already inside the grounds, we were screwed.

Liv jerked her head at the cantrip I'd dropped. "Where'd you get that?"

I raised my chin. "The Death King's storeroom."

No point in hiding anything now. Once all the cards were on the table, she could decide for herself if she wanted to be a hindrance or a help. Out of the corner of my eye, I saw two guards escorting Harper and Mav from the grounds—yet still, Shawn and his allies were nowhere to be seen. Either Sledge had given the wrong signal, accidentally or otherwise, or there'd been a change of plans which nobody had enlightened me on.

"You and Harper were in on the same plan," said Liv. "Care to tell me who else was involved?"

I wish I knew. Our plan lay in tatters, and around the castle, the liches were on the move. Dark shadows swept across the castle's grounds, blocking the gates and masking Harper from view. The only way out was the node behind me, which Liv had somehow switched off. Unless my transporter spell might still work. I took a step in that direction, but Liv got in the way.

"You aren't getting away that easily," she said.

There came a flash of light from outside the gates, a current of energy flaring up to the sky on the other side of the fence. The other node. *Please say it's someone on our side.*

When Liv glanced over the fence, I reached into my pendant. "Sorry, Liv, but I have backup."

I flung a paralysis cantrip at her and took off at a run, hoping I could beat her to the gates. Whoever had shown up, friend or foe, I needed to get the hell out of here while I could.

I skidded to a halt at the gates. A group of tall, graceful, smartly dressed individuals gathered outside. *Vampires?*

What the hell was going on? Whatever it was, it wasn't the diversion I'd planned, and it definitely wasn't Shawn and his pack of spirit mages. Liv appeared as dumbfounded as me when she set eyes on the newcomers.

"We have come here for justice," said the leading vampire. "Hand over Olivia Cartwright and Brant Edwards, and we will spare your lives."

And that's my cue to leave.

I fumbled for an invisibility cantrip and switched it on, waiting for an opening to run through the gates. Harper must be somewhere on the other side after she'd got kicked out, but the vampires blocked my path, arguing with the Death King. He seemed to be negotiating about whether to trade Liv and some guy called Brant over to the vampires, which might have caught my attention under any other circumstances. Had Liv seriously managed to make an enemy of the vampires who ran the city of Arcadia? Whatever the case, the time for bargaining for the help of the Death King's people was over.

Once a gap in the crowd appeared, I wove through the liches and out of the gates into the swampland. There, I released a breath, scanning the area for any signs of Harper. If it turned out Sledge hadn't screwed up the signal, he'd be pissed off at me for ditching him, but it was that or end up in a cell of my own.

The Death King and the vampire lord continued to argue at a high volume as I trod through the swamp— where, to my intense relief, I saw Miles hovering near the node. I quickened my pace and turned off the invisibility cantrip when I was close enough to the node not to be spotted by any of the Death King's people. "Miles? What in hell are you doing here? Where's Shawn?"

"With any luck, hiding." He grinned. "Like my diversion?"

"Your what?" Then it hit me. "*You* called the vampires?"

"Well, yes," he said. "I figured the one thing that would draw him out of his castle would be the arrival of his biggest rival. Even Shawn can't take on the vampires *and* the Death King and his entire lich army at once."

"Right." The Death King and the vampires were not friends. "Were you aware that they wanted to arrest Liv for some reason? Also, she thinks I'm the villain, I might add. Things kinda went wrong in there."

"You're telling me," he said. "I never got your signal."

"That's because Liv captured Mav and booted her and

Harper out of the contest." I looked around the swamp-land again. "Have you seen them?"

"Not yet." He tensed, glancing at the node behind him. "I'll take care of Liv, too. I don't know her personally, but I figure she isn't the villain here."

"Except where the vampires are concerned." I turned on the invisibility cantrip again as the node lit up behind him.

"That's the signal," he breathed. "The others are coming. We'll take Liv. You find your friend, and if Shawn shows up…"

"I'll shove him into the line of fire." I doubted he'd show his face at this point, though. Ordinarily, I might have been annoyed with Miles for going off script and bringing a group of vampires along with him, but it was more Sledge's fault than anything for screwing up the signal.

The node ignited and Miles's friend Shelley appeared, followed by several of his other fellow Spirit Agents. Hoping their presence would distract the liches who weren't wrapped up in watching the vampires' argument with their master, I moved across the swamp, looking for Harper. *She can't have gone far, surely.*

As I did so, the liches' attention turned towards the node, and Liv's brows rose at the sight of the new arrivals.

"I'm not sure I like the idea of your justice," she told the vampire. "You're working with a group of murderers and traitors."

"Murderers?" said Miles. "I wouldn't say that."

"Quiet, Miles," said Shelley.

Lord Blackbourne shot them a disgruntled look. "I would prefer it if you were to stay out of this one."

So Miles did personally know the vampire lords? I'd have to ask him about that one later. Liv's hands glowed with spirit magic, and while the vampires and mages had her surrounded, she looked more exasperated than scared.

Two vampires closed in, but Liv got there first, blasting them off their feet into the swamp. Miles laughed. "Damn, she *is* good."

Now isn't the time to underestimate her. She fired off another bolt of spirit magic from her hands, and Miles deflected it. Despite her obvious disadvantage, Liv's stare was unwavering. "Whoever you are, I'm not coming with you."

"You don't have a choice," he said. "Besides, I'm told we're not all bad."

The mages closed in around her, and the glow brightened as the node's strength bolstered her own. Static power vibrated through the air, making my teeth rattle. Liv was far outnumbered, but if she hurt Miles or his allies, then it wouldn't do any of us any favours.

Still invisible, I walked around Liv from behind. Then I conjured flames to my hands, switching off the cantrip when they reached their peak and stepping directly in front of Liv. "Hey, there."

Liv's eyes bulged at the sight of me. "You."

I darted out of sight, but the distraction was enough for Miles to get in a hit. Spirit magic shot from several directions at once and blasted Liv clean off her feet. She hit the ground on her back, hard, and didn't get up.

"Thanks," Miles said, sounding surprised.

"Anytime you need assistance, ask me." I eyed Liv's prone form on the ground. "Where are you taking her?"

"Back to our base," he responded. "You'd better go find your friend."

Right… Harper was still missing. "Sure. Let me know if you need me to kidnap anyone else."

I turned the cantrip back on and left Liv with the Spirit Agents by the node. Invisible, I walked away from the castle, keeping both eyes open for any signs of movement. A flicker above a bush drew my attention to a humanoid figure floating in the air. *Mav. She's okay.*

I ran over to her, switching off the invisibility cantrip when I saw Harper hiding in the bushes nearby. "There you are. Don't worry—Miles and his friends took Liv with them, and Shawn won't dare attack with the vampires *and* the liches roaming around the place."

"I wouldn't speak too soon," she murmured.

I rotated on the spot. A flicker of fire stirred in the bushes nearby, and suspicion roared to life inside me. There was a fire mage outside… hidden by an invisibility spell.

"The fuck?" Ignoring Harper's hiss of alarm, I advanced on the bushes. "Who's there?"

Several fire mages popped out of the air… including Sledge.

"Someone let you out of your cage, did they?" I said. "Whatever happened to waiting for the signal?"

He bared his teeth. "You bitch. You abandoned us."

"If you were paying any attention, you'd have seen the reason we had to change tactics." I folded my arms across my chest. "Besides, you were supposed to set off the signal when you saw Shawn or his friends coming through the node, not randomly yell and blow our cover."

"There's been a change of plans," said Herod, one of

the other mages from the contest. "Specifically, a change of leadership."

There came the flicker of a dozen invisibility cantrips turning off. More mages appeared, surrounding Harper's hiding spot. Some were fire mages from among the contenders, some were Shawn's friends… and one was Harper's brother.

Harper rose to her feet. "Please tell me you didn't."

"Sorry, Harper," he said. "If I were you, I'd duck."

Water rose from his hands and shot at me, dampening the flames that sprang to my palms. Then came a torrent of fire, blazing to the sky, as Herod and Sledge turned on their cantrips.

Harper shouted in alarm, but Percy grabbed her by her shoulders and yanked her aside. Herod ran at me, his mouth twisted in a grin as the inferno slammed into me like a truck.

The flames were everywhere, ripping through my body until nothing remained but darkness.

16

My eyes flew open to see a shadow blotting out the sky. Cold wetness covered my back where I'd hit the swampy ground, while ashes drifted in the air. The Death King leant over me, and I blinked up at him. "What the hell is going on?"

"I should be asking you the same question," he said. "I thought you had a plan to stop my castle being overrun by traitors. Now a considerable number of my liches have been burned to a crisp and half my contenders are missing."

"We hit a snag." I pushed upright into a sitting position and then got to my feet, brushing dirt off my legs. Swamp water soaked my clothes, but that was the least of my problems. "Half your contenders decided to throw their lot in with Shawn instead."

I looked around for any signs of Harper, but she'd gone. Her brother had betrayed us both, and the other mages had left me for dead. Had she gone with him? Maybe she'd had no choice.

"I'm not surprised," he said. "Walking away from a situation which endangers one's loved ones is not a decision taken lightly."

"Harper's brother turned against us," I said. "The bloody fool wanted to protect her, but she's in even more danger if she goes with him. They'll know she helped me."

"I was concerned that would be the result," he said. "I hoped she might escape in time to avoid that scenario."

"That's why you kicked her out," I said, comprehension dawning. "You knew it was him dampening everyone's magic today, not Mav. Didn't you?"

"Harper's sprite?" He beckoned, and Mav floated out from behind him. "She's safe."

"No thanks to you," I said, momentarily forgetting who I was talking to. "Did you just let Shawn's allies run off with Harper? Were you too busy arguing with the vampires to notice?"

The vampires, I noted, seemed to have disappeared at some point while I'd been out of commission as well. The two of us stood alone in the swampland, aside from the liches guarding the castle gates.

"If you're suggesting I ought to have walked into the middle of that young man's inferno spell, then you have the wrong idea about what advantages being the king of the liches provides," he said. "I am not, unfortunately, fireproof."

That was when I saw Herod—or what was left of him. His body had burned to a crisp, ragged clothes hanging off scorched red flesh. Nausea rose in my throat, followed by panic. In the Death King's eyes, I ought to have looked the same, and I had no reasonable explanation to offer him.

I scrambled for a change of subject. "I'm guessing that's why the vampires took off, then. Did you and Miles plan to invite them all along, to deter the spirit mages from breaking into your territory?"

"Not hardly," he said. "Miles informed me of his plan less than an hour before he implemented it. The vampires, unfortunately, were already searching for my spirit mage, so at my request, the Spirit Agents offered to help hide Olivia until the vampires give up their search for her."

"Wait, Miles came to talk to you in person?" Why hadn't he told me? Admittedly, we'd been short on time, but it'd have been nice to know the vampires were coming. Though it didn't seem that the Death King had told Liv he'd arranged for her to be kidnapped by the Spirit Agents, either.

"We go back a long way," he said, "but you have a problem on your hands."

"You're telling me." I turned to the water sprite. "Did you see where Sledge and the others took Harper?"

Mav let out a sob. "No. They took her through the node… I couldn't stop them."

As long as she's not dead… but why had the other contenders ultimately chosen to believe Shawn over me? Maybe they'd thought they had no choice but to take his side, but Harper had been faced with the exact same dilemma and she'd come out on my side.

"I need to find her," I told the Death King. "It's not her fault this happened. The others were supposed to give us a warning if Shawn showed up, so we could team up against him. They weren't meant to join him again."

"People often disappoint."

No kidding. For all I knew, that was precisely why he'd

exiled himself to the middle of nowhere with a bunch of liches and wights and undead horses. I didn't blame him a bit, considering how many of his potential Fire Elements had turned out to be lying bastards.

"I'm pretty sure Liv thinks I'm the bad guy," I added. "But she got in my way at the worst time."

"That's unfortunate," he said. "Perhaps you will be able to mend your differences later."

"I doubt it." Getting my friends back was more important. "I'm going after Shawn and the others. Can I expect backup?"

"You might have noticed I have a considerable number of enemies who have picked this moment to strike," he said. "I'm sure Miles is aware of your dilemma, and I'll send him in your direction when he returns from restraining my spirit mage. I take it you know where Shawn and his allies are hiding?"

"They're in the citadel," I told him. "In Arcadia. The doors are barred, but that shouldn't be a problem for you."

"My skills may be considerable," he said, "but I lack the ability to be in several places at once, and I have other matters to attend to."

Great. Shawn and his friends likely didn't even register as a threat to him. But then again, it wasn't his loved ones they had captive.

I'm coming, Harper. For all I knew, Tay was with them, too.

"They aren't alone," I told him. "Last I saw, they had a giant wyrm tied up in their hideout, and I'd bet they're preparing to unleash it on the public."

"Then you'd better stop them before they do."

Thanks for the help. I could see why Liv had such a

contentious approach to working with the Death King, and yet he was off to save her neck right now while the rest of us were in trouble. She and the Death King had a hell of a weird relationship, that was for sure. More to the point, he'd had Shawn and the others figured out from the start, down to the last part of their plan. I could see why he'd maintained control over an army of the dead for so long. Nothing slipped his notice.

Except…

"You didn't ask how I survived the fire mages' attack," I said.

"I didn't need to."

And with that, he walked away, leaving me wondering if there was anything the Death King hadn't already figured out. Including Herod and the others' betrayal. I wouldn't deny it, that part stung. I'd really thought I'd got them on my side and convinced them to go with me rather than with Shawn and his dickhead friends.

Nevertheless, I understood why they'd made the choice they had. They'd been downtrodden for so long they couldn't conceive of having a choice to turn their back on those who threatened them. They thought their destiny was predetermined.

I'd thought that way once. But I'd learned the hard way that even if I felt like someone else was guiding my choices, the consequences would be on me alone.

A flash of red light zipped across my vision, and Dex flew down to my side. "What have you done now?"

I gave him an accusing look. "Your friend Liv screwed up my plans, majorly. On top of that, Harper's brother turned traitor and his allies took her away with them, and your boss won't help me find her."

Miles would be willing to help, true, but how many spirit mages were left on his side? Perhaps enough to help me find Harper, but if that wyrm escaped the citadel, we'd be in a world of trouble.

"Hey, don't blame me," said Dex. "I can't control what Liv does. As for the boss, he relieved me from guard duty, so I'm willing to help you on your ill-advised rescue mission."

"We'd be grateful if you did." In truth, we were far outnumbered. Shawn had too many allies, including Harper's brother and the other ex-contenders—not to mention that wyrm.

On the other hand, I refused to abandon another friend.

With the water sprite and the fire sprite at my side, I headed for the node and travelled through to Arcadia. The instant we landed on the other side, a chorus of screams came from behind us. I wheeled around on the spot, squinting through the node's glare at the clouds of smoke pouring out from a side street.

The Withered Oak was on fire. Smoke billowed over the rooftops, while the patrons fled into the street. I ran towards the pub, my heart lurching. *Did Shawn and the others come here?*

I halted outside. Through the window, jets of flame shot in all directions, causing the patrons to flee or duck behind tables to avoid being hit.

"Mav," I said to the water sprite. "Can you help? Is that magic-boosting spell still in effect?"

"It is." She flew through the door in a cloud of mist, and the effect was like a sprinkler system on the fire mages below. Water doused some of the flames, but one of the fire mages ducked underneath the sprite, spotting me outside. It seemed Sledge's friend Bark had found a new hideout.

"You're that bitch who got me kicked out the contest," he said accusingly.

Flames leapt to my hands, rivalling his own. "Want to take this outside?"

He met me at the door and aimed a flaming punch, which I ducked with ease, spinning into a kick to the back of his leg which sent him staggering. I didn't need to hold back. We weren't in the trials any longer.

"I *knew* you weren't human," he said. "You're too fast."

"Maybe you're just slow." I kicked his other leg, and as he stumbled, I swung a flaming uppercut into his jaw. He flew back into the doorway. Catching his balance, he dug a hand into his pocket. There came the faint click of a cantrip, and a torrent of fire returned to his hands. Oh, hell.

He leapt to his feet, flames dancing in his eyes, and bared his teeth in a grin. "Beat this, bitch."

I backed into the street, dodging punches and fireballs one after another. I was more worried for the bystanders than myself, because his entire body was outlined in flames that seemed inches away from devouring him like Herod's fatal attack back in the swamp.

"You should be burning!" he bellowed. "You're no ordinary fire mage."

"Really? I had no idea." I was done playing games. A flame leapt to my own palms, and I pivoted with inhuman speed, slamming into him from behind. My fire joined his, and the mage recoiled, yelling as his own flames turned against him and burned his hands to a crisp.

He was right. I was no ordinary fire mage. Not by a long shot.

The mage fled down the street, and I lowered my hands. The bar was almost deserted, but I spotted Mav in the hallway. "Anyone upstairs?"

"No, they're all out," she said.

"I sent them on the run," said Dex, with a cackle. "Don't worry, the fire's out. Crisis averted."

"Good." I headed outside again, seeing the patrons scattered throughout the surrounding area. Some people cast confused glances in my direction. I hadn't intended to make a public spectacle. Hopefully, they'd be too relieved at their lucky escape to question how I'd escaped being burned to a crisp.

"Where are the spirit mages hiding?" said Mav. "Are they really in the citadel?"

"I think so."

"*That* citadel?" said Dex. "The haunted one?"

"The one and only." I released a breath. "They have Harper. Maybe my best friend, too. The place links up to the other citadels around the Parallel, so the rogue spirit mages are using it to hide from the authorities."

"Convenient," said the fire sprite. "All right, let's burn them."

Miles was still nowhere to be seen, but we couldn't delay any longer. Followed by the sprites, I made my way towards the towering shape of the citadel. I wished I'd just told Harper and the others the location of their hideout to begin with. If they'd seen the wyrm, though, they might have thought twice about offering me help. But in the end, whether they'd taken his side or not, Shawn would have got his way one way or another. People like him would always find supporters among the desperate and downtrodden.

I would not let Harper be forced to do his bidding, too. No way in hell.

"Here we are." I reached the citadel, peering up at the towering structure. "There's a side entrance, but it was booby trapped the last time I was here."

Dex flew up to the building. "It doesn't feel booby trapped."

"Let me check." I reached gingerly for the door, but no shock came. The handle turned at my touch. *Okay. That's weird.* Had they abandoned the place already?

I entered the wide room where the spiralling staircase led to the upper floor... and a pair of giant eyes looked down on me.

The wyrm was out of its cage.

I held my breath. The citadel's interior was dark enough that the wyrm might not have spotted me yet, but it wouldn't last. The sprites shrank back behind me, and I dropped my voice to a faint whisper. "Guys, if you can divert its attention while I run upstairs, it'd be appreciated."

"Go on!" Mav hissed in my ear. "We'll keep it distracted."

"With pleasure," put in Dex.

"Thanks." I turned on an invisibility cantrip. Once I was sure my body was unseen, I trod across the floor towards the foot of the stairs. As long as I didn't make a sound, I ought to be able to get to the top without the beast realising I was there, but the tower caught every sound and multiplied it. *This is gonna be tricky.*

I began to climb as the sprites circled the beast's head, conjuring sparks before its eyes. The wyrm turned its head to watch the sparks, not comprehending what they were at first. Then it released a bellow of fury and reared back.

I ducked as its tail swiped overhead, crashing into the staircase and missing me by inches. I leapt to a higher step, and the creature hissed as sparks flew into its eyes, courtesy of Dex. Yet its tail kept thrashing, slamming into the stairs so hard it threatened to hurl me towards a painful landing. I waited for a moment for the path to clear, and its head swung around in my direction, its nostrils dilating. Even invisible, the wyrm had sniffed out its prey.

The sprites descended into its eyes, and it reeled back, giving me the chance to climb up another few stairs. The door was just above my head. One more loop of the room ought to do it. Almost there…

The wyrm wheeled around in my direction again, its eyes narrowed and sore-looking from the sparks Dex had thrown at it. Reaching into my pocket, I threw a paralysing cantrip at its head. That ought to hold it for a bit.

I sprinted for the top, pushed the door open and darted through, breathing hard. The room within appeared empty at first glance, aside from the abandoned machinery… and the cage from the lower level. Except instead of a wyrm, the cage contained several mages, Harper among them. Not Tay… and not Miles or his fellow Spirit Agents.

Harper startled at the sight of me when I turned off the invisibility cantrip. "How'd you get past that beast?"

"Your sprite gave me a hand." I crossed the room to the cage. "Where's your brother?"

"The bastard's with *them*," she whispered. "He left me

in here and went with the spirit mages through the trans-porter, but they'll be back any second now."

"All right," I said. "Hang on. I'll get you out."

The cage door was a simple lock, so I used the cantrip tool to pick it open. The other mages watched me with wide eyes. Some looked barely out of their teens. Others were younger. A spasm of rage shook me.

A flash of light bloomed on the raised platform in the room's centre, and several people appeared from the transporter. Shawn stood at the centre of the group, along with Harper's brother. Percy's jaw tightened at the sight of me, but it was Shawn whose expression was pure murder.

"There you are, Bria," he said. "Or should I call you… the heir to the Family?"

Icy fear clenched my stomach and locked my feet to the spot. He knew… which meant he'd talked to one of *them*.

"I'm not the heir to anything." I rose to my feet. "The Death King's army is on its way here right now, along with his other allies. You've lost."

The sound of the beast thrashing around below reached our ears. I edged around the cage, hoping to give Harper the chance to run for it—though hell if I knew how we'd get past that giant monster *and* Shawn's allies at the same time.

Now would be a really good time to come here with backup, Miles.

"I don't see an army," said Shawn. "I think you're lying. Nobody is coming to help you."

I let my gaze pan across his group. Six of them, including Percy. Fewer than I'd expected. "Where's *your* army? Did you leave them behind, or did they get sick of your bullshit and quit?"

"If you mean the other fire mages who you failed to convince to take your side," he said, "they're dealing with the Death King. Shouldn't take too long… he's lost too much of his army already, and the former Fire Element is more than prepared to take him down."

Davies. I'd bet the former Fire Element had rallied the ex-contenders around him. That's why the Death King had stayed behind rather than coming to help me out— he'd known his presence would draw the fire mages here. Instead, I was faced with only six enemies… oh, and the giant wyrm. That, too.

I made a sceptical noise. "Have you seen the Death King in action? He can rip out your soul in a heartbeat."

"Oh, I can do the same." Despite his light tone, a chilling look burned in Shawn's eyes. "There's a reason my existence is punishable by death in the world on the other side of the nodes."

I tilted my head. "Is this where you tell me *why* you made yourself an enemy of the most powerful person in the Parallel?"

"The Death King is a traitor and a liar," he said. "By taking his side, Miles and his fellow Spirit Agents declared themselves to be the same."

I forced a laugh. "Is this all because they didn't support your little coup? Judging by the obvious chip on your shoulder and your interesting choice of venue, I assume you're trying to bring about a second elemental war, like your ancestors did."

"My ancestors didn't do anything wrong." A couple of his friends nodded in agreement. "They weren't even spirit mages. We're being punished for crimes we never committed."

I raised my hands. "Dude, I had exactly zero to do with that—and by the way, you *did* commit the crime of locking up a bunch of defenceless mages in a cage, including children, and capturing a dangerous magical creature inside a tower which is supposed to be out of bounds to the public. So I feel justified in kicking your arse."

"So do I." Harper leapt up, her hands blazing with fire magic, and threw a handful of flames at her brother. He ducked, and her attack fizzled out on contact with the machinery behind him. The whole place must be magic-proofed… but Shawn and his friends weren't.

I threw my own flames at Shawn, forcing him to duck behind the cage to dodge. In the room below, I heard the wyrm roar. Dammit, there must be a way to get it out of our path. Unless we used the transporter—

Shawn caught Harper's brother in a headlock from behind. "Surrender, or I'll rip out your brother's soul."

"Hey!" Percy squirmed. "Keep me out of this."

Harper's expression was murderous, but she lowered her hands. Even after he'd betrayed her, she wouldn't risk her brother's life. I didn't blame her, but we were seriously short on allies.

The machinery lit up, bright lights spinning on its surface.

"Oh, look," said Shawn, a smirk on his face. "Backup has arrived."

Shit. The light brightened to a glare, and several people appeared in the middle of the room… including Tay.

Not in a cage. Not tortured, or desperate, but free.

When she spotted me, she stopped mid-step, her mouth parting in surprise. My heart thundered in my ears. *No. It can't be.*

Her expression smoothed out. "Hey, Bria."

A roaring sensation filled my ears, and even the murmur of the mages' voices and the sound of the beast thrashing around downstairs faded into the background as I looked at her in stunned disbelief. "You—you do realise he had you kidnapped, didn't you?"

"Is that what he told you?" she looked from me to him. "Funny, because he told me *you* went off to the Death King's territory instead of coming to find me."

"I thought you were in the House of Fire's custody!" I caught a glimpse of Shawn's smirk, but my attention was fixed on Tay. "The authorities were on the street looking for both of us. I turned two of Striker's vamps into ashes and I had to run. I always planned to come back for you. What I don't understand is why you believed his lies."

"Lies?" she said. "Like the ones you told me when we met? You never shared a thing about who raised you."

"If you'd wanted to know, you should have asked." I couldn't believe she was confronting me about my family history at a time like this. "As opposed to joining forces with a maniac who wants to steal the Death King's soul and start a war."

"That's really not what's going on here," she said. "If you think so, though, by all means, do what the House of Fire did and take me down."

My gut tightened. *I can't.* Elements, the one thing I couldn't do was hurt her. Even if she seemed to have taken Shawn's side, there had to be a mistake. After everything we'd been through together, why would she side with the Family?

Around us, everyone watched the show. To Shawn and his friends, our pain was their entertainment, but I refused to believe Tay had turned on me of her own free will. There must be more at play here.

"Tay," I said. "I'm going to say this to you one last time… don't do this."

"It's already too late," she said. "You know how the mages are going to be the first to suffer if the Houses get their way."

"You told her that bullshit about the Houses, too?" I said to Shawn. "Tay, he's a compulsive liar. Nothing he says is remotely true."

"They want us dead, Bria," said Tay. "The Houses of the Elements, and everyone in power in the Parallel. You know it's true."

"He's lying to you," I warned. "Don't—"

Her hands lit up. Electric sparks flew from her fingertips, and a pulse of dread pounded through me. She never used her magic openly. Most people didn't know she was even a mage.

I'd kept her secret for years. I'd thought she trusted me with her life.

Everyone stilled, quietness spreading through the room. For an instant, I thought it was because they were mesmerised by her power… then I heard the sound of footsteps on the stairs. And the wyrm had gone awfully quiet.

"What was that?" Shawn demanded. "Who else is in here?"

"Isn't this place supposed to be haunted?" I backed up a

step towards the stairs, hoping the freed prisoners would take the opportunity to run. "Haunted by the ghosts of the mages killed in the elemental war? If I were them, I'd be pissed off at the new generation of mages making the exact same mistakes all over again."

"Very funny." Shawn's mouth twisted. "Right. You—"

The door crashed wide open, and Shawn yelped as he was flung off his feet and into the air. Miles entered, accompanied by several other spirit mages. Thank the Elements.

"Still afraid of the ghosts of your predecessors?" said Miles. "Bria is right. I wouldn't be happy with you either, if I were them."

"Enough of this bullshit," said Shawn. "Go on. Kill them."

Before anyone could move, a deafening roar and crash sounded. The mages scattered as the wyrm wriggled through the doorway, its scaled form squirming up the stairs. Even Tay looked cowed at the sight of the fanged beast dragging itself into the room, teeth bared and ready to kill. *How did Miles get it up here?*

"Your guest is pissed at you," Miles said.

The wyrm gave one last lunge through the door, its tail flicking up, and everyone flung themselves flat to avoid getting hit.

"This way!" Shawn leapt onto the platform, his hands alight with magic. The transporter flashed once, and several spirit mages vanished along with him.

The beast roared, and Harper caught my arm. "I don't think it cares if we're friends or foes. Better run."

"Wise idea." The path to the stairs was clear, so I ran for the door behind Harper, guiding her down the stairs in front of me. The other prisoners sprinted out, too, and Miles and his friends brought up the rear as we climbed down the spiralling staircase. I barely breathed until we hit the bottom of the staircase, giving me the chance to waylay Miles. "How did you get that thing to obey you?"

"Used a cantrip." He walked to the door leading outside and pushed it open, beckoning to the former prisoners. "Go on. Get out of here, lie low. Oh, and don't go to the Withered Oak."

"Thanks," I said to him. "I thought you'd ditched me."

"As if I would," said Miles. "It took a little longer to convince the others to join me than I anticipated. And that creature was a major pain in the arse to get past."

"Yeah." Harper slumped against the wall. "My brother went with them."

"So did Tay." I couldn't even wrap my head around her decision. Shawn must have brainwashed her somehow, but she never used her magic in public. What kind of lies had he poisoned her mind with?

Miles's brows rose. "Wait, was that your friend? It was dark in there, but I thought I recognised her from the day we met."

"She fell for Shawn's bullshit, hook, line and sinker."

He winced. "I wish I'd realised and kicked Shawn and his allies out of the Spirit Agents sooner. He's been playing a long game."

"Not to mention using the citadels to hide," I added. "Did you know he can travel between them?"

"Yeah, they must have figured out how to use the transporter a while back," he said. "I don't get why they captured a wyrm, though."

"Never mind that," Harper said. "Where are we

supposed to go now? The fire mages set the Withered Oak on fire."

"And some of the others went after the Death King." I recalled the mages' words from earlier. "Shawn ... he implied the ex-Fire Element was leading the army to kill his former master. He might have been lying, but…"

But if he wasn't? Killing the Death King would leave a power vacuum, and I did not want Shawn or his allies getting their hands on any more power. Especially if they were taking orders from the Family.

Miles turned to the tower as the door opened again and his spirit mage friend, Shelley, ran outside.

"He's gone," said Shelley. "Shawn used the transporter and they all scarpered. We tried to follow, but we've no idea how to operate that thing."

"They'll be back," said Miles. "Bria, want to come with us to find them? Liv went back to the Death King, so it's just us now, but I reckon we can take them."

"I have to help the Death King." I didn't know why the impulse hit me, but the idea of the fire mages who'd turned their backs on my plan winning the battle filled me with a mixture of guilt and rage. "He could use all the allies he can get, given how many of his potential Fire Elements turned traitor."

"Does that mean you're going to tell me how you survived that inferno cantrip?" said Shelley. "Because you were burned to a crisp, I saw. Are you sure you aren't a lich?"

Ah. I'd forgotten that little detail.

"Long story," I said. "I'll tell you later. Go with Miles— it'll be safer than coming with me."

Harper gave me a quick hug. "I never said thank you for getting me out of that cage."

"Anytime," I said. "I'm sorry about your brother."

"I'm sorry, too," she said. "About… Tay."

My chest tightened. "I can't wrap my head around it. Shawn really unleashed the bullshit on her. I mean, I knew she always hated the Houses, but she can't possibly think joining a group of rogues is going to end well."

I wanted to speak to her before I made a decision I couldn't take back, but if she'd joined the fire mages in fighting against the Death King, there could only be one outcome.

"No," said Miles. "I'll drop Harper off at the base, then I'm coming with you, Bria."

"What?" I shook my head. "No. I can't ask you to risk your neck on my behalf. You—"

"I owe the Death King," he interjected. "Instead of assuming I'd betrayed him along with Shawn, he gave me the chance to explain myself. I can't ditch him now. Besides, if he dies, then we'll be next."

"Then I'm coming with you, too," said Harper. "If I'm to stand any chance of getting the position of the Death King's Fire Element out of all this, I have to help him fight off those traitors."

Dammit. "You should stay out of the battle, Harper."

"No chance," said Harper. "You saved my life, and if not for the Death King, you'd never have had that chance. I'm coming with you."

"No more arguing," Miles said firmly. "We're in."

Their words bolstered me more than I'd anticipated, coming on the heels of Tay's betrayal. I didn't know what I'd do if I ran into her on the battlefield, but Miles was right. We had to take down the rogues before they could get their hands on any more power.

The three of us stepped into the node's path, and the current of energy carried us away, towards the swampland… and a battlefield.

Bolts of fire shot across the swampland, clashing in mid-air as the fire mages fought the shadowy forces of the Death King's liches. One of them must be Davies, the ex-Fire Element, and as I'd feared, he'd brought an army with him.

Liv and the Death King stood side by side, using the node's power to send blasts of spirit magic at their adversaries. Not just fire mages, but some liches fought on the side of the enemy as well. This, I realised, was exactly what Liv had tried to warn me about. Some of the Death King's own forces had gone to join the ex-Fire Element and his allies, and even with an undead army at his back, the King of the Dead was surrounded. There must be something I could do to help, but considering our earlier encounter, I bet Liv would think I was fighting against her if I went within her line of sight. If only she'd trusted me, then we could have teamed up against the enemy.

We still have that chance. If we survive this.

A clamour shook the swampland as a group of skeletal

beasts on horseback rode through the gates of the castle, wielding swords and spears. It seemed the Death King had called on all his forces to help, and the tide of the battle turned as the wight army joined the liches.

A fire mage stepped into my way, hands blazing, a cantrip glowing around his neck. I dodged the oncoming inferno and retaliated with a strike of my own. Damn, those cantrips were strong. Was it any wonder, considering who'd created them?

Mav flew around, using her water magic to dampen the enemy's fire. My heart lurched when I saw Harper surrounded by liches, fighting side by side with Dex's firepower. Ahead of her, another fire mage stood in the midst of the liches, wearing armoured clothing in the style of the Elemental Soldiers.

It's him. Davies. The Death King's former Fire Element. He must have kept the uniform as a final 'fuck you' to his former employer... and his attention was on Harper.

"You." He approached her, conjuring fire to his hands. "Thought you'd come back, did you? I could have given you a far better deal than the Death King, you know."

Harper, no!

I put on a burst of speed, but a wall of shadowy liches blocked my path, cold hands grasping for my life essence. The world distorted in a haze of shadow as I fought to cling to consciousness. I spotted Liv punch Davies hard enough to break his nose, but I didn't stop to join in. Instead, I slammed a fireball into the liches' path, sending them scattering in all directions. Reaching Harper's side, I dropped to a crouch beside her. She lay on her back, still and quiet.

No. Please, no.

Another fireball leapt to my palms, and I fired it straight at the liches blocking my path. Then I hauled Harper's body over my shoulder and sprinted for the node. Too fast, but—*fuck it.* I wouldn't let her die.

The node's light flared around me, then I reappeared in the street of Arcadia, close to the citadel. Harper's dead weight made my shoulders scream with pain, but I hardly noticed. In seconds, I ran across the square, reached the back door of the citadel, and kicked it open.

For an instant, I thought I'd crashed into another battle. Miles and another spirit mage were shouting at one another at the foot of the stairs—at least until he saw me. "Shit, Bria. What happened to her?"

"She's dying," I gasped out. "The Death King's liches turned traitor—and the ex-Fire Element had them attack her."

"I told you," he shot at one of the others. Then he added, "They refused to come and help us."

"Because it's a death sentence!" protested one of the other spirit mages. "Fire mages with amplifying cantrips, full-powered liches *and* that scumbag of an ex-Fire Element—we're outgunned."

"So you're going to wait for them to come for you instead?" I laid down Harper's body, my shoulders aching, my eyes burning with tears. "You're *spirit mages.* How can you sit this one out?"

"We're spirit mages, not trained for war," said Shelley.

"Some of us are." Miles reached to Harper's body, his brow furrowed as though focusing on something I couldn't see. "This is bad."

My heart lurched. "Can you save her?"

"Her soul is badly damaged," he said. "I can try, but… it might be too late."

My brief flare of hope extinguished in a flash. "It's my fault. She came with me because she wanted to help."

"She died because the liches turned on the Death King," said Miles. "I have no intention of doing the same. If any of you have a problem with that, then you're free to leave."

None of the spirit mages moved. He must have assembled his remaining allies in here, but with the monster rampaging around upstairs and Shawn on the other side of the transporter, they wouldn't be able to stay here forever.

Shelley shook her head. "She's all but dead. It's too late."

"Not necessarily." Miles pulled something out of his pocket. My gaze caught on the shape of a skull engraved into a disc-like shape. A soul amulet.

"What the…?" *Oh.* "You want to turn her into a lich."

"I want to offer her the choice." He glanced at Shelley. "Don't look at me like that, Shelley. This is Bria's and Harper's business. Do you trust me?"

You know what? I did trust him, despite it all. I looked down at Harper's cold, still form. "I never should have brought her back here. If I hadn't…"

"It's not your fault," Miles insisted. "C'mon, Bria. Can you hold the amulet?"

I looked up at the skull etched into its surface. "I'm not a spirit mage."

"Go with it," he whispered in my ear, pushing the amulet into my hand. "I'll save her."

His hands glowed with light as he leaned over her

body. A moment later, a tall, pale figure appeared, transparent and floating above his hands. *Harper.*

"What's going on?" Panic lit up her gaze when she caught sight of her body lying on the ground below her. "I'm dead, aren't I?"

"Harper, hang on," I urged her. "Miles is going to save you."

"I have to ask you first," he said to her. "Are you okay with coming back as… as a lich?"

"Am I *what?*" she said.

A fist clenched over my heart as I recalled the rumours that the Death King had created his army by ripping out the souls of those who defied him, condemning them to serve him forever. While I didn't think there was any truth to the rumours after what I'd seen of him, the fact remained that I was asking Harper to give up a natural life in order to survive… or else disappear forever.

"It's okay if you don't want to," I said to her. "Miles and I wanted to offer you the chance. If you don't, you can move on peacefully. If you do decide to stay, you'll lose your fire magic as well as your old life."

She looked between us, her mouth pinched with indecision. "If I disappear now… I'll never see my brother again. I won't get to say goodbye. I'll do it."

"Are. you sure?"

"No, but I only get one chance to make the choice, don't I?" She nodded to Miles. "Do it."

"Okay." He lifted her transparent figure and gingerly carried her towards the amulet in my hands. Despite myself, hope bloomed inside me when her spirit sank beneath the surface of the disc. Miles muttered something inaudible under his breath, and light suffused the lines of the amulet.

Slowly, a shadow began to take form in the place where Harper had floated. A cloaked shadow shaped like a person but with no features, no life shining behind the shadowy mask. I glanced to the side at her body and shock hit me when I saw she'd *gone,* leaving nothing but her clothes behind.

"Hey there," said Harper's voice from the shadowy figure of the lich. "Damn, this is weird. Am I floating, or am I just taller than before?"

"Both," said Miles, nodding to the amulet in my hand. I saw the tremor in his shoulders and realised the spell had taken more out of him than I'd thought.

Harper turned her shadowy head as though examining her new body. "I see why the liches always look so intimidating."

"You'll have a few new tricks up your sleeve, too," added Miles. "Sorry you had to give up your fire magic, but in my humble opinion, spirit magic is better."

"I can use *spirit magic* now?" she said. "Holy crap."

"Don't do it in here," said Shelley, in tones laced with disapproval. "When you've quite finished raising the dead, Miles, we have a decision to make."

"Keep your hair on," he said. "We have one more ally now. Let's head back to the base and find the others. Then we can help the Death King."

I wasn't certain that Harper would remain sure of her decision, but that could wait until later. For now, we had a battle to win.

19

Miles led the way across the square to the node. The others followed, grumbling among themselves. It seemed not everyone agreed with our plan, but hiding in the citadel with a monster loose above their heads wasn't much of a battle strategy, either.

I turned to Miles to find him watching me with concern in his expression, which prompted me to speak. "Did… did you know? About Tay?"

"I suspected from the start," he said. "But I didn't know you at the time, and it didn't feel right telling you my suspicions when I had no proof. All I knew is that she was missing, and I didn't see who took her."

I opened my mouth, then closed it again. The time for grudges was over. The only person who could tell me the truth was Tay herself.

We halted at the alley's entrance to find the Death King of all people standing in our way. His gaze went to

Harper, who gasped and tried to hide behind Miles. Unsuccessfully.

"That was risky," he said, addressing Miles.

"Don't you have a battle to fight?" I told him, standing defensively in front of Harper. "I thought you were in the middle of a war."

"It's over," he said, his tone without any inflection. "Davies is dead."

And so is Harper. "It's not over. Shawn and his allies are still out there."

"Then I expect you want to deal with them yourselves," he said. "If you want me to take her soul amulet back to the castle to put with the others, then I can do that."

I looked from him to Harper and back again. "What?"

"Don't play at ignorance," he said. "It's not becoming of you."

"It's Harper's choice," said Miles, "but the amulet will be safer in the castle."

"I'm not giving my soul to him," came Harper's indignant voice from behind me.

"Would you rather take it into battle with you and risk one of the other spirit mages finishing what Davies and his allies started?" he enquired.

Harper was silent for a moment. "No. Bria, give him the amulet."

"You sure?" I pulled the disc-shaped object out of my pocket, acutely aware I was literally handing her life over to the Death King. But what choice did we have? If I kept it with me and the Family found me... it didn't bear thinking about. I would not let Harper's free will be taken away again.

The Death King took the soul amulet from me with

cold, transparent fingers, making me shiver. "Come and speak to me later, Bria, and bring your friend with you."

As he swept away, Miles chuckled under his breath.

I tilted my head at him. "What's so funny?"

"He's not going to arrest us," he said. "Not going to conscript us into his army, either."

"I bloody hope not, considering I just handed him my soul," said Harper from behind us. "Also, how in hell did he know you were the one who turned me into a lich?"

"He's the king of the liches," I said. "Or maybe being a lich gives you mind-reading powers, who knows."

"Hasn't happened to me yet," she said. "I want a refund."

"Come on." Shelley stepped into the lead. "Let's head back to our base."

Harper didn't move. "Can I travel like this? Aren't I supposed to go to live in the Court of the Dead with the other liches?"

"You don't have to," said Miles.

"You'd be fine," I said. "Everyone will be terrified of you now."

"Yeah, well. I'm not so sure about this."

My heart dropped. "You think you made a mistake?"

"I don't know," she said. "I'll come with you, and then... we'll see."

A twinge of worry reminded me her decision might not be permanent, and we might have to say goodbye later after all, but I pushed it aside as we followed Miles and the others through the node.

Once we'd reappeared in a flash of light, Miles led the way to a decently sized house with whitewashed walls. It looked almost like a transplant from back in the other world, complete with a garden, and, inexplicably, a number of vampire chickens roaming the yard.

"I'm going to ask for an explanation of *that* as soon as we're inside," I warned him. "Were you the ones breeding the vampire chickens from the start?"

"No." He opened the gates and led the way to the doorstep, while the rest of us followed behind him. Then he knocked on the door.

A tall black man with hair shaved to stubble and a pierced ear answered. "Miles."

"Hey, Tate," said Miles. "Shawn's on the run. Fancy chasing him down?"

The mage on the doorstep glared at us. "She's not coming in."

"I know Harper looks like a lich, but she's an ally," I said.

"Not her," he said. "You."

My heart dropped. "Excuse me?"

"You used to be with the Family."

Shit. Did everyone know about my history now?

"I also heard another of your friends is working for the enemy," he added.

"That wasn't something I planned for," I told him. "Tay betrayed me. And everyone else, too. Harper died for it."

"I have no idea who that is."

"Me," said Harper.

"You brought a lich with you, too?"

"Come on, Tate," said Miles. "We need a plan. If you let us in, I can explain it all. None of us are going to hurt any of you."

"I'm more worried about her." He jabbed a finger at me.

I frowned. "I'm on your side, and nobody is following me. I've been with Miles since the battle."

"Let them in," said another mage from behind him. "You'll draw more attention hanging around outside. We won't let anyone get hurt."

To my relief, the group of mages moved aside and let us into the house. The white-painted hallway and furnished rooms were as incongruous to me as the Death King's castle, compared to my usual haunts. The Spirit Agents had more resources than I'd known. Yet Shawn and his mates had thrown it all away.

Even so, the number of remaining Spirit Agents was higher than I'd expected. I counted over a dozen of them between our two groups. Some regarded me with suspicion, and a couple outright recoiled when Harper entered the room.

"Why is there a lich in here?"

"She's with us," I told them.

"She was killed by one of Shawn's lot." added Miles. "Not an hour ago."

"So you decided to turn her into a lich?" said Tate. "Miles, we've talked about this."

This wasn't the first time he'd raised the dead? I'd have asked, but the others descended on him, asking questions, while Harper shrank back into the doorway.

"Maybe this was a mistake," she said quietly.

"Nah, they're just on edge," I whispered. "Besides, I think I'm the one in trouble. And Miles."

At least the others had momentarily been distracted from questioning me about the Family by Miles's apparent habit of binding people to soul amulets. I'd forgotten to ask where he'd even got it from, but it was clear this place was as full of secrets as the Death King's castle.

"Enough," Miles said, cutting through the others' arguments. "Whatever you think of Bria and Harper's presence here, the fact remains that Shawn screwed us all over, and took half our allies along with him. We scared him out of the citadel by setting his own wyrm on the loose, but they'll be back."

"And he has a fucking wyrm, too?" said Tate. "I'd say that's a good reason to leave them to it."

"They want us dead," Miles said. "We need to get that monster out of the citadel, for a start, before it attacks someone."

"Exactly," I put in. "They're in hiding, but I bet they'll go back to Arcadia as soon as they think the coast is clear."

"And what if that traitor friend of yours is back there waiting for us?" said Shelley.

She had a point. "I doubt she is."

But I didn't know what I'd do when I inevitably came face to face with Tay again. It was still too raw to think about her betrayal, and I didn't blame the others for being suspicious.

"The wyrm is Shawn's responsibility, not ours, anyway," said Shelley. "What're we supposed to do with the damn thing, keep it in the garden with the vampire chickens?"

Harper snorted, and several of the others looked startled to hear the noise coming from a lich.

Another mage asked Miles, "Where are Shawn and his friends now?"

"No idea," said Miles. "They activated the transporter in the citadel. They might have gone anywhere."

Tate swore. "So they might be back any second now?"

"Yeah, if they want to get eaten by the wyrm," said Miles. "Besides, I'd say bringing the Death King and his allies along with us might deter them a little."

"The Death King promised to support us?" said Tate. "You know what happened last time. He promises the world and delivers nothing."

"He tries," said Miles. "A damn sight more than Shawn ever did. Look, I have a way to bring down the wyrm, okay? We already managed to get past it once."

"Yeah, right," said another mage. "Is it like the time you tried to take on that nest of revenants?"

"Hey, that wasn't my fault," he protested. "Look, we have a whole stash of cantrips for controlling animals, don't we?"

"For the vampire chickens," corrected Tate. "Are you ever going to tell us what you wanted to do with the chickens, anyway?"

"I'd also like to know," I added.

"Later," said Miles. "Guys, seriously. I think a small team of us can get the wyrm under our control and out of the citadel if we use the cantrips. We might even be able to turn it on its captors."

"If the spells actually work on a beast of that size," said Shelley. "We'll have to hijack the transporter machine to get it out of there."

"It's worth trying," I said. "If we stop that thing from being unleashed in Arcadia, we'll save lives, and we'll be ready to face Shawn without his monstrous ally getting in the way."

Murmurs of agreement rose, and relief welled in my chest to have their support. I didn't know if I really believed Tay could be saved at this point, but Harper? She was worth hanging on for.

"Bria saved my arse at least twice, so listen to her," added Miles. "She's on our side. No more arguments."

Some of the mages still wore suspicious looks, but Miles wrangled a small group together, including Shelley. He then handed each of us a cantrip equipped with a minor influence spell for controlling animals.

"That's our entire stash, Miles," Shelley said.

"With luck, we'll only need one of them," he responded. "Once you get close to that beast, throw it into its eyes. Preferably without getting bitten first."

"Not helping," I muttered to him. "You used those cantrips on the vampire chickens?"

"With help," said another mage, older, with greying dark hair. "Catching those little shits earned me a stint in one of the Order's jails."

Miles grimaced. "I already said I'm sorry. I didn't know the Order would take the issue so personally."

"You mean the Order of the Elements?" I glanced at Miles. "They locked you up?"

"I had a narrow escape," said the mage. "The Order's having issues of its own, thanks to those traitorous spirit mages, so they thought I was with them."

"I'd have come back for you if you hadn't already given them the slip," said Miles.

"I'm lost." I looked between them. "Why are the vampire chickens even here?"

"Because it's the only safe place to keep them before we figure out how to post them back to the breeder," he responded. "That was the original plan, but we didn't count on half of them escaping on the wrong side of the node. I found someone willing to meet me in Arcadia, but then those assassins attacked us in the Withered Oak before my contact showed up."

"You don't think someone might walk past the house and figure out what they are?" I said. "Like Striker?"

"Nah, the guy's lying low, if he has any sense," said Miles. "Haven't heard anything new from him lately."

"Wish we could set the wyrm on him." It was a satisfying thought to consider enacting my revenge on the guy who'd cost me my job and my best friend all at once, but I had quite enough enemies to deal with already.

"Are those cantrips likely to work on the wyrm, then?" asked Harper.

"They worked once before," said Miles. "I'll catch you up, okay? Go to the node with the others. I'll be right behind you, Bria."

Together with the other spirit mages, Harper and I approached the same node we'd entered through.

"More than half of the other spirit mages stayed behind," Harper observed.

"There's still enough of us," I said. "If we get that monster subdued, Shawn and his friends will lose at least one of their major weapons."

"And if not?" she said. "They must have realised leaving it behind in the middle of Arcadia wasn't a smart move."

"Shawn doesn't strike me as smart," I responded. "Persistent, righteous, but not smart."

Movement stirred in the corner of my eye. Someone

was behind us. Not a spirit mage, I didn't think… but not a lich, either.

Then a cold hand locked around my wrist, dragging me backwards. Another clamped over my mouth to muffle my scream, as someone yanked me into an alley.

"You were hard to find," a voice growled in my ear. "Did you think getting this band of vagabonds on your side would keep you safe from me?"

Striker. Speak of the devil. He must have been waiting for me to return to Elysium so he could wring my neck over the vampire chickens.

I bit down on his hand, teeth sinking into flesh, and he bellowed and let go. Spinning around, I conjured fire to my fingertips. "I'm not beholden to you anymore."

"I kept you alive." He swore, shaking his injured hand. "You ungrateful bitch."

"You turned in Tay to the House of Fire," I said. "You gave her no choice but to join up with the Family, didn't you? Then you ran off and left us to take the fall."

"You cost me everything, Bria," he responded. "You damn near got me locked up by those shitheads. They're coming for all the mages soon, you know, and you're already theirs. I won't let them get me, too."

"Too bad I can do worse," Harper said from behind him. "I don't know you, but you seem like a royal dick-head who deserves to be stripped of his soul."

Striker stiffened as her shadowy form towered over him, and brightness suffused her hands. Then he pivoted away, and she lost her grip.

"A newly reformed lich?" he said. "Is that the best you have?"

"She also has me." Miles ran towards us, and Striker recoiled from a blast of spirit magic that knocked him sideways into the wall. The distant sound of squawking followed. Miles, it seemed, had left the gate to the house open.

Striker's mouth fell open. "What have you done?"

"Those vampire chickens," said Miles. "They were yours, weren't they? I seem to remember you forcing Bria and her friend to transport them around the city, risking arrest."

His face flushed. "You stole my vampire chickens?"

I burst out laughing. "There's something you don't hear every day."

Striker cursed and ran towards the squawking noise, but the vampire chickens had tasted freedom and liked it. I doubted he'd have much luck catching them all.

"Wonder if he'll outrun the authorities this time?" Miles said.

Harper sighed. "I thought I had him then. Spirit magic's harder than I thought."

"I can teach you," said Miles. "I'd let you practise on Striker, but I think he'll be occupied for a while. The authorities are on high alert after the vampire chickens escaped the Order and were sighted in the city."

"Yet they never noticed they were in your garden?" I said. "How did you get away with hiding them in plain sight, anyway?"

"They didn't have reason to check up on our house," he said. "We're not known troublemakers… or we weren't before Shawn decided to set up shop in the citadels, anyway."

"And before you met me," I added.

Or rather, before they'd drawn the attention of the Family.

"I won't hold it against you." He flashed me a grin. "I've had worse days."

"Speak for yourself," Harper said.

I snorted, my heart lifting despite the guilt burning within me. We'd lost so much in such a short time, but there'd be time enough to grieve later. If we all got out alive.

A deafening roar split through the sky ahead of us, and the spirit mages scattered as the wyrm shot straight out of the node and into the air.

"It already escaped," I breathed.

Never mind the vampire chickens. Now we had a real animal-related problem on our hands.

20

The creature took to the sky, tail lashing at the buildings below. Miles backed up, swearing. "We'd better move."

"Leave it," said Shelley. "There's no catching it now."

The wyrm turned in mid-air, diving straight at us. We threw ourselves to either side to dodge its swiping tail, then ducked into an alley it was too big to get through.

"I think it recognises us as the people who set it loose," said Miles.

Harper hovered behind us. "Can it see us?"

"It recognises faces," said Miles. "That's why we need to get the hell—"

The creature shrieked and dive-bombed us again, its body wedging into the alley and its teeth snapping at our heels. After a couple more half-hearted attempts to get through, it took to the sky once more.

"I don't think it's going to listen to reason," I said. "Come on. Let's move before it decides to snack on us after all."

"Hang on," Harper said. "Looks like it found a new target."

"Where?" I backed up to the alley's entrance, standing on tiptoe to see over the rooftops.

Miles caught me up. "Holy shit."

The creature soared over the rooftops and landed atop the spired citadel. A deafening clang echoed above as its body slammed into the roof.

"Why is it targeting that place?" I asked. "Does it think it's the same as the other citadel?"

"Damn, that thing is smart," said Miles. "I think it just pointed out Shawn and his friends' hiding spot."

"That's where they ran off to?" The beast slammed into the roof again, its claws bouncing straight off its smooth exterior.

A calculating expression crossed Miles's face. "Guys, change of plans."

"We're not running up to that monster," said Shelley.

"I don't see why not." Miles pulled a cantrip out of his pocket. "It's already got Shawn and the others on the run."

"And I'd rather not join them," Shelley said firmly. "I vote we stay back here and let the monster eat them."

"Don't you think they have a plan for dealing with their predator if it escapes?" I said. "They can always hide in the citadel until it calms down. I doubt it'll break in."

"I bet they don't have a plan," said Miles. "They're not forward-thinkers. Neither am I, but the difference is, I didn't lock up a deadly predator."

Really, Miles. I still hadn't figured out what his reasoning had been when it came to those bloody vampire chickens. Had he really tried to make up for the chaos he'd unintentionally caused earlier this week, or was there some other reason? Either way, they were on the loose again, and the odds were high that Striker would be caught by the authorities. I wouldn't lie, that painted an appealing picture.

As for Tay, I couldn't picture her staying in hiding while her new allies let their plans collapse around their ears, but then again, I hadn't been able to picture her betraying me, either. Some things were just impossible to imagine until they slammed into you and left you scrambling to pick up the pieces.

"Might they transport themselves back to Arcadia?" one of the other spirit mages asked.

"They might," said Miles. "We need to get rid of that wyrm before they do. Use the cantrips. We play our cards right and we'll be heroes."

"Or dead," Shelley supplied. "Not all of us want to trade our lives for an afterlife as a lich."

"I think Miles is right," I said. "We have them trapped in that tower. If we get that beast out the way, they'll be cornered by the authorities."

"The authorities might catch us, too," said Shelley. "Sure you're not just trying to get back to that friend of yours?"

I shook my head. "I don't know if she's in there. If I were her, I'd have run. Besides, if they use the transporter to get away, we'll lose our shot and that beast might start attacking civilians. We have the means of subduing it without anyone getting hurt."

"And we have an advantage," Miles said. "Shawn will assume any lich in this city is here to help him."

All eyes turned to Harper.

"What?" she said. "You want me to pretend to be Shawn's ally?"

"If you want to," said Miles. "That beast can't harm you as a lich, you know. All you have to do is run up to the citadel and pretend you're the backup. Then they'll open the door, and…"

"Good idea," I said. "If Harper's up for it, that is."

"I'm not the one in danger of getting eaten by a monster," she said.

"Exactly," said one of the other spirit mages. "I'm heading through the node. We can meet on the other side."

Miles frowned. "You don't know what's going on in Arcadia."

"I'll risk it." Several of the mages walked back in the direction of the node, while the rest of us remained behind. Harper took the lead, gliding shadow-like through the streets.

"How many places does the citadel's transporter link to?" I asked Miles.

"They used to be able to link to any citadel anywhere in the Parallel," he said. "Back in the old days, before the war, it was how the spirit mages got around."

"I can see why." We closed in on the citadel, ducking low so the beast didn't spot us. Cantrips in hand, we readied ourselves to surround the wyrm from below. Miles whispered orders to the others, while I stuck with Harper. "You okay?"

"Of course," she said. "I could get used to this. Not being afraid, I mean."

"Stay focused," Miles said. "Okay… go."

Harper glided towards the citadel, halting for a brief

moment when the beast turned its attention to her. One swipe of the claws had no effect on her transparent form, at which point it lost interest and turned its attention back to the citadel. Harper floated up to the doors, unharmed, and said in a clear, carrying voice, "Backup's here. Let me in."

The doors didn't open.

"Oh well," said Miles. "It was worth a shot—"

The beast roared and dove at the tower, clawing at its metal exterior. I readied my cantrip, and a blast of fire grazed my shoulder.

"Incoming!" someone yelled.

I spun around to see the spirit mages who'd left through the node running back, pursued by a group of fire mages along with two masked individuals wearing long coats and boots. Fear sliced through me as keenly as the point of a knife.

One of masked men flung a knife at me, which I dodged despite the dread seeping through to my core.

"They aren't mages." Miles conjured spirit magic to his hands and deflected another weapon. "Not cool. Who even are you?"

I had the sinking suspicion I knew who. "Assassins-for hire."

Spirit magic blasted from his hands and narrowly missed one of the assassins, who leapt onto the rooftop with eerie grace. "Whoa. Not humans?"

"Not regular humans."

A roar sounded above. The beast circled us, drawn by the new arrivals, and the door to the citadel flew open.

"Oh, thank fuck," said one of Shawn's people, spotting Harper and the mages. "Hawker sent backup."

Not quite. But with fire mages and assassins surrounding my friends, our group had scattered, our formation had broken, and my attention was torn in a dozen directions at once. One eye on the monster, the other on the tower, while the sound of the spirit mages fighting with the newcomers echoed in the background.

Flames shot from my palms at the two assassins, who fell under the spirit mages' assault. Then I turned my attention to the wyrm. When it dove down, I took my cantrip in hand and sped towards it. The cantrip flew into the air, hit the beast dead-on, and it froze mid-flight.

Miles clapped his hands. "Good one, Bria."

I looked into the beast's eyes. "Go back into the tower and attack Shawn and his friends."

The beast roared. Then it dove through the half-open door, grabbing a spirit mage fleeing into the tower. Snapping and crunching noises followed as the beast's tail disappeared into the room within.

The sounds of screaming intensified, and several seconds later, a blinding flash of light came from inside the tower. I ran towards it, and Miles snagged my arm. "I reckon Shawn used the transporter to run."

"Dammit." I turned back to the battlefield, where the Miles's allies gathered around the bodies of the fallen assassins. It didn't look like anyone from our side was dead, but the tower had gone eerily quiet.

"The beast must have followed them through the transporter," I said. "Shit, I ought to have told it to fly away instead."

"Then this isn't over," said Miles. "C'mon. That noise will have drawn the authorities' attention, I guarantee it."

We moved for the tower door, and Harper floated

ahead of us and into a wide room. The place was a mirror of Arcadia's Citadel, including the staircase spiralling to the upper floor.

"Where d'you reckon they went?" I reached the top of the stairs first, which contained a copy of the same transporter as the one in Arcadia. "Anyone know how to use this?"

"I think I can figure it out," said Miles. "It's our best bet at this point."

"Arcadia?" asked Shelley. "Not exactly a safe haven."

"Safer than here if the Houses catch up to us." Miles took central stage, examining the transporter. "I need a spirit mage to turn it on. Harper, can you give me a hand here?"

"I would if I had the slightest clue what I was doing." She flew over to his side. "Do you want me to come with you?"

The other spirit mages examined the machinery at the back, and Miles pointed to a button which stood out among the others. "I saw one of Shawn's mates hit that when they vanished before. Can one of you try it?"

Shelley hit the button. There came a flash of light, and two of the spirit mages vanished from the platform.

"Oops," said Miles. "Okay… we'll go in next."

We climbed onto the platform, at which point Shelley hit the button again. A moment later, light flashed and the three of us reappeared in the room of Arcadia's citadel. The empty cage where Harper and the other mages had been held captive lay on the floor, while the faint sound of fighting echoed through the half-open door leading downstairs.

"Is that monster outside?" asked Harper.

"Can't be, we'd hear it." Question was, where in the world had it gone? And did that mean Shawn and the others had fled elsewhere?

I made for the open door to the stairs, peering into the gloom. The room below appeared to be empty, but the sounds of battle grew louder. They came from outside. Harper glided ahead of me downstairs.

"Slow down." I followed her, while Miles waited at the top of the stairs for the other spirit mages to catch up. "What's going on out there?"

"I think we've found the Death King's army," she said.

I reached the ground floor and pulled open the front door. Outside, liches, fire mages and assassins clashed with one another, and fire leapt to my fingertips as I struggled to make sense of who was fighting on which side.

Then my gaze landed on Liv, who was looking straight at me as though *I* was the enemy.

21

I stared at Liv. She stared back. "Oh, *fuck,*" she said.

"Liv?" I approached her, my hands still blazing.

"I guess you saved me the bother of coming to find you." Spirit magic blasted from her hands, and I rolled to the side to avoid it, the fire going out. *Okay, maybe now wasn't the best time to try explaining myself.*

"Wait! I'm on your side!"

She didn't seem to hear. The Death King's Air Element ran behind her and levitated two assassins into the air, while sparks of fire ignited among the mages and knives flew in gleaming arcs. As one of the assassins threw a knife at me, I dodged and blasted him with flames.

"Hey!" Liv shouted at me. "Whose side are you even on?"

"Not theirs." I hadn't the time to argue with her, and before I could offer an explanation, a blast of spirit magic shot between us, forcing us both to dive to avoid it.

A blaze of fire slammed into the ground at my feet, and I deflected the attack with my own flames. When I looked up, Liv had disappeared somewhere among the fighting. I'd explain myself to her later, assuming she survived.

Amidst the chaos, I spotted Harper's shadowy form, which was considerably more difficult to see with the oncoming darkness of night. That proved advantageous for her, as she was able to sneak up on the enemy without being detected until the last possible second. However, she hadn't got the hang of her new magic yet, so she could only stall the enemy spirit mages instead of bringing them down. The liches accompanying them ensured they outnumbered our own team, while I saw no signs of the Death King and his own liches.

"Retreat!" Shelley called, backing towards the citadel's shadow.

"You do realise we're not supposed to be in there?" I said, my words drowned out by the general clamour. "If we go back in there, the vampires might come and arrest us for trespassing."

Shelley's response was drowned out by the echoing sound of metal clanking on metal, and a torrent of bright light shot from the citadel to the sky.

"Was that the transporter?" I looked around for Miles, but I'd lost sight of him somewhere in the fighting. *That isn't good.*

A knife flew overhead, passing straight through Harper's transparent body.

"Hey!" she said indignantly. "Nice try, but I'm dead."

The light grew blinding. "I'm gonna check that out."

I ran for the citadel and a blast of magic knocked me backwards. Four other mages ran out of the door, including Shawn. *There he is.* The bastard had slithered away, but I should have known he'd be back. I tackled the nearest mage—Garber—and slammed my fire magic into him. He reeled back, his eyes widening at my speed. "Tay said you weren't human, but I didn't believe her."

Another blow hit my heart at the notion of her casually betraying me to the enemy. "At least I'm not the scum of the earth. What the hell is happening in that tower?"

"The second war is about to kick off." The light of the citadel gleamed in his eyes, making him look quite deranged. "This won't end like the last one."

"Every single spirit mage died in the last war." Fire leapt to my palms, and he recoiled with a hiss of pain. "So did millions of other people, you selfish dickhead. You're the reason spirit mages have a bad name."

He leapt to his feet with a roar, only for me to kick his legs out from underneath him. I spotted Miles duelling another spirit mage. I ran to his side as his opponent fell down at his feet, and he caught my eye, breathing hard. "Never thought I'd see the day where I'm forced to fight my own allies."

"Shawn claimed to be starting a second spirit war," I said to him. "They want a repeat of the last time."

"Apparently they haven't learned from how that turned out." Miles shielded his eyes against the glowing tower. "The hell is happening in there?"

"I have no idea." He and I wove through the fighting towards the citadel door, which I kicked open. While the light wasn't as bright inside, several bodies lay scattered at the foot of the spiral staircase.

Then Shawn leapt at me from behind, his teeth bared in a feral expression. His punch sank right through me, and a sudden spasm of weakness shook my entire body.

He was draining my life force in the way only a spirit mage could.

"Cut that out!" Harper flew up to him, breaking the connection so I could breathe again. I reeled on the spot, and Harper took my place, blasting spirit magic at Shawn.

I caught my breath, grabbing for a cantrip. I was almost out of them, but I refused to let Shawn escape our grasp again. He dodged Harper's attempts to hit him with spirit magic, but before I could intervene, Miles ran into view and slammed an uppercut into Shawn's chest that sent him flying back into the staircase. Around us, the citadel gave another tremble.

"What the hell is that?" I asked Shawn. "And don't fob me off with an excuse this time. What are you doing in here?"

Shawn pushed upright. "You set that beast on us, didn't you?"

"Me?" I said. "You're the one who brought the wyrm here in the first place. If you're looking for sympathy from any of us, you're barking up the wrong tree."

A horrible screeching noise came from above, followed by clanking which sounded too mechanical to belong to anything living.

"Bria," Harper called from somewhere in the gloom. "The transporter is making that noise. I think it's broken."

"Oh, hell." I kicked at Shawn when he tried to punch me again, and Miles got in behind him.

The light of a paralysing cantrip shone in his hands, and Shawn froze to the spot.

"Hang on." Miles grabbed Shawn's arm and fumbled in his pocket with his free hand, pulling out a rope. "I'll leave him tied up in here. I'm sure the vampires will be thrilled to find someone to blame for attacking their city."

"You wouldn't dare," said Shawn. "Bastard."

"This place is supposed to be haunted, did you know?" Miles used the rope to tie Shawn's arms and legs together. "Hope the ghosts of the spirit mages killed in the war kick the crap out of you."

At a run, Miles and I headed for the stairs. Harper floated ahead of us and through the door at the top.

Inside the room, the transporter was trembling all over, emitting frequent flashes of bright light. Harper halted in front of the bank of machinery. "How do we shut it down?"

"I reckon only a spirit mage can do it." Miles stepped around the machine's side, ducking a bolt of light. "Or a lich. Harper, you and I will have to switch it off."

They took up positions on either side of the glowing platform. I watched them, a flicker of unease travelling through my nerve endings. Light washed over me. Rustling sounded at my back.

As I spun around, a hand grasped my wrist and dragged me into the light. I heard Miles's exclamation of shock, but whiteness blanked out my vision, and the room disappeared.

The hand let go of me. Miles and Harper had vanished from sight, but I wasn't alone. The coiled shape of the wyrm waited ahead of me, its body crushing the machinery. An alarming flare of orange-white light shone from the transporter, and its eyes locked onto me.

"Steady now," I murmured to the wyrm. "I'm not your enemy, but I think you should probably get off that transporter before you get electrocuted to death."

A familiar voice spoke from behind me. "He won't, but you might not be so lucky."

"You know, when I said we'd deal with our crap later, I meant when we weren't in the middle of a war," I said, knowing it was Tay without turning around. "What now? Going to try to kill me, or did you just want to gloat?"

The beast didn't budge, but a faint growling came from between its teeth. It'd definitely broken free of the cantrip I'd used on it, but something held it subdued, and I wasn't sure I wanted to know what. Or who.

"You know, I did think you'd come and find me as soon as you realised I was gone," Tay said. "That would have made it easier."

"I didn't know where you were," I said. "I thought the House of Fire had you, and then I found out about the Family being involved later down the line. If it had just been the House, I'd have gone there straight away, but then I'd have ended up arrested. Was that what you wanted?"

"You'd be safer behind bars," she said. "So would the rest of us."

"Wait, is that what this is about?" My hands fisted. "I thought you didn't judge me for my history. Just like I didn't judge *you* for what you did with your own magic."

"You held it against me for years." Her jaw trembled. "Don't deny it."

"Tay." I softened my voice. "I didn't. I swear."

"You don't understand," she said. "They took everything from us, Bria. And now I see you working with the Death King as though he isn't complicit."

"I wouldn't have had to ask for his help if you hadn't

let me think you were kidnapped," I said. "You turned your back on me."

Magic crackled from her hands, and dread bloomed in my chest. I'd never really believed she would hurt me on purpose, but she'd confided her past where I'd hidden mine, and I hadn't known how deeply she'd resented me for it until now.

A jolt of electricity shot from her palms, bouncing off the wyrm's scales. It recoiled, hissing in agony, as the waves of power travelled over its skin. "You know, it feels good to be able to cut loose again, and not worry about watching my back."

"Stop that!" I dodged the next bolt of power that shot from her hands. "Tay, you told me why it's too risky to use that power."

Her type of magic was lethal in more than one way. When used too frequently, it rebounded on the caster… or anyone else standing in the vicinity. When she was a teenager, her first loss of control had ended in tragedy.

I didn't believe she'd really meant to kill her younger sister. Her parents had said otherwise.

"Not anymore." She revealed a cantrip, attached to a piece of string looped around her neck. "Your family had the means of controlling this power all along, yet you refused to share them with me."

"I didn't know," I said. "Look, everyone working with Shawn and his friends is a liar, including whoever gave you that cantrip."

"*You* lied to me." Her voice cracked like a whip. "Every day we spent together."

The beast snarled, recovering from Tay's attack. I backed up a step. "I didn't lie."

"You've seen one of these before, haven't you?" she said. "Your brother said."

My chest tightened. *She's spoken to them, all right.*

"He's not my brother."

If she meant who I thought she meant, I hadn't thought of him that way for a long time. We'd grown up together, but I shared no more DNA with him than I did with the spirit mages. We just had the same family. Or rather, Family, with a capital F. They'd raised us, nurtured us, tortured and experimented on us in equal turns. I'd assumed the House of Fire had confiscated all the cantrips they'd created through their experiments, but it seemed someone had taken up the practice again.

"That's not what he said," she said, her mouth twisting with bitterness. "Was there anyone you didn't lie to?"

"I always told you I hated my family," I said to her. "I told you they were awful people. Yet you really believed him over me?"

"He told the truth," she said. "You walked away from a great thing, Bria."

"What spell did they hit you with?" I said. Or are you that desperate to repay your debts that you'd screw over your only friend?"

"You must know I didn't have a choice, Bria," she said. "The second spirit war is coming. Only one side will be victorious, and if it's the Houses, they'll see to it that we don't live to see another day."

I took a step forwards, and her magic tingled in the air like static. "Tay, stop this. I'm not siding with the Family, but I won't hurt you, either."

"Then tell me," she said. "How did you really get away from the Family?"

My throat closed up. I hadn't told her the full story. Hadn't told anyone. Nor had I known she'd taken it so personally. "Does it matter now? You've already made up your mind."

"Tell me," she said. "You knew what those cantrips were, didn't you? You know who was responsible for creating them."

I shook my head. "Their resources were cut off. They should be behind bars."

"Because you're the one who put them there," she said.

"If they were free, I'd know," I added. "They'd have already killed me for it."

"Our parents would rather see you suffer extensively for what you did to us." The voice was strange and familiar all at once. A cold, horrible voice I hadn't heard for years except in my dreams.

Oh, Elements. He's here.

My brother had found me.

22

Adair strode into view. Tall and lean, he had the grace of an elf coupled with the intensity of a mage. Dark hair shaved to stubble, pale skin marked with fewer scars than it should have been, and expensive-looking clothes. His ears were pointed at the ends, and unlike me, he didn't wear a pendant containing a cantrip which masked his real features.

The last time I'd seen him, he'd been cuffed with magic-sapping handcuffs and dressed in the House of Fire's crimson prison uniform, his blue eyes narrowed in anger at me as I watched them take him away. He was never supposed to walk free. But if he was here… the others wouldn't be far behind.

He looked me up and down. "Nothing to say?"

"Nothing I haven't already said." In truth, I had a dozen questions, but Tay's presence was too much of a distraction. "That's a low blow, targeting Tay to get to me."

He shrugged. "Want to come home with me, or do I have to use force?"

The wyrm growled. It hadn't moved an inch since he'd shown up. He was the one controlling it, then.

"What if it breaks free from your control?" I said.

"It won't."

No. His control was perfect. He'd pulled the same trick on me for years, after all, and now he'd used the same spell to ensnare Tay.

Light flashed in the room's centre.

"Incoming!" Harper's voice came from thin air, as she and Miles appeared on the transporter's platform.

All hell broke loose again. Miles's spirit magic slammed into the monster, which reared up, forcing Tay to move aside to avoid being hit by its flailing tail. Adair grabbed for me, but I shot out of his grip, throwing a handful of fire at him. Miles looked startled at how fast I'd moved, and his eyes flew wide as Adair leapt across the room with the blinding speed of the magically enhanced. Straight at Miles.

I got there first, crashing headlong into Adair. I landed on top of him, pinning him to the floor with my knees.

"Still as fierce as ever, I see," he said.

"Get fucked." I rolled to the side as he threw me off him, narrowly missing another hit from the beast's tail. "You can't use your spell on me any longer."

Miles stared at Adair. "Who are you?"

"Hasn't she told you who she is?" he said. "Or should that be *what* she is?"

"Honestly, I'm more concerned about what *you* are," he responded. "We were fighting a war back there, and you rudely interrupted us."

"Exactly," I said to Adair. "If you don't mind, we have something more important to deal with."

"What could be more important than family?" he said.

Chills raced down my spine. "I told you, you're not my family. You're a weapon and a tool."

"Speak for yourself."

"Guys, can you save it till later?" Miles ducked and rolled as the beast lashed its tail at him again.

"Watch out," I told Miles. "The monster is under his control. Let's just say he's not like anyone you've met."

"Figured that much out for myself." His hands glowed with spirit magic.

"So you found some allies, did you?" Adair said to me. "They'll all turn on you. Like she did."

He indicated Tay, who'd backed to the other side of the room, not looking me in the eye.

My hands fisted. "Give me one good reason not to feed you to that beast."

"All I did was keep the promise I made when you turned me in," he said. "I will turn everyone against you. I will be the arbiter of your demise."

"Seriously?" Miles arched a brow at me. "Does he always talk like this?"

"Unfortunately, yes," I said.

Adair bared his teeth at us, and a shadow fell over him from behind. *Harper.* Cold light bloomed from the spot where her hands had once been. She'd figured out how to harness the power of the nodes, spirit-mage-style.

"Duck!" she yelled at me.

I threw myself on top of Miles as she blasted spirit magic at Adair. He dodged, only for the beast to take the brunt of the attack instead. The wyrm swung its tail and knocked Adair off his feet. Spitting out curses, he climbed upright and put a hand on the beast's head to calm it down. "Word of advice, Bria? Ditch the spirit mages. Come back home where you belong."

"It's not up to you to tell me where I belong, Adair," I said. "I want no part in your twisted games."

"So you picked them instead?" he said. "A living disgrace and a dead one. They're not long for this world."

"Speak for yourself," said Harper.

Spirit energy burst from her hands, but her attack bounced straight off him. We backed up, side by side, dodging the monster's lashing tail.

"He's pretty much impervious to magic," I warned her. "He's not like other mages."

"Like you?" she asked. "I saw how fast you moved."

"Later," I said. "We have to get him subdued, preferably without setting him loose on the unsuspecting public."

Most people wouldn't be prepared to deal with someone with his particular skillset. The bastard had always been a tough one to beat even when we sparred for fun. But when I'd turned him in, I'd been elevated to the top of his list of enemies.

Why was he here in the city? There was something more going on than a simple family visit, that was for sure.

"Why now?" I approached him at a wary distance, flames leaping into my hands. "You could have come looking for me at any time, yet you had to drag in my best friend and employer—not to mention the spirit mages."

"Why do you think?" he said. "It's started."

My heart dived. "What's started?"

He smiled at me. "The second spirit war. You know it's

coming, and you know you'll have to pick a side. Choose ours."

"No, thanks."

"It wasn't a request." Hate simmered in his eyes. He was still mad at me for what I'd done, and he'd stay mad even if I ultimately took his side.

As if I'd ever let the Family control me again.

He lunged. I did likewise, but my flaming hands caught on empty air. He'd aimed for Miles instead at the last second, and the spirit mage immediately froze on the spot, his gaze fixed at a point in the distance. Under his control.

"Let him go," I warned.

"Only if you agree to join the Family again." Adair pressed a knife to Miles's throat. "Do it."

23

I remained still for a moment, trying to catch Miles's eye. To my relief, the glazed expression was fading already, but the knife bit into the side of his neck, a bead of blood rising to the surface.

"Go on," said Adair. "You can't stay loyal to him, not when he'll inevitably betray you like the others."

"Really bright and cheerful, isn't he?" said Miles, as though there wasn't a knife pressed to his throat. "Honestly, I think you're losing the war. From what I've seen, anyway."

"The war is just starting." He indicated the bank of machinery behind him, and the wyrm coiled around it, as though waiting to pounce. "We'll bring down the Houses and the Death King and everyone else who wants to claim dominion over the mages of the Parallel."

"You're talking about unleashing anarchy at a time when things are unstable already," I said. "People will die."

"We won't."

He was right on that one, unfortunately, but that didn't

mean I wanted to be involved in this. "You want to be the last man standing?"

"Pretty much." The knife bit into Miles's throat. "Go on. Say you'll join me."

Damn him. The two of us were equally matched, but I didn't dare risk Miles's life. The beast coiled in the background watched me hungrily. And Tay…

There came a spark of light. Then, electricity flared, igniting at Adair's feet. He jumped back with a curse, and Miles spun away from him, his hands glowing with spirit magic. His punch sent Adair sprawling, tripping back onto the platform. Harper closed in on the bank of machinery, her own magic igniting the transporter. Adair leapt to his feet, but the transporter's light caught him, and he was gone.

"This isn't over," I said. "He must have ended up in one of the other citadels, and there's a fair chance it might be Arcadia."

"I figured." Miles reached into his pocket and tossed a paralysing spell into the wyrm's face. "That ought to hold it for a bit."

"Tay," I said. "Did you…?"

She stepped forward, her face flushing. "Word of advice? If you don't want to go back to your family, run far away."

"You were my family," I told her. "But I guess that doesn't matter now."

She flinched, which was my intention. I'd wanted her to think really carefully about what choice she made, because once she did, there would be no going back. Perhaps it was already too late, but I didn't really believe that. The fact that she'd come out on my side over Adair proved that.

Miles grabbed my arm. "She's right. We need to go. The others are still fighting in Arcadia."

I know. Miles and I had abandoned the other spirit mages on the battlefield, including Shawn. Time to abandon ship.

Miles led the way, and Harper and I followed him through the transporter. When the light faded, we found ourselves faced with the empty room of Arcadia's upper floor.

Harper faced me. "Who was that guy back there?"

I'd known the pair of them had a million questions, not least because they'd witnessed our fight for themselves and were no doubt making connections between me and the impossible speed and grace that they'd witnessed from Adair... and from the assassins.

"My... my brother," I told them. "Kind of. We grew up together, but we're not technically related. He has a gift for magically induced influence. A mild form of mind control. I learned how to resist it, but it's not easy if you don't know the tricks."

"Damn," he said. "He moves as fast as you do, too. And the ears..."

I moved a self-conscious hand to my own. "Yeah. We're both half-elf, I think. I use a spell to hide mine, but I guess he doesn't care if anyone notices."

"Half-elf?" he said.

"And half-mage," I said, "though it was a toss-up as to whether I'd come out with the right talent or not."

Miles's brow wrinkled. "Right talent?"

"The Family was—is—very precise about what kind of

skills they wanted their subjects to come out with," I explained. "Adair came out with mind control abilities. We both got the ability to regenerate from deadly wounds. The Family used unlicensed experimental cantrips on us and sold them behind the scenes. That's how Tay ended up the way she is."

"Come again?" said Miles. "I saw her use some kind of electric power. You mean to say your family did that to her—*gave* her magic?"

I dipped my head. "Her guardian bought one of the Family's cantrips and used it on her. I didn't know she still held a grudge, but it doesn't help that the Houses see anyone with unconventional magic as an abomination. Anyway, I ran at the first opportunity when I broke free of Adair's influence and got him and our parents locked up by the House of Fire."

"He's walking free, though," said Miles. "Why're they working with Shawn and the others? They're not spirit mages."

"No, that's why I didn't know they were the ones pulling the strings at first," I said. "If the Houses of the Elements crack down on mages, though, they'll hit what's left of the Family doubly hard. It makes sense that they'd side with the people they think are going to win the second war. Meaning, the spirit mages."

"Damn," he said. "And Adair thinks you want to join him?"

"He's deluded," I said firmly. "Never mind him. We have to get back to the others."

The sound of footsteps came from the stairs. I halted, my heart sinking. *Is that Shawn?*

"I knew we should have killed the bastard." Miles ran for the door, which flew open as a flash of light ignited.

Shawn ran at me, but Miles slammed into him from the side before he could unleash his attack on me. The two spirit mages fought bitterly, and another spirit mage ran at me. I hit him hard and fast, no longer bothering to hold back. Flames leapt around me, surrounding me in a circle and preventing them from getting close enough to drain my life force. They must be close to running out of steam now.

"Retreat!" Shawn yelled from the top of the transporter.

"Get back here!" Miles ran at him, but the transporter's glow had already flared up.

I crashed into Miles, he pinned down Shawn, and the transporter's energy engulfed us all, taking us back to Elysium.

The monster had gone. That was the first thing I noticed.

The second was that Adair was back, and his expression promised me pain, and a lot of it. "You'll pay for that one."

Shawn rolled out from underneath Miles, and the two began firing off attacks at one another again. Adair, meanwhile, advanced on me. "Come on, Bria, it won't be so bad. We always planned to join forces, didn't we?"

"Those were just games, Adair," I said. "They ended when you started hurting real people. I was a kid, but you should have known better."

But I knew better than to expect him to change. Our creators had designed us to be two halves of a violent whole, only one of us had been able to see past our shared destiny. Adair wasn't capable of being anyone else.

"You're going to lose, Bria," he said. "I picked the winning team."

"Like I said, this isn't a game," I replied. "Not anymore."

He lunged. I rolled to the side and fetched up against the wall. A hand closed around my wrist—*Tay.* I tensed, but she pressed a cantrip into my hand. I felt its cool magic stirring against the magic in my own palm.

She'd given me her only spell, and I had to make it count.

Fire ignited in my hands, and Adair's eyes flew wide as the cantrip stoked the flames into an inferno. The jet of fire flung him backwards into the bank of machinery which operated the transporter. Fire danced across the surface, its amplified strength combining with the damage wrought by the wyrm. Lights flickered on and off, while sputtering noises sounded from the transporter.

Good luck calling your army now.

Adair's screams died in an instant, while flashes sputtered from the flaming hunk of metal at the back of the room. His army wouldn't be using that as an escape route again anytime soon.

Breathing hard, I turned around to see Miles and the other spirit mages in the act of restraining Shawn. The spirit mage released a furious cry at the sight of Adair's body lying across the wrecked transporter, but Miles firmly tied his hands behind his back.

Tay strode out of the corner and into view, and her eyes went to Adair. "You killed him?"

My jaw tightened. "You might have gathered my family's a little more resilient than most. He'll get over it.

Before he does, I'm going to call someone to pick him up, along with those guys." I jerked my head at the fallen spirit mages. "It's up to you to decide if you want to be here when they show up."

Pain flashed in her eyes. Then she turned and left the room without another word.

"She won't make it far," Miles said. "The authorities are already combing the streets. The only reason they aren't in here is because they think it's haunted."

I rubbed my eyes. "To be honest, I think she'd be safer with them than the alternative. When you're with the Family, you either stay with them or die."

He rose to his feet. "Not sure if this will make you feel better, but Shawn and I were once allies, too. People can disappoint you. Not everyone, mind, but some people."

"Family certainly can," I murmured. "Adair needs to be locked up before he recovers."

"I'll take care of it," he said. "We'd better head back to Arcadia and check on the others."

With the transporter broken, we had little choice but to leave the tower via the front door. Miles astral projected outside to check the coast was clear, and when we had a clear route free, we walked to the nearest node and travelled back to Arcadia.

From the node, we hurried into the square, where the surviving spirit mages gathered around Shelley.

"Garber is dead," Miles said to her. "Shawn is tied up and waiting for the authorities to show up. Have we lost any of ours?"

"Tate is checking," said Shelley. "I heard Sledge copped it, too. Blew himself up with one of those inferno cantrips."

I grimaced. "That figures."

The square was a confusion of bodies, some living, some dead. Spirit mages, former wannabe-Fire Elements, assassins, and whoever else had joined their ill-conceived attempt at a coup.

Harper drifted along the ground, then let out a soft gasp. Her brother's body lay in the dirt among the others.

"Harper." I strode to her side, tried to put an arm around her, but it passed straight through her transparent form. She sobbed, without tears, unable to accept the comfort I offered.

My heart ached for her. Had there ever been another fate after he'd turned against the Family, though? They took no prisoners and left none alive who defied them.

Except for me.

"Let's head home before we get arrested," I said. "Harper... we can take his body with us. I won't let anything happen to him, I promise."

"Not so fast." The Air Element strode forward, covered in blood and debris. "My master wishes to speak with you."

Oh, hell. "Can't it wait?"

They glanced between Harper and me. "Come to the Court of the Dead tomorrow. Alone."

24

The authorities caught Tay within an hour of her escape from the citadel. Turned out Miles's guess was right on the mark, but not being surprised didn't make it hurt any less. A half-dozen spirit mages had died during the battle—not counting the defectors who'd supported Shawn and the Family—and the authorities had taken care to round up the survivors.

As for me, I spent the night lying low at the Spirit Agents' house. Miles offered me a room, but I didn't sleep. There seemed little point when I had to meet with the Death King tomorrow, and besides, a fair few of the Spirit Agents would have been more than happy to see me leave.

At dawn, I gave up pretending to sleep and went in search of Harper. Since I found no signs of her in the house, I assumed she'd already gone to the Death King's castle.

Okay. Time to get this over with.

While part of me was reluctant to leave without at least saying goodbye to Miles, I didn't know which room was his, and I'd prefer not to wake the others. I slipped out of the house and headed for the node, my rucksack over my shoulder. Just like when Tay and I had left our hideout, though I fully expected I'd have to come back with my tail between my legs when the Death King sent me packing.

When I reached the gates to the Court of the Dead, two liches parted to let me through, their faces hidden beneath their shadowy masks. Creepy, not that I'd admit so to Harper. I looked around for her, but I saw only the Air Element waiting on the stone stairs leading up to the castle doors. When I turned their way, they caught my gaze and nodded, stepping aside to let me pass. That struck me as a good sign. It couldn't be bad news, right?

I headed for the oak doors and opened them, revealing the wide hall. The hall of souls was locked, but no longer guarded. And the Death King stood on the dais at the back of the hall.

Several long seconds passed as I walked, each step echoing, and halted in front of him.

"You might be wondering why I've called you here," said the Death King. "I'm here to offer you a position in my Court."

"You want me to work as your Fire Element?" He had to be joking. Right? "I didn't even finish the trials."

Nobody else had, either, but I could think of a dozen reasons why I wasn't qualified. Not least of which was the fact that I'd trusted the wrong person, several times over.

"You are the only surviving potential Fire Element who passed all the trials whose loyalties didn't come into question," he added. "You came back to fight on my side despite the risks. That's the sort of loyalty I look for in my Elemental Soldiers."

My mouth parted. "I have enemies."

"Who doesn't?" he said.

"Fair point, but… have you asked any of the others?" I was scrambling now, unable to make sense of his decision. "I made too many mistakes. To tell you the truth, the whole thing was a complete mess. People died."

"Many lives were lost in the battle," he said, his voice tightening. "Many sacrifices were made. I believe you were the only person who was already aware of the potential pitfalls when you walked in here."

Seriously? I shouldn't complain, but a job offer was the last thing I'd expected to result from this whole clusterfuck.

"I'm not saying no," I added. "I just need to think about it. Do the other Elemental Soldiers know? Because at least two of them don't like me."

"I've spoken to them," he said, "but yes, you can meet with them yourself before you decide to take the job, if you're inclined to."

There had to be a catch. Admittedly, I'd be trading in a future with a group of magical criminals hellbent on world domination for a job working for an immortal death lord who might be hellbent on his own kind of world domination, for all I knew. But I'd take anyone over the Family, and the Death King, despite it all, wasn't my enemy.

"I can do that," I said, "but I'd like to know what the catch is. You don't just want me to defend the castle, do you? You hired me for a reason."

The Death King looked at me. "I need someone to

infiltrate the Houses of the Elements and ensure they don't take the side of the enemy in the oncoming war."

He wants me to spy on the House of Fire? "You want me to be a spy?"

"I want you to do what you do best," he said. "You already helped me by bringing your Spirit Agent allies to assist in the fight. I understand that despite your gifts, you aren't a spirit mage, but it would be beneficial for me to retain that connection."

"I can try," I said, "but I can't promise there aren't still enemies within their ranks."

"That's a problem I'm familiar with myself," he said. "Oh, and your friend, Harper, is welcome to stay. I believe she'd be more comfortable here than living among humans."

Poor Harper. Her brother's death had hit her twice as hard now the aftermath of the battle was over, and she hadn't spoken much to me since. I still didn't know what her eventual decision would be, but I wouldn't get in her way.

As for Tay, I'd give her time to think on her mistakes while in the House of Fire's jail. It was the safest place she could be, really.

"Go with Ryan," the Death King added. "They'll take you to get your uniform."

Uniform? I'd get some of that fancy armour the other Elemental Soldiers wore? I wouldn't say no to that, for sure, but part of me was still convinced this was some kind of elaborate prank. I mean, the non-humans had been kicked out in the first round of the trials. He *must* know what I was, and he'd given me the job anyway.

Dazedly, I followed the Air Element out of the room. A moment passed before they spoke.

"Did you really go head to head with a full-grown *wyrm?*" they finally asked.

"Yes," I responded. "If you're asking where it went, I haven't a clue. I imagine it flew away to freedom. Where was the Death King through most of the battle, anyway?"

Their eyes shadowed. "If I were you, I wouldn't ask him. The enemy got away, and someone close to him was badly hurt."

"Oh." I was doubly glad I hadn't pressed him for details. "Same happened with me."

"That Harper... she's a lich, isn't she?"

I nodded. "Yeah. Why?"

"It's hard to adjust, I gather," they said. "A close friend of mine ended up the same way. I'm still not sure which decision she'll make."

"Sorry to hear that." It was a hell of a depressing thing to bond over, but then again, wars had a way of doing that. As well as destroying lives and ripping apart families.

Except for mine, regrettably. My weird, messed-up magical family was still out there, no longer contained. If anything, the Court of the Dead was the safest place I could possibly hide... for me, and for them.

———

I surveyed my reflection in the mirror once I'd changed into my new uniform. Not only did I get armoured clothing, I also got a snazzy crimson-lined cape embossed with the Death King's personal seal—four elemental rings surrounding a symbol of a skull representing the

Court of the Dead. The new uniform was a definite plus, but the other Elemental Soldiers would be reluctant at best to accept me as one of their own. The Air Element had been civil, but the others hadn't said a word to me yet.

"Is she even a fire mage?" I heard Cal, the Earth Element, saying to Felicity, the Water Element, as I went to join the others in the break room.

"Yes, she is," said Felicity. "She got the job fair and square."

Shoulders tensed, I let the door close behind me and took in the sight of a room filled with plush sofas and gleaming fittings. I had to admit, the place was pretty fancy, considering it was a castle designed for the dead rather than the living, but it would be nice if the inhabitants were a bit friendlier.

"Hey, Bria," said Felicity. "Glad to see you accepted the job."

Okay, maybe one of the other Elemental Soldiers wanted me here. The Earth Element would take longer to convince, I could tell, but I had time to work on him. As for the liches, they tended to keep to themselves, none more so than their leader.

As though conjured up by my thoughts, a lich entered the room behind me. "What the *hell* is she—?"

The Death King strode behind the lich, "I need to talk to you."

The lich shot me a look I could have sworn was a glare, then walked off behind the Death King. *Guess not all the liches are pleased that I got the job, huh.*

"Sorry about that." Felicity rose to her feet and held out a key. "This is for your quarters."

"Thanks," I said. "Is there anything else I should know?"

"House rules?" said Cal. "Don't steal my shit from the cupboards. I'll know. Also, the chores rota is back there."

I scanned the kitchen area at the back of the break room and spotted a piece of paper affixed to the fridge. "We have to cook? Seriously?"

"What did you expect, the liches to do it for us?" Cal gave an eye-roll. "Felicity is the only one of us who can cook worth a damn, so we mostly live on takeout."

"Yeah, it's not my strong point." I hadn't foreseen chores being part of my job description, but then again, I still hadn't adjusted to the idea of being in the Death King's employment at all. More to get away from the others' stares than anything, I said, "I'm going to check out my new room. I'll be back soon."

I headed for the door and made my way to the Elemental Soldiers' quarters. The door to my own room was unlocked, so I dropped off my bag inside. It was the nicest place I'd ever lived, yet utterly empty. I sat down in one of the plush armchairs, then stood up again.

What the hell was I thinking?

I should at least have said goodbye to Miles before I'd taken off on him. Not that I'd expected to get the job, or the perks that came with it…

A faint breeze ruffled my hair, and I turned my head. A lich had floated through the door, facing me across the room.

"Hey," I said. "I'm assuming you're Harper, because this would be kind of awkward if you weren't."

"Yes, it's me," said Harper. "Nice outfit."

"Isn't it?" I gave a twirl in the cape. "Gotta get some perks from the job, considering this is my home now. If I want to keep everyone safe from my nutcase family, anyway."

"What about Miles?" she said.

"What about him?"

"You and he hit it off, don't deny it," she said. "I'm surprised you didn't stay there with the Spirit Agents."

"His friends don't like me," I responded. "Okay, some of them do, but you've seen the number of enemies who have me on their hit lists. I'm better off staying here. Besides, he's a spirit mage."

"You're not an ordinary fire mage," she said. "You can tell me the truth, you know."

My gut clenched at the memory of Tay's betrayal. "People who get close to me… bad things tend to happen to them."

"I'm dead," she said. "Can't get much worse than that."

I looked away. "I'm sorry. For what happened."

She was silent for a moment. "It's really not that bad. Might be because everything seems kind of… muted, since I turned. I always thought liches were inhuman, but… it's kind of true."

"You're still a person," I said. "You just had an upgrade."

"That's one way of putting it," she said. "I'm not sure Percy would have made the same choice. He never liked the liches. Or this place."

"But do you?"

"Not sure I'd use the word 'like'," she said. "I guess it's fitting for the living dead, though."

"And a few of the living." I walked across the room to the door. "I'm going for a walk."

Harper drifted alongside me as I left the castle via the

back door. The grounds were deserted, aside from a few liches, and…

Miles. Here in person, no less.

"How in the world did you get in here?" I asked. "You walked in through the gates?"

He must have done. The node was off-limits, and he didn't have another transporter spell, as far as I was aware.

"The Death King gave me permission to come in," he said. "Hey, Harper."

"Hey." Harper floated past. "Don't mind me. I'll leave you two alone."

I turned back to Miles. "Sorry I took off on you. I'm surprised the Death King let you in."

"Hey, I had to come and congratulate you on the new job," he said. "Also, you ran off without saying goodbye."

"I hardly expected to be offered a job, did I?" I said. "I thought he was going to chew me out and send me packing. Besides, I'm still having second thoughts about the whole thing."

"Well, you have a room back at the Spirit Agents' place, if you ever want to use it," he said. "Harper, too."

I tilted my head. "And there I thought you were giving me special treatment."

He grinned. "Nah, but Harper's watching us right now."

So she was. "That might be another of the Death King's liches. They look pretty similar."

"She's staying here, then?"

"Yeah, she needs to learn some tricks from the Death King."

"Bet he'll teach you some, too," he said. "Except for the ones you already have."

I fingered the pendant around my neck. "I guess you heard what my brother said."

His gaze went to the pendant. "Which part? He's in jail, by the way… I thought you ought to know."

"He got out once already." I slid open the pendant and revealed the cantrips inside it. "You know I'm not fully human."

"You said," he said. "It's fine. I don't judge."

I flicked the cantrip. The illusion around me dimmed, revealing pointed ears, finer features than I let the world see. Miles's gaze panned over me, but he didn't speak.

I turned the cantrip back on. "I need to replace the cantrip every month or so, but it's long-term. Figured the elf side of me was easier to hide than the rest."

"You shouldn't have to," he said. "Not here. I mean, that castle is ruled by a zombie. Pretty sure he'd be fine with a half-elf Fire Element."

"You aren't wrong." A sense of lightness descended, as though telling him had removed a heavy burden from my shoulders. "So… still want to associate with a freak of nature like me?"

"I wouldn't object if you came to visit me during your time off," he said.

"Considering my new job is to spy on the House of Fire?" I said. "I might need your help."

Despite the risk, I was warming up to the idea of being the Death King's Fire Element more and more by the second. It wouldn't be an easy job, with the sheer number of enemies out there for both of us to handle. The rogue spirit mages seemed to have been dealt with for now, but the fact remained that the Family were trying to instigate a second war, and they wanted me to be on the battlefield at their side.

But with the Death King at my back, I'd be able to keep them at bay. And with a little luck, I'd be able to bring down the House of Fire and the Family all at once.

ABOUT THE AUTHOR

Emma is the New York Times and USA Today Bestselling author of the Changeling Chronicles urban fantasy series.

Emma spent her childhood creating imaginary worlds to compensate for a disappointingly average reality, so it was probably inevitable that she ended up writing fantasy novels. When she's not immersed in her own fictional universes, Emma can be found with her head in a book or wandering around the world in search of adventure.

Find out more about Emma's books at
www.emmaladams.com.

PROLOGUE

THE YEAR WAS 1658. During times of unrest in Italy, unable to defend themselves against local uprisings defying religion and power, churches were targeted for their land and wealth.

One particular priest, Father D'Ascenzo, feared for the boys entrusted into his care. After one last vicious raid where priests and children were kidnapped or killed, he collected some items of value, the last of their money, and fled to the mountains with the remaining three small boys.

They found refuge in an abandoned villa, shelter from the impending winter. An older stone home on the side of a mountain, in much need of repair but hidden from the world. The priest and the three boys set to work, mending the roof and tending vegetables inside gardens and relining the basement and cellar.

Father D'Ascenzo was a good man. He taught the boys Latin, English and discipline, and kept them schooled in the ways of their religion. And as the years passed and peace returned to Italy, he used the money he'd taken from their old church to invest in the property, and after only a few years, he had acquired some wealth. So he bought more land, and his wealth grew further still.

Father D'Ascenzo insisted the boys each learn of the arts, economics, politics, and law, and also be the keepers of their lands. They would tend to the vast gardens, chores and maintenance, taking pride in themselves and their home.

But above all, Father D'Ascenzo maintained strict discipline. The boys were to kneel when he entered the room, keep their heads bowed, or they would receive lashings from a leather strap for insubordination.

Going against the Father's orders was rare. The three boys *wanted* to please him.

As the boys became young men, they noticed changes in their mentor; the way he would watch them, how his gentle touches would linger.

In the secrecy of their dorm late at night, the three young men would whisper to each other soft words of yearning to please him. It gave them such a sense of pride and completion to make him happy. They admired him, craved his praise, his touch. They *longed* for him.

Though the boys matched his size and strength, their discipline never changed. They still knelt, they still bowed their heads. They still sought salvation through his teachings. They still kissed his feet, his hands. They still bore lashings from leather.

Father D'Ascenzo could see how much they yearned for it. How discipline had become pleasure. How they thrived under his hand. When their pleasure became his, Father D'Ascenzo renounced the cloth; he would now be addressed as Master D'Ascenzo.

Yet the words of faith so ingrained in them didn't change. Words of Latin were still murmured, but their focus sought a new direction. They never turned their back on God but found a new sense of purpose within their own discipline.

It wasn't blasphemy. It was right. The Good Lord had meant for it to be. How else could they explain their Master's presence, if not for God? He'd saved them. He'd protected them. Cared for them and kept them safe. He gave them a discipline in which they prospered.

It was a natural progression for the three young men. They had urges, desires. They found comfort in leather bonds, in strict obedience, in reassurance and praise from their Master. It was their submission, the yield of their bodies and their minds, which gave them a greater sense of being. To please their Master was its own reward.

They'd found their true calling.

Master D'Ascenzo had shown them that the foundation of his happiness was their happiness, and vice versa. One did not exist without the other. The union of a Dominant Master and submissive was a sacred bond, built on respect and trust. And as the years went on, others were welcomed into their Sanctus. Each of the three men now had their own three submissives, and Master D'Ascenzo's teachings were handed down.

Guided by a higher calling, they had created their own dominion. A sanctuary where Masters and submissives were safe, where they could thrive under the teachings Master D'Ascenzo had instilled in them. A haven for those who were deemed good enough, disciplined enough, deserving enough . . .

And so, *Sanctus Infinitus Redemptio*—the sanctuary of infinite redemption—was born, and after almost four centuries of prestigious tradition, so it still remains today.

With dominions all around the world, the real estate

was vast, their wealth immeasurable. With enough power to topple governments, to manoeuvre presidents and economies alike, Sanctus Infinitus Redemptio was a secret society that could rival the Vatican.

In keeping with Master D'Ascenzo's strict traditions, each dominion is headed by three Grand Masters. Each Grand Master has three subs. They abide by laws and practices four hundred years old. Initiations and unions are still forged from respect and trust.

Exclusive, elite, and private, each Sanctus Infinitus Redemptio dominion is its own functioning society. Most are gated communities, and its members include doctors, lawyers, bankers, pilots. Self-sufficient, limiting exposure to the outside world. The original Sanctus still exists, the Casa di Salvezza—the home of salvation—was the most revered of all dominions.

The realm of past submissives was great, most of whom have become Dominants in their own right. All of them practise the way of the Sanctus Infinitus Redemptio: trust, respect, consent, and care.

The Sanctus prides itself on its successes, on the bonds forged between Master and submissive. Such unions are prized and celebrated, and in all the Sanctus's history, disputes between Masters and their subs were rare. No Grand Master had ever had to void a union. No sub had ever required to be recalled, re-Mastered.

Until now.

Current Day

The air carried a chill which had nothing to do with the cool spring breeze. The Casa di Salvezza was more of a castle than a chalet, nestled in the Italian Alps and surrounded by gates and security. It was private and exclusive. And it was also the European headquarters of the *Sanctus Infinitus Redemptio.*

Grand Masters Colton and Valente waited on the threshold of the huge oak doors for their guests to arrive. They each stood with their feet apart, hands clasped behind their backs. Their dark coats complemented their dark moods. Not even the wind dared disturb them.

Colton had spoken to Lazzaro personally, requesting he be here at five sharp, and he was to bring his submissive with him. No other explanation was given.

Lazzaro was a small, slender man, with his long blond hair always pulled into a severe ponytail; his stare could cut glass. During his training, Valente had found him to be a submissive who thrived under strong domination. He enjoyed sadism and masochism more than most. He'd liked canings; he'd enjoyed being bound and whipped. Valente had told Colton Lazzaro would make a strong Dominant in the S&M arena, and his submissives would require a definite love for structured and reinforced discipline.

When Hunter had first been called into the Sanctus dominion, his old Master knew Hunter required firm domination; he feared the boy unable to survive without it, and he believed he could no longer give the boy what he needed. Hunter passed all psych evaluations and his health report and blood work were both fine. Hunter was a great submissive; very dedicated. Even with his hard limits, he was a pleasure. His Dom was sad to see him go, but it was his responsibility to see Hunter's needs be met.

Colton had thought the pairing of Hunter and Lazzaro would be well suited. Although the boy was quiet natured, both Dom and sub required strong determination, and both craved structured discipline.

Lazzaro had been well informed of his new sub's hard limits and had vowed under the Sanctum's code of law he'd respect the boy taken into his care.

So it was of great concern to Colton when he'd seen Lazzaro and his sub at the role-play scene here at the castle the night before, and had noticed faded welts on the boy's back.

Certain welts made from certain props.

Lazzaro had whipped him.

And in doing so, breached his hard limit.

Lazzaro arrived right on time, dressed in a black coat, tight black pants, and black boots, walking with an air of superiority to the entrance of the grand stone hall, his submissive at his heel. Though most Doms could school all outward emotion, he was unable to mask his shock at seeing two of the Sanctum's Grand Masters awaiting him.

They stepped inside and the doors were closed behind them. Two clothed submissives stood at the far wall. One of Colton's, one of Valente's. They stood feet apart, hands behind their backs, faces slightly tilted downward, expressions stoic. Lazzaro never even looked at them, but they weren't there for his benefit.

Without niceties or any kind of greeting, Lazzaro was ordered to his knees and told to remain silent, though any kind of excuse was hardly needed. His guilt was written clearly on his face, in the fear in his eyes.

His submissive, who had knelt behind him, was then asked to stand and granted permission to answer freely.

"Did your Master violate your trust and breach your hard limit?" Colton asked, his voice cutting through the silence. "You bear welts on your back from a leather strap, if I'm not mistaken."

Hunter nodded, though clearly scared and timid. "Yes, Master."

"Hard limits are taken seriously by the Sanctus, and to breach such a trust is a violation of Sanctus law," Colton said. "Hunter, my boy, I assure you, you've done no wrong. Lazzaro, on the other hand . . ."

Lazzaro looked up, fearful, shaking his head furiously. He opened his mouth to speak but he'd been ordered to remain silent, and not even he was stupid enough to defy such a direct order.

Valente stepped toward him, as though Lazzaro's intent to speak was as bad as speaking itself. "Under code law of the Sanctus Infinitus Redemptio," he barked, the sound booming off the stone walls, "I am enforcing an immediate cease of union. Your status and rank are hereby removed. Your entrusted submissive is relinquished into our care, and you are now demoted to submissive in training."

Lazzaro's eyes went wide. He shook his head no. "But Master—"

"Do not speak!" Valente roared.

Lazzaro shrank back, bowing his head, but Colton noticed Hunter's reaction as well. The sub closed his eyes and gasped quietly, almost swaying on his feet. *This poor boy . . .*

Valente escorted Lazzaro out and Colton went to Hunter. The sub's head was down, and when Colton put his fingers gently to Hunter's chin to raise it, a tear rolled down his cheek. "Fear not, boy," Colton soothed. "You did nothing wrong. We failed you, and we take responsibility for Lazzaro's actions. But Hunter . . ."

The boy frowned as if he knew what was coming, and Colton could feel the grief and fear rolling off him.

"We must remove your collar," Colton whispered, and another tear escaped Hunter's eye.

Colton knew Hunter would never defy him—it wasn't in his nature—but he could see how much this hurt him. Colton took Hunter's hand. "Come sit with me," he said, leading him into the Sanctus Masters' private room. It was a large space with a stone floor, walls with soft lighting and occasional furniture, antique artworks, and tapestries on the walls. There were two male subs, naked and kneeling by the fire. The flames gave them a warm glow, and Colton smiled with pride when he saw them. His boys made him proud every day . . .

"Sit with me," Colton murmured to Hunter. They sat on a velvet chaise by the fire. "I know you're not comfortable right now, but I want you to know you are safe. No one will touch you without your consent."

Hunter nodded. "But my collar . . ." He touched the leather band around his neck absentmindedly.

"It's Lazzaro's collar, and he is no longer your Dom. I will need to remove it, okay?"

Hunter's fingers trembled and he clasped his hands in his lap, wringing them nervously before he caught himself and stilled. "Yes, Master," he breathed.

Colton cut the collar with leather shears as gently as he could, and Hunter began to twitch and fidget, and then he rubbed his neck, and finally he started to cry. "Please, Sir, Master . . . I can't . . . I need . . ."

Colton watched as the boy struggled to breathe, and his

heart ached with the need to mollify him. Placing a calming hand on the boy's head, he soothed him. Hunter was relatively new to the dominion and Colton remembered how the boy's last Dom had said Hunter needed strict dominance to survive. "You need a Dominant to feel safe?" Colton whispered.

Hunter nodded.

"You need a Dom to feel worthy?"

Hunter nodded again and fresh tears welled in his eyes.

"You need to be under the rule of someone who allows you to thrive and grow within firm ordinance?"

Hunter nodded again and breathed the word, "Yes," like a man dying of thirst would when asked if he wanted water.

Colton tilted the boy's chin up so he could look at him. "I feel responsible for this failure."

Hunter shook his head, almost fearfully, and another tear slid down his cheek.

Colton wiped away Hunter's tears with a gentle touch. "Not you, boy. You've not failed. I have failed. I paired you with him," he said sadly. "I want to right this wrong, and I have something in mind . . . Normally I would have you stay here with us, until I was sure you're well enough to be placed with another Dom."

Hunter blinked several times. "H-h-how long?"

Colton had seen this many times in his years at the Sanctus. Some submissives needed to be collared, needed to have a Dom. Without, they felt adrift and lost. And this poor boy had been through enough already.

There was one man who kept coming to mind. One Dom who would suit Hunter's needs and be able to monitor him from a medical standpoint as well. If Hunter needed time to heal, then there was only one man who Colton would trust with such a responsibility.

"Hunter, if I said I knew a Dom who was firm but fair, kind and gentle, strict but as generous with his praise as he is with discipline, would you be interested?"

Hunter swallowed. "I would trust your judgement."

Colton supressed his sigh. This poor boy . . . he'd been through enough and it only reinforced Colton's conviction that this was the best move for him. "There is no one I would trust more. He is caring and gentle, and seeing his subs thrive is his greatest joy. This Dom already has a sub, a very good one," Colton said. "You'll be second sub, but he'll respect your needs, and more importantly, your hard limits. This Dom is one of the best there is. I should know. I trained him myself."

Hunter's tears streamed down his face. He wrung his hands in his lap and nodded weakly. "Please."

Colton nodded. He knew it was a grand request, but he also knew this Dom wouldn't deny him. "I'd like you to spend a week with him and his sub at his estate. There will be no sexual interaction during this week. I want you to get a feel for his methods of domination before I commit you to his care full-time." This was not standard procedure, but Colton was adamant he'd never let anyone hurt Hunter again. "I will speak to you in one week's time and you can make the decision then. If it's not a match, you can stay here with us until we find a suitable Dom."

A flicker of confusion flashed in Hunter's eyes. "Master?"

"The blame of Lazzaro's mistreatment of you falls with me," Colton said. "I want to be certain this time. I would take you on myself, boy, but I have my three subs. So the man I'm choosing for you is my second choice, only behind myself. But I think you'll thrive with him."

Hunter nodded; fresh tears of gratitude welled in his eyes. "You are too kind."

"Stefan, Mikhail," Colton called to the two naked, kneeling subs. "Please take Hunter to the dining room, and make sure he eats. Then take him to the preparation room. Get him ready." Before the two obedient submissives could help Hunter to his feet, Colton touched his face. Hunter leaned into the touch. "You'll have the right Dom before the night is out, dear boy. I will set this right."

Hunter smiled and bowed his head. "Thank you, Master. Thank you."

When the three boys had left the room, Colton took out his phone. He dialled a number he knew well. After only two rings, a familiar voice answered. "Master?"

Colton smiled at the familiar timbre, the immediate subservience. "Sig."

CHAPTER ONE

SIG BRUCKNER

THE MERCEDES SLOWED around the grand driveway, stopping in front of the huge manor. The Casa di Salvezza was a remarkable nod to history and grand architecture, and a buzz thrilled through me every time I came here. One of Colton's boys, Phillip, opened my door. He offered a polite smile before bowing his head. "Good evening, Sir."

I nodded my acknowledgement and stepped out of the car. I straightened my jacket and ran my hand through my hair. A touch of grey flecked at my temples, but the brown mostly matched my eyes. It was otherwise short and tidy; impeccably neat, like everything in my life. Structured, organised, understated but distinguished. I glanced up at the huge stone building, the windows glowing warm and inviting, and I walked to the door, knowing Levin would follow. Without prompting, without even a look, he read my cues.

The perfect submissive.

My perfect submissive.

Levin had been in my care for two years. He had dark hair, blue eyes, and fair skin that flushed beautifully when he laughed and when he orgasmed. Other Doms would probably say I was too lenient on the boy or I spoiled him, but Levin was different. He was smart, sometimes a little cheeky, warm and kind, and completely insatiable. He had been chosen for me by Colton. Colton, my old Master, my Master still, had an uncanny ability to choose the perfect partner.

Dominant to submissive, Master Colton had a gift for forging bonds between pairings. As far as I knew, he'd never failed.

I hadn't been Colton's sub for nearly a decade. He taught me everything I know. I had no obligation to fall to my knees in front of him, but I would. No matter how long it had been since he called me his sub, he would always be my Master.

Even though I'd been a Master in my own right for ten years, we would still meet regularly and talk over coffee. At least every six weeks, not including play sessions. He was my mentor, my adviser, but I'd like to think he was also my friend. We'd discuss the trials and tribulations of being a Master, of having the responsibility of subs, the latest goings on in this dominion, and in the other dominions in other countries.

This dominion I was part of, like all dominions in the Sanctus, had three Grand Masters: Jürg, Valente, and Colton. Each had a specialty, an area of expertise. All three were exceptional men. With traditions spanning centuries and unimaginable wealth, the Sanctus was an exclusive, elite community, and one I was honoured to be part of.

Each member was chosen with a specific purpose— mine being medicine—ensuring the dominion remained self-sufficient. We didn't have to look outside of our own dominion for expertise. Real estate, stock markets, even our mechanics and house cleaners were all part of the dominion.

There were rules. Many rules, but none more important than the first.

Silence.

Keep the secret.

As I approached the huge wooden front doors to Master Colton's manor, I knew Levin was following. I could hear his quiet footfalls two steps behind me. I didn't have to turn around to know he'd be walking with his head slightly bowed, his shoulders squared, and his hands clasped behind his back.

Master Colton was right.

Levin was perfect for me. He read me, as I did him. He was dedicated and willing, his submission to me a true gift.

Colton had matched other Doms perfectly with their subs, which was why I was surprised he called me, requesting to see me urgently.

He'd gotten one wrong, he'd said.

He needed me to come, it was a matter of importance, he'd said.

Bring Levin, he'd told me.

Which was why we were here.

The doors opened before me, and we stepped inside. The marble foyer was impressive, as was the entire estate. Stefan, Colton's first sub, a pretty, dark-haired boy, greeted us with a nod. "Master will be pleased," he said quietly, and ignoring the immense staircase in front of us, we turned to the left and walked through to the sitting room, where I was asked to wait. The doors closed silently behind him.

The room was delicately dressed in fine antiques; ironic, considering the furniture in the several playrooms downstairs. There were two French provincial chairs, and I deduced I was to sit on one of them.

Levin silently knelt beside me. Dressed in my standard required attire of faded jeans, he also wore a black T-shirt, a coat, and boots for the weather. He rested on his heels.

A sight to behold, my sub.

He hid his anxiety well. Kneeling beside me now, no one would guess he was nervous about coming here. He'd wondered why Colton had insisted on his presence. He thought for one horrible, fleeting second that he was being recalled.

"I don't want you to leave me," he'd whispered. "I could never belong to anyone else. Not as I belong to you."

I'd dismissed that, reassuring him Master Colton had not implied any such thing. I'd reassured him ultimately it was my decision if I kept him as my own or even his decision if he wished to remove his collar. "Never," he'd whispered, so then I'd reassured him with my cock.

Just how he liked it.

When the doors reopened and Colton walked in, he held a piece of paper, and I could tell he was uneasy. Colton sat in the chair across from me, worry lines marring his brow. His third sub, Mikhail, knelt quickly beside him, assuming the same position as my Levin.

"Thank you for coming on such short notice," Colton said.

"Of course."

"Sig," he started. "You know me well."

I nodded. "And I can tell you are troubled."

He frowned again and sighed. "I am."

"What is it?"

"I failed a submissive," he said quietly.

Instinctively, I was quick to leave the chair and kneel in

front of him, in a pose that mirrored Levin's. "I don't believe it."

"It's true," he admitted. "I paired a Dom and sub, and they were . . . not compatible."

Compatible. I didn't like how the word sounded. Not all bonds are for life; some last years, some don't. But this sounded . . . different. I couldn't quite marry what he was saying with the man I knew. "Please explain so I understand."

"A boy was brought into the Sanctus a few weeks ago. I oversaw him. He's a dear boy; a boy who needs strict boundaries. I paired him with Lazzaro."

I winced at the mention of his name. I knew many Doms who practised S&M and they were good people. But Lazzaro had a coldness about him. He had the hollow stare of a manipulator, a sociopath.

Colton didn't miss my reaction to the mention of Lazzaro's name and he let out a sad sigh. "Yes. Last night, Lazzaro brought him here to do a scene and I noticed marks on him that contravened his hard limit. Valente and I recalled him. Lazzaro has been relegated to a sub in training with Valente."

Quite a demotion indeed. Stripped of his rank, stripped of his sub, and sent back to training. Valente would not tolerate such blatant abuse of power and disrespect of a sub in his care. His retraining would be harsh and thorough. Though Lazzaro was not my concern.

"Does the boy need medical attention?" I asked, my first priority.

Colton gave a slight shake of his head. "Please, sit as equal with me," he said, nodding to the seat I'd been sitting in.

Equal? Never . . .

Though I did as he asked, choosing silence over disagreeing with him. "The boy is physically fine. He'd used a whip on him, and that breached his hard limits. The welts weren't that bad; he'd provided good aftercare."

Sig frowned. "If he broke his trust and hurt him, then provided aftercare . . . That's an abusive powerplay. Did he hurt him then soothe him and tell him it was his fault, that he wouldn't have been whipped if he'd behaved better? Master Colton, that's—"

He raised his hand. "I know. And Lazzaro will learn this lesson, believe me." He sighed heavily. "But now the boy has been recalled. He's had his trust breached, he had his submission thrown back in his face, and now, he's struggling mentally."

My field was medical; I was a doctor, not a psychologist. "Why have you called me? If the boy needs a psychologist, surely Ephraim is better equipped."

Colton smiled, almost sadly. "I need you to take him. I need you to take him as a second submissive."

I blinked, turning his request over in my head before glancing toward Levin, who had not moved a muscle.

"I know Levin is your first concern," Colton admitted. "I know you to be a strict but fair Dominant. But I also know you're compassionate; one who punishes and uses as required but who also cares deeply for his subs."

"Tell me about him."

Colton handed me the piece of paper he was holding. "His name is Hunter Vargo. He's twenty-three. He'd been with a Dom outside of our dominion who feared he lacked the skills required for such a boy. He needs twenty-four seven submission. I took him in; he's very dedicated. I found him to thrive under strict domination, but . . ."

"But?"

"Look at his form," Colton said, nodding to the piece of paper. It was a sexual soft and hard limit form. Each and every person who entered into the Sanctus was required to fill it out, and any Dom worth his salt would insist a sub's forms were redone often, discussed and negotiated at length.

This form was decidedly empty, except for one hard limit. "He has a hard limit of whipping," Colton said.

"That's not uncommon," I conceded.

"Whipping of any kind," Colton added quietly. "When you see him, you'll understand."

I nodded. If Colton said as much, then I took it as truth and would wait until I saw the boy for myself. But this form . . . I turned the paper over in my hand. It was blank. "There's nothing else marked or noted."

"Yes. An oversight. The system we have in place has never failed anyone before . . ."

I frowned. "But his one and only hard limit was breached? The failure was with Lazzaro."

"All responsibility and failures stop with me. I allowed Lazzaro a position of Dom, and clearly he's not worthy. When Hunter was ready to go with a Dom, after his initial training with me, he said he understood everything, he was ready . . ." Master Colton shook his head. "I think he told me what I wanted to hear. He wanted to please me, so he agreed. I should have seen that. I should have known better. For me now, the incident with Lazzaro is a separate issue. The first issue is mine. I failed this boy. Not just the Sanctus and our traditions. Me."

We were both quiet for a moment. While Master Colton was responsible for all members in this dominion and would bear the weight of blame, I had a hard time agreeing that he was entirely at fault.

Colton sighed. "I want you to take Hunter. I wouldn't ask anyone else. He's a special case. And he needs a Dominant I can trust, Sig. And there is no one I would trust more."

"I'm honoured."

But a second submissive?

"I already have three subs. I am unable to take on another," Master Colton continued. "Otherwise I would. I let this boy down, and now I feel obligated to ensure his care. Someone who I know will do right by him."

As alarming as this was, I could never have denied Colton. He asked me to take this boy on. And so, I would. Again, I left my chair and knelt before my old Master. "It would be an honour to do as you have asked of me."

A smile graced his voice when he spoke again. "One of my greatest subs," he whispered. Colton threaded his fingers through my hair, pulling my head up so I looked at him. "It's why I ask you to do this. Because I know you will teach him as I taught you. Care for him as I cared for you."

A rush of pride warmed my chest. I smiled at the compliment, at the gentle touch of his hand. "Of course."

"I have told Hunter that in light of his recent mistreatment and the betrayal of his Dom, I would impose a one-week trial with you."

I looked up at that, shocked. The Sanctus rarely applied such trials. "Oh?"

"Yes. And I know you like to pet your boy and reward him with a hand in his hair. And I will allow that. You can reassure him and reward him with gentle touch, though I would impose a rule of no sexual contact in that time. I want him to trust you and be sure it's right. I want him to feel safe before he is used again in that way. Let him see how you operate before he decides if you're a match."

I gave him a nod. "A cautious and fair decision."

Colton's fingers found my hair again. "Though you can let him watch, if he wishes. I'm sure Levin would like that."

I smiled and kissed Colton's palm.

"Come," Colton said as he stood. "I want you to meet your new sub."

LEVIN AND STEFAN followed us downstairs, and along the familiar hidden corridor, to a room in which I'd been many times. It was a playroom; a wall of whips, canes, floggers, shackles from the ceiling, a padded bench, a table, a chair in the corner, and a cabinet of toys. The centre of the room was marked, as were all playrooms under the Sanctus dominion, by a large wooden St Andrew's cross.

But that was not the feature of this room. Because on his knees, naked—in the inspection position—was my new submissive. Upon immediate impression, I could see he was fit and lean, physically in good condition. His short blond hair was closer to my brown, and a stark contrast to my Levin's black.

I stood in front of him, looking him over. He was on display for me. His uncut cock was long, limp, and heavy. His shoulders were broad, his thighs were defined, his waist slim.

But when I walked around him, I could see exactly why Colton had made the comment about me understanding why the boy had a hard limit of whipping.

His back was covered in scars. A real-life spiderweb of horrors.

Old scars. From his childhood.

As a doctor, I knew how a body healed and which

injuries left which mark. I knew, without doubt, this boy had been whipped to within an inch of his life. Not once, but several times.

No wonder he had a hard limit.

I stood in front of him once more and gently lifted his chin with my finger. He was beautiful in a refined, even dainty, way. His cheekbones were high, his nose straight, his eyes a haunted blue. Beautiful, yes, but damaged and in need of my care.

"Hello, sweet boy. My name is Sig Bruckner. Master Colton has asked me to help you, and I would be honoured if you would let me try."

He swallowed and nodded.

Then Colton said, "I would insist you all return here in one week, and Hunter can decide if he wants to give you his submission."

I bowed my head. "Agreed."

Colton put his hand to Hunter's head, a gentle, reassuring touch. "You are in safe hands, Hunter. I give you my word."

Hunter almost sagged with relief, then Colton gave me a hard nod. "Please keep me informed."

"Of course," I replied without hesitation.

He left, his subs following him dutifully, leaving me and Levin alone with a still-kneeling, still-naked Hunter. There was a neatly folded robe on the padded bench. "Levin, please get the robe."

Levin quickly wrapped it around Hunter's shoulders, and only when he was sure Hunter was covered, he turned to face me, then knelt beside Hunter. My heart swelled with pride, and I lightly touched his hair. "You are a good sub," I whispered.

Levin preened a little at my praise, so I lifted his chin

and bent to kiss him. He hummed, so in tune with every touch, every look, every kiss.

I took my place before them. Taking on another sub had been the last thing I'd expected coming here tonight, but now, seeing them side by side, kneeling before me, it did something to the Dom in me.

"Hunter," I said, firm but gentle. "Your place in my home is welcome. Your choosing to or not to remain in my care after your trial week has no bearing on how you will be treated. And should you wish to remain after your first week, the decision is yours and yours alone."

Hunter gave a slight nod to acknowledge what I'd said.

"For this week, I am not your Master, and you can address me as Sir."

His answer was immediate, his voice rough. "Yes, Sir."

"I will honour Master Colton's wishes and see you are not touched sexually in your initial week. You will be safe. You have my word."

He bowed his head. "Thank you, Sir."

"You will still have safe words, even though there will be no sexual scenes between us this week; they are your power to stop whatever we are doing. Those safe words for all things are yellow to slow, red to stop. Can you repeat them for me?"

"Yellow to slow, red to stop."

I hummed approvingly and trailed my fingers through his hair. "Good boy."

"Levin is my first sub, and you will be second sub for the duration of your stay. Follow his lead and his instruction as you would mine."

"Yes, Sir."

"It's gotten late, and I imagine you've had an exhausting day," I added gently. "Let us get you to your new home and settled in. We can discuss rules and answer any questions you might have first thing tomorrow."

"Yes, Sir."

I turned to Levin. "Please help Hunter to the car."

Like the perfect submissive he was, he helped Hunter to his feet and fixed his robe, then with an arm around his back, led him back through the hall to the entrance foyer and into the waiting car.

CHAPTER TWO

THE DRIVE to my estate from the Sanctus didn't take long; barely fifteen minutes through the winding Alps. The Sanctus had accumulated much land through these mountains over the centuries, setting up private estates in smaller lots for Doms and their subs.

My estate was set on five acres and consisted of a main chalet and a smaller cottage. The chalet was stone and timber, double storey, and spacious. I knew I'd been given one of the nicer properties because Colton favoured me.

Or maybe because I favoured him. I idolised him. I still did.

I was close to the Sanctus's headquarters for my medical training but also for playdates and parties. I was privileged, and taking home a second sub reminded me of that.

The car pulled into the drive to my estate. I instructed Paul, my driver to take us to the front and to open the doors for us. All in all, Hunter had been very quiet. Not that I expected him to be loud, but even his demeanour was reserved. He wasn't frightened. He was unsure.

"Come," I told them both. "Let's show Hunter his room."

The room was modest but lovely, neutrally furnished. Tones of blues and gold, carpeted floor, a queen-sized bed, side table, lamp, and nondescript artwork on the wall, the large window draped with heavy curtains. "Your own bathroom is through here," I pointed to the first door, then the second one. "And your personal closet through this door. We can arrange clothes for you tomorrow."

Hunter walked into the room and I watched him. He was still quiet, but when he turned to look at me, his eyes were filled with tears, his voice was whisper quiet. "All this is for me? Really?"

His reaction concerned me. As though he'd never been given anything. "Yes. Hunter, have you never had your own room?"

He looked to the floor, and he shook his head.

I was very well aware not all Dominants could offer wealth and luxury, but his reaction went deeper than that. "Have you ever had any personal belongings?" I asked.

He shook his head again and wrapped the robe tighter around him. "Not many, Sir."

My heart clenched at his troubled past. What kind of life had he had? What brought him to this point in his life? What had dulled the fire in his eyes? I was almost certain it ran deeper than a worthless Dom like Lazzaro who'd mistreated him. "Levin will provide you with enough clothes until we organise your own."

Levin disappeared from the room, and I knew he'd taken my words as an order and was collecting some personal belongings for Hunter to call his own.

But given what I'd seen and what Colton had told me, I knew the boy would feel more relaxed knowing some immediate boundaries and rules. "Hunter, while you are here, this is your room and your space to be as you please. You will be downstairs at 6.30am sharp. Your daily outfit will consist of jeans. You won't wear underwear. You won't wear a shirt or shoes unless we are leaving the house. Learn from Levin; watch him and do what he tells you to do. He's the best submissive I've seen; do as he does, and you'll please me greatly."

Hunter nodded and Levin walked in and placed some neatly folded clothing on the dresser before resuming his standing idle position; feet apart, head bowed, hand clasped behind his back.

"Hunter, have you eaten?"

He gave a nod. "Yes, Sir. Master Colton gave me soup and bread."

"Okay. We have much to discuss, many details and rules to examine. But I'd rather you sleep first. It's not fair on you to make decisions when you're clearly exhausted. Levin and I will leave you now, and you're free to shower; there are shower gels and shampoos and unused tooth-brushes and toothpastes. Consider them yours. Or, if you're simply too tired, just climb straight into bed. Which-ever you want. And during the night, if you need for anything, Levin's room is next to yours. He will help you. Set your alarm for six. Levin will come and get you and run you through the morning routine before you come downstairs."

"Yes, Sir."

"Goodnight, Hunter. I'm glad you're here."

Just as I was about to leave, Hunter took a small step toward me. "Sir?"

For a boy who was naturally timid, I knew this had to be important. "Yes?"

His voice was quiet, and he spoke to the floor. "Have I done something to displease you?"

Displease me?

Then, so quietly I almost didn't hear him, he added, "Sir."

Sir.

Sir.

It wasn't the word. I'd told him to address me as such, but it was how he said it. I stepped in front of him. He lowered his head but didn't move. "Look at me," I said, my voice low and demanding. "If you have concerns, please voice them."

He looked up, and his eyes were wide; scared, vulnerable, pleading. He swallowed hard. "I . . . I . . . it's nothing," he whispered, but his fingers went to his neck absently.

Where his collar used to be.

Colton had said this boy needed collaring.

My voice was commanding, a tone he obviously responded well to. "Hunter, for the duration of this week, I am your Dom but not your Master. I cannot collar you. It is not the way of the Sanctus."

He blinked quickly. "I . . . I understand," he whispered. This time his fingers dug a little harder at his neck, leaving pink lines on his skin.

Oh hell.

"But I can see you're uncomfortable," I soothed him with my voice. I touched the top of his head, softly fingering his hair. "You don't like being uncollared, do you, boy?"

He shook his head. "I can't . . . f-f-focus . . ."

His reaction wasn't a good one, and I knew it would need addressing, but for now, I needed him to be safe.

"Levin," I said, looking over to him where he stood,

unmoving. His gaze met mine when I spoke his name. "The leather wrist cuff in the playroom. Please get it for me."

Levin disappeared out the door and I turned back to Hunter. This boy was a mess. I cupped his cheek and he leaned into my touch. "Sssshhh," I whispered. "Hunter, this is your home for as long as you want it. I want you to feel safe here."

I lifted his chin and he nodded. "Yes, Sir. Thank you, Sir."

Levin appeared with the leather cuff. It was two inches wide with a metal O-ring stitched into it. Levin handed it to me before he stepped back and resumed his idle position.

"Hunter," I began. "If you need this cuff to feel validated and safe here, then I'll gladly give it you. It's not the same collar Levin wears, and there will be no collaring or claiming ceremony tonight, but for this week, this cuff is yours." Then I spoke more reverently. "To mark your place here, as my submissive, this cuff is to remain on your body, to show you belong to me. You will serve me; you will do as I ask. I will respect you and guide and support you. Do you agree to these conditions, sub?"

"Yes, Sir," he whispered.

"Give me your right hand."

He offered his hand to me, and he held his breath as I slid it around his wrist and clasped the buckle. Once it was secure, he breathed out in a rush. He was immediately more relaxed and calm.

"Your submission to me is a gift, thank you," I whispered, still holding his hand. "Do you feel better?"

"Yes, Sir," he replied quickly.

"You need to know your safe words have power here. If anything I request of you is too much, you must use them," I said. He gave a nod. "And if you wish to cease this agreement at any time, all you have to do is remove this cuff."

He gave another nod. "Thank you, Sir."

"Get some rest. You will have a busy day tomorrow, sub."

He smiled, a genuine smile, and beneath the anxiety, beneath the vulnerability was a beautiful boy.

I turned to leave and smiled at Levin, still standing perfectly. "Levin, follow me," I said, and we left Hunter to check out his room. I went into my bedroom and Levin followed dutifully. It wasn't often he joined me here, but I needed to speak to him. I took off my coat, and without me asking, he took it and hung it up. Then I sat on the seat by the dresser, and he knelt before me and undid my laces.

He was gorgeous. And still far too overdressed . . . but tonight had been out of the ordinary and his first concern was for Hunter, and that pleased me.

I watched Levin as he used his skilled fingers to untie my shoes and take them off. He set them down to the side then took off my socks, and I couldn't take my eyes off him. I was incredibly aroused. Being offered a second sub—that I couldn't touch, no less—was heady, and then watching my Levin tend to him and be the utmost perfect sub . . . always standing correctly, kneeling perfectly, never once faltering.

He needed to be rewarded, and just the thought of that aroused me.

Still between my legs, he sat back on his heels, head bowed, hands clasped in his lap. I could order him to take my cock out and suck it, but I had obligations first. Though he'd never show it, me taking on a second submissive must've been unsettling for him.

If I were to have asked him, he'd say he was proud that

his Master was bestowed a second submissive. The perfect submissive response; a very Levin response.

But I wanted to—needed to—reassure him of his position. Submissives were ultimately creatures of habit and found comfort in repetitive structure. So while his home environment had changed to include another, he needed reassurance from his Master; he had done no wrong, his needs would still be met.

Knowing Levin as well as I did, I knew he'd respond best if I included him.

"Taking on a second sub is a great responsibility. I will require your help with this boy," I said. "It will be your role as first sub, to assist in my training him. He will look to you for leadership. Are you ready to be a first sub, Levin?"

"My Master has taught me well. I am ready."

His words made my cock throb. "You made me proud at the Sanctus tonight," I said gruffly. "You are an exemplary submissive, and Hunter is lucky to have you to look up to."

He beamed with pride but tried to contain it. "Thank you, Master."

I spread my legs a little wider. "Do you know what happens to subs who make their Masters proud?"

Levin licked his bottom lip. "Do they get rewards, Master?"

I leaned in and spread my thumb across where his tongue had just been and drew his face close to mine. "They most certainly do." He made a whining sound when I ghosted his lips with mine. Such a good boy. "Levin, go to the playroom. When I walk in, you'll be in the waiting position in front of the apparatus of your choice."

"As you wish, Master," he replied breathily, and then he was gone.

I smiled as I stood and undressed from my suit, slipping

into my leather pants; my playroom attire. My cock was hard, knowing what was about to transpire. So I gave myself a hard squeeze to try and stave off the desire to walk into that playroom and fuck Levin for my own pleasure. He needed his reward, and I would make sure I gave it to him.

Once I'd given Levin adequate time to prepare, I quietly checked on Hunter, only to find him fast asleep, and made my way to my playroom. I'd told Levin to choose whichever apparatus he wanted, and I was keen to see what he favoured tonight.

The lights were low, but there he was, naked and kneeling in front of the padded bench, his head bowed, his hands behind his back. There was a Fleshlight placed on top of the bench.

Although my favourite apparatus was the wooden cross, Levin had always favoured the bench; I wasn't at all surprised he'd chosen it. He loved to be bent over it, restrained to it, and fucked.

I was also hyper aware that after taking on a second sub, Levin needed me to reassure him of his place. Not with the words I'd said a few moments ago, but with my body. He needed me to reaffirm my dominance over him, and he needed to reaffirm his submission to me.

I walked straight to him and lifted his chin with my finger. "The bench *and* a Fleshlight as well?" I asked, my voice low and smooth.

His eyes almost rolled, and a look of serenity washed over his face. He leaned into me; this boy, this man, who would allow me to do anything to him.

"Have you fitted a plug?" I asked.

"Yes, Master."

Of course he had. He knew what I liked.

"You've been a very good sub today," I praised him. "I'll

allow you the Fleshlight." I rubbed my hand down the side of his face and massaged his throat. "Now, take out my cock and suck it."

With eager hands he undid the button fly and slid his long fingers around my shaft, freeing my cock. He engulfed me easily, immediately. He was well-practised and very talented at oral pleasure, this boy. He slid his mouth over the head and wrapped his delectable lips around me. His tongue swirled as he sucked, and my balls began that familiar, welcome drawing up.

He moaned as he devoured me, my cock sliding into his open throat. I could have easily let him finish me like this; I loved emptying my cock in his mouth. But this was not about me tonight.

"Enough," I demanded. He released me, licking his swollen lips, pleased with himself.

"Set up your Fleshlight," I ordered as I turned around to retrieve some supplies. I chose the fur shackles for his wrists, lubrication, and a soft suede flogger.

The custom-made bench had a hole in the end panel, which fit a Fleshlight. When he was bent over the bench, he'd be fucking the sex toy, while I fucked him.

It was his most favourite pastime.

When I turned back to the bench, he'd slotted the Fleshlight into place and was standing in the waiting position. His feet were shoulder-width apart, his head bowed, and his hands were behind his back. His cock jutted out proudly from his body.

I placed my items atop the far end of the bench and picked up the lube. Drizzling enough on my hand, I wrapped my fingers around his cock and watched his reaction; his eyes rolled, his dick pulsed in my hand, his breath hitched, and he whined.

"You like your Master's touch," I said.

"Oh, yes, Master," he murmured and nodded eagerly.

"Get into position, sub," I ordered. "I want to watch your cock enter the toy," I told him. "Fuck it, nice and slow."

He stood at the foot of the bench, and with one hand around his shaft, he positioned the head of his cock at the waiting hole and oh-so slowly slid himself into it.

It was beautiful to watch. The most glorious sight was to watch a cock entering a tight hole. How it twitched, how it pushed, how it slid in.

With a long moan, he rose up on his toes and pushed the remaining inches of his cock down into the toy ass. When he was fully embedded in the Fleshlight, he adjusted his weight, and with a quick look into my eyes, he nodded to tell me he was ready.

"Good boy," I said, my voice gruff.

He leaned over the padded top, placing his feet on the footrests, with his arms dangling down the sides. I picked up the fur shackles and cuffed his left hand to the C-bolt in the wooden panelled side of the bench, then did the same to his right hand.

"Are you comfortable?" I asked him quietly.

"Yes, Master," he breathed, almost like a moan.

Taking the suede flogger with me, I dragged the soft end down his back, across his skin, teasing him. Gooseflesh covered his skin where it touched him.

He moaned louder.

I rubbed the soft suede across his lower back, down to his ass. "You look so good, sub," I murmured. "So ready for me."

He moaned again.

I continued to rub the suede over his ass, over the silver bullet plugged in his hole, down to the seam between his hole and his balls. He shuddered and moaned again.

"How does your cock feel, boy?" I whispered, my voice rough. "Feel good buried in that sex toy?"

He pulled against the restraints. "Good, Master," he moaned out. "So good."

I tapped the flogger against his skin now; for pleasure, not punishment. First the flesh of his ass, then I tapped the plug. He whimpered and writhed, flexing his hips to fuck the toy.

When I tapped the flogger against his balls, he yelped out a moan, so I rubbed the soft suede across his balls to where his cock was implanted in the Fleshlight. He cried out, pulling hard on his arms.

He looked so fucking perfect, bent over and restrained for me. His hole was ready, his cock was hard, and he was fucking a sex toy, waiting for me to impale him. "Mmmm," I hummed. "Such a good cock whore."

He whined at the name I called him, and the sound throbbed in my balls. I stood between his thighs, laid the flogger on his back, and rubbed my hands over his ass. He groaned again, taking in ragged breaths. Every slight movement he made had him fucking the toy.

"Do you want to come, sub?"

He pulled against the shackles and rolled his hips, driving his cock into the Fleshlight. He nodded quickly. "Yes, Master."

I smiled. He was so well-trained. He was such a testament to the Sanctus dominion, such a testament to his training, such a testament to me.

His submission was my ultimate gratification.

"Come as often as you want," I allowed. He could obviously hear the pride in my voice. "I want to hear you, boy."

He groaned. "Thank you, Master."

I removed the plug and slapped his ass. He cried out, flexing his hips to push his cock deeper into the Fleshlight. I lathered my cock in lube and rubbed his hole again, slipping my fingers inside him. He bucked and moaned again.

"Master . . . Master . . ." He was getting desperate.

So I grabbed his hips and, aligning him perfectly, I drove my cock into him, and he bucked, crying out and coming on contact. Every inch of my cock, in one slick movement, I buried in his tight hole, and I pinned his hips down as he spasmed through his orgasm. My cock nailed him to the bench; his hole tightened around me while he emptied his load into the sex toy.

"Oh, yeah," I groaned with him. "Such a dirty cock whore. You come as soon as my cock touches you."

He was moaning almost non-stop now; his cock was still buried in the sex toy. He was crying and mumbling through his aftershocks, but he was far from finished.

I slid out of him, to the tip of my cock, and rammed back in. I didn't give him time to recover from his orgasm; I simply just fucked him harder.

Just how he liked it.

His moans got louder, then they got longer. And then he was begging and pleading for more. His hands gripped the shackles and he was rocking his hips into the toy, onto my cock. "What feels better?" I asked as I fucked him. "Your cock in the toy or my cock in your ass?"

"Oh, Master," he ground out. "Your cock. Always your cock."

I gave him a few hard thrusts for his answer. "That's right boy," I said as I fucked him. "You take it so well. Nine inches buried in your ass, and you moan like a good little cock whore."

He cried out and pushed his ass against me.

"*My* cock whore."

His whine became a moan. "Yes. Yours."

I fucked him harder, giving it to him how he liked it. His hands pulled against the shackles with every thrust, the sound of the metal bolts and buckles spurred me on. And he started to rock his hips again, fucking the Fleshlight while I fucked him. "The toy is slick with your come. Can you feel your cock sliding in your own come?"

He gasped and whimpered. "Yesss."

I leaned back and watched my cock as it entered him, sliding in and out. Knowing I'd soon be coming in his ass made me moan. "You want me to fill you with my come? Remind you who you belong to?" I grunted out, and all he could do was groan a reply.

And the muscles in his back stretched tight, his shoulders flexed as he pulled against his bindings. And with a strangled cry, he came again.

He convulsed as pleasure ripped through him. He threw his head back and groaned, pumping his seed into the toy. I fucked his ass relentlessly, again and again until my cock lurched, filling him with my seed. There would be no doubt to whom he belonged now.

Covered in sweat, he collapsed onto the padded bench, turning his head so I could see him smile.

But I ran my hands over his back and shoulders, massaging his spent muscles while I slid my softening length out of him. I unbuckled his restraints and helped him stand. I held his face and said, "Thank you," before kissing his soft lips. Then I wrapped my arms around him and held him, as I always did after our sessions. "Did you want to lie down and cuddle, or would you rather a bath?"

He moaned. "Bath."

I smiled. "Then I'll run it for you."

He sighed contentedly. "Thank you, Master."

He smiled as he followed me to his private suite. I started the bath and, as always, Levin stood, leaning forward over the bathroom counter. With a light oil, I massaged his shoulders, his arms, his lower back, his beautiful ass and his thighs, kneading his muscles free of knots. The sight of his glistening hole, knowing my come was inside him, stirred something within me. A need to protect him, to cherish him and adore him. I kissed his shoulder, between his shoulder blades, the nape of his neck.

When the bath was ready, I helped him step into the large tub, and then I got in with him. I washed him, reverently, affectionately, soaping him up and rinsing him clean. He revelled in my attention. He leaned against me, his back to my chest, my arms around him. His eyes were closed, and he hummed and smiled at my touch.

"Levin?" I murmured.

He turned and looked up at me. "Yes, Master?"

"It's been quite a day. Do you have any questions for me?" I asked. "About Hunter?"

"No, Master."

"He will need our help this week."

"He will."

"Would you have any concerns if he decided he wanted to stay on with us?"

Levin shook his head. "No. I think he belongs with us, Master." He leaned back against me snuggling down a little into the water and his voice was soft. "I trust you to do the right thing by him. And me." There was a fractional pause, the slightest hesitation, before he bowed his head again.

"Levin, look at me."

He sat up and met my gaze, of course, almost without

expression. But I knew my boy. He couldn't expect to be my submissive for two years and have me not able to read him; how his eyes flashed, how he swallowed, how his pulse quickened.

"Speak of your troubles, sub."

He looked up at me again, his dark brown eyes huge with worry. "It's not *my* troubles, Master. He . . ." His voice was hesitant. "His scars . . ."

"I know," I whispered. "He's been wronged, terribly."

"Do you know how . . . who?" he asked, his voice just as quiet as mine.

"No, sweet boy," I replied, tracing the side of his face with a gentle touch. "But we will find out tomorrow."

CHAPTER THREE

KNOWING we were in for a long day, I walked downstairs just after six thirty. I headed straight for the kitchen, as I did every morning, and when I saw Levin, I couldn't hide my grin.

Because beside him, posed the same, kneeling in the same waiting position, was Hunter. Both dressed only in jeans; no shirt, no shoes. My favourite dress code for subs, and doubly impressive with the two of them side by side.

I stood before them and touched the top of Levin's head first. "Good morning, sub."

"Good morning, Master."

Then I placed my hand atop Hunter's head. "Good morning, sub."

"Good morning, Sir."

I stepped back and looked them over. If having one sub dressed and in the waiting position was a sight to behold, having two was intoxicating. Levin looked up first, then Hunter, and I smiled. "A good morning, indeed." I shook my head in wonder before walking toward the kitchen. "Come, boys. Breakfast."

I sat at the head of the table, Levin sat to my right where he always sat, and when Hunter moved to sit beside him, I stopped him. "Hunter, sit here." I motioned to my left so he'd be across from Levin. "This table is neutral ground. You can speak freely here. Although I need not remind you, you must show respect at all times."

He took his seat and nodded. And it was then I noticed the leather cuff on his wrist. A warm thrill shot through me. It was different to Levin's collar, which was a thinner leather necklace with an O-ring that looked perfect on his shirtless torso. But Hunter's wrist cuff was his tie to me, no matter how temporary.

"I trust you slept well?" I asked him.

"Yes, Sir," he replied quietly. "Very well, thank you."

"And Levin helped you this morning?"

Hunter nodded. "He showed me his morning routine. He was very kind."

I smiled at Levin so he could see the pride in my plea-sure. "Master," Levin said. "I took the liberty to ask Michael to prepare breakfast for three. I didn't want to overstep any boundaries, but I also did not want for you to be running late because breakfast was not ready."

I patted his hand and gave it a squeeze. "Very consid-erate of you Levin, for my time and Michael's. But I won't be working today or tomorrow. Hunter will need time to settle in," I added.

Hunter looked at me, a little startled. "I don't want to be a nuisance," he said quickly.

"No, it's fine. You're no nuisance at all," I reassured him. "When Levin first joined me, I didn't work for almost a week. You won't need me here for that long because your time with us this week doesn't include the playroom. And you have Levin to help you and guide you while I'm not here."

Just then, Michael, one of the many dominion cooks, served breakfast. He himself was part of the Sanctus; he and Paul, my driver, were partners. Paul had been my first permanent sub, and now he and Michael lived in the cottage on the estate.

Michael, a tall, well-built man with black hair, pale Irish skin, and a kind smile, placed plates of cut fruit, yoghurts, muesli, and warm toast on the table. Introductions were made, and I explained to Michael I'd leave a list of grocery items in the kitchen once we'd worked out a dietary programme for Hunter.

Hunter's eyes widened. "I don't need anything special," he was quick to say. "I'll be happy with whatever's available. I won't be a bother, Sir."

"You're no bother." I patted his hand but smiled at both him and Levin. "Eat up, boys."

They started to eat their breakfast, and after Michael had served coffee and juice, I explained to Hunter what I meant exactly when I said *dietary programme*. "You'll require a certain intake of kilojoules per day, to fuel the energy outtake you will expend. I expect you and Levin to spend a minimum of one hour in the gym: cardio, muscle toning, and endurance, every day. I have high expectations of what Levin's body can tolerate, so he needs above-average fitness. And while you're here, you can begin a programme. Not for endurance so to speak, but for your general health and well-being."

I looked at Levin and he smiled and nodded his agreement while eating a hearty breakfast. Hunter, on the other hand, ate like a bird.

"I expect you to eat, to look after your body," I urged

him. "I won't have you unwell. And I'll have you know," I said with a smile, "if Levin doesn't wake up hungry, I know I didn't work him over hard enough the night before."

Hunter stared at me with disbelieving eyes, but he relaxed when he saw I was smiling. Levin chuckled, and Hunter almost smiled.

Almost.

I continued, "I'll make a list of likes and dislikes and inform Michael to incorporate that into a daily intake of fruits, vegetables, protein, and carbohydrates."

Hunter swallowed his food and took a sip of juice. "What food I like?"

"Yes," I replied with a nod. "I certainly don't want you to suffer through anything you don't like. Hunter, I'm not sure what kind of relationships you've had with past Doms, but how this dominion works—and how I work—is for my sub, or subs as it would be now, to be happy." I shrugged. "How can I be happy or have my needs met when my subs are not happy?"

Hunter stared at me as though he couldn't believe my words. I smiled. "Levin hates mushrooms and salmon. He'll tolerate celery." I glanced at Levin to see him playfully scrunch his nose and shake his head. It made Hunter smile. Then I added, "And I don't like cantaloupe or cilantro. Everyone has likes and dislikes. I don't want you to feel you have to eat anything you'd rather not."

He blinked a few times, and I could see he was getting ready to say something. "I . . . I don't like oatmeal," he murmured.

I smiled at this small victory. "Then you won't ever have to eat oatmeal."

His lip quirked in another almost-smile, and I hoped he would see how easy it was.

"Now," I continued. "The foods you enjoy?"

He blinked, seemingly a little stuck, so I offered a prompt. "Levin loves creamed honey on toast."

Levin's eyes lit up and he nodded. "Love it."

Hunter blushed and his lip drew down. "I've never tried that."

Levin gasped. "Never? My grandmother used to buy a special kind with orange blossom, and Master tracked down the same kind because he knows how much I love it." Levin looked at me, a little shy, a little proud. "He spoils me."

"Because you please me," I replied.

Levin beamed. "But Master, Hunter's never tried it," he added with pleading eyes.

I smiled and rolled my eyes. "Michael?" I called out. "Please bring the creamed honey." Then I explained to Hunter, "Levin would eat the entire jar in one sitting, so I have Michael hide it."

Michael brought out the creamed honey and Levin happily prepared two slices of toast, handing one to Hunter.

Levin bit into his, and he smiled as he chewed, delighted. Hunter took a smaller bite, but he hummed when the honey hit his tongue, and after he swallowed the mouthful, he appeared a little embarrassed. "It's very good, Sir."

I finished my cup of coffee and smiled at both boys. But, knowing today wouldn't be all-smiles, I took a moment to appreciate the simple joy of a new day, the rising sun, and having two subs in my home. "Please finish your breakfast and meet me in the lounge in five minutes," I said.

"Yes, Master," Levin said, his cheeks rosy. He always had a way to read my moods and my happiness reflected onto him.

"Yes, Sir." Hunter ducked his head, his voice small. These two couldn't be more chalk and cheese, but I had hope of helping Hunter out of his shell a little more. It wasn't something that could be forced. It had to burgeon naturally, like a flower needing the right conditions to bloom.

I headed to my study to phone in, advising my office of my two-day hiatus from work. I checked messages and emails and decided it could all wait.

I found the paperwork I was after, and when I walked back into the large open lounge area, both subs were in the kneeling, waiting position. Again, I acknowledged both boys with a gentle touch to the tops of their heads. "We will start in here, if you'd both sit on the sofa, please," I said, sitting on the large leather sofa. "We have rules, guidelines, and expectations to discuss, and I'd prefer to do this openly."

I waited for them to sit on the sofa opposite me. Levin did first and Hunter followed his lead, and I waited for them both to look at me before speaking. "First, I want to tell you the house rules, Hunter, so there's no misunderstanding." He nodded and I continued. "You will be respectful at all times and use appropriate manners. If I ask you a question, you will answer with yes or no, Sir. You will not back chat or speak out of turn. I allow you to speak freely when we are at the dining table or if we're having an open discussion and I give permission. You can always ask me questions if you're not sure. Or you can ask Levin. If I'm not here, you will look to him for guidance, and you will obey his instruction."

Hunter gave a nod. "Yes, Sir."

"I also want to talk about your role here, Hunter," I said, my voice low and smooth with authority. "What expectations you might have, what your needs are, what you require from me as your Dom. You need to be comfortable in your time here, and remember, while you can speak freely, I expect honest, respectful answers."

"Yes, Sir," he replied.

"Being a twenty-four seven submissive is demanding, and some find it too challenging," I stated. "Some prefer weekend-only play, some prefer weekends off. But you find it difficult to be uncollared, yes?"

Hunter absentmindedly touched the leather cuff on his wrist and he nodded. "Yes, Sir. I feel . . . overwhelmed. I um, I can't think straight without a Master or a Dominant, Sir," he mumbled and cringed.

I nodded because I'd seen that before. It was a common trait in subs who had been collared by a Dom who didn't nurture or teach self-respect within the realm of submission. It was one thing to dominate; it was another to control without respect. It bothered me that he was almost scared to speak.

"Hunter, I want you to speak loud and clear," I said. "I know it's not easy sometimes, but when we have open discussions, I value your opinion, and if you struggle to find the right words, take your time. You won't get in trouble. It's not just out of respect to me, but for yourself. I will help you see how worthy you can be. You will learn in your time here that your submission is far from a sign of weakness."

He swallowed hard and nodded but hardly looked convinced.

"If you have any questions, at any time, please ask them. Okay?"

Hunter gave another nod. "Yes, Sir."

"So, first of all, we need to discuss hard limits." I knew this was uncomfortable ground for him, considering his hard limit form he'd filled out previously, but it needed to be done. "Everyone has limits, whether they be hard or soft limits, and not all hard limits are sexual, but they're all very important. Between the three of us, there should be no secrets and no shame. Having soft and hard limits is what keeps us safe."

I handed them both a sheet of paper. "Levin, this will be a good time for us to re-evaluate our needs and our limits. I know you're familiar with this form, but for the sake of transparency, you'll see lists of activities and scenes, certain props. Mark each hard limit with an *H*, soft limits with an S, and tick anything you'd like to explore."

"Hunter, your form is different to Levin's. Your form has no sexual lists, and it's more of an introductory form, likes and dislikes, needs and wants, that kind of thing." I smiled watching him read through the list. "If you decide you wish to stay after your initial week, and if you'd like to incorporate sex into your role as submissive, then we can do your sexual limit list next week, okay?"

"Yes, Sir."

"Now, I want to ask you something, Hunter, before you begin. If I were to take Levin into the playroom or bend him over the table or have him perform fellatio on me on the sofa, would you be comfortable in watching? Or should I ask you to go to your room?"

He blushed and swallowed hard. "I'm comfortable in watching, Sir."

I didn't even try to hide my smile. "Good."

He blushed again, furiously, but picked up a pen and started to complete the form. I noticed two things about him immediately, the first being he was left handed. And the second thing I noticed about him was that he wasn't particularly strong at either reading or writing.

Although Levin finished his form with ease, having done it many times, I gave Hunter all the time he needed. I filled in mine as well, and when Hunter was done, I took the forms and read Hunter's first.

Oh dear.

His writing wasn't great, more childlike than that of an adult. Some words I couldn't quite make out and some were spelled wrong.

"You've listed humiliation as a hard limit," I noted. This was not a sexualised list. "Do you mean not in a sexual way?"

He squinted a little and spoke to his hands. "I don't like it when I'm made an example of. Or asked to stand out in a crowd. Like taking me to the front of the room and saying, "Look at this, everyone, this is how not to do something.""

My gut twisted. "People made fun of you?"

"Some." He nodded. "I don't like being in front of crowds. It makes me panic."

"Hunter, no one here will ever make fun of you, I promise." I went back to his form, and noted one thing was very clearly *not* on his list. He hadn't marked anything down as hobbies, likes, or goals. Nothing he enjoyed, nothing he found pleasure in, no gratification, which was something I'd be coming back to. Though some things had a cross next to them, like tennis and dogs.

"You don't like dogs?"

"I was bitten once," he whispered. "It was big, and it chased me. I was about seven, I think."

"Fair enough," I replied. "I'm pretty sure I wouldn't like something either if it chased and bit me."

He gave me a grateful smile.

"Tennis?"

"Um, well . . . no sports with a racquet or bat really." He swallowed hard.

Christ.

"There were boys older than me at my first home, and they would hit me . . ."

I let out a slow breath. Right. Nothing that could be used as a weapon. "Rest assured, that won't happen here. You're safe here, I promise you that. And thank you for telling me."

He gave a nod. He wrung his hands in his lap, his long dainty fingers tied up in knots.

"You've left all likes and goals unanswered," I said gently. I didn't want to make an issue out of it, and I didn't want him to think he'd done anything wrong. "That tells me you're uncertain, and maybe you don't know what you're allowed to like."

He took in a sharp breath and I knew my words had hit their mark.

"So," I said, giving him a reassuring smile. "That means we can spend this week exploring the things you like. Movies, walks outside, reading, archery, baking. Whatever you want. And we might even establish some goals. Short-term goals could be to run a mile or read a book. Or long-term goals like getting a university degree or becoming a plumber or dressmaker." He looked at me like I'd sprouted a second head. "I don't know yet what your dreams and aspirations are, Hunter. But I'd like to find out."

He shot a glance at Levin, then turned back to me. "I um . . . I . . ." He cleared his throat. "No one's ever asked me what I wanted, Sir. Not like hobbies or if I wanted to learn something. I wasn't sure..."

My heart sank. "Then I'm glad I asked you today."

Levin frowned at him. "Lazzaro never asked you what you wanted from your relationship with him?"

Hunter shook his head. "No."

Levin shot a hard glare at me, and I nodded. Yes, I

would be telling Colton. "He should have," I said. "And I'm sorry he didn't."

The mood had soured a little, so I went back to our forms. I'd hold onto Hunter's and go over it when I had more time to evaluate it properly.

I held up Levin's form with a smile. "Now, Levin's form is sexual, soft and hard limits, including sex toys. He's checked off . . ." I scanned Levin's list. "Balls, Fleshlights, dildos, rings, vibrators, wands . . . Actually, Levin just ticks yes to the entire toy list."

Hunter looked at Levin, and Levin grinned. "I love it."

I chuckled, explaining to Hunter, "Levin is a greedy boy." Levin scrambled off the sofa to kneel at my feet, his face raised for kissing. "See what I mean?" I asked Hunter, but I slid my hand around Levin's neck and pulled his smiling mouth to mine. I kissed him, and the cheeky boy moved to deepen the kiss. I pulled back from him and placed my thumb on his bottom lip. "Not now, boy. We have work to do first."

He pouted but obliged. I took his chin between my thumb and forefinger. "You're in a very playful mood today, sub. Making you come twice last night has put a skip in your step." Levin moaned and I kissed him again. "Now back to your seat."

Hunter stared at us, surprised and with wonder. I smiled right back at him. "He was a very good boy yesterday. And Levin, tell Hunter what good boys get?"

Levin's lips twisted, smug and knowing. "Rewards."

Hunter blushed and let out a pent-up breath, quickly looking back to his hands. I liked his reaction, and by his smile, Levin did too. He clearly seemed to like the idea of rewards, but the rule of no touching was in place for good reason . . .

I went back to the forms in my hands. "Levin's hard limits are still unchanged. No scat play, no weapons, no blood play, no fisting, no bestiality, no sharing."

Levin nodded. "They still stand."

I gave a nod. "Agreed."

"His soft limits are watersports and breath play. Would be tolerated but he's not a fan, and they're not high on my list of priorities, so I would never ask him to partake in those." I looked to Hunter, wanting to remind him he was safe here. "It's my role as his Dominant to push him, to show him his strengths, but never to abuse that."

Hunter held my gaze as though he was trying to figure out a puzzle.

"Now for my list," I said.

"You filled one out too?" Hunter asked.

"Absolutely. Levin must know what my limits are." Christ. I was beginning to wonder what training this boy had had. Where had he been so failed? His lack of preparation and knowledge wasn't just Lazzaro's doing. Master Colton was right, though. The Sanctus had fallen short also. "My soft and hard limits are important too, and Levin must know when to call the shots. He can end a scene at any time. He can use his safe word at any time. As can you, Hunter." I held his gaze this time. "Anytime, anywhere, and whatever we're doing stops. If Levin decides I'm about to cross a line or if I'm not in the right headspace, he's the one who holds the power to end it all. Same with you, okay?"

He turned to Levin, who gave him a nod, then he turned to me. "Y-yes, Sir."

I made a mental note to go over this again, every day if I had to, until he understood.

"Okay, so getting back to my list." This was mostly for Hunter's benefit. I needed him to know what kind of Dom I was, or more importantly, how different to Lazzaro I was. "First, my natural inclination is for sensual domination. Basically, I love to tie up my subs and wring orgasms out of them. I enjoy come play and voyeurism and restraints. I love the sounds of chains. I like to fuck my sub and I love to watch as they orgasm and ejaculate. I love restraining them, I love coming inside them, and I love making them orgasm."

Levin groaned real low, and Hunter slow-blinked, his cheeks splotched beautiful shades of pink. *Oh boy . . .*

"My hard limits are unchanged. I will not share my sub, or subs, as the case may be. I will not tolerate another person touching or marking my subs. I have claimed your body as part of the sacred Sanctus Dom/sub union, and that will be respected. Even at a scene party or meeting, no one will touch either of you but me." I paused for a moment so I could look each of them in the eye. "And I have a hard limit of brutality and beating. I have nothing against the act if it's consensual and safe, but it is not in my nature to hurt someone, be it for pleasure or punishment. I'm a doctor, and inflicting pain on others goes against my grain. That eliminates knives, fire play, blood play and air deprivation, and I've treated one too many patients from the use of meat hooks, so that was also added to my list. Also scat play, fisting, and watersports. Some love it, but the first thing I think of is . . . hepatitis." Levin smirked. He was used to the doctor side of my Dom nature. Then I added, "Soft limits are also unchanged. Wax play and foot licking."

"The idea of licking toes grosses him out," Levin explained, earning a small smile from Hunter.

"Yes, thank you, Levin," I added. "I will rim you until you orgasm, but I'm not a fan of toes."

Levin laughed. "Which is why he's so particular about

douching and cleaning, but believe me, the reward is worth the effort."

Hunter put his hand to his mouth, his eyes wide, and he chuckled. My God, he actually laughed. Levin grinned at me and leaned in toward Hunter, giving him a playful nudge.

Happiness and warmth filled my chest. "Like I said, happy sub, happy Dom."

Levin raised his hand and bit his bottom lip. "A correction, if I may, Master."

A correction? This should be interesting . . . "You may."

"Subs, as in plural. There are two of us now." Levin linked his arm with Hunter's and curled into him like a cat, smiling at me. "Happy subs, happy Dom."

I met his gaze and shook my head, unable to not smile. "I stand corrected. Thank you, sub."

He beamed and I could see Hunter was unsure what to make of us. We did have an unusual relationship. I afforded Levin more leeway than many other Doms would have, but he was playful by nature and inquisitive and smart, and I wanted to nurture that. Though I could tell with Hunter, we'd gain more ground with smaller steps. "How about we make the most of the sun this morning?" I said. "I'd like us to talk more this afternoon. I think we should address any further questions we might have, but for now, let's show Hunter around the grounds."

Levin's eyes lit up. "Can I give the tour, Master?"

His smile was bright with happiness, and I preened a little at his joy. If he wanted to teach the second sub, in his capacity as first sub, I should allow it. I nodded my consent. "Very good, first sub."

Levin gasped and his eyes met mine, ever so briefly. Maybe, for a short while, he'd forgotten his responsibility.

"Thank you, Master." He got to his feet and, taking Hunter's hand, helped him stand. "We'll start with the back. There's so much to show you."

Levin led him through to the rear atrium where they slipped on some gardening shoes. "Michael won't mind you wearing his for today, but Master will get you some," Levin explained. "He's very generous." They were still shirtless, wearing only their required uniform of jeans, but the sun was out and there was very little breeze.

Hunter smiled, and a moment later, Levin opened up the atrium doors that led to the back garden. I gave him room to lead, to instruct, and to show Hunter at his own pace. It was a small test for Levin, in his role as first sub, but I knew he'd do well. I had no doubt . . .

Levin pointed out the edge of the property, a boundary of trees, and fencing to the right of the chalet. It sloped down the mountainside and raised sharply again at the side of the next mountain. The mountains to the rear of the property were still snow-capped but wouldn't be for long. The sun was warming nicely.

Hunter marvelled at the greenery, and I could see how the sunshine pleased him. He walked close to Levin, and I followed a short distance behind them, observing them. The sunlight on Hunter's skin highlighted the scars on his back. A spiderweb of horrors, indeed. I could see where they crisscrossed, and I was certain they were scars that had healed without medical attention.

The idea that Lazzaro knew his hard limit was whipping and the fact he had seen his back and decided to whip him anyway made me very, very angry. I hoped Lazarro's retraining at the hands of Valente was without mercy. And knowing Valente and how he valued the Sanctus and the code of hard limits and his love of strict sadism and masochism, I imagined it would be. It still gave me little satisfaction though.

Levin pointed to the direction of Sion; although we couldn't see it, he promised Hunter it was just over the mountains. "And Como is that way," Levin said, pointing in the opposite direction. Then he pointed to different types of plants, quoting botanical names, and as he saw birds, he pointed them out as well. As we walked further around the estate, Levin told Hunter the cottage at the western side of the chalet was where Michael and Paul lived. "Paul is our driver, but he also tends to the gardens and lawns and general maintenance. Michael is the chef; you've met him."

Hunter gave a nod. "And they live together?"

"Yes. Within the Sanctus dominion, but as partners. They still attend some playroom parties that Colton puts on, but they're not that active anymore. They keep it private."

"Is that allowed?" Hunter asked, his eyes wide.

"Oh, yes," Levin replied easily. Hunter stared at him for a moment, though Levin continued with his tour. He showed him the ponds, pointing out the types of fish. He pointed back to the chalet, to each door, explaining where they led, which windows belonged to which rooms. He was very thorough and patient, answering any questions Hunter could think to ask.

When we came back toward the house and got to the pool, Levin explained, "Master allows laps as part of the fitness regime. It will be warm enough soon, yes, Master?"

The pool was heated, but it was still only practical during the warmer months. I nodded, "Yes, soon."

Hunter looked from Levin to me. "I can't swim, Sir."

I smiled at him. "Then we shall teach you. Maybe that can be one of your goals. Something you'd like to achieve."

He beamed, a real, genuine smile. A beautiful smile. "You're very kind, Sir," he said.

I grinned back at him. His happiness pleased me in ways I wasn't expecting. From what I could tell, this boy hadn't known much joy in his life, and seeing him happy stirred that part of me that wanted to protect and provide for him. As though each smile, every sliver of happiness was a gift. And I could tell from the happiness in Levin's eyes, it pleased him as well.

By the time we'd strolled the perimeter of the five-acre estate and made it back to the house, it was midmorning. I was proud of how they'd interacted. I was proud of how Levin stepped up, and I was proud of how Hunter asked questions, willing to listen and learn.

I followed them inside, and after they'd taken their shoes off and Levin showed Hunter how to line them up, Levin noticed me watching and was quick to pull Hunter to his side and assume the waiting position. Feet apart, hands clasped at their backs, heads slightly lowered.

Perfect.

I walked over and stood before them. I paused a moment to note their breathing, the set of their shoulders. Levin was completely relaxed, and Hunter was wary. I put my hand to Levin's hair, then cupped his face and lifted his chin. "I am very proud of you. You're a good boy, aren't you?"

"Yes, Master," he breathed.

I stepped in close, right into his personal space, but not quite touching, and claimed his mouth. He didn't kiss me back, he let himself be kissed, let me take what I wanted. He was flushed, his lips plump and wet, almost smiling. His chest rose and fell with his breaths, his head bowed. "Such a good sub," I murmured.

Then I stepped in front of Hunter. I touched his hair, then cupped his face. I met his gaze and held it. I wanted him to see me as a Dom; if that was what he needed, then I would make sure he got it. We may not be sexual, but he still needed discipline and reassurance. "I'm proud of you, Hunter," I said, my voice low. "You're a good sub too, aren't you?"

His pupils dilated, his reply just a breath. "Yes, Sir." Then he licked his lips, as though he was preparing to be kissed . . . He leaned in, just a fraction, as though he wanted me to kiss him. And Christ, I wanted him. I wanted to take his mouth right then and there. I wanted to devour his mouth, and I wanted to command him to his knees and push my cock in between those sweet, sweet lips . . .

But I had my orders.

I pulled back, and Hunter almost fell forward but caught himself and swiftly resumed the waiting position. A flash of disappointment caught in his eyes before he schooled himself.

Yes, he wanted me to kiss him. Yet it was forbidden, for now. And I needed to regain some control.

"You're both very good subs, and you've pleased me today," I said, rewarding them with praise. "Levin, take Hunter to the gym room for one hour. Change into workout wear. Show him the equipment and encourage him to become familiar. Nothing strenuous."

Levin gave a nod. "Yes, Master."

Hunter did the same. "Thank you, Sir."

I watched them leave and took a moment to collect myself before going into my office and picking up my phone. I dialled the familiar number. "Sig," he answered.

"Master Colton," I replied. His voice always soothed me.

"How is your new sub settling in?"

"He's doing just fine."

"Sig? I know that tone . . ."

I resisted sighing, barely. "He has some issues, and I have some concerns." I told him what Lazzaro had—or in this case had not—taught him or discussed with him, and Colton promised to inform Valente. I felt marginally better.

"That's not all, is it?" Colton said.

He knew me far too well. "Levin has adapted very well, and I quite like the idea of having a second sub. I hadn't given it a single thought until you asked me to take him, and I find myself hoping he decides to stay on after the initial trial week." I let out a breath. "Though I'm fully aware he comes with a history, I do think he could be very good."

"You've barely had him for fifteen hours."

"I know." I scrubbed my hand over my face. "He needs a lot of work. He can't read or write very well, and he's never once been asked what he wants to do with his life. I dread asking him about his past, his abuse. He needs to see Ephraim."

"He's had a psych eval," Colton said.

"Yes, I assumed as much." It was standard procedure that all incoming prospective subs and Doms undergo a psychiatric assessment. "Though I think regular scheduled appointments would help him a lot, and I'm pissed off that Lazzaro even laid a finger on him. The boy needs controlled discipline, guidance, and help. Not to have his trust and emotional damage thrown back in his face."

"Hmm," Colton hummed. "You're fond of him already."

There was no point in denying it. "I want what's best for him."

"That's why I chose you for him, Sig."

His praise plucked a chord in me. "Thank you, Master. And that's why I seek your guidance."

"Guidance for what?" he asked, his tone serious now.

"Nothing I can't handle. Your confidence in me reassures me."

"Hmm," Colton hummed again, and this time I could almost picture the knowing look on his face. "Struggling with temptation, Sig?"

"Master?"

"I know you. You're struggling having a sub you can't fuck, aren't you?"

I groaned and pinched the bridge of my nose. "Just a few moments ago, he looked at me in such a way, his eyes full of need and his mouth open, that I almost ordered him to his knees. I didn't, of course. And I won't. Talking to you has calmed me, thank you."

"I trust you, Sig," Colton said. "I know you won't touch him. And anyway, that first sub of yours craves your cock as if it gives him air. If you struggle with temptation again, take your boy, chain him to something, and fuck him senseless."

That was a really good idea. "Thank you, Master. I will." Then I wondered . . . "You did say Hunter could watch, yes?"

Colton laughed. "I think he would like that. He's a very sexual creature, or so his former Dom said. He just needs time to gain some trust and to restore his faith in the Sanctus. We let him down, and I want to do right by him this time."

"So do I."

"I know you do."

"Thank you, Master. I will make you proud of me."

"I'm already proud of you."

I smiled; that long-buried submissive inside me still glowed at his approval. "I will be in touch again tomorrow."

"Good."

The call clicked off in my ear and the next number I dialled was Ephraim's. "Sig," he answered. His deep tone was warm and rich. "What can I do for you?"

"I need some information," I said. "I know you can't divulge details, but I've been given a second sub to take into my care, and he . . . he has some issues. I'd like you to see him."

"Of course. What's his name?"

"Hunter Vargo."

Silence.

"Ephraim?"

"I remember him," he said. "And he's with you now?"

"Yes."

"I'm glad. He'll do well with you."

"Thank you. What can you tell me about him?"

"You know there are things I can't tell you, Sig."

"I know. But I have concerns for this boy. From a doctor to another doctor."

"I can't tell you the how or why, but I can tell you this: he needs discipline and structure. A firm but gentle hand."

"Yes, I'd gathered that. He needs to have a Dom. He said he did, that he feels out of control without one—like he can't focus—which was a red flag for me. When he realised I wasn't going to collar him immediately, he freaked out. So I gave him a wrist cuff to wear, not my usual collar, but he calmed right down. His relief was instantaneous."

"Mm, yes." Ephraim was quiet for a moment and I let him gather his thoughts. "From a doctor to a doctor, he's a typical submissive, has a service-oriented mindset, and finds peace in taking instructions and routine. And from my assessment of him, I think he can't express himself or his needs very well."

"Did you tell Colton that?" I asked. "Because his hard limit form was as good as blank."

"Jesus."

"Exactly. Then Colton told me he thought, with hindsight, that Hunter didn't really understand what he was agreeing to. He just wanted to make Colton happy."

"Colton got my full report, Sig."

"This boy slipped through the cracks, Ephraim. He needs the best care I can give him. Should I request your report from Colton?" Sig knew that was a low blow because they both knew Colton would give it to him.

Ephraim sighed. "Christ, Sig. Hunter's issue isn't that he needs a Dominant. It's that he needs to feel wanted and supported. He needs someone to take care of him, in all matters. And he doesn't just need it, he loves it. With the right Dominant, he will thrive."

"I'm hoping that's the case. And thank you."

"I would suggest you get the boy to open up. Ask him about his past and his reasons why he chose this path. I can't tell you the intimate details, Sig, but he can."

"I'd still like you to see him on a weekly basis. I don't even know if he'll be in my care after this week—it's not a permanent placement yet, which is why I haven't collared him properly—but even if he decides to move on, I'll be asking Master Colton to see the boy seeks permanent, scheduled counselling."

"Master Colton has already asked me."

I smiled. "Good."

"I'm not sure if I should have told you that, but he never expressly said not to."

"It's fine Ephraim. I just want the best care for Hunter.

If Colton decides to put me over his knee and spank me . . . I'll take it."

Ephraim laughed. "I know you would, why do you think I love you?"

I laughed, feeling much better now. "Thank you, Ephraim. You have reassured me and put my mind at ease."

"Anytime," he replied smoothly. "You can call me anytime if you have concerns or questions."

"If you and Louella would like to join us for dinner sometime, just let me know. It might give our subs some time to talk. It's good for them to blow off some steam."

"Sounds lovely. And you're right. They can spend a few hours gossiping about us while we pretend not to hear, and we'll have to spank them later."

I chuckled. "Yes, Levin does that so I *will* spank him."

Now Ephraim laughed. "Louella as well. Naughty brats, the pair of them." He paused, then followed with, "Though you have your own pair now. Lucky you."

I huffed out a laugh. "Well, I don't expect any bratty behaviour out of Hunter."

"If anyone can get the boy to see his own potential, it's you, Sig," he said. "Just be patient with him. I know we Doms like to think we're in charge, but you're on his schedule now. He'll only be ready when he's ready. In the meantime, get him to talk, and give him all the care and attention in the world."

I smiled again. "I plan to do exactly that."

"HOW WAS your time in the gym?" I asked Hunter. We were sitting at the dining table, our lunch eaten. He ate a little more but not as much as I'd have liked.

"Very good, Sir," he replied. "Levin showed me how to use all the equipment. He was very patient with me."

I smiled at Levin and he gave me a nod. "He was a good student," Levin said. "He already has it all figured out."

"Good," I said. "That pleases me."

Hunter blushed at my praise. Pink splotches coloured his cheeks and ran down his neck. I could imagine how flushed he'd be when I fucked him, how warm his skin would be . . . It made my dick stir, and my balls twinged with need. This boy was going to test me, of that I was certain.

Michael came in and cleared our plates, and I was grateful for the distraction. "Boys," I said, "wait for me in my office." They left the table, Levin leading the way out of the room. It gave me a moment to centre and calm myself. When I walked in, they were both kneeling beside the main sofa. It took my breath away and didn't help my control issues at all. I walked over to them and stroked both their heads before I took my place on the sofa. "Please take your seats, boys," I said, motioning to the two-seater across from me. "I'd like us to talk some more. It will give us an opportunity to learn about each other and what motivates us. You're free to speak and to ask any questions you might have."

I wanted no secrecy between us, and I wanted Hunter to know he was safe here and perhaps reassuring him that we were decidedly normal would help. "I'll go first," I began. "My name is Sigmund Bruckner. My friends call me Sig. I'm thirty-seven. I was born in England, though by the time I turned sixteen, I'd lived in fourteen countries all over the world. My father was in a special branch of the military, so we moved a lot, which probably explains my accent. A touch British, mostly not.

"At fourteen, I found myself in military school and—" I

smiled. "—I found myself surrounded by men in tight uniforms and black leather boots who lived by codes of strict discipline. And I liked it."

Levin chuckled. He'd heard this before and he clearly loved hearing it again.

"I liked it so much," I continued, "over the next two years, I found myself pushing boundaries that shouldn't have been pushed, just to get a reaction out of my superiors. Some of them gave me what I wanted, some of them took turns. And I wanted more."

Levin groaned and squirmed a little. He grinned when Hunter and I looked at him. "I can't help it."

"Behave," I said, a little stern but with a touch of affection.

He gave a nod and recomposed himself. "Master."

I began again. "My father insisted on medical training, which I did in New York. And it was disciplined and structured, but not the kind I needed. Once I'd had a taste of this lifestyle, first it was men who would restrain me, who would take what they needed, and then it was me restraining them and taking what I needed, and I knew it was for me. I sought out clubs and dungeons in the US, but I needed something more permanent. Once I'd graduated, I spent a few years in London working in emergency departments, and I would destress and unwind in BDSM clubs. I liked subbing and relinquishing my control to someone else. With my work and exams, it helped me be free of that responsibility. I'd heard whispers of a special club in Italy, so I found myself in Milan in a private play party where I caught the eye of a beautiful dark-haired man named Colton. He took a certain liking to me, to my skills as a doctor, and to my need for dominance, twenty-four seven. He thought I belonged in the Sanctus, and he was right."

"You were a sub?" Hunter asked disbelievingly, then he blinked and bowed his head. "Apologies for speaking out of turn, Sir."

"No apologies required," I replied. "I said you could speak and ask questions. And yes, I was a sub to Colton for six years. I call him Master still. He will always be my Master. He trained me, moulded me, made me better."

"Master Colton is a good man," Hunter said softly.

"He is." I smiled at him. "Though after a while, Master Colton saw something in me that I hadn't perhaps seen in myself. I was topping other subs more and more, getting more satisfaction in the change of role. I had the nature, the self-control, and patience of a Dom, and so he shifted my training into a new focus. And that's when I knew I'd found my true place. For a sub to gift me with his mind and body . . ." I shook my head slowly, smiling at Levin. "It's a beautiful thing."

Levin gave a dreamy sigh and leaned into Hunter. "Pretty sure I'm the lucky one."

Hunter blushed and chewed on his lip, but then he looked to Levin expectantly, waiting to hear his story.

"My turn?" Levin asked. I gave him a nod to continue and turned a little so he could speak mostly to Hunter. "My full name is Levin Andrych. It's Polish. My grandparents moved to Switzerland before my dad was born, and that's where my family all come from. I'm twenty-five. I graduated early from high school at sixteen, but I had no clue what I wanted to do. Nothing grabbed me. I had no desire for more studies, so my parents suggested I take a sabbatical in Paris. Which I did." He smiled that cheeky smirk. "But one night, I found myself in trouble with the police." He put his hand to his chest. "I was completely innocent, by the way."

Now it was me who chuckled. Hunter looked on, intrigued.

Levin loved having this little audience. He pouted mischievously. "And I did *not* resist arrest, but when a certain well-muscled officer handcuffed me, spread my legs, and pushed me over the front of the police car, I had an awakening from God."

I snorted, and Levin shot me a look. "It's true!" he said. "I'd always liked watching porn with rough sex or fantasised of having a bigger guy do whatever he wanted to me, but that cop flipped a switch in my head. So I resisted a little more, and he got rougher, holding me down, and breathed threats of violence in my ear. He wasn't being sexual at all. He was just rough and demanding, but I'd never been manhandled in such a way before. So I struggled some more, he got rougher, and I came in my pants."

Hunter's mouth fell open. "You . . ."

Levin nodded. "Yep. Came so hard, the cop let me go. I think he was embarrassed."

Hunter snorted out a laugh and covered his mouth with his hand. "I'm sorry. I'm not laughing at you."

Levin chuckled and gave him a nudge with his shoulder. "It's okay. It's a funny story. But after that, I researched more, but the porn I watched wasn't enough. I frequented clubs and I loved it all, but then that wasn't enough. When the scenes were over, my emotions would crash really hard. I didn't just want to play the games; I wanted to live it." He sighed. "I was lucky, so very lucky, because I happened to be stuck in an airport going back to see my family and I struck up a conversation with the man next to me. He was a German man by the name of Jürg."

Hunter's eyes widened. "Master Jürg?" Jürg was the third Grand Master of the Sanctus. He, Valente, and

Colton were the governing body of the Sanctus' headquarters in Italy.

Levin nodded. "The one and the same. There was a blizzard and all planes were grounded, so we chatted for hours. But he had that air about him that spoke of dominance without having to say it. That *something* that only people in the lifestyle recognise, and I called him Sir. I didn't even mean to . . ."

"What happened?" Hunter said, hanging on every word. It made me smile.

"He just about set me on fire with only a look. Asked me if I knew what that title meant. I said yes. He asked why I was travelling alone, and I told him I was without a keeper. How I wanted one so bad I ached for it. How playing scenes wasn't enough and how I wanted to live it." Levin sighed. "He took out a card, wrote an address with a date and time on it, and told me if I was serious, I'd be there."

Hunter's eyes were wide. "You went?"

"Oh, yes," Levin said, biting his bottom lip. "And I never left."

I smiled at them. "Master Jürg later said he wanted to fuck you in the middle of the crowded airport."

"I would have let him," Levin replied simply.

"I know," I answered with a laugh. "And that was why Master Jürg gave you his card."

Levin looked to Hunter then and gave him a cheeky smile. "Master Jürg trained me so very well. Until I was ready for my new Master." He gave me a shy look, almost fluttering his eyelashes.

"Such a cheeky boy."

Levin curled his legs up underneath him and sat side on so he could give Hunter his full attention. "What's your story, Hunter? How did you end up in the Sanctus?"

I steeled myself because I knew this wasn't going to be good.

Hunter swallowed hard and absently turned his leather wrist cuff. He chewed his bottom lip and frowned. And then he began to speak.

CHAPTER FOUR

"MY NAME IS HUNTER VARGO," he began, so quiet and unsure. "I'm twenty-three. I was born in Slovenia, though my mother was English. I don't know anything about my father. I spoke mostly English at home, which made schooling hard. I, uh. I found I had a liking for boys, or men, I should say, when I was about fifteen, though I never acted on it. Not then anyway. I was in a boys' home in Venice—I was moved around a lot—run by the church, but I found myself reacting to instructions and discipline in ways no other boys did." He gave a sad smile. "They hated the way the teachers would discipline them. I . . . did not."

There were vast years missing from that short summary of his life, but I didn't interrupt.

Hunter swallowed hard. "One of the guardians noticed how my body reacted, and after a while he would take me into his prayer room for what he called *inner-reflective discipline*. He'd have me kneel, naked, with my hands behind my back. Sometimes on the floor, sometimes on a bench seat. He would have me tell him all the impure thoughts I'd had, and then I'd suck him. Sometimes he'd suck me or watch me pleasure myself, and when I begged him to fuck me, he did."

Fuck.

"He gave me a necklace and told me it made me his. And I loved it. I finally had someone who wanted me as theirs, and I belonged to him. But then I had one birthday too many, and my time at the home was up. I had to enter the priesthood or leave. I considered it, but not for the right reasons. I liked the idea of the discipline, of the strict rules and regimented life, but it wasn't for me. I wanted more of his private discipline, but he said no. So he took back the necklace, and I didn't really understand why. But then he took me to a man he knew; a retired priest. He'd left the church because of his . . . urges."

Hunter licked his lips and I could see it in his eyes that he remembered this man fondly. It wasn't lost on me that for such a difficult subject, he spoke with ease. And I couldn't help but wonder, or even hope, that was because he felt safe here.

"And he took me in and gave me what I needed. He gave me a leather band to wear so I would know to whom I answered, but it wasn't long before I needed more than he could give. Like you, Levin," Hunter said shyly, "I didn't want scenes or games to play. I needed more. I wanted to live it."

"He was a kind man?" Levin asked.

Hunter nodded. "Yes. But he found the twenty-four-a-day lifestyle too much. It wasn't for him, and he said he could no longer do the right thing by me. But he knew someone who could."

"Master Colton," I said.

Hunter smiled at me and nodded. "Yes. He took me in, and I knew it was right for me. Him, the Sanctus, full submission. I wanted to stay with him as one of his. But he had his three subs already."

"So he handed you to Lazzaro," I said, trying not to let my emotions show.

Hunter frowned. "He was strict and it was okay, in the beginning," he whispered. "Until he kept pushing me to test myself, and then it wasn't good. He told me I'd surrender all hard limits to prove my submission. That was . . ." He shuddered. "I was scared of what he might do next."

"Lazzaro was wrong," I said, my voice firm and serious. "And he's being punished accordingly. He won't harm anyone again; I can assure you. His role as your Dom was to nurture and provide a safe environment, and he failed."

He nodded but kept his eyes downcast. But then Levin reached over and took Hunter's hand. It surprised me as much as it did Hunter. "Hunter," he said gently. "I want you to know that you deserve better. You deserve to have a Dom who treats you with respect, who knows what you need and gives it freely. There shouldn't ever be a price on your submission."

Hearing Levin say that gave me a rush of pride and a sense of responsibility to do right by both of them. I needed to know about his pain so I could help him heal . . .

"Hunter, I want to ask you something, and we'll discuss it only this once. Unless you need to talk about it, of course." I could see it in his eyes that he knew I was going to ask about his scars. He blinked, twice. Levin squeezed his hand.

"In my role as a doctor, I've seen many types of scars before. None as bad or extensive as yours, though." I spoke gently but with a firm tone. "Who beat you?"

He blinked again, and although it took him a second to answer, he wasn't trying to hesitate or defy me; he was merely trying to find the courage to speak. He'd paled, his voice was just a whisper. "My mother."

Oh, heaven's mercy.

"How old were you when it started?"

He shook his head a little. "That I remember? Three or four."

My jaw clenched and my nostrils flared. Hearing his admission made my blood boil, but I rationalised that my anger was misplaced here, so I swallowed it down. "What happened to your mother?" I asked, keeping my voice neutral.

He shrugged. "I don't know, Sir. They took her away when I was five. I was sent to a . . . home."

"Was the home any better?" I asked, knowing sometimes they weren't.

"In some ways, yes, Sir," he answered. "I liked the routines. Set times for everything. It was very structured, and I liked the discipline. I liked making the teachers happy. They'd smile and it gave me purpose." Then he added, "And there was food."

"Did your mother not provide food for you?"

"She'd cook oatmeal, once a week," he replied. His voice was detached and quiet, but I couldn't imagine the courage it took to tell us this.

So as a small boy he had to fend for himself, eating fetid oatmeal by the week's end. He was probably whipped for crying. And I was beginning to understand him; his reserved nature, his quiet demeanour, his ingrained need for discipline, his hatred of oatmeal, his hard limit of whipping.

Levin held both of Hunter's hands in his now, and I couldn't even be mad. I was proud of him for giving Hunter encouragement. As my first sub, it was Levin's duty to look out for Hunter and to provide him with additional support.

And I made a promise to myself: I would see to it personally that this boy's self-esteem and self-image would be repaired. He would see his own worth.

"Thank you, Hunter," I said. "That can't have been easy. Thank you for trusting us."

He gave me a nod and weak smile.

"I'd like you to see a doctor friend of mine," I added. "His name is Ephraim; he's a psychologist."

Hunter's eyes widened and he blinked. "Is there something wrong with me, Sir?"

"Hardly, my dear boy," I said. I stood up and both boys got to their feet as well. I put my hands on Hunter's shoulders, then cupped his face. "Your story, your scars, tell me that you're stronger than you give yourself credit for. But it's my responsibility to care for your well-being, and that includes ensuring your mental health needs are met as much as your physical needs. Our minds need as much care as our bodies."

Hunter looked at me with such vulnerability and fear in his eyes. "If you think I should."

"Hunter, Ephraim is a trusted associate of mine, and he's a Dominant in our dominion," I explained. "He will understand. He won't judge you, and everything you tell him is completely confidential. You've met him before when you first came into the Sanctus, remember?" I asked, and he nodded. I ran my fingers through his hair. "Levin and I both see him periodically."

He turned to Levin. "You do?"

"Sure, I do," Levin replied. "He's great."

"And I see him so Levin knows I'll be in the best headspace for him. If I have any grievances, I unload them to Ephraim over coffee, not on Levin in the playroom."

Hunter blushed at the mention of the playroom and I

couldn't resist thumbing his cheek. He looked at me again with that same heat and longing in his eyes, his lips parted, and I could have so easily kissed him. But my resolve held.

"I'll speak with Ephraim later and set up your first appointment in a day or two. You'll have some time to settle in first." Then I turned to Levin and found him smiling at me. A look I couldn't quite discern. "How about we show Hunter the rest of the house. I'm not sure if he's seen everywhere. Last night must have been a bit of a blur for him."

"Yes, Master," Levin said excitedly. He took Hunter's hand, a contact the boy seemed to like. "Where to first?"

"This way," I answered, leading the two boys to the den from my office. "Levin and I will sometimes sit in here and read." Then I took them to the right wing of the house. Across the foyer was a large sitting room with a guest room and a bathroom. "These rooms are hardly used, and quite often, the doors to this part of the house are closed," I explained as we went.

And Levin showed him certain framed paintings or statues and which rooms had the best sunlight in winter. It was a grand chalet of wood and stone and lush carpets, white walls. It was expensive, lavish even, but it was also comfortable. Home.

Hunter had already seen the kitchen and dining and the informal family room, so I led the boys upstairs. I went left first, pointing to where Hunter was already familiar with. "Your room," I pointed to different doors leading off the hall. "Levin's bedroom, another guest room, and the last door is my room. You can come to me at any time, though you must knock first and wait to be called in."

Hunter nodded seriously. "Yes, Sir."

Then Levin added, "Doors are to remain unlocked—"

Then he stopped. "Well, mine is. So I can be woken, if the need arises."

Levin didn't need to explain. Hunter understood. He even smirked.

"Come," I said, walking back down the hall. I walked past the stairs and toward the right wing of the upper floor. There were two doors on the left side of the hall. "A master bathroom and another guest room," I explained. "And this door leads to the playroom," I said, opening the double doors on the right.

I walked in, savouring the sight, the smell of this room. It was an identical replica of any Sanctus dominion play-room. There was an array of floor equipment, wooden benches, padded seats, a sling, a wooden St Andrew's cross. A wall of props, floggers, canes, crops. A cabinet of toys and supplies, and a wooden trolley to wheel whatever I needed to any of the equipment, and mirrors on every available wall space.

A feeling of calm settled over me whenever I walked into this room, and when I turned to face the two subs behind me, I could see the same serenity on their faces.

I cradled Levin's face gently. "Tell me what you like about this room."

He closed his eyes and inhaled, measured and deep. He spoke slowly, reverently. "I like how it smells. I feel at ease here. I like what happens in here." Then he looked up to me and smiled. "I like what you do to me in here."

No, Levin never joined the dominion because of unhealthy familial, childhood issues. He joined because he was a sexual creature who craved being dominated. I smiled and kissed his lips. "Such a good sub."

Then I tenderly touched Hunter's cheek. "And you,

sub? What do you like about a playroom? How does it make you feel?"

He closed his eyes and a serene expression settled on his face. "I feel a part of something bigger than me. I feel . . . centred. Like I belong to something magical."

I nodded. "We are not too dissimilar, you and I," I replied. "Being in a playroom, in particular a Sanctus playroom, grounds me." I turned around and faced the cross and inscription engraved into it. *Salus ex cruce venit*. "From the cross comes salvation," I translated the Latin out loud. I inhaled deeply, feeling the devotion of those words. "The religious counterpart to the dominion is very satisfying for me. I feel part of something bigger than me, as well. I love the exchange that happens in here, the trust and the gift of submission that Levin gives to me. It's personified in here."

I walked up to the large cross and traced my fingers along the grain. I thought for sure they'd both be watching me. But when I turned to face them, I saw Hunter wasn't looking at me at all. He was looking at the wall of canes, whips, and floggers.

"Hunter, look at me," I ordered, my tone demanding. He was quick to face me, responding well to my authority. I walked over to him and he could see the seriousness in my face and hear the promise in my tone. "You're safe here. If we are ever in the playroom and I bring out a flogger, it will be for Levin only. I will not touch you with it. Hunter, you have my word. If we don't have trust, we have nothing."

He exhaled and nodded.

"You must understand, Hunter," I reiterated, "even if a punishment is warranted, I will not breach your hard limits. I may spank you with my hand, no paddle, to your buttocks only. If you are to be punished, it will be immediate and brief, and then it's over."

He stood with his feet apart, his hands behind his back, head bowed, and his eyes looked to the floor between us. He'd assumed the ready position from my tone alone. My cock liked his receptiveness.

But I needed to make sure Hunter understood. "I don't believe in relegating you to sit in another room, or to deprive you of anything, or to withhold affection from you as a form of punishment," I said. "I don't play mind games. I take my rules seriously and my punishments against broken rules even more so. But I will never break your hard limits."

"I understand, thank you, Sir."

I lifted his chin. "Good boy." I smiled so he could see I was pleased.

I looked at Levin and noted his eyes downcast. At the word punishment, I was certain he was remembering the one and only time he disobeyed me and was punished accordingly. "Levin, tell Hunter of the time you were punished."

Levin assumed the same position as Hunter; feet apart, hands behind his back, and his head bowed. His voice was so quiet, still burdened by the experience. "I broke one of Master's rules."

"Yes, you did. Tell Hunter what you did."

He spoke quietly. "I back-chatted. I spoke out of turn and without respect. And I was spanked with the paddle accordingly." He met Hunter's eyes. "It was fair and over swiftly. Master took good care of me."

Levin didn't explain further, so I did. "The whole incident had been very out of character for him. He'd been here for just a few months and we'd been seated at the dining table; I'd been telling him how the pool was scheduled for a clean and Paul could be expected to do it tomorrow. Levin dropped his fork, clanging it on his plate, and told me Paul wouldn't need to clean it if he didn't swim in it."

Hunter's lips parted with a quiet gasp. Levin put his head down.

"His reply had nothing to do with Paul. It had nothing to do with the pool." I added, "He wanted to push his limits. He'd been here long enough to feel safe and comfortable with me. He'd seen first-hand how I played, how I showed affection. He wanted to see how I punished. So I showed him."

I remembered it with such clarity, as if it were yesterday. I'd put my cutlery down gently, and using a calm, quiet voice, I told him to go to the playroom and wait. His eyes had flinched, half a dozen emotions flickering across his face, and he'd pushed his chair out and raced upstairs. I'd followed, of course, selected a flat wooden paddle, and put him across my knee. Pulling the denim down to expose the creamy flesh of his ass, I'd spanked him.

While I wanted Hunter to know I would punish if necessary, I didn't want him to think it was anything close to torture. So I explained, "I'd explained calmly and quietly, his behaviour was not acceptable and wouldn't be tolerated. I'd told him he'd receive six paddles and insisted he count them out loud."

"It was awful," Levin whispered. His frown was deep, his gaze sad.

He'd taken his punishment, and he'd withheld his emotions during the spanking but had cried when I bathed him afterward. He'd sobbed his apologies, and I couldn't doubt his sincerity. "He'd not meant to offend me or insult me in any way, I knew that. He'd simply been testing his grounds."

I'd rubbed in a medicated salve over his reddened

buttocks and through his tears he'd apologised again and again. The very worst part of the whole ordeal, for me, was listening to him cry himself to sleep. As much as I'd wanted to go to him, I didn't. He needed to know my punishments held as much water as my affection.

Just like Hunter needed to know. I looked at Levin. "It wasn't pleasant, was it?"

He shook his head and said a quiet, "No, Master."

I turned to Hunter and explained, "Levin has only disrespected me once in two years." But I lifted Levin's chin and kissed him lightly again. "He's a very good boy."

Levin smiled at my compliment. "Rewards are much more fun than punishments." I chuckled and kissed him again, a little deeper this time, and I could quite easily have told him to take his place on the padded bench . . .

Hunter hesitated. "Sir?"

"Yes, Hunter?"

"I don't want you to punish me," he replied hastily. Then he corrected himself. "Wh-what I mean to say is I won't disrespect you. You won't ever have to punish me. I'll be good, I promise. I don't want you to *have* to punish me . . ."

I pressed my finger to his lips. "Sssh, sub. I know what you're trying to say. You don't want to burden me with having to punish a disobedient sub."

He shook his head. "Never."

"Hunter, I detest punishment. But I won't have defiance and disrespect in my house. I believe your sincerity, and I hope I don't ever have to punish you. But I will if it's warranted, and I promise you I never punish in anger."

"I understand, Sir."

"As I explained before, follow Levin's lead, and you'll do just fine."

Both boys smiled, and it appealed to the Dom in me. We'd accomplished much this afternoon and I felt a stronger connection to both of them. I felt Hunter had taken a huge leap forward in such a short time, and I knew Levin was responsible, in part.

Then what Master Colton had said came back to me . . . And being in this room, having two subs in this room, set off my senses.

"Hmm," I said, my voice deep. My balls drew down just thinking what was about to happen. "Levin, you've made me very proud today. You've taken to your position as first sub very well, and I think you deserve a reward."

He stayed in the sub position, but his chest rose and fell with heavy breaths. "I aim to please you, Master."

I smiled. "Yes, you do."

I could see the bulge in Levin's jeans already. Being in this room had the same effect on him as it did me. "What would you have me do, Master?" he asked, a tone I knew well. Breathy, filled with anticipation; the cat who knew damn well he was about to get the cream.

"I think I shall reward you a few times today," I said. My balls were heavy and aching, my cock hard. "Once won't be enough."

Levin's delectable lips curled into a smile.

"First, I will fuck that mouth of yours until you drink your reward," I murmured. His breath hitched. "Then I will take your ass."

"Thank you, Master," he breathed.

I took a step closer and brought his chin up so I could kiss him, hard. He took my tongue into his mouth with a groan and I pulled his bottom lip between mine. His pupils dilated and he moaned. I hummed, almost desperate to be inside some part of him. "Get your padded knee rest. And get undressed."

He was quick to retrieve the padded knee rest, placing it on the floor without a sound, then stepping out of his jeans and neatly folding them, putting them aside. Oh yes, his cock was rock hard, jutting gloriously out from his body.

I turned to Hunter, who was standing perfectly still, except for the rapid rise and fall of his chest. I went to him and lifted his chin. His darkened eyes and the bulge in his jeans, how his nipples had pebbled, told me he was aroused.

"I am under strict instruction not to touch you in a sexual manner," I whispered. "So I'm giving you a choice."

He blinked. "Sir."

"You can leave the playroom and go to your room until I'm done with Levin," I offered. "Or you can get on your knees—" He gasped, lips parted with desire. "—and watch."

He licked his lips and swallowed. "Thank you, Sir."

Then, while I still had my hand under his chin and not breaking eye contact once, he ever so slowly went to his knees.

Oh, fuck.

He wanted to watch.

This boy was sent to test me, I was sure of it. Was he teasing me? Going to his knees like that in front of me made me want to fill his mouth. I wanted to. Every part of my body wanted to.

But I had my orders. So, turning on my heel, I went to Levin. Naked, on his knees, his hands behind his back, his cock jerked in anticipation. I slid my hand along his jaw and drew his face up so he'd look at me. "Do you want my reward, sub?"

"Oh yes, Master," he murmured.

"Then take out my cock."

His agile fingers made quick work of my button and fly, then he freed my erection. I was engorged and aching, leaking precome. But he didn't touch, he didn't lick or taste me. He did exactly as I'd instructed.

Such a good boy.

"Open your pretty mouth," I rasped.

He did, so I laid the tip of my cock on his bottom lip. Such a beautiful sight. "I want you to suck me. Show Hunter how good you are and suck me until I come down your throat."

Levin's eyes glazed over with lust, the way they did when he was in the moment. "Please, Master," he whispered.

I pushed into his mouth and his lips went around me, and he began to suck. Wet lips and tongue, sucking hard and stroking the underside of my shaft with his tongue, and then he opened his throat and took me all the way in.

Fuck. Yes.

I needed to come so bad.

I looked over to Hunter. He was still in the waiting pose, his hands behind his back, but his mouth was open as though he was imagining my cock in his mouth. His jeans were straining. I smiled at the sight just as Levin swallowed around me. I let my head fall back, succumbing to the pleasure. I fisted Levin's hair and he moaned, and I didn't even try to fight it.

I gave him his reward, and he hummed as he drank it down.

It was just a taste of what was to come. I needed to take the edge off so I could give Levin his proper reward, the one he loved the most. I pulled out of his mouth and tucked my cock, still half-hard, into my open pants. I didn't bother doing them up. It wouldn't take long to be ready again. My balls were already aching with more need.

I cupped Levin's chin and swiped my thumb across his bottom lip. "Such a good sub."

He smirked, just a little. His eyes were still glazed over because we weren't finished yet, and he knew it.

"I want you in the sling."

He smiled as he got to his feet. "Yes, Master."

I helped him into it. Him lying on his back with his knees bent and spread, secured, so he was held in that position. He relaxed, knowing his weight was held by the leather and chains. His ass at the perfect height for me to fuck him. I pulled on the chain fastener. "Does that feel okay?"

"Yes, Master."

"Not too tight or loose?"

"No, Master," he whispered. "It's perfect." He arched his back a little, a sign of his impatience. His cock lay up to his belly, hard and with precome glistening at the tip.

I walked up to his face and bent to kiss him. He opened his mouth, willing, wanting, and tried to follow my mouth when I pulled back. "You're beautiful, sub."

He relaxed back into the sling and took a deep breath, so I slid my hand down his chest to his cock and rubbed it against him. I tweaked his nipples, I ran my hands all over his chest, his stomach, up his thighs. He was completely restrained and I could touch him wherever I wanted. And I wanted his whole body to sing. I took my time, touching him, adoring him, and when I pulled on his balls and stroked his cock, he arched his back a little again and breathed through the pleasure of it. Then I moved around to his ass and applied some lube, pressing my finger into him, then another. He groaned as I stretched him, not with pleasure but with exasperation. So I pulled my fingers out and gave his cock a stroke. "Patience, boy."

I spared a glance at Hunter. He was panting now, and I could see him straining not to move, and then I noticed why. His cockhead was poking out of his jeans above his hip. He was so turned on, but I'd only asked him if he wanted to watch. I never told him he could touch himself. So very eager to please . . .

But we'd also not discussed the finer rules of the playroom, and we'd not reiterated his playroom limits or boundaries, even if I never touched him. I could have kicked myself for being so careless. So I went to the toy cabinet and took out a Fleshlight and a bottle of lube and placed them in front of him. "The rule was that I couldn't touch you," I said gruffly, "but there was no rule about you not touching yourself. You can use these. Or not. You can still stay to watch, or you can wait in your room. The choice is yours."

Hunter's nostrils flared. "I'd like to stay, Sir."

"Would you like to come?"

He shivered and his breath hitched. "Yes, Sir."

I smiled. "Then use the Fleshlight. Come as many times as you'd like."

His breathing was ragged by now, and he kept eyeing my cock, where it was half hidden in my still-open pants. "Thank you, Sir."

I turned and went back to Levin. He'd turned his head to watch our exchange and he was smiling. "I think he likes what I do to you," I said to Levin.

Levin chewed on his bottom lip. "I think so too, Master." But then his gaze flicked back to Hunter and I followed his line of sight, just in time to see Hunter slide his cock into the Fleshlight.

The look on his face was pure ecstasy, and when I turned back to Levin, I saw a similar expression.

How had I been gifted with two such beautiful subs?

I pulled out my cock, applied some more lubricant, and pressed the blunt head against Levin's hole. "Watch him fuck that toy while I fuck you," I murmured, and I thrust into him.

Levin cried out as I buried myself in his ass, and Hunter stifled a groan as he came inside the Fleshlight.

Oh fuck.

Hunter shuddered and gasped as his orgasm took hold. He was even more beautiful when he came. Then Levin's moans, the sounds of the chains rattling as I fucked him filled the air. I was driving into him, the way he craved it, and begged for it. I was taking him to that place between heaven and hell, teetering on the edge of both. I gripped his hips and he took every inch of me, over and over, again and again.

He never took his eyes off Hunter. I'd told him to watch, and he was doing exactly as I'd ordered. Hunter still had his dick inside the toy, sliding it up and down, his expression one of concentration. I'd told him to come as many times as he wanted. He wasn't about to disappoint me.

I slowed my pace but drove into Levin with intense, deep thrusts. I fisted his cock and he cried out at the contact, his body contorting within the confines of his restraints. "You love my cock buried inside you," I whispered, knowing how much he responded to dirty talk.

"Yes, Master," he bit out. His cock swelled in my hand, leaking precome onto his belly. His moans were loud, punctuated with every thrust of my hips. He was about ready to come. I knew his body. I knew the sounds he made. I was attuned to him; I was getting closer and closer to my release, and he wanted me to give it to him.

"You want your reward now?" I asked.

"Please, Master," he begged. "Inside me. Come inside me." Then he arched, almost violently, pulling on all his restraints, and his cock swelled and pulsed in my hand as he cried out and moaned. His come shot in spurts onto his chest, and I drove into him harder, wringing his orgasm out of him, and I was so far inside him, his tight body milking me . . .

And I gave him his reward.

Powerful waves of bliss tore through me and I gripped Levin's hips, holding him to me as I came. He groaned with each pulse, and I grunted with the force of it. When I looked over to Hunter, he was coming into the toy a second time.

His head thrown back, both hands around the Fleshlight as he emptied himself into it again.

Fuck.

The room was filled with heavy breaths and quiet whimpers, the smell of sex, the soft rattle of chains. Familiar sounds, gratifying and lovely.

I was reluctant to pull out of Levin. I could stay inside him forever. But I did, and tucked myself away before I quickly untied his restraints, then helped him to his feet. He almost fell into me, thoroughly spent. I pulled him close and supported him. "Can you stand?" I asked.

"Hmm." He nodded. "Yes, Master."

I kissed the side of his head. "You did great today. I'm very proud."

Then I turned my attention to Hunter. He was still on his knees, his jeans undone and his dick still hanging out, limp and heavy. He was breathing hard, his head was bowed, and the Fleshlight and lube sat on the ground beside him.

"Hmm, yes," I said approvingly. "I have such good submissives." With one arm still around Levin, we crossed the floor to where Hunter still knelt. I put my hand in his hair. "You did great too, sub," I said, praising him. I slid my hand to his jaw and made him look up at us. "Did you like that?"

"Yes, Sir," he said, his voice strained. "Very much, Sir."

"I'm glad." Then I put both arms around Levin, rubbing his back, and he snuggled into me. "Levin likes some reassurance after I've fucked him," I told Hunter. "Would you like me to hold you too?"

Hunter blinked. His mouth opened like he might answer, but instead, he slowly got to his feet. Levin unfolded his arm, so I did the same. And Hunter took a small step in, still so very unsure.

And then another, and another, until he was close enough for our torsos to touch. Levin put his arm around him first, then I did, and little by little, breath by breath, Hunter allowed himself to be held. He leaned against me, into me. And Levin, being the brat he was, snuggled and hummed happily. I rubbed their backs and kissed the side of Levin's head. "Feel better?"

"Much," he replied. "I like cuddles with the three of us, Master."

"Of course you do." I chuckled and pulled back enough so I could kiss him. A brief hint of my tongue had him chasing for more. "Such a greedy boy."

Then I turned my attention to Hunter. I wanted to kiss him, I wanted to claim his mouth, claim his body. And if I'd not been instructed otherwise, I would have done both several times by now. Instead, I cupped his face and pressed a kiss to his forehead. I wasn't sure who was more disappointed, him or me.

"You both can clean up the playroom. Hunter, Levin will show you how. And I will run you both a bath," I whispered. "It will soothe any aching muscles. Then you two can have the rest of the day in free time."

I turned and walked to the door, and later when the bath was ready, they came into the bathroom, Levin leading the way, holding Hunter's hand.

It warmed me through. Pride and happiness, fulfilment and a true sense of what it meant to be a Dom within the Sanctus. These boys trusted me and gave me their submission as a gift. I couldn't deny it. I wanted Hunter to stay. I wanted him to be a part of my house, and I wanted Levin to revel in his role as first sub. I wanted Levin to grow and to be happy.

Yet, what I wanted and what I would get were quite possibly two different things. I had to put Hunter's happiness first. His needs, his well-being. I just hoped by the week's end, he'd see that maybe his needs and well-being were our only priority, and that he'd find his happiness with us.

CHAPTER FIVE

"HOW'S HE SETTLING IN?" Master Colton asked me. I fought the urge to sigh, and watched Levin and Hunter talking in the garden instead. They looked happy in the sunlight, their bare torsos warming in the spring morning. Levin was showing Hunter something in the garden—a type of plant, probably—and Hunter was smiling.

"Very well," I answered into the phone. "Levin is very good with him. We had a bit of a breakthrough yesterday, I think. Just getting Hunter to talk and sharing his past with us and trying to get him to see there is no shame here."

And for a brief moment, I considered not telling him about how he went in the playroom yesterday, until I remembered it was Colton's idea. And he was my Master. I would never have held back information from him before. So why would I start now?

Because you're scared of losing Hunter.

"I rewarded Levin in the playroom," I began. "And gave Hunter the option of watching."

"And did he?"

"Oh yes."

Colton laughed. "Enjoy the show, did he?"

I smiled, relieved, but also a little guilty for not trusting Colton. "Very much. He came twice."

Silence, and my heart rate took off. Had I said the wrong thing?

"Just by watching?"

"Yes," I replied. "I gave him a Fleshlight to use on himself, only if he wished to. I told him if he wanted the privacy of his own room, he could leave. It was fine. He most definitely wanted to stay. Dropped to his knees right in front of me."

Another breath of silence and I closed my eyes, waiting for his admonition. "Did you act on it?"

I frowned. "Of course not. I take your orders seriously, Master Colton."

He surprised me by laughing. "Oh, Sig. Your self-control is second to none."

"Yes, and at this rate, I may as well keep Levin tied to the padded bench. I want to fuck something every minute of the day."

"He wouldn't object."

I smiled despite my frustration. "No, he wouldn't. Doesn't help though."

Colton chuckled a little but soon turned serious. His tone was a quiet authority I knew well. "My rule for the boy stands. He needs more than sexual domination right now. He needs to settle back into the right headspace and to have no fear that his trust won't be broken again."

"That's what I'm doing, is it not?" I asked. "Gaining his trust?"

"I should hope so. Let him find a friend and confidant in your boy, as long as he finds a strong Dom in you." He sighed. "And I mean strong and assertive, not cruel. I know what you're thinking, Sig."

I couldn't even argue. He knew me too well. "If you wanted cruel, you asked the wrong Dom."

I meant it as a joke, and thankfully Colton laughed. "I know! Just don't forget to reaffirm who you are. He's not there for a holiday."

"I'm supposed to go to work tomorrow," I said.

"Then establish some rules for your absence. And for the love of the cross, Sig, stop doubting yourself."

The call wrapped up and I stayed there, watching the two boys talking in the sun outside, letting Colton's words play over in my head.

As long as he finds a strong Dom in you . . .

Strong and assertive.

Establish some rules for my absence.

Stop doubting myself.

Why was I doubting myself? Why was I so unsure? Because Hunter's life hinged on it. Because his time with us depended on it. If I let him down, his trust in any future Dom would be hindered forever, and his trust in himself would be damaged irreparably. If I let him down, he'd leave us.

I needed to do this right.

I called the boys inside, and they came in smiling until they saw my stance. I stood with my feet apart, hands clasped behind my back, face stoic. Levin quickly assumed the waiting position, on his knees, head bowed, and Hunter was fast to follow his lead.

I smiled, not that they saw. "I have tasks for you both, and I expect them done well and within the time frame I give you." The one thing I'd learned as my years as a sub, and as a

Dominant, was that if a submissive needed structure and was failed on this need, they would be forced to create their own. Something I didn't want Hunter to ever have to worry about.

"Levin, you have a daily roster," I said. "Can you please get it for me and make a copy so we can amend one?"

"Yes, Master," he said with a nod and ran out of the room.

"I think a day and a half has been enough time for you to get a feel of how my house operates," I said to Hunter. "And as I'll be going back to work tomorrow, I want you to feel comfortable in my absence, in knowing what your role is, and what is expected. All tasks will be explained, as will the desired results and time frame allowed. Then there's no confusion and no miscommunication. How do you feel about that?"

Hunter looked up at me. "It sounds fair, Sir. I like knowing exactly what is expected. I don't want to disappoint you."

"I'm sure you won't," I allowed. "And if the tasks I set aren't getting completed because of time or lack of training, perhaps the error is mine and not yours. We can re-evaluate at any time and I'll readjust accordingly."

Hunter wasn't sure what to make of that, I could tell.

Levin came back in with two sheets of paper and handed them both to me. "Thank you, Levin," I said. "Please, will both of you join me at the table?"

Levin pulled my seat out for me; a quirk of his lips gave his pride away for doing such a thing for me. He sat on my right. Hunter sat on my left. I put one of the schedules in the middle of us. "This is Levin's daily schedule. Yours will be similar. Start at six like Levin has shown you, doing all the morning tasks you've done the last two days. Personal hygiene and preparing for breakfast, et cetera."

Hunter nodded. "Yes, Sir."

"Then we have breakfast and open discussion at the table," I continued. "I leave the house at seven thirty. Then Levin has his set schedule." I pointed out time slots on different days where he did prescribed tasks. Study, exercise, cleaning and dusting, laundry. It was Levin's responsibility to ensure all supplies in the playroom were stocked and in order.

Hunter nodded again, though I could see the unasked question in his eyes. "You're free to ask questions, Hunter," I offered. "I will need your input on this."

"Well, Sir," he began, timidly. "I'm not sure . . . if Levin does all this, what can I do? I want to be useful, and I want to please you. I mean, make you happy."

I reached over and gave his shoulder a gentle squeeze. "You are useful, and you do make me happy, Hunter. Your worth, and Levin's worth, is more than tasks on a schedule, okay?"

He nodded but didn't speak.

"I've been thinking about tasks for you," I furthered. "And I've been observing. You enjoy being outside?"

His gaze met mine, still so unsure. "Yes, Sir."

"Then I think I shall ask Paul to include you in his gardening. You will help him do tasks he sets out for you."

Hunter blinked and shot Levin a look before his eyes met mine. "Yes, Sir. I would like that."

"And because you will be helping Levin with the cleaning and laundry, it will afford him the time to tutor you. One hour every day on reading and writing skills."

Hunter swallowed, but Levin beamed. "Thank you Master," he said. "For letting me help."

But Hunter's brows furrowed. "Hunter?" I pressed. "How do you feel about that?"

He looked at us both but settled on me. "I never went to school very much. I was in and out of homes, and I picked up what I could, but I . . ."

"Oh, my sweet boy," I murmured. "It's nothing to be ashamed of. I see a young man who is resilient and strong, who has overcome many things, and who strives to be the best he can be."

Hunter blushed and his eyes became glassy.

"I want to help you, and I think Levin will make a great teacher," I said. "You'll probably feel more comfortable with him helping you, but if you'd rather a tutor come to the house—"

"Oh no," he replied quickly. "Levin, please. I wasn't doubting his ability to teach me. I just . . ." His brow furrowed. "I just don't want you to think I'm stupid."

Levin frowned sadly, and I put my hand on Hunter's shoulder. "Hunter, look at me. You're not stupid. Far from it. We all have our strengths and weaknesses, and we're all human. We all make mistakes, and I do not expect perfection. As your Dom, I expect effort and willingness to improve on areas that might need improving, that's all. I want you to set some goals, and we can work on small steps on achieving them. I'm not talking about climbing Everest. A goal you set for yourself this month might be to run three miles on the treadmill or to make the perfect cup of tea." I smiled at him. "Or it might be to complete a word puzzle or read a chapter a day."

Hunter smiled and his eyes glistened. "Okay, thank you, Sir."

"Does that sound manageable?"

He gave a nod and took a deep breath, composing himself. "Yes, Sir."

"So this week, I want you to do something for me."

"Yes, Sir," he answered obediently.

"I want you to think of the one thing, the one goal you'd like to achieve. Your dream goal. I want you to think about it, and we can start implementing smaller goals to help you achieve the long-term goal. It might be . . ." I racked my brain. "Anything. Painting, car mechanic, teaching, psychology, engineering, plumbing. It doesn't matter if you think it's too big or too small. Levin wanted to study law, so that's what he's doing. It requires discipline and attention to detail, and he's been working hard on getting his units done."

Hunter stared at Levin. "You study law?"

Levin nodded and smiled. "Yes. Second year, and I complete my units externally and we have online classrooms and lectures. Master has allocated time into my schedule and he allows for exams and assessments."

"And if he has too much on," I explained, and I can see he's struggling with stress or pressure, I pull back on his other tasks. It's about finding a balance that's good for him. And Hunter, I want you to know . . . if you decide next week that you'd rather not join this house on a permanent basis, I can pass your goal and schedule onto your new Dom, and Master Colton will see that it's implemented."

Hunter frowned again and he concentrated on the table for a long moment. Levin gave me a sad look that told me he didn't like the idea of Hunter leaving. I didn't either, but I needed to be strong for both of them.

"Are you okay, Hunter?" I asked. He nodded. "I can fill in your schedule and we can discuss it more at any time. In the meantime, why don't you go with Levin and he can show you what chores you'll be helping him with."

"I don't need a week," Hunter murmured. "To tell you my goal."

I thought he was going to say he didn't need a week to decide if he wanted to stay with us or not, and I couldn't deny the stab of unease it brought with it. "Do you know what you'd like to do?" I clarified. "You can change it later if you decide it's not for you."

"Hair," he replied in a whisper. He swallowed hard and met my eyes. "I've always wanted to do hair. A hair stylist. Even when I was very little, I wanted to do people's hair, but teachers and carers at the home told me no. It wasn't a manly enough job, or it wasn't good enough. I mean, it's not a lawyer or a doctor, like you both, but in my dreams, I work at a salon and my Master is proud of me. It's stupid, I know, but I . . ." He blinked back more tears. "I haven't told anyone that in a long time, but I can choose something else if you say it's not good enough."

This poor, poor boy . . . I wanted to pull him in my lap and comfort him, but we hadn't discussed those boundaries yet. So, instead, I slid my chair out and angled myself so I was closer to him, looking him square on. I took his hand and gentled his long, slender fingers. "Hunter, my sweet boy. It's plenty good enough. *You're* plenty good enough. And I will make some calls this afternoon to see what we can do to begin helping you achieve your goal." I added my other hand, holding his in both of mine. "Thank you. Thank you for trusting me, and Levin. Thank you for trusting us. That can't have been easy, and it took courage."

He nodded, but his eyes brimmed with tears. "I stopped telling people what I wanted," he said, and his chin wobbled.

"Hunter, would you like to sit on my lap?" I asked, and he almost shot out of his chair into my arms. He folded himself against me, his head against my neck, and I wrapped my arms around him.

He allowed himself to cry a little and he was totally relaxed against me. Perhaps he cried for what he was able to admit just now, or perhaps it was for his time spent with Lazzaro that he'd kept pent up inside. I glanced to Levin, who was frowning with tears in his eyes too. So I extended my right arm and he quickly stood at my side, and it became a three-way embrace. Levin rubbed Hunter's shoulder, ran his fingers through his hair, comforting him as a first sub should.

And I revelled in the moment, of holding my two subs at once. Of Levin supporting Hunter, of Hunter opening up and telling us what he wanted, of him finding his voice. For a long while, I rubbed Hunter's back, touching his scars for the first time, keeping an even, warm pressure of my palm in reassuring circles. "I'm proud of both of you," I murmured.

"I'm proud of Hunter too," Levin said, softly combing Hunter's hair with his fingers. "Master, do you think Christa and Tanja will take him on?"

"I'll ask," I replied, and Hunter sat up, still sitting on my knee but looking at me.

"Who are Christa and Tanja?"

I wiped a smeared tear from his cheek with my thumb. "Christa owns the hairdressing studio in the village. She's a Dom. Tanja's her submissive, so she'd be a perfect teacher for you. Though I've not seen her or Christa in a little while, so it might be worth a phone call first."

"Would you really do that for me?" Hunter asked.

"Of course I would."

Levin leaned into me, his fingers now in my hair. "Master takes very good care of his subs."

I shot him a look. "You're being bold today. A little too confident, I think."

He bowed his head, but his lips hinted at a smile. "Would a spanking remind me of my place?"

The cheek of him! I was almost certain he was doing this to make Hunter feel better. I took Levin's chin between my thumb and finger and made him look into my eyes. "Don't tempt me, sub. And don't take my good mood as leeway for insubordination."

He knew by my tone there wasn't any weight to my warning, but still, Levin checked himself, dropping his hands to his sides. He nodded. "Sorry, Master."

I put my arm around Levin's waist and smiled at Hunter. "This one's getting a little bratty." I lightly, playfully, smacked Levin's bottom, not even hard enough to swat a fly, and Levin moaned, spreading his legs a little, raising his ass for another. "See what I mean?"

Hunter gave a shy smile. Our playfulness made him relaxed and happy. "Thank you, Sir."

"Now, I want both of you to go upstairs. Levin, show Hunter how to help with your chores for today."

All playfulness gone, Levin gave me a nod. "Yes, Master." And he and Hunter disappeared through to the stairs.

I took a moment to let what just happened settle over me; Hunter's honesty, his bravery. Levin's ability to comfort and support, then joke and make Hunter smile. And me holding both of my boys at once.

It felt kind of surreal.

So I let myself bask in that, for just a moment, then I finished drafting Hunter's schedule and made phone calls for his future.

CHAPTER SIX

THE NEXT MORNING, I left with a smile on my face. Both subs were in high spirits; they had their schedules and a keen desire to begin their day. I'd explained my wishes for Hunter's tasks to Paul and set a plan for him to include Hunter in his gardening routine. Paul had welcomed the help, and if I'd worried that Hunter might be reluctant, I was wrong. He warmed to Paul immediately.

After that, I'd asked Michael if he could include Hunter in a cooking session. Twice in the week he was staying with us, he was to help with preparation and cooking. I'd explained to both Paul and Michael that if Hunter decided to stay longer, his new routine would become permanent. They were fine with it, of course. Happy even.

And so was Hunter. Giving him duties, responsibility, and purpose helped him a great deal. So I left for work feeling confident he and Levin would have a good first day without me.

As soon as I got to the clinic, I put my bag in my office, then went in search of Qingshan. She was the other Sanctus doctor in our dominion, and the one who must have done

Hunter's physical, because I hadn't. As Sanctus doctors, we both had access to all files of dominion members, and I could have simply looked up his file, but I didn't want to disrespect my colleague.

I rapped on her open door and she looked up and smiled at me. "Morning, Sig."

"Morning. I have a question," I began, sitting opposite her at her desk. "You treated a new submissive. His name is Hunter Vargo. Just wondering if there was anything I should know about?"

"Is he your new sub?" she asked with a hint of a smile. She was already tapping on her keyboard.

"Yes. He's a . . . special case."

Qingshan smiled at that and turned her computer screen around so I could see it. "All bloods were clear, though he could use some more iron. Still in the normal range though."

"Yes, he doesn't eat much of anything really. But I'll have Michael introduce some iron-rich foods." That was easy enough to fix. "And his physical?"

Qingshan clicked on her notes. "In good health. Good teeth and clear eyes. BP normal, blood sugar was great. No tears or fissures."

I'd assumed all of this because he'd been given the greenlight to be subbed out. "And his scarring?"

"Oh, yes." She frowned. Another click or two later and photos came up on screen. Hunter, naked, his arms outstretched, his scars on display. "Terrible. Scarring is old. But he has no discomfort, no pain. The scar tissue lacks elasticity, but it doesn't restrict movement at all."

"Hmm," I said. "Wounds made by a wide leather strap. A belt, most likely."

She nodded. "I hope whoever did this to him has

suffered in return, tenfold."

"Me too." In all honesty, I hoped Hunter's mother was tied to a flagpole and had the skin flayed off her back, but that thought wasn't helpful. I sighed. "Thank you."

"I don't need to tell you, Sig. Aftercare on this boy's back will require special care."

I gave her a nod, though I didn't explain I wasn't allowed to touch the boy. "Yes, I know."

She smiled. "I'm glad he's with you. I know you'll take good care of him."

"Thank you."

I went back to my office to begin my work day. I still worried about my boys, though. My thoughts drifted to them often, and I doubted I was very useful at work. At lunchtime, I had my phone in my hand and was considering calling them when it rang.

Colton's name flashed on screen. "Master," I answered.

"Sig."

"Everything okay?" I asked, not that it was unusual for him to call.

"Everything's fine. I was calling to see how you were."

I smiled, and his care and protection settled over me. "I am . . . very well, actually. I was just considering calling home to see how the boys are getting on."

He chuckled, the sound deep and pleasing in my ear. "And the reason you haven't?"

"You know why," I replied with a smile. "They need to know I trust them. And I need to trust they'd call me should they need to."

"Ah, yes," he said, his voice tight. Then he spoke to someone who was in the room with him. It wasn't meant for my ears, but I heard it nonetheless. Low, gruff, commanding. "Yes, boy. Like that. Gooooood."

My belly warmed when I realised what he was doing. "Being serviced by one of your subs while you speak to me?"

"I can multitask," he replied. "And so can Mikhail, apparently."

I laughed. "Then I shall let you get back to it. Just know I had another breakthrough with Hunter yesterday. We can discuss it . . . at a more convenient time." He hissed. Not at me, but at Mikhail. I knew that sound. "You're doing little to help my libido."

He groaned out a laugh. "Have you thought about taking Levin to work with you? It's beneficial for everyone." Then he grunted and murmured something I couldn't decipher. I might not have known the words, but I knew those sounds. He was getting close to climax. "Saturday night, six o'clock. Sub social night. Informal. Dinner . . . Fuck yes, you little cock whore. All the way in."

My cock was hard by the sound of his sex-voice, the slurping and slapping I could hear in the background. "We'll be there," I replied.

The line went dead in my ear, and I shook my head and laughed. Great. Now I didn't just want to call home, I wanted to *go* home. My dick had been permanently hard pretty much the entire time since Hunter's arrival.

And in the name of self-control, I never took Levin into the playroom last night. He could have probably done with the break—he'd had two intense sessions the two days before—but I needed to resume control, and for me that began with self.

Self-control. Wanting something but withholding as a way to test my resolve. To prove to myself that I could control my urges. And I could. I was well-practised and extremely patient. I could compartmentalise and think rationally, even when desire licked at every nerve ending in my body.

So I told myself to enjoy it. Enjoy the self-control. Feel its power and the strength that came from within. Revel in the knowledge that I was in complete control. Not only control over Levin and Hunter, but control over myself. It was a powerful, heady thing. And the low buzz of arousal in my balls, my permanent hard-on, wasn't exactly unpleasant.

So yes, I could relish the power of control. And, apparently, I could also miss Levin and Hunter like crazy and watch the clock until it was time to go home.

When Paul drove us into the estate, my stomach was in knots. Anxious, nervous for some reason, and anticipation curled around my insides. On the drive home, Paul had said both boys had helped Michael in the kitchen today and that Hunter was a keen learner.

It just made me want to see them more.

I walked in, aiming for composed, to find them both kneeling in the waiting position. And my anxiety and restlessness were extinguished, replaced by the warm embers of relief and pride, longing and desire.

I went straight to them, put my briefcase down beside Levin, and touched his head, his face, tilting it upward. I leaned down and kissed his lips, and then I touched Hunter's head, cupped his face, and leaned down to kiss his forehead. I wanted to kiss his lips, and I was certain from the look in his eyes, he wanted it too.

"You're both such good subs," I said, forcing myself to control this exchange. "I've missed you both today. How about we take ten minutes to cuddle on the couch while you both tell me about your day?"

Levin grinned, shot to his feet, grabbing my briefcase and sliding it onto the table on his way to the couch. He was excited, and it was hard to rebuke him for getting ahead of himself. Hunter stayed behind me, half a step, and when I sat on the sofa, I extended both arms and Levin slotted himself on my right side. Hunter followed his lead on the left.

Relief and contentment settled in my bones, and I sighed.

"Long day, Master?" Levin asked.

"Nothing out of the ordinary. It's good to be home though." I rubbed their shoulders. "I'm very interested to hear all about your day though."

"The schedule worked well," Levin said. "By splitting the chores, we had extra time. I finished my assignment, though I want to read over it one more time before I send it. And we helped make dinner."

"You did?" I acted surprised. "Then I look forward to it."

"Wait until you try it before you say that." Levin snuggled into my side, his head on my chest. "Our time increments worked well, and they flowed well. I think it was an easy adjustment, Master."

I kissed the top of his head. "I'm glad to hear that. Hunter, what about you? How did you find your first day without me here?"

"It was great, Sir," he said. His voice was a little quiet, and I wondered if they weren't telling me something. "Paul was patient with me, and I quite liked cooking with Michael. It was good to be helpful. And Levin was very kind."

That was an odd way to describe it. "Kind? How so?"

"With my . . . class. The reading and writing."

Levin sat up and looked at me. "He thinks he's not very good, Master. But he is. He's very clever. It just might take some practice, but we'll get there." Levin reached over and took Hunter's hand, linking them on my stomach, before settling back against me. "You'll get there, Hunter. We can work on it every day."

I gave them both a squeeze and kissed the side of Hunter's head. I rather enjoyed them holding hands on me. "Be patient, boy."

"I will try, Sir."

"I have some news," I began. "I spoke to Colton today."

Hunter froze, and I gave him a squeeze. "There's no need for concern. It's good news. They're having a sub social on Saturday night."

Levin sat up again, his eyes almost as wide as his smile. "They are?"

Hunter sat up, more hesitant though. "What's a sub social?"

"It's an informal gathering at the Casa," I explained, realising Hunter hadn't been in our dominion that long. "A few times a year, the dominion holds a party, of sorts, where the subs can let their hair down."

"And do what?" Hunter asked.

"Nothing sexual or anything like that," I reassured him.

"We can eat what we want, we dance, we laugh," Levin said. "It's a lot of fun."

"All the subs talk and chatter about sub life while we Doms sit in a stuffy room talking politics and economics."

Levin laughed and snuggled back into me, claiming Hunter's hand again. "It's a lot of fun. They have pizza and a DJ and a dance floor. And I can introduce you to everyone. They'll love you, Hunter." Then Levin looked up at me, a happy faraway glint to his eyes. "I can see you now, Master, walking in with two subs behind you."

"Will everyone be watching us?" Hunter asked quietly.

I rubbed his back and held him tight. "Not in any intrusive way. Hunter, people will be very happy to meet you. I know you're not comfortable being the centre of attention, so perhaps we can get you inside without walking through the front door."

Now it was Hunter who sat up and looked at me. "You'd allow that?"

I rubbed his arm. "Of course. You told me being under the scrutiny of an entire room was a hard limit, so it's my responsibility to make sure you're not subjected to that."

"We can come in through the kitchen," Levin suggested. He looked me right in the eyes. "I'll make sure he's okay. We can stay in the corner where it's dark, and I'll make sure he's not inundated. I promise. What anyone else thinks doesn't matter. That Hunter feels comfortable is what's important."

I cupped Levin's jaw. "You are a good first sub."

"I want to please you," Levin whispered. "Both of you."

I brought him in for a kiss. Gentle lips and a touch of tongue. "You make me very happy."

Then I turned my attention to Hunter. "Do you think you'll be comfortable with Levin at the party? If we enter through the kitchen and stay out of the limelight? If you'd rather not, I can tell Colton we're unable to attend. He'll understand."

His gaze darted to Levin, then to me. "If Levin's okay with that. I don't want to be any trouble, and I don't want to let you down."

"You're no trouble at all," I replied. "I trust Levin to look after you, and we don't have to stay long if you feel overwhelmed. But Hunter, I trust you to look after Levin as well. That's how your relationship works. He will lead you, and you can look to him for guidance. But he might look to you for guidance too. If you're uncomfortable, you'll need to let him know. We can use our safe words, okay? If you're anxious but it's still manageable, it's yellow. If it becomes too much, call red. Okay?"

Hunter nodded, a little more relaxed. "I can do that."

"Good." Being with them both, being close and touching them both, set my body on fire. Awakened my desires and fuelled my needs. My cock began to fill, harden. "Are you boys hungry?"

Levin moaned and leaned his body into mine. "Starving," he breathed.

I chuckled. "You're not talking about food, are you, sub?"

He shook his head real slow. "No, Master."

I pulled him in close enough so my lips were to his ear. "Then be a good boy and go fetch the leash. Two leashes."

He didn't even reply. He scooted off the sofa so fast it left a rush of cool air in his place. I chuckled and rubbed Hunter's back. "He's a naughty boy."

Hunter blushed and kept his gaze down. I took his hand and fingered the cuff at his wrist. "Is this comfortable?"

His response was breathy. "Yes, Sir."

I touched the O-ring on the cuff. "Does this bother you?"

"No, Sir."

"I'd like to leash your wrist cuff and lead you to the playroom," I murmured. "But only if you want. You can tell me no."

He swallowed hard. "I want it, Sir."

"I'm still forbidden to touch you sexually. But I'm going to play with Levin and you can watch again. Maybe even pick out your own toy. Only if you want."

"I want," he breathed. Then he swallowed, his nostrils flared. "Thank you, Sir."

Levin came back in holding two thin leashes, both leather. I stood and gave them a direct order. "Assume the waiting position, and wait for my return."

I left them without another word and took the stairs to my bedroom. I chose my favourite leather pants and changed into them. The feel of them made me shiver with anticipation. Shirtless, shoeless, I took a deep breath, gave my cock a hard squeeze, and centred myself before walking out and going back down the stairs, slowly, getting more into my headspace with each step.

They were both on their knees, side by side, heads bowed and hands behind their backs. *So fucking beautiful.* The leashes sat on the floor beside Levin. I stood before them, watching the rise and fall of their chests, Hunter's a little faster than Levin's. I stroked his hair. "You're a good boy," I said, reassuring him. He inhaled deeply. Then I focused on Levin and lifted his chin so his eyes met mine. "You've been a little eager, haven't you, sub?"

"Yes, Master. I crave it."

I smiled. "I know you do. Hand me the leash."

He picked up one of them and offered it to me. "I'm going to leash you, and you will walk, following me like a good boy."

His eyes glazed over as he slipped into his happy place. "Yes, Master."

I clipped the leash onto the O-ring of his neck collar and gave it a gentle tug, making him moan and me smile. Then I took the second leash and turned to Hunter. "Raise your cuff." He lifted his hand and I clipped the second leash onto it. His gaze never left mine, darkening, and he gasped as the clip clicked into place.

Fuck.

"Stand," I ordered. They stood. I gave Hunter's leash to

Levin, and I pulled on Levin's leash, and together we walked, slowly, reverently, up the stairs and into the playroom. I went straight to the toy cabinet and opened the top drawers. Levin almost raised his hand, but he caught himself. He saw that I saw, too. "Hunter gets to choose whichever toy he wants to use on himself." I gave Levin's leash a little tug. "You, sub, get only my cock and my come."

Gooseflesh broke out over Levin's skin, and he kept his gaze down. Smart boy. Though he couldn't help but moan. I knew he was eager; the bulge in his pants told me all I needed to know.

"Hunter, choose the one you want the most, and take it out," I said; my throat felt harsh and raw. I was so turned on.

There were clamps, Fleshlights, blindfolds, cock rings, ball spreaders, pinwheels, dildos, wands, vibrators, straps, beads; a range of textures and sizes . . . I was dying to know which one he'd choose.

He slowly reached in with his uncuffed hand and chose. And I couldn't help but smile. He'd chosen the vibrating anal wand with a remote control. "Hmm," I hummed into Levin's hair. "Seems our new sub likes to come."

Then Hunter did the boldest thing. He turned to me, his head down, feet apart, but he raised his cuffed hand and offered me the small black remote. "For you, Sir. You're not allowed to touch me, but you can still control my body."

Fuck. It felt like the oxygen was sucked out of the room, and electricity sparked between us.

I took the remote, and standing directly in front of him so he could see even with his head down, I slipped the remote into the pocket of my leather pants, then palmed my erection. "Very thoughtful, sub," I murmured. "For being such a good boy, how many times would you like to come tonight?"

He sucked in a breath. "Two times, please, Sir."

I took his leash and led him to the adjustable bench. It was padded, like a weight bench, with different settings for heights and angles, with feet rests and restraining links. I raised one end so Hunter could be half sitting up, giving him a better reach for the wand. "Undress," I ordered. While he did that, I collected some lube for him and put it on the bench. He was naked now, his erection was flushed and full, making my mouth water. I wanted to taste him, his cock, his ass, his sweet mouth. I was beginning to think I never would.

"Sit on the bench and lean against the backrest," I ordered. "You can use the foot rests if you need to."

He lifted his right leg to the foot rest, spreading his legs. Fuck, this boy was going to be the end of me. "You're so fucking tempting," I mumbled. Then I took his cuffed wrist and hooked the leash to the top of the bench above his head. "You can unhook this at any time," I said, showing him how all he had to do was stand up and lift the leash higher than the hook. "Tell me your safe words."

He was breathing a little hard. "Yellow to slow."

"And to stop?"

"Red."

"Good boy," I said, running my thumb along his jaw, then his bottom lip. His cock leaked precome from my touch on his mouth alone. "You have lube and the wand. You can begin at any time, but I will control your orgasms."

"Yes, Sir," he replied quickly. "Thank you, Sir."

I stalked back to Levin, who was watching us with heated eyes. I took his leash and pulled upward, just a touch. It brought him to his toes, his lips closer to mine. "You're in for quite the reward tonight." I kissed him, hard, giving him my tongue while I tugged on the leash, and he groaned into my mouth. When I pulled away, he was breathing hard, and his lips were plump and wet. "Undress for me."

While he did that, I took a plug from the drawer, pumped some lube on it and turned Levin around. Bending him over a little, I knelt behind him, spread him wide and stroked my thumb over his sensitive flesh. Then I licked his hole, pressing my tongue in, and when he gasped, I replaced my tongue with the slicked plug. He gasped, his thighs shook, and the hook on the plug shuddered.

So goddamn beautiful.

I stood, turned him around, and taking his leash, drew him up to his full height. "Does that feel okay?"

"Yes, Master." His cheeks were flushed, his lips parted, his cock leaking a little. I knew my boy; I knew his body.

"Such a good sub."

I went to the wall of harnesses. Considering he was already wearing the collar, it was an easy choice. I chose the wrist restraint; a leather strap that hooked onto the back of his collar and a wide leather strap ran down his spine to restrain his two wrists behind his back. I showed it to him. "Yes?"

"Oh, yes, Master," he breathed. He was sliding into that sub headspace, that dreamy place where he relinquished his control and his body to me. Where he trusted me to bring him the most pleasure his body could take.

I fitted the wrist restraint and double checked the cuffs at his wrists weren't too tight behind his back. "That feel okay, sub?"

"Yes, Master."

I took the Fleshlight from the drawer, and taking Levin's leash, I led him to the pommel horse bench that he loved so much. We were at the end of Hunter's bench, with a glorious view of him working the wand into his ass with one hand, his other hand still restrained above his head. "Hunter, look at Levin. Isn't he beautiful, restrained and leashed?"

Hunter's back arched. "Oh, yes, Sir."

Fuck. The smell of arousal in the room made my balls ache.

I slotted the Fleshlight into the aperture and then, pouring lube onto my hand, I fisted Levin's cock. He moaned and winced, and I smiled. "You need to come, sub?"

"Yes, Master," he answered quickly.

Hunter made a long low sound, half pleasure, half pain. I spared him a glance, but kept the remote in my pocket for now. He was pulling on his balls, the wand protruding from his ass, and his cock was leaking a stream of precome.

Oh, yes. I liked this very much.

I led Levin up to the pommel horse by his leash until his cock was at the opening of the Fleshlight. Then I pulled on his leash until he slid into it, his cockhead resisting at first, but after the initial give, he slipped in easily.

He let out a high-pitched moan as he did, and Hunter groaned at the sound.

My head swam with the rush of it.

I moved Levin's legs up onto the leg rests. With his arms restrained behind him and his cock buried in the toy, he was completely at my mercy. I gave his ass cheek a slap, then the other, and he gasped with each contact. He fucking loved it. So I wiggled his butt plug before slowly extracting it, and he hissed. His balls drew up and he panted, but he didn't come.

I took the remote control from my pocket and undid my leather pants, pulling my cock free. I added a little more lube but had to give myself a squeeze to stem the desire to come already. I stood behind Levin, my cock at his hole. I held his leather restraint in one hand, Hunter's remote in my other, and I pushed into him in one long thrust and gave Hunter's wand a buzz at the same time.

They both cried out in pleasure together.

Hunter's leash rattled as he pulled on it, his back arching, his cock straining as the wand vibrated against his prostate. He almost screamed as he came, a guttural, throaty sound that drove me straight to the edge.

I switched the remote off and let him enjoy the aftershocks of his orgasm, and I concentrated on Levin. I drove into him, deep and hard, holding his restraints as I did, and it only took a few thrusts until he was coming into the Fleshlight. He moaned and grunted, begged and groaned as he filled the toy with his load. Such a vocal boy.

I stayed balls deep inside him, not even pulling out an inch, enjoying how his body throbbed around my cock. Then I took the remote and gave Hunter another buzz. "Oh!" he cried out, his leash straining as he arched. And I kept it on the pulse setting, the sound of the vibration lost to his groans. His cock was still hard, bulging in his fist, and I knew he was close.

I knew how good those wands were. The pleasure was excruciating.

So while Hunter kept pulsing and grunting out a rhythm, I fucked Levin, deep, long, and hard. Hunter cried out again, his voice hoarse, and the sound of him coming again sent me over the edge. My orgasm rocked me from my bones, pure pleasure overtook me as I emptied my cock into Levin, and he grunted with every spill.

Hunter made a tight whining sound that made me look at him. He'd pulled the still-pulsing wand out, his hand visibly shaking, and an amazed and sated expression on his face. But his arm was still hitched above his head, so I slowly pulled out of Levin and went to Hunter. I unhooked his hand and rubbed his shoulder. "Can you stand?"

He was staring at my cock. Half-hard and glistening, protruding from my opened leather pants, and right in front of him. He licked his lips and then, as though it just registered I'd asked him a question, he looked up at me. "Yes, Sir."

I helped him to his feet and walked him to the bed. "Lie down here."

I quickly went back to Levin and helped him stand. I pulled his softening dick out of the Fleshlight and uncuffed his hands. I rubbed the tops of his arms, his forearms and wrists. "Can you walk?"

He was all languid but smiley. "Yes, Master."

"Come this way," I said, helping him walk to the bed. "Let's lie down."

I lay in the middle, and each sub put their head on my chest. I rubbed their backs and held them close, letting them come down from their subspace highs in their own time. Levin snuggled in close, as he always did, but Hunter was a little more rigid.

I kissed the side of his head. "Is this okay?"

He took a moment. "Yes, Sir."

"Do you like cuddling and baths after time in the playroom?" I asked.

"Yes," he replied, though there was something unsaid.

"But?"

His voice was small and detached. "It's not something I'm used to, Sir."

Levin's head shot up and he stared at Hunter. "You never got . . . anything? No cuddles or baths or massages?"

Hunter gave him a sad smile. "Not really. I do like it though."

Levin looked at me. "Master, may I please give him a proper cuddle?"

I chuckled and gave a nod. As Levin scrambled over our bodies, I whispered to Hunter, "He really does give very good cuddles."

With a laugh, Levin wriggled into the other side of Hunter and together, we cocooned him, giving him a double cuddle. Hunter smiled and settled his head into the crook of my arm. It was the closest I'd been to him. He was completely naked, I was half-naked, my pants still undone, and we were in contact from head to foot. I would keep my orders not to touch him though, because this wasn't sexual. This was comfort and an unspoken promise that I would protect them, keep them safe, and keep their needs met.

And I would always comfort my sub, or subs, as the case was now. I hoped Hunter would make it a permanent arrangement, I truly did. I wanted him to be a part of this house, and I wanted to give him the life he deserved.

I also didn't want to neglect Levin in any way, and while my concerns were with Hunter, I needed to make sure Levin was coping as well. Leaning up a little, I reached across Hunter and put my hands to Levin's face. "How are you feeling, my boy?"

He smiled warmly. "I'm very good, Master."

Snuggled into Hunter like that, he did look like the cat that got the canary. And we stayed like that for a while, until our breathing was deep and peaceful.

"How about we shower?" I suggested eventually.

"Mmm," Levin hummed. "I love showers with you, Master."

I put my thumb to his lip. "I wasn't finished. How about

we get cleaned up, then we have dinner? I want to taste what you both helped cook today."

The shower in my private bathroom was the biggest—a walk-in shower with waterfall showerheads—so I took them in there. I soaped both of them up, gently massaging their shoulders and arms where they'd been restrained. Levin had moaned and rolled his neck, leaning into me as I touched him. He was half-hard again, which was almost a permanent state of being for Levin. He was insatiable.

Hunter was, as always, more reserved. I don't think he liked me washing his back too much, but as I softly swiped the soapy loofah across his skin, I replaced it with a light kiss to each scar. I wanted him to know I found him beautiful, scars and all. That while I saw the marks on his skin and I saw what he'd endured and how strong he was to live through that, I also saw the man underneath. The bright-eyed boy, who was timid but determined. I saw *him*.

And of course, being naked in the shower with two soaped-up, sexy subs was a little too much. My dick was far too interested, even though my mind knew there were boundaries.

I took a subtle step back, and Levin shampooed Hunter's hair, and that made him smile. Needing a distraction, I stepped out and dried off a little before wrapping a towel around my waist, then waited for them to be done, and I handed them a towel each.

And so help me, I wanted this on a permanent basis. I wanted this every night. I knew it wouldn't all be so rosy, and I knew there would be times of problems and adjustments. But I wanted them both. Both of them in my house, in my playroom. In my life.

"Master?" Levin's voice broke me from my thoughts.

"Sorry, I was just thinking," I said. "Both of you go get

dressed and I'll meet you at the dinner table in five minutes."

They both nodded and slipped out of the room. I made myself move and get dressed, but I knew I'd have to speak to Colton about how I was feeling. I just needed to speak to Levin first.

Dinner was a zucchini and ricotta lasagne with a crisp salad. It had Michael's touch, that much I could tell, but both boys had helped. It was delicious. I'd had a few mouthfuls before I spoke. "Tell me how you made it."

Hunter gave me a strange look. "You want to know?"

"Yes. You created food for our table. I'd love to hear about it."

So he told me how Michael had him peel slices of zucchini as substitute pasta and how he'd helped season the ricotta. It was good to hear him talking and to see his confidence grow. Even just the smallest bit, every day he'd been here had been a step forward.

"Oh, that reminds me," I said, putting my fork on my empty plate. "Hunter, I spoke with Christa and asked if she had a position available for a trainee at the salon."

His eyes widened. "You did? Oh, Sir . . . I, uh, I don't know what to say. Thank you, Sir."

"She wasn't sure when the college class starts, but she wants to meet with you next week."

His smile quickly died. "Oh."

"No, Hunter," Levin said. "You'll nail it. But if you like, I can help you with any coursework. I can take you through it step by step."

I had a sinking feeling it wasn't the mention of coursework that bothered him. "Is something else the matter?"

He looked down as he spoke. "Well, next week . . . what if I'm not here next week?"

My heart squeezed, though I managed to not let it show outwardly. The idea of him not being here next week was almost too much to bear. "The offer of your employment and studies will continue, no matter whom you choose to stay with."

"It's just that . . . ," he said. "I mean, please don't think I'm not grateful, because I am. I really am . . ." He frowned and finally made eye contact with me. "I don't know . . ."

"Are you saying you'd rather not stay with us?" I asked, my voice neutral. "I'm sorry if I pressured you. That was never my intention."

"Oh no, that's not it," he shot back quickly. He shook his head, flustered. "I don't know . . . There're things I don't know. I really like being here, and I trust you, Sir. I know you won't hurt me, and I have Levin to help me." His smile was sad. "What if Master Colton decides for me."

"He said it was your decision," I said gently. "And he's a man of his word."

He nodded, though his expression said all I needed to know. And it was clear from Levin's face that he saw it too.

Later that night, when I went to say goodnight to Levin, I poked my head into his room. He was in bed reading, but he put the book aside. "Master, can I ask you something?"

"Of course." I went and sat on the edge of the mattress and waited. "I wanted to speak to you too. But you go first."

"Does Hunter not want to stay with us?"

I sighed heavily. "I don't know. I'm beginning to think maybe he doesn't."

Levin frowned. "I like him."

"Me too."

"I don't know why he doesn't feel welcome here," he mused, sadly. "You've been so patient with him and caring."

"As have you."

"And it's still not enough."

"Maybe he needs something we can't give him. And that's okay." *Or maybe I haven't given him what he needs . . .*

His brow furrowed as though he agreed with my thoughts. "I'll be sad if he says no."

I touched his hair, his face. "Me too."

"Then make him stay. You can tell him he has to."

I chuckled. "It doesn't work that way." The truth was, I wished it *did* work that way. I wished I could make Hunter stay and show him how happy he could be here.

He pouted. "I know . . ." Then he sighed. "What did you want to speak to me about, Master?"

"It was about Hunter, and if you wanted him to stay. But you just said you did."

He nodded. "I do."

"I wanted to know if you were comfortable with him being brought into the house," I furthered. "I need to know if you have any hesitation or reluctance."

He shook his head. "No, Master. None."

"Because you know that his being here doesn't detract from you. It doesn't mean my time and attention to you will be any less. His happiness doesn't come at the price of yours."

"I know that, Master," he murmured. "Thank you for asking."

"If you feel, in any way, that his being with us isn't right for you, I need you to tell me. Now, or in six months, or a year, okay?"

"I will," he replied. "Master, can I be honest with you?"

"I would insist on it."

He gave me a smile. "I kinda feel like . . . like what I have with you isn't different now Hunter's here, yet it *is* different. And I don't want to say it's better, because that would imply it was lacking before, which it wasn't, and it won't be lacking should he not wish to stay. What we have with him being here is . . . deeper. And I don't know if that's the right word either, Master. Like you give me one hundred percent, and now that Hunter's here, you don't give us fifty percent each, you give us *both* one hundred percent. And that makes me happy. As a submissive, I know the man who I give my submission to is worthy. Does that make sense?"

His words hit me right in the solar plexus. "Perfect sense. And thank you, Levin. Your praise is its own reward for me. It means a great deal to hear that from you." The truth was, it humbled me a little. My heart squeezed for this boy in ways it wasn't accustomed to. "I don't know what I did to deserve a sub like you, Levin. But I am grateful."

He blushed; the soft light of his room made him look angelic. "If you'd like to reward me, I wouldn't object," he murmured, then moved his leg so the blanket pulled away, revealing his very naked body underneath. His dick lay on his leg, half-hard and enticing.

I growled. "You're beginning to take liberties, sub."

He almost smiled, but he bowed his head. His dick twitched and he squirmed a little. "If you think I should be spanked or punished, Master."

Christ. "Did you not have enough of me before?"

He shook his head. "Never, Master." His ragged breath was the only sound in the room, and God, how I couldn't get enough of him either. "I still have your come inside me from before."

Oh, fuck. He knew which buttons to push.

"Should I put you across my knee?" I whispered roughly. "Or just bend you over the edge of your bed?"

He let out a whimper and his cock hardened. Such a

greedy sub. I didn't give him time to answer. I grabbed his ankle and pulled his leg off the bed while pushing his shoulder into the mattress. He gave a surprised yelp, which became a moan. I kept one hand on his back, but he straightened himself a little, his hips at the edge of the mattress, his ass at the perfect height. I pulled down the front of my pants with my free hand and guided my cock into his hole. In one brutal thrust, I was buried inside him. His back arched and he cried out, and he clawed at the sheets. But he spread his legs wider and began to rock, moaning like the cock whore he was.

So I drove into him again, and with a hand around his neck, I lifted his chest up off the bed so his back was arched, my cock fully embedded in him, and whispered into his ear. "I'm going to put another load in you, boy. And you'll sleep with it inside you."

And just like that, he came.

His punishment became a reward.

I let him slump onto the mattress and took his hips in both hands and I wasn't gentle. I took what was mine, and I gave him what I'd promised him.

When I left his room, he was already asleep with a smile on his face. And I fell into my bed much the same way. Happy, thoroughly sated, and content. Despite the uncertainty of Hunter's stay with us, I would allow myself to enjoy it for now.

Though I dreamed of having him. His ass, his mouth, those lips . . . And Levin too. Both of them, together, the sounds, the smell of sex. Linked fingers, whispered moans, throaty groans. Not even in my sleep was I free from wanting them.

CHAPTER SEVEN

I TOOK a half day at work the next day. I'd left the boys at breakfast, telling them to be dressed suitably for a day downtown. If Hunter had been unsure, Levin's grin put him at ease.

I saw a few patients at the clinic, mostly running blood work and seeing a few minor issues. The majority of my patients were from the Sanctus, but not all. It was a quiet clinic, far from fast-paced emergency rooms. But then again, this village, these mountains, and everything about them was idyllic.

Life was pretty damn perfect.

When Paul drove into the estate, excitement and anticipation put a smile on my face. "Please stop at the front door and wait. We won't be long."

"Yes, Sir."

I went inside to find them both kneeling, waiting. Levin wore his jeans, a black T-shirt and a light grey coat, and his heavy black boots. His hair was combed neatly, a hint of a smile at his lips.

Hunter wore the faded blue jeans, a grey T-shirt, and a black jacket. He had a pair of Levin's leather loafers on his feet, his blond hair styled, and even though his head was down, I could see that he, too, was smiling. I did like to see them dressed with such care to detail, and while I couldn't see Levin's collar or Hunter's cuff, I knew they were there.

"Oh, boys," I said. "You're both very beautiful. Both such good subs." I gave them a gentle stroke along their cheekbones. "I wanted to treat you both to an afternoon in the village. We can have lunch and do some shopping. I thought Hunter might like to pick out some clothes and shoes."

Levin's smile got the better of him. "Thank you, Master."

Hunter paused for a moment. He probably would have liked to object, but we were not at the table, and I'd not asked for his opinion. "Thank you, Sir."

"So come," I said, taking a step back. "The car is waiting."

The drive into the village took all of ten minutes. The view along the winding mountainside was spectacular. Green and lush, white snow tops, blue skies, and grand chalets dotted along the way.

Hunter took it all in, and Levin explained who from the Sanctus lived where and what to expect in the village. I let him lead. The responsibility for Hunter's care rested with Levin as well, and his role as first sub was almost as important as my role as Dom.

I was happy to observe. Even as we left the car and entered the picturesque streets on foot, I was happy to let Levin take charge. The streets were narrow and cobblestoned, with lampposts and huge pots of spring flowers, with a backdrop of mountaintops. Each store was boutique and expensive. The entire place was utterly charming.

Tourists strolled and smiled as they parted with their money, funding what were mostly Sanctum-owned businesses, run by Doms and subs alike. It was no wonder it felt like home.

I took them into The Rickety Chair, a delightful little café with dark teal walls, leather sofas, and coffee tables with Moroccan tile tops. Suspended from the ceiling was a wooden chair, and to any normal tourist, it might look like a well-loved antique. But anyone in the dominion would know what the scuff marks around the front legs and along the arm rests were from. And there it hung in plain sight, suspended by old chains and leather cuffs.

Leo, the owner and a Dom I knew well, grinned when he saw me. He was an Italian man, short and a little round in the middle, but he could wield a bullwhip like no one else I'd ever seen. He walked out from behind the counter and kissed me on both cheeks. "Sig, my old friend. Long time, no see."

"I've been . . . busy," I offered.

Leo eyed Levin, then noticed Hunter and how they held hands. He shot me a surprised look. "I can see that. You have two?"

"It's early days," I said, somewhat cryptically but giving enough away.

He let out a low breath. "It suits you, Sig. You look great."

I gave a nod and a smile. "You too."

"Come, sit," Leo said, leading us to a table. "Espresso?"

We sat, both Levin and Hunter opposite me. I ordered for everyone, espressos, different toasted focaccias, and water. Leo gave a nod and a promise to soon return with our order. Levin spoke in a whisper, pointing out that Leo was a Dom, the barista was a sub—who right then looked our way and gave us a nod—and then he pointed to the chair strung from the ceiling.

Hunter's eyes went wide, and he smiled. "Everyone in this village is . . . ?"

I gave a nod. "Nearly everyone. There are a few hundred non-dominion people. None of them know though."

He made a face. "How can they not know?"

Levin laughed. "They're oblivious. They don't know our world exists."

"You mustn't assume everyone is part of it," I explained. "We get a lot of tourists here, and they can't know about us."

Hunter gave a nod. "Understood, Sir."

Leo brought us our drinks, and soon after that, our lunch arrived. To any outsider, we would have appeared completely normal. Just three men having a pleasant meal together. They couldn't have noticed how both boys waited for me to eat first, for me to give them a nod for them to start. Hunter followed Levin's lead flawlessly, he watched and learned. Subtle and astute. Perfect.

The Dom in me delighted at their excellence. It made me sit a little taller, a little prouder. If I wanted to hand feed them right here, I could. If I wanted them naked, they'd strip, no hesitation. God, I could even demand Levin onto his knees and to suck me off right there in broad daylight in a busy café, and he'd gladly do it. I wouldn't ask that of him. I wouldn't ever expose my boys or the Sanctus like that.

But I could.

And knowing that, knowing I held the authority and the

power, to have these two boys obey every word, was enough. It was intoxicating, and invigorating. The Dom in me loved it.

I could so easily get used to this. I wanted it. I wanted two subs, and not just any two. These two. Levin always, but Hunter now as well. And of course, my cock liked the idea. I only had to think of it for a moment and I was half-hard. I was beginning to think that this constant state of arousal would be permanent, and I couldn't decide if it was heaven or hell.

When we'd finished, I paid the bill, and with a wave to Leo, we stepped back out into the street. Levin took Hunter's hand, and they stopped in front of windows, deciding on which stores to go into. And I let them have their time together. They complemented each other: Levin was outgoing, Hunter was quieter, but they smiled and talked, laughing. They asked me questions, they included me, but honestly, it gave me greater joy to simply watch.

Levin picked out new clothes for Hunter. Jeans, shirts, a coat, a woollen sweater. He made Hunter try them on, and I was rewarded with a fashion show. By the end of it, Hunter was positively beaming.

In one store, they were inspecting a row of boots. Hunter's eyes kept going to a black pair that would lace up to his shins, with buckles and an O-ring at the back of the heel. "You like these?" I asked him.

Each pair on this shelf was several hundred euros; the ones he'd picked up were over a thousand. "Sir," he whispered, uneasy.

I stepped in close. "Boy, I didn't ask you to look at the price. I asked you if you liked them?"

He dropped his gaze. "Apologies, Sir." He swallowed hard. "Yes, I like them."

I picked the boot up, pulling hard on the O-ring, imagining him wearing them, restrained by them, in the sling with his legs spread. "Then you shall have them." Just thinking of him in leather boots . . . Christ, I loved men in boots. "I think Levin needs a pair as well."

Levin chuckled beside me.

"Something funny, sub?"

"Absolutely not, Master," he said, almost purring. "I can't wait to wear them for you."

I couldn't deny him. The way he leaned into me, the way he looked at me with desire in his eyes. He wanted to please me. He wanted my attention, and I wanted to give it to him, right here in the store. I looked around the store to see how many customers there were. I was sure the fitting rooms were big enough for two though they were hardly soundproofed, and I knew all too well that Levin could never be quiet . . . unless I filled his mouth with something.

"Can I help you, sir?" the salesman said. I knew him. He was an older gentleman, a sub I'd seen in play sessions at the Casa.

"Yes," I replied, just about to ask for the biggest changing room they had when the front door opened. Two young girls walked in, chatting and laughing. Not from the dominion. Damn. "I'll take two pairs of these. One for each of them."

He bowed his head and smiled knowingly. "Excellent choice, Sir."

The boys tried them on for size, and I looked on, supervising, observing. I handed my card over and paid, and we were soon back out on the street, my boys holding hands and looking in shop windows, chatting and smiling.

I could watch them forever. And even though Levin got to hold Hunter's hand and I didn't, I wasn't jealous at all. In fact, it made me happy to see them interact like that. I kept coming back to the word *proud*, but watching them together pleased me, it satisfied some part of me that longed to see my boys thrive.

"Sig?"

I turned. "Christa!" I gave her a kiss on her cheek. "So good to see you!"

She was a tall, thin woman, who I'd only ever seen wear black. She had poise and grace, her lips painted red, with jet-black hair straight to her shoulders, her fringe severe, her appearance always angular and immaculate. "I don't see you for six months, then within a few days, I get a phone call and I run into you." She smiled. "You look great. What's your secret?"

I gave a pointed nod to Levin and Hunter who were one shop up, looking in the front window.

"Ah," she said, giving me a knowing look. "I see. This is the boy you phoned about?"

"Yes." I called out to them. "Boys!"

They turned immediately at my voice and came to us. "Levin," Christa said. "You look amazing, as always. Sig must really have a magic touch."

Levin grinned but bowed his head. "He most certainly does."

"And you must be Hunter," Christa said.

Hunter lowered his gaze. "Madam."

Christa smiled at me. "Oh, I like him already."

I chuckled. "Hunter, Christa owns the hair salon," I said, nodding to the salon across and up the street.

Hunter gave her a startled, apologetic look. "Oh! I believe Sir has made a call on my behalf and I'm very grateful."

Christa smiled but I noticed a certain look in her eyes.

"How about I take you to meet Tanja. Levin, lead the way," she said, waving to the salon.

He glanced at me and I nodded, so doing as he was told, still holding Hunter's hand, he led him across the street. Christa watched them, then watched me. "I have to say, Sig. I saw you watching them, and I thought, 'There's a real Dom. Letting them run and play while you stand back and observe'." We began to cross the road. "There's so much fire in your eyes I'm surprised you don't combust."

I snorted. "That obvious, am I?"

We got to the sidewalk and she looked up at me. "But then he called you Sir."

I sighed. "I thought you noticed that."

"Rather hard not to."

"He's not mine. Not permanently, anyway. Not yet."

Christa's eyes narrowed and she pursed her lips, her expression confused. "Are you trialling him?"

"More like he's trialling us." I glanced up to where Levin and Hunter both waited outside the salon. "It's a long story."

"And yet you ask about me taking him on to get qualified in hairdressing?"

"He's been deprived of a lot of things in his life, and doing hair is a dream of his. I'd like to see it happen, and even if he doesn't stay with us, I would ask Master Colton to see his training and studies continue with whomever takes him on."

Christa's lips pulled up in a smile. "You're a good one, Sig. I hope you remind him of that when you get him home."

I groaned. "Don't mention it. I'm not to touch him while he's temporary."

Christa shot me a look. "Ouch."

I laughed. "Oh, you have no idea."

She laughed as well. "Come on, let's introduce him to my Tanja."

Tanja was a Russian woman who could have been a 1950s pin-up girl. She had flame-red hair in scrolls that defied gravity, gorgeous curves, and a contagious smile with a stud pierced into her dimple. She was finishing serving a client, finalising payment, as we walked in. The client left with a smile and wave, their hair done to perfection, and Tanja turned to us. Her attention trained straight on Christa, and she bowed her head.

"*Pokornyy*," Christa whispered, her hand extended toward Tanja.

Tanja took her offered hand and kissed her knuckles. "*Vladelets*," she whispered.

Submissive.

Owner.

It was a private moment between them, and it was a privilege to witness. Christa put her hand around Tanja's waist and introduced us. "You've met Sig and Levin before," she said. "But this is Hunter. The one I told you about. He wants to learn hairdressing."

"Oh, my darling," she said, taking Hunter's hand. "You're beautiful."

Hunter blushed, Levin grinned, and I tried not to smile. Levin took Hunter's shopping bags. "Give them to me." When his other hand was free, Tanja took that one as well.

Tanja turned to Christa and gave her puppy dog eyes. "Daniella finished two months ago, so you know we have a place. And another sub, *Vladelets*, please . . ."

Christa held her breath for a long moment, then sighed. "We will need to discuss conditions."

Tanja took Hunter by the arm and led him to the chairs and basins. "My darling, let me show you . . ."

Christa turned to me and shrugged. "How can I resist her?"

I smiled. "I have the same problem."

"Though she might need a lesson in manners when I get her home."

I chuckled. "A good lesson in manners never hurt a sub . . . much."

Christa laughed. "This is true. Though we will need to discuss it further. I'll gather up some information about the course he'll need to complete, and we can discuss any of his needs."

"I am indebted to you, Christa."

She gave me a wink. "Don't make promises you can't keep, Sig."

I stood with Levin while Hunter spoke with Tanja and Christa. "He'd be happy here, Master," Levin said.

"Yes, he would."

He turned into my side and put his forehead on my shoulder. "I want him to stay with us."

"I do too."

He looked up at me, his brown eyes imploring. "Today has been wonderful. Thank you, Master."

I pulled him in for a sound kiss. "Yes it has. And you deserve it, sub."

He smiled and put his head to my chest. I held him for a moment, and when Hunter came back to us, Levin held out his hand. Hunter took it gratefully, but he smiled at me. "Thank you, Sir."

"You're very welcome." I wanted to pull him in for a kiss. Actually, I wanted to put him in one of those salon chairs and fuck him every way I could. Instead, I put a hand to his arm. "We'll be speaking with Christa and Tanja again soon."

Another client came in, a face I recognised from the Casa. "I apologise for being late," she said. "I got . . . tied up."

Tanja giggled and led the woman to a chair, and we gave them a wave and made our exit. Hunter was beaming, his excitement hard to contain. The wind tousled his hair, the sun shone on his skin, his eyes were bright, and his smile wide; he was simply gorgeous. Yet it was more than looks. For the first time since I'd known him, he looked like a weight had been lifted, like he dared to hope.

Levin saw it too. He looked at Hunter the same way I imagined I did. As if we were seeing the rarest flower bloom. Holding his hand, he pulled him in close. "We haven't looked down this side of the street."

So again, I stayed a step behind, watching them, adoring them. Until Levin, laughing, pulled Hunter into a pet store. I followed, keeping enough distance to supervise but leaving them free to explore. I was confident I knew which section they were going to.

And I was right.

There was a whole aisle of dog collars and leashes, and considering this store was Sanctus owned and operated, their products suited all . . . clients. They also had pup and kitty treats suitable for human consumption, and a lot of Doms brought their pets in here. It was innocent enough to the unsuspecting, unknowing folks, but it really did help the mindset of all pups and kitties for them to be able to be taken to the store and to be given a bone or fish shaped treat in public. Role play was important, and being able to do that out in the open was a luxury.

Levin showed Hunter different collars: leather, neoprene, choker chains. And all the different leashes, which Hunter seemed keen to feel and hold. He took one off the rack, black leather with some chain link at the clip. "I like this one," he said.

And just like that, my cock throbbed, filling and lengthening in my pants.

This boy . . . he was killing me.

Then a guy, who I had seen at the Casa but whose name escaped me, came up behind them. He hadn't seen me. "So, two pups allowed off the chain," he said. He put his sleazy arm around Hunter's shoulder. "Want to try that on?"

Maybe he recognised Levin, maybe he didn't. Maybe he was an asshole who needed a swift lesson in fucking manners.

Hunter turned and took a reflexive step back. He didn't like the man, that much was clear. I took a step toward them, but Levin was right there. He put himself between them, staring at the man. His expression was murderous. "Back the fuck up. Don't touch what's not yours."

To say I was shocked would have been an understatement. I'd never heard him speak or seen him behave like that. He was protective, in charge, well within his rights to give this piece of shit the lesson he needed.

The man moved back a little and tried to laugh it off. Levin never broke his gaze, but then the guy saw me and his whole demeanour changed. He put both hands up and took a step back. His expression was panicked. "I didn't know. I wasn't told. I—"

"You will listen to what Levin told you," I said, staring hard at him as I walked closer. "And you *will* back the fuck up. Or I will make you."

He kept walking backwards, his hands up, palms forward. "Master Sig, apologies," he murmured, then turned and scurried away.

I put my arm around Hunter. "Are you okay?"

His eyes were wide. "I didn't ask him . . . I've never seen him before. I don't—"

"Shhh," I whispered, pulling him into my side and pressing a kiss to the side of his head. "You did nothing wrong." Then I looked at Levin. "And you . . . ?"

He put his head down. "Sorry, Master. I thought he posed a threat, and I thought Hunter was scared—"

I put my hand to his jaw, making him look at me. "What you did right now was amazing. You defended him, and you protected what's ours. I'm very proud of you. And I'm incredibly fucking turned on." I kissed him soundly. "We need to leave."

The store owner came out. I knew him. He was a Dom, but a weak one at best. "Master Sig," he said. "Please let me apologise."

"I don't want you to apologise, David," I said coolly, an arm around each of my boys. "I want you to train your dog how to behave. May I suggest you start with a caning. And a cage."

He bowed his head and we left. I called Paul, and five minutes later we were in the car and on our way home. I sat in between them and held their hands.

"I ruined our day," Levin mumbled.

"Not at all," I replied. "You impressed me. You continue to impress me."

He sighed. "Thank you, Master. I still feel bad though."

"Hunter," I said. "Are you okay?"

"I'm fine, Sir. He startled me. He was closer than I was

expecting, that's all. And he was slimy," he answered. Then he looked around me, to Levin. "Thank you, Levin. You were kind of badass." His eyes shot to mine, but I laughed.

"He *was* kind of badass," I agreed, and Levin eventually smiled. "And if you feel that bad, Levin," I added, "perhaps you need to tell me what would make you feel better."

His smile became more genuine and he leaned his head on my shoulder. "I'm sure I can think of something." Then he looked up at me. "How much time will we have?"

I smiled, confident I knew what he was thinking. There was one session that took quite a long time, and it was a favourite of his. "All the time in the world."

Thirty minutes later, we were in the playroom. I was wearing my leather pants and nothing else. Hunter sat on the bench, naked, his hand leashed above his head again. I'd given him a Fleshlight, a dildo, and lube. "We might be a while," I'd said. "You can come as many times as you like."

And Levin . . . well, Levin was a work of art.

He was on the bed, his arms spread wide, his wrists shackled to the top corners of the bed. His thighs were restrained with thick leather cuffs, bringing his knees up to his chest, a spreader bar between his knees kept him secure and completely immobile.

He was fitted with a cock ring and a small black plug. I put all kinds of toys beside him on the bed, but I gave him time as I walked back and forth. He could see me, and he watched my every move. His breathing evened out as he let himself drift into his subspace.

The last item I collected was the blindfold.

I walked to him, holding it up. "Soon, sub. First, I want you to watch Hunter while he fucks himself with that dildo."

Half the pleasure of this session was the anticipation. The time it took to prepare him, strap him in, restrain him. I allowed him to watch as Hunter came the first time, the dildo fully embedded in his ass, the Fleshlight stroking his cock. The sight, the sounds he made, everything about it was delicious, and Levin was already leaking precome.

Then I blindfolded him, took my time, relishing every minute, every inch of his skin, every goose bump, every moan. With pegs on his nipples, a prostate massager, and my mouth, I got to tease him, edge him, make him beg, make him come. And when he thought he couldn't take any more, when he was a quivering mess, his body flinching and pulling on the restraints, I freed his legs, flipped him over, and fucked him all over again.

When I gave Levin a load of come deep inside him, Hunter came again as well.

It was hours of perfection, and so were the hours that followed.

I bathed them, massaged them, fed them dinner, and we cuddled on the couch in front of the TV. Levin fell asleep on me, and I considered staying right there all night. This time Hunter helped me get him upstairs and into bed. He watched as I pulled up the covers and kissed Levin's forehead, and I wanted to do the same for him.

I held his hand and took him to his room. I pulled back his covers and watched, silent, as he stripped naked to get into bed. I pulled the covers up and cradled his face, watching emotions flicker in his eyes. I wanted, more than anything else, just to kiss him. But I couldn't.

So instead, I kissed his forehead. "Sleep well, sweet boy. Goodnight."

He smiled and slow-blinked, tired. I got up and walked to the door.

"Sir?"

I stopped and turned. "Yes, sub?"

"Goodnight."

I smiled and walked out with my heart tripping over in my chest.

CHAPTER EIGHT

THE NEXT TWO days were blissful. Work was without stress, and as much as I loved my job, loved treating people and helping others, I'd never wanted to be at home more. Levin had stepped into his role as first sub seamlessly. Actually, he was so good at it, I wondered if I'd missed the signs earlier, that perhaps I should have seen.

Hunter clearly enjoyed his new schedule. His days were more structured, and he knew where he was supposed to be and what he was supposed to be doing. It gave him purpose and direction, and like most subs, it made him feel safe.

I'd come home every day to the both of them kneeling in their places by the door, and a sense of calm blanketed me as soon as I saw them and stroked their hair. I would give them both a kiss—Levin on the mouth, Hunter on his forehead—and we'd sit on the sofa and I'd have them tell me about their day.

I gave Levin a break from fucking, but on the second night, I had him kneel and suck me instead while Hunter watched. I'd not told him he could touch himself or use a toy, so he knelt in the waiting position, his hands behind his back, his eyes dark, lips parted, and his jeans tented at the front.

And he watched me in a way that felt like his hands were on my body. His eye contact was direct and imploring and I could almost imagine it was his mouth I was fucking.

My imagination and his heated gaze finished me, and when I was done, I saw Levin was fully aroused as well. So, I gave Levin the Fleshlight and lube, but gave Hunter only lube, and told them to masturbate where they knelt.

I wanted to watch Hunter. I wanted to know what he liked and how he liked it. He didn't disappoint. He worked his shaft and head with one hand and fondled his balls and perineum with his other. They watched each other as they pleasured themselves, and it was a heady mix of voyeurism and control. Levin came first and Hunter followed seconds later. I was almost ready to go again, but I took stock of my body, squared the desire away, and focused on my self-control.

I showered them and put them to bed, and there was a weird paradox to Hunter. There was something I couldn't quite put my finger on, but I stared at the ceiling most of the night until I put the pieces together. I'd never felt closer to him, or further away, at the same time. As though there was a wall around him, and every time a block or two came down, another two popped up somewhere else. I didn't know how to breach it, or if he even wanted us to. Tomorrow was the sub social party, and the day after that was the day Hunter was to make his decision. We were fast running out of time.

The next morning, after breakfast, both boys went about their chores and I went into my office and closed the door. I took my phone out, scrolled through my contacts, and hit Call.

"Sig," Ephraim answered, his deep voice a welcome sound. "Everything okay?"

"Yes, I think so," I replied. "I'm not sure. Am I interrupting?"

"Not at all. What's on your mind?"

"Hunter," I murmured. Both he and Levin were upstairs cleaning so I knew they couldn't hear me, but still . . . It wasn't an easy conversation.

"How's he adapting?"

"The schedule and roster worked well. He's responded better than expected, really. He's opened up, been honest with me, and told me about his past."

Ephraim paused. "So what's the problem, Sig?"

"It feels the closer we get to him, the more he pulls away." I sighed. "I think he's distancing himself because he's going to say no. He's going to say he doesn't want to stay."

"You knew that was a possibility, Sig," Ephraim said. "It was always a possibility."

"I know."

"You've grown attached to him."

"I have. And Levin has too." I sighed. "He's grown rather fond of him, and he really is a remarkable first sub. The other day we were in the village and a man approached Hunter in a . . . not exactly pleasant manner. Levin got between them and defended him. It surprised me, to be honest. But he's very protective of him."

"I probably wouldn't be too surprised, Sig. You put him in charge of the boy's safety. He was following instruction."

I frowned. "Perhaps. It felt more than that. It felt personal. I don't know . . ." I sighed. "Do you think I missed something with Levin? Did I miss the signs that he needed to be a first sub? Did he need this and I didn't see it?"

"I don't think so," Ephraim answered. "Sometimes we don't know what we need until we're given it."

I sighed again. "I can't help but feel he needed to be challenged and be given more responsibility and I didn't see it. I'm his Dom and I should have known what he needed."

Ephraim was quiet for a moment. "Sig, it sounds to me that you're still doubting yourself."

He was right. Both Ephraim and Colton had said the same thing. "I am. Having two subs is a responsibility I wasn't quite prepared for."

"Doesn't mean you're not capable. Master Colton wouldn't have trusted you if he didn't think you could handle it. You trust his judgement, yes?"

"Of course."

"You want to know what I think?"

Not really. "Yes."

"I think you're scared, Sig. Scared of what it means for you and Levin if Hunter says no. And scared if he says yes. It's completely normal to feel that way," he said. "Change is daunting, especially for us. Even more so for submissives. And, I think it'd be safe to say if you're scared, then Hunter is terrified."

"Fucking hell," I mumbled, digging the heel of my hand into my eye.

"He's had a rough time."

"I know."

"And now he's been placed with you, Sig. Probably the kindest Dominant in the Sanctus. He's waiting for the rug to be pulled out from under him."

"The kindest . . .?"

"Yes. And the best."

"Ephraim, I—"

"Take the compliment," he said, his voice deep and stern. It was his Dom voice. Then he softened. "We all know it, Sig. You're sexy as hell, hung like a horse, and you're great at what you do. Some Doms get off on pain, some need torture. You, on the other hand, you get off on the orgasms of your subs. Believe me, if you were in the market for a new sub, there'd be a line a mile long."

I snorted. "I certainly don't need a new sub."

He chuckled. "No, you don't. You need to talk to Hunter. Ask him what he wants."

"I don't want to pressure him."

"He's pressured already."

"Have we made it worse for him?" I asked. "Should we have removed his choice? He really is better with reaffirmed structure and disciplined instruction."

"No, I think the choice was good. It's giving him the power to decide his own path. Something that he hasn't had a great deal of experience with."

I sighed and we were both quiet for a while. "What if he says no?" I asked. "Levin will be devastated."

"And you."

I nodded. "Yeah. And me. There's something about this boy, Ephraim. Something that makes me want to care for him."

"The sub social is on tonight," Ephraim said.

"Yes . . ."

"We have to drive past your house on the way," he said. "How about we come early and I can speak to Hunter?"

"I would appreciate that. I'm not sure if Hunter will though. Levin's hyped up the sub social and Hunter's even a little excited for it now, so it might be a bit of a downer."

"I'll keep it light," he said. "But Sig, I can't sway him

either way. If he doesn't want to make his position with you permanent, that's his decision to make."

"I know. I would never ask you to."

"I'll be there around four."

"Thank you, Ephraim."

"Any time, Sig."

I disconnected the call and stared into that void between close-up and far away, putting together the pieces of what Ephraim had said and what I had to do.

WHEN LEVIN and Hunter came down for lunch, I stood by the table with my feet apart and my hands behind my back, my chin raised.

Their reaction was instantaneous. Gone was the inquisitive glancing around and smiles, replaced with composure, calm, and complete submission. Levin stopped in front of me and went to his knees, Hunter followed immediately after.

I needed them in a subspace. I wanted them in that mental place, that realm of quiet and peace where nothing outside of it exists.

I couldn't influence or pressure Hunter, and I couldn't control the outcome. But I could control this feeling of being adrift, and the worry and fear of the future we were facing. And I could only control it the one way I knew how.

"Good subs," I murmured. I acknowledged Levin with my fingers in his hair, then Hunter. I lifted his chin and he met my gaze. I thumbed his bottom lip, the lip I wanted to kiss, suck into my mouth. "You will both sit at the table in your usual seat, and I will feed you."

"Yes, Master," Levin replied.

"Yes, Sir," Hunter said.

I took my seat at the head of the table and they took theirs without a sound. I had a plate of cut fruit, cheeses, and rice crackers, some deli meats, and taking a piece of sliced apricot, I held it to Levin's mouth. He took no liberties, kept his hands in his lap and simply opened his mouth and allowed me to slip the fruit between his lips. He made my heart soar.

Then I did the same for Hunter.

And piece by piece, alternating between them, they finished the plate. Apricot, apple, cheese, prosciutto, crackers. It wasn't supposed to be sexual, and technically it wasn't. But there was something to be said about feeding them, providing sustenance and care, and complete control. It appealed to me on a baser level.

The Dom in me preened.

"Have you had enough, subs?"

"Yes. Thank you, Master."

"Yes, Sir. Thank you."

"You have both pleased me," I said. "I have separate tasks for you this afternoon. You will resume your separate schedules until three o'clock when you will shower and prepare for your night at the social. Hunter, I have asked Ephraim to join us early. It's more of a social visit, but I thought you might appreciate the time to talk to him about any concerns you might have."

His brow furrowed. I knew he would simply do as I had instructed, but I wanted him to be clear.

"If you're worried or stressed about tonight or the decision you need to make tomorrow."

He opened his mouth, then closed it and looked down at the table. "Thank you, Sir."

"Hunter, look at me," I said, and he did. "I don't want to

pressure you. The decision needs to be yours. Ephraim can help you with any questions, as a third party with no personal interest. He's assured me he won't influence your decision."

Hunter frowned, and Levin had his chin to his chest. I needed to provide support and guidance, and I could only do that being their Dom. "You will meet with him in my office at four o'clock."

He gave a nod. "Yes, Sir."

Yes, he responded to domination, and yes, he might have even needed it. But I struggled to be as detached as Master Colton insisted. It wasn't how I treated my subs. "Hunter," I said gently. "I need you to know something. No matter what you decide, you have a place in the dominion. Whether that's with us or with someone else, that's up to you. But you needn't worry about having a place to be. You'll always have a place in the Sanctus. You just need to find a Dom that speaks to your sub."

He nodded but kept his head down.

"Hunter, are you scared?" I coaxed.

He swallowed hard. "Yes."

I reached out and put my hand to his shoulder. "Doing what's in your heart isn't easy."

He glanced up sharply. "Sir?"

"Yes, sub?"

"What do you think I should do?"

My heart beat triple time even though my stomach sank. "I can't answer that. I wish I could, but I can't sway you in either direction." I took a deep breath and put on a brave face. Despite me wanting to demand he stay with us or even beg him to, I knew I couldn't. "I just want you to be happy and in a healthy mental space."

"Will Ephraim tell Master Colton I'm not ready?"

"Absolutely not." I took Hunter's hand and looked him square in the eye. "Ephraim will be here as a friend. I want you to feel confident walking into that meeting tomorrow, and talking with Ephraim might clear up a few things in your mind. So you can enjoy the social tonight and wake up tomorrow ready to make your decision. That's all."

Then his actual words replayed in my mind.

"Hunter, do you feel you're not ready?"

He turned his cuff around and around his wrist. "I don't know."

I heard Levin's sharp intake of breath and had no doubt Hunter heard it too. Levin looked about ready to cry, and it broke my heart.

Hunter frowned. "I never meant to make you sad," he said to Levin.

"Master, please," Levin said, his tone, his eyes begging.

I knew what he was asking. He wanted me to try and influence Hunter into staying. "I can't," I replied gently.

Hunter's bottom lip trembled. "I promise I won't make you sad anymore," he whispered.

Levin shot to his feet. "Master, tell him," he cried, his eyes brimming with tears. "Tell him to stay!"

I put my hands on the table and stood up as well. "That's enough, sub!" I yelled back at him.

I'd never raised my voice at him, ever. My tone made him recoil and he dropped his head, but then he put his hands to his face and sobbed. "Sorry, Master."

I kept my anger in check, though he'd crossed a line and he knew it. "You will go upstairs right now, sub. Collect the flogger and kneel at the foot of the cross."

Levin took a step backwards, but before he could leave, Hunter got to his feet, his eyes teary and wide with fear. "Please Sir. Please don't whip him." He shook his head and almost knocked his chair over, but he scrambled to right it. He shook his head again, tears now streaming down his face. He was pale, and he could barely even speak. He struggled to breathe, and I'd never, ever, seen such terror and panic in a person before. It scared me to see it now.

He gasped back a wild breath. "Don't whip him because of me. Please, please."

"Hunter," I said, putting my hand out, but he recoiled, stepping back into his chair and he almost fell. Levin caught him and he resisted the contact at first, but then clung to him and sobbed.

Levin held him tight, protecting him. He was crying too, tears trailing down his face, and he looked at me over the top of Hunter's head and said one word that stopped my world from turning.

"Red."

CHAPTER NINE

I'D NEVER FELT SO out of my depth. I had no idea what I was doing. I had lost control—of my subs, of my house, of my heart.

And for a Dominant, control was everything.

Levin and Hunter both sat on the sofa in the sitting room, both still upset and horribly sad. But that wasn't the part that broke my heart the most. It was the fact they sat together, holding hands.

I stood staring out the window, engulfed by the sun, yet I felt as though I was stumbling blind in the dark. And as hard as it was, I needed to be the Dom these boys deserved.

I walked to the sofa opposite them, sat down and wiped my hands on my thighs. "First, and most importantly, I want to thank Levin for using his safe word."

Levin's eyes welled with tears. "I didn't do it for me."

"I know." I tried to smile for him but couldn't really manage it. "You saw a situation where one of us felt unsafe and made the right decision. Thank you. And I also need to apologise."

They both stared.

"I was wrong. I thought I could handle this, I thought I knew what I was doing, but . . ." I swallowed, my mouth dry. "I was wrong."

Levin opened his mouth to say something, but I raised my hand, making him pause. I wasn't finished.

"Hunter, you needed a home where you felt safe, and I failed to provide that. And Levin, I threw you in the deep end without any preparation, and that is a failure on my behalf. I truly am very sorry."

Levin shook his head, his chin wobbled as new tears rolled down his cheeks. "It wasn't your fault, Master. None of us could have prepared for this."

"I should have. I have a duty of care and consent to you both." I swallowed down the lump in my throat. "And I failed. I should have seen this coming. I should have been the one to safe word. I shouldn't have put you in a position where you had to, Levin. So I failed. And I'm so very sorry."

Hunter struggled to speak. "Is this my fault?"

"No!" Levin and I said together.

Levin took Hunter's hand in both of his, turning to face him. "No, Hunter. No."

I shook my head slowly. "Hunter, this was in no way your fault. Levin and I weren't expecting . . ." *God, was I really going to say this?* Then it occurred to me, that if I didn't speak the truth now, I'd have failed him again. "Hunter, we weren't expecting the emotional connection with you. It surprised us both. And then coupled with the fact you could be leaving, and with that uncertainty hanging over our heads . . ." I let out a slow breath. "I've been trying so hard to buffer you from any emotion we might feel because I didn't want to influence you, but I can see now that was a mistake. I should have trusted in your ability to make a fair judgement call on your own future. I was trying to remain impartial, and . . . I was wrong."

I ran my hand through my hair and let out a shaky breath. Fuck it all to hell.

"Master?" Levin asked, his voice whisper quiet. "What are you saying?"

"I've never failed before," I admitted. "At anything. And I failed epically here."

Then Levin's breathing changed and his chest started to heave. His face drained of colour, panic setting in. "What does that mean? What are you not saying? I used a safe word, I didn't remove my collar . . ."

Fucking hell, no. I got up from my seat and crossed the floor and went to my knees in front of them. I put one hand over their joined hands and the other on Levin's knee. "Breathe for me, Levin. Breathe in, nice and slow. Let it out."

He did as I instructed, and after a few times, he calmed down. "I can't lose you," he whispered with honest to God fear in his eyes. "You sound like you're leaving me."

"Levin, you're not losing me, and I'm not leaving you." I put my hand to his beautiful face. "Ever. Okay? I made a promise to you when I claimed you that I would take care of you forever, and I meant it. And I will prove to you that I can right the wrongs from today. Using a safe word doesn't diminish your collar. If anything, it reinforces its very purpose. You're not losing me, and I'm not leaving you. Please tell me you believe me."

Levin finally smiled, with more tears, but he nodded. "Yes, Master. Thank you."

Hunter sniffled, wiping his face. "I'm sorry," he mumbled. "I didn't mean for any of this to happen."

I took his hand. "Hunter, you have nothing to apologise for. You were treated horribly by your last Dom, and then you come here only to have the wheels fall off again. That's not fair on you, and I am truly sorry. I promise, we're better than this. I'm better than this. I fucked up today, and believe me, I'll learn from it."

It wasn't lost on me that I was kneeling in front of them. Yet it somehow seemed fitting. So I sat back on my heels, put my hands in my lap, closed my eyes, and inhaled deeply. I needed to centre myself, and I needed to feel the gravity of what had happened. I needed to own it, and I needed to learn.

I opened my eyes and tried a new approach. "Hunter, if you're not ready to make a decision or if you need more time, I'll tell Master Colton, and you will get whatever you need. A week, a month, whatever. You can stay here for as long as you need to decide. Or I can get you a room back at the Casa for whenever you wish. Your prospect of doing hair design remains, regardless of where you choose to stay. You don't lose anything I've offered, should you wish to look for a new Dom."

"Thank you," he whispered.

"The social is on tonight," I furthered. "But given the course of events today, if you'd both rather not attend, I'll send a belated apology. No questions asked. And I can ask Ephraim to reschedule his visit. I'm not sure if you're feeling up for that on top of everything else we've been through this afternoon."

"I'll still talk to Ephraim," Hunter said. "I think it might help."

I smiled up at him, and Levin smiled too, squeezing his

hand.

"I think it wouldn't hurt," Hunter said, his bottom lip pulling down. "Um, I actually think we could all probably do with a session with Ephraim."

Levin put his hand to his mouth and snorted out a teary laugh, and I tried not to smile. Because he was right. "I think you're right, Hunter. I think that's a very good idea."

The heavy, sullen mood lifted a little, and Levin let out a long sigh. "Master, I'd like to apologise also. For how I spoke to you at the table. I was very rude and disrespectful, and if my punishment still stands, I won't object."

I put one hand on each of their knees. "I'm willing to let it go, Levin. Quite frankly, what you said needed saying. And although our methods were wrong, I'm kind of glad we cleared the air. I feel a bit better now we've spoken about it." Then I looked to Hunter. "And I need you to please know, I would never, ever whip or flog Levin out of anger. I'm sorry that frightened you before. I should have been more mindful."

"I know you wouldn't," he whispered. "I do know that. I just panicked. I've never heard you raise your voice before and you mentioned flogging him and, and, I . . ."

"Shh," I soothed. "You don't need to explain. I understand. It was my fault. We're all feeling pressured at the moment, but that's no excuse."

"Hunter," Levin said, squeezing his hand. "I know you don't like it, and I know you have your reasons. But I do like the flogger and the crop and paddle. They give me sharper focus, and sometimes when I'm floundering or feel like I'm lost, it really helps me. Master is very good and never unkind. He specialises in the bondage and domination, not the sadism and masochistic side. Same coin, but very different sides. And if he says he'll never use a flogger or whip on you, then you can believe him. He would never breach your trust like that. But if I need it and if I ask him, he will give it to me."

Hunter looked right at him and nodded. "Okay."

Levin sighed and stretched his neck, then rolled each shoulder. He was out of sorts, off kilter. I knew exactly how he felt.

"Just thinking about it . . . ," Levin whispered. He shuddered, looking uncomfortable, then looked at me, his gaze beseeching. "Master?"

"Would it help?" I asked. "It's intense, and you've already had an emotional dump today."

Then, what he did, almost brought me undone. It unpicked my seams, yet bolstered me, fortified me.

He let go of Hunter's hand and slid off the sofa to kneel in front of me. He had one knee between mine, almost wedged between me and the couch, and he put his forehead to my chest. "I need you to remind me who I am," he whispered. "Bring me into line, make nothing else exist. Please. I need this. And so do you."

And so do you . . .

Christ. He was right. He knew what I needed like I knew what he needed. It was both gratifying and humbling. I put my hand at the back of his head, gently massaging his nape. He was tense, stressed, and strung tight.

He needed to let go, and I needed to be the one to help him.

I cupped his jaw and lifted his face. "Are you sure?"

He didn't even blink. "Yes, Master."

I kissed him. "Go upstairs. Strip naked and stand by the cross. Wait for me."

He shivered and pushed himself up and walked out of the room, leaving me with Hunter. "Hunter," I murmured,

"I want you to watch. I'm aware the idea of seeing this makes you anxious, but I think not seeing it, hearing him moan and yelp and *imagining* what I'm doing to him would be worse. You can wear a shirt if that makes you feel safer. And sit along the far wall near the door, if it becomes too much, you can get up and go to your room. No questions asked. But I think seeing what I do and how he responds will help. That way you will know I'm not hurting him."

He swallowed. "Okay, Sir."

"Good boy. And remember, you can leave the room at any time."

He nodded. "Thank you, Sir."

Sir.

I didn't know whether I loved or hated that word.

I got to my feet and held out my hand. "Come. He doesn't like to be kept waiting."

Hunter smiled at that and gave me his hand. I laced our fingers, which surprised him, and held his hand all the way up the stairs where I stopped. "Would you feel more comfortable being fully dressed?" I thought perhaps covering his back would be like an added layer of protection, more mental than physical, but protection nonetheless.

His eyebrows drew together. "Sir, if I can't trust you when I'm fully dressed, how can I trust you when I'm naked?"

My breath caught. I cupped his face and brought him into my embrace, sighing at how right it felt. "You are a remarkable boy." I kissed his forehead. "Thank you."

Taking his hand again, I walked him into the playroom. Levin stood next to the cross, naked, his head bowed, his cock half-hard, hanging long between his legs. It was such a beautiful sight.

But I didn't take Hunter to his seat near the door. Still

holding his hand, I led him to the wall where the props hung. His breathing was a little shallower, but I needed to reassure him that what Levin was about to go through wasn't pain.

I ran my finger down the leather flogger. "This is a punishment flogger. Feel how the single strand is hard, more rigid and heavy," I murmured.

He touched it, gingerly. Then he nodded.

Then I felt the suede flogger. "And this is soft and light. Almost like a feather. It has more tails, which gives it a sweeter bite."

He touched it and nodded.

"It's Levin's favourite," I explained, pulling the suede strands through my hand. "He prefers more sensation play than impact play, and it's the one I'll be using today. And this," I added, touching the riding crop with the suede leather tip. "See how it's soft too?" Hunter nodded. "Levin loves it. So you can see I'm using the soft ones, his favourites."

Hunter nodded again, but he didn't seem too comfortable, so, still holding his hand, I led him to the seat by the door. He sat down and I put a finger to his chin, making direct eye contact. "I'm going to get him ready now. Are you feeling okay?"

"Yes, Sir," he replied.

"Hunter, so we're both clear . . ." I paused so as not to rush him. "You can leave this room at any time during this session. You don't need to safe word; you can just leave and go to your room."

"Yes, Sir. I can."

I almost leaned down and kissed him but stopped myself. Instead, I thumbed his bottom lip. "Good boy."

Then I went to Levin. He'd been waiting long enough. I

took his face in my hands and kissed him. "I've asked Hunter to watch so he knows I'm not hurting you. Is that okay with you?"

"Oh yes, Master," he breathed.

I smiled. "Good sub. I'm going to prepare you now. I want you to breathe deep for me while I get your things ready."

I went to the wall and wheeled over the wooden trolley. I collected the flogger and the crop, but also two spreader rods with shackles, a blindfold, and Levin's favourite prostate wand, then wheeled the trolley back to Levin. The St Andrew's cross was one of my favourite apparatus. It was solid oak construction with soft leather padding at the junction, eye bolts all the way down the sides for different heights, and this one had a chain between the top of the X, for times such as these.

"Your hands," I ordered Levin. He put both hands in front of him and I took the spreader rod, explaining for Hunter as I buckled Levin into it. "It has cuffs, similar to the one on your wrist. The rod keeps his arms spread, and when I clip it to the chain at the top of the cross, it means I can turn him around."

Levin was almost panting, his eyes dark, his lips parted.

"You need this, don't you sub?" I murmured.

"Yes, Master. I do."

I gave the spreader rod a tug. "Does this feel secure?"

"Yes, Master."

"Are you ready?"

"Please, Master."

"What are your safe words?"

"Yellow to slow," he breathed. "Red to stop."

"Good boy." I took the blindfold next and slipped it over his head, fixing it so he could still blink but was completely blacked out. I glanced back to Hunter. "By restricting his movement and removing his sight, the only thing he will feel and hear is me."

Then I turned Levin around so he was facing the cross and gradually raised his arms up over his head and clipped him into place. He arched his back, pulling on the cuffs, testing their strength, and he whined. Then I cuffed his ankles with the other spreader rod and stood back to admire him.

He was long and lean, pale and strong. His arms and legs spread wide, his figure in the shape of the X he was secured to. He was on the balls of his feet, his back curved, his ass out. His cock was fully hard now and a deep pink at the tip.

He was so fucking beautiful.

I ran my hand down his shoulder, down his ribs and over the swell of his ass, making him moan. I stepped in close, letting him feel my body behind his. "I'm going to put the wand in your ass now."

He whined again and pushed his ass out.

Greedy boy.

I took the wand and lubed it well. It was black silicone, ribbed and shaped for direct prostate contact. The handle was tear shaped with three buttons: on/off, low, and high. I spread Levin's ass cheeks and rubbed lube over his hole, then pressed the tip of the wand inside him. I slowly angled it in, and by the time it was fully seated, Levin was panting and whining. I hadn't even turned it on yet. Let alone touched him with the flogger.

He wasn't joking when he said he needed this.

I stood up and gripped his hips, rubbing my crotch over the wand, and he cried out. "You can come as often as you like," I whispered in his ear.

He shuddered violently but didn't ejaculate.

I took the crop first and ran the soft suede flap down the length of his back, over his ass cheek, down the back of his thigh and lightly tapped the inside of his leg. Then I drew it up his other leg to his ass, tapping it lightly. "Keep your ass out."

He did, so then I ran the crop over the flesh of his ass and gently patted the wand with the suede tip. He bucked and cried out, trying to find more friction. Tucking the crop under my arm, I took his hips again and stilled him. "Stop moving, or I won't turn the wand on."

He stilled.

"You want me to turn it on?"

"Yes, Master."

I turned back to the trolley. Hunter was still watching, his eyes dark. I deliberately didn't offer him the option of masturbating because I didn't want this to be sexual for him. I wanted him to watch and learn, to trust. It was the same reason I wouldn't be coming either. This was solely for Levin. I needed to be his Dominant, his Master. And Levin needed to know that title meant more to me than an orgasm.

Keeping the crop under my arm, I picked up the flogger and turned back to Levin. I ran it across his shoulders, letting the soft suede fingers caress him, and he moaned. Then down his back and across his ass, letting him feel the softness of it, the tickle, then I gave him a swish of it across his ass, across the wand. He cried out, and I knew he was close.

"You're doing great," I murmured. "You like how I touch you? You like how that feels?"

"Yes, Master!"

I gave him another swish, a little harder, and he gasped and shuddered. I turned him around so he faced me, because I wanted Hunter to see everything I was doing. His cock was leaking precome, so I tapped underneath his balls with the crop. He shot back and cried out, unable to move away, not really wanting to either.

"Please!"

"Please, what?"

"Please, Master."

I gave his chest a swat with the flogger and he groaned. Then his stomach, again, then his ass, and then finally his cock.

"Master, please," he begged.

I gripped the wand and turned it on. His reaction was immediate. He yelped, arched his back, pulling on all restraints. His body went rigid, and his engorged cock began to stream. He cried out as he came, and I gave his ass another swat with the flogger. And just when he thought I might have turned the wand off and let him calm down, I turned it onto high.

He let out a hoarse scream as his whole body was wracked with tremors and his cock swelled and surged, spilling more come onto the floor.

I turned the wand off and slowly pulled it out. He sagged as much as his restraints would allow, still moaning. I put all the props on the trolley so I could take his blindfold off, and I cupped Levin's face with my hands. "You did great, sub."

He shuddered again, and tears rolled down his cheek. "Thank you, Master."

"I'm going to uncuff you now," I whispered, kissing his eyelids. I did his ankles first, planting his feet flat on the floor, then I uncuffed his wrists and slowly brought his arms down. "How do you feel?"

"I feel good, Master," he answered, crying, still a little drunk from his high.

I wrapped my arms around him, taking his weight and holding him tight. For a long moment, we stayed just like that. I rubbed his back, I caressed his hair, I kissed his temple, murmuring sweet nothings in his ear. Telling him how good he was, how perfect, how he made me so proud. It had been an intense day, to say the very least, and we both needed the contact. When his tears stopped, I gave him a soft, warm kiss. "I want to massage you now, then run you a bath," I murmured. "Can you walk to the table?"

"Hmm." He nodded but snuggled back in against my chest, clearly preferring to be held for a little while longer.

"Whatever you need," I whispered, wrapping my arms around him.

I noticed then that Hunter was standing. I thought for a fleeting moment he was about to walk out, but he stepped toward us. "Tell me what to do, Sir."

I smiled at him. "In the cabinet, two towels and the bottle with the blue label would be helpful, thank you."

He went to get them, and Levin unfurled himself from me, so I helped him onto the table. We also used this table for fucking in a variety of positions, but its padded top made for a great massage table after a restraining session.

Levin lay down, face first, his hands by his sides, and Hunter returned with the supplies I'd asked for. "Thank you, sub," I said. He nodded. I wanted to talk about what he'd just watched, but now was not the time.

I laid a towel over Levin's legs and one over his ass, not wanting him to get cold. Then I drizzled some oil onto Levin's shoulders and began to rub. "These muscles have been extended," I explained to Hunter, my voice soothing. "From being over his head and restrained. It wasn't an overly long session, but he was pulling pretty hard. And this oil helps soothe his skin where he was hit with the flogger."

Levin's skin where I'd whipped him was a warm, flushed pink. It was barely even raised, but I was gentle nonetheless.

"Levin, how does that feel?"

"Mmm," he mumbled, almost asleep.

"That good, I take it?"

Levin chuckled. "So good, Master."

Hunter even smiled at that, then he turned to me. "Shall I run him a bath, Sir?"

His compassion and caring nature filled me with warmth. "Yes, please. And thank you, sub. Your thoughtfulness is most appreciated."

He smiled and ducked his head before turning and walking out. I turned my attention back to Levin, ensuring he was well-cared for. I rubbed the salve on his ass cheeks, then turned him over and applied it to his chest and stomach. "Can you sit up?" I asked.

He did, giving me a lazy smile. "Thank you, Master."

"How do you feel now?"

His smile became a smirk. "I feel like I'm flying."

I chuckled and put my hand to his face, making him look directly into my eyes. "I didn't mean physically. You were troubled before, on edge. You wanted me to remind you of who you are."

"I have been reminded," he replied. His eyes were still dark, but this time with something else. It took me a moment to see it for what it was. It was conviction. "And I know now, if Hunter decides not to stay, that we'll be fine. I don't know why I doubted us. Because I belong here, as your submissive. I wouldn't be anywhere else. Thank you, Master. For knowing what I needed and for giving it to me."

I kissed him soundly and pulled him into my neck. "Thank you for knowing that I needed to give it to you." I helped him down from the table. "To the bath with you."

Hunter was checking the water temperature when we walked in, and he was quick to straighten up. "It's not too hot," he said.

"Thank you," Levin replied. He put his hand on Hunter's arm as he went to step into the bath, and Hunter instinctively helped him. He held his arm as Levin lowered himself into the water. And it warmed me through; it made me proud. Levin's words came back to me . . .

"I know now, if Hunter decides not to stay, that we'll be fine. I don't know why I doubted us. Because I belong here, as your submissive. I wouldn't be anywhere else."

And like Levin, I now knew the same truth. Did I want Hunter to stay? Absolutely. But if he left tomorrow, would Levin and I be okay?

Yes, we would.

Having Hunter here and the uncertainty of his stay had unearthed a lot of things between myself and Levin. Bringing in someone new made us question our own positions and needs, and our emotions had been strung tight. But Levin and I were the base, the foundation on which Hunter, or any other man, could rise.

I had faith in Levin and me, in us, and trust. It didn't mean we wouldn't miss Hunter, should he choose not to stay, because we would. But Levin and I were rock solid. I knew that, and I too was sorry I ever doubted us. Maybe doubt was the wrong word. Maybe taken for granted was more apt. I'd always known Levin was perfect for me, but I'd never really dissected and studied the emotional connection we had.

Levin had wiggled his way into my heart, this cheeky,

greedy sub. I was still his Dom, he was still my sub, but he owned me. He owned my heart.

"Sir," Hunter said. "Should I go and clean the playroom?"

He made me smile. "Thank you. I appreciate your initiative."

He disappeared and Levin stretched out in the bath, sinking up to his chin. His eyes were closed, a contented smile on his face. I sat with him a while, bathed him, and asked again if he felt sore anywhere.

"Not at all, Master. I feel great," he murmured. There was a peacefulness to him now, as though he was sailing with an even keel, and when he said he wanted to shower to scrub all the oils and lube away, I left him to it and went in search of Hunter.

He'd had enough time to clean the playroom, I would have thought, but the door was still open so I poked my head in. And what I saw stopped me right where I stood. He was in front of the cross, on his knees but resting back on his heels. The cleaning towels were in a pile beside him as though he'd finished cleaning and had taken a moment to stop and think.

I considered leaving him to his thoughts, but I needed to make sure he was okay. I walked in and he startled, quickly grabbing up the towels. I put my hand up. "Stop. Stay as you were," I said, walking over to him. He paused and went back to how he was resting before. I traced my fingers through his hair, and then I knelt down beside him. I looked up at the cross. "It feels a lot like being in church," I whispered.

He almost smiled. "It does."

"In a lot of ways this has become my church," I mused. "Not in a blasphemous way. I was never overly religious, and I have nothing against it. People find peace and comfort in their faith. And that's what I find here. Not everyone understands that."

"I do," he whispered. "I understand that. I find peace here too. Where I belong. Where people are like me."

"Sexual?"

He nodded, a soft blush pinking his cheeks. I smiled at him. This boy and I were so alike . . . We came from different worlds, but we were similar in many ways. "Did you want to talk about Levin's session?"

He looked from me back up at the cross. "It was . . . different than what I expected."

"Better different? Worse? Or are you still processing it?"

He took a deep breath and let it out slowly. "Better. You were right. I think I needed to see it. I wasn't sure if I'd be able to stay in the room, but then I saw how he responded." He swallowed. "You helped him. I didn't know a flogger could be used for pleasure."

Fucking hell. This poor, poor boy.

I took a deep breath and let it out slowly. "Every single thing in this room is for pleasure. Some people need and enjoy certain levels of pain with their pleasure. I know my limits as a sub and a Dom. I don't mind small doses, in the right measure and by the right hand."

"You . . . as a sub? I just can't imagine it, Sir."

I chuckled. "Oh yes. Master Colton knew which strings to pluck. He could play me like a harp."

Hunter's eyes went wide before he blinked. "Oh."

"But as a Dom, that's not my area of expertise. If someone needed more pain than I would be comfortable in delivering, I'd refer them to a Dom who was more attuned to that skill." I gave him a smile. "I like giving pleasure. So yes, every prop you see here is for the purpose of bondage and domination, to restrain a sub and help them reach that level of high as Levin did earlier."

Hunter's brow furrowed, just a fraction. "Sir, if I . . . if I stayed on here, would you do that to me?" He swallowed, then shot me a frantic look. "Not the whip, not the flogger, that's not what I meant, I—"

I put my hand on his shoulder for just a moment. "I know what you meant. Would I help you find that high? That peace? Yes, I would. As often as you needed it. Any furniture you wish, any prop of your choice. If you want to be restrained, however you want to be restrained. The bench, the cross, the chair, the pommel horse. Blindfold, dildos, wands, Fleshlights, collars. It doesn't even have to be sexual. Whatever you need. Whatever it takes for you to reach that place inside you, where you're free. That's where I will take you."

He swallowed hard, his eyes a little teary, then he nodded. "Thank you, Sir."

"Do you have any other questions? About what happens if you choose to stay with us?"

His eyebrows pinched and he suddenly seemed a little nervous. "Would . . . You said you don't share your subs. And I just wondered if that meant me and Levin? Together, I mean. I would be second sub, right? So you could tell him to fuck me . . ."

The blush on his cheeks deepened as though he liked the idea. He'd clearly given it some thought. "Would you like that?"

"If you ordered him or asked him, then yes."

"No, that's not what I meant. I meant if you and I were in this room and I was helping you reach that place where you're free, would you like Levin to participate?"

"Oh." His blushed deepened. "Uh, yes."

I grinned. "I would like that very much too." Christ. Watching those two together might just do me in. "And I know Levin would like it, a lot."

He smiled shyly and ducked his head.

"You like Levin, don't you?"

His eyes shot to mine, a dash of fear. "He is very kind and thoughtful."

"And sexy, and gorgeous, and sassy, and smart," I added. I gave him a wink. "It's okay. I'm rather fond of him too."

Hunter chuckled. "He's very lucky."

If he thought Levin was lucky, maybe that was a sign he wanted to stay . . . ?

"If you do decide to stay, we'll redo our soft and hard limit forms," I said. "You could add that you want to include Levin in our scenes. And anything else you want or don't want. It's all up to you."

He smiled. "Thank you, Sir."

"Do you feel better now?" I asked. "It's been a crazy day, huh?"

He let out a bit of a laugh. "It has. But yes, I do feel better. Thank you for asking me, Sir."

Then I heard something. I tilted my head and listened to be sure. "Can you hear that?"

It was faint through the chalet walls, but he could hear what I heard. His eyes darted to mine. "What is that?"

I grinned. "Levin's singing in the shower."

Hunter laughed and put his hand over his mouth, and I clapped him gently on the shoulder and got to my feet. "I better go hurry him along before it becomes a full-blown musical production."

Hunter laughed again, and I felt better seeing him smile, even though this day was far from over.

CHAPTER TEN

I OPENED the door to my friend and grinned. "Ephraim, come in. It's been too long." He was a tall Black man in his forties. American born, played basketball through college, where he studied psychology. He had high cheekbones, a jaw that could cut glass, and full, plump lips. I'd often joked with him, saying it was a shame he was straight because I'd loved to have seen those lips around my cock. And he'd always laughed and replied saying I didn't have enough orifices for his liking.

Crude, yes. But meant in fun, and a little Dom humour. We'd known each other for years, and I wouldn't hesitate to call him a friend.

We shook hands as he stepped inside, Louella a close step behind him. She was a tall girl, late twenties, with long brown hair pulled into a ponytail. She had porcelain skin, pouty lips, and mischief in her eyes. She kept Ephraim on his toes, that was for sure.

"Looking lovely tonight," I said to her. Ephraim took Louella's coat and handed it to me.

"Thank you, Sir," she said, her head bowed. She wore a red dress that was fun and flirty and a silver chain around her neck with two interlocking circles. To anyone outside the dominion, it would look like an expensive diamond necklace. Which it was. But it was also her collar. Ephraim wore a ring on his right hand that had two interlocking circles. And I noticed for the first time that she also wore a matching ring. Ephraim always liked to spoil her.

"Come into the lounge," I said to them both. "There's someone I'd like you both to meet."

Levin and Hunter stood, side by side, their hair colour the only noticeable difference between them. They wore matching black jeans, matching grey T-shirts, their new black boots. And they also stood identically: feet apart, hands behind their backs, gazes to the floor. The sight took my breath away.

"Well, Sig," Ephraim mused, his smile wide. "I didn't know you had a kink for twins."

I laughed at that. "I can assure you they're very different." I walked to Hunter's side. "You've met him before, but I'd like to introduce you again. Hunter, this is Doctor Ephraim Deans. Ephraim, this is Hunter Vargo. He's a very special addition to our house." They both nodded to each other. "And this is Louella. She's Ephraim's submissive, and Levin's partner in crime."

Both Levin and Louella smiled at that. "It's very nice to meet you," Hunter said, his voice quiet.

"Why don't you three go into the den," I suggested. "Hunter, I'll call for you in a few minutes. I need to speak to Ephraim first."

The three subs disappeared, and Levin's and Louella's laughter sounded before they even closed the door to the den. I smiled after them before turning to Ephraim and letting out the mother of all sighs.

"Come on, friend," he said, his voice deep and soothing. "Into your office and you can tell me all about it."

We walked into my office, I closed the door behind us, and turned to face him. "Levin safe worded," I blurted out. "He safe worded on behalf of Hunter."

Ephraim's eyes almost popped out of his head. Then he blinked and stared. It took him a second to regroup. "Start at the beginning."

So that's what I did. The very quick, condensed version, but I covered everything.

"You care for the boy," he said.

"I do. I really do. And I tried so hard to protect him, keeping him at arm's length, and I lost it. Levin yelled at me, Hunter freaked out, Levin safe worded, and every single life choice I'd ever made flashed through my mind." I met his eyes. "I failed them both."

"Insulating Hunter from emotional attachment was an interesting decision."

I snorted at his way of saying it was stupid. "It was hardly interesting. It was fucking wrong. I know that now. I thought I was protecting him by not influencing his decision."

"But you course-corrected."

"Yes. Thank God for Levin. He made me refocus."

"He's a good one," Ephraim said.

"He's the best. I think Hunter feels better. He says he does. He's still guarded though. It's hard to tell."

"Of course he's guarded. You just spent the last week keeping him at arm's length."

I sighed. "I showed him affection, all the gentle touches,

to his hair, his face. But nothing more. Do you have any idea how many times I had to stop myself from kissing him? I've thought about fucking him, but that mouth . . ." I let out a breath. "Master Colton told me not to touch him. Said the boy needed to recover and find his trust. And look at what I did." I frowned. "Fucking hell. Do you think Master Colton will remove him regardless?"

Ephraim blinked his surprise. That wasn't something he'd thought of, obviously. He shook his head. "No. He said the decision was Hunter's, and so it will be."

"But I fucked this up, Ephraim. He came from the mess that was Lazzaro to the mess that is me."

Ephraim almost laughed. "Oh please. You're not even comparable. Lazzaro abused that boy. You tried too hard not to hurt him."

"But I still did."

"And you apologised. On your fucking knees, no less." He shook his head, disbelievingly. "Do you know how much weight that carries? An honest, heartfelt apology, where you admitted your wrongs and promised to do better, to *be* better? Sig," he said, shaking his head again. "If that won't make the boy stay, hearing his Dominant apologise? Then he was never going to stay in the first place."

I sighed, long and loud. "I just want him to be happy."

"I know you do."

"He said we all needed to have appointments with you, by the way."

Ephraim laughed. "He said that to you?"

"Yep. After I lost my shit and we spoke freely."

Ephraim chuckled and nodded. "I like this boy already. And I'll book you all in for next week, shall I?"

I wasn't sure if that would be for two or three of us. "Yes, please."

"Call him in," Ephraim said. "Or we'll be late to this party. You know how Master Colton hates tardiness."

I got to the door. "I know I can't tell you what to say or influence him or you in any way," I said. "Just tell him . . . I just want him to be happy."

I LEFT Hunter in my office with Ephraim and went out into the back garden to give them complete privacy. The mountains were stunning, the light breeze was cool, but the afternoon sun was still warm. Bees and butterflies were buzzing around the plants, and it really was beautiful. Everything was tranquil, serene.

So very opposite to the inner turmoil I felt. Today had been one helluva day.

"Everything okay, Master?"

I hadn't heard him come up to me. I turned and gave him a smile. "Paul, you know you can call me Sig."

He laughed, surprised. "Yes, as if you could call Master Colton by any different name."

That made me laugh. "True."

"Do you still require a car to the main house this evening?"

"Still unsure. Sorry for the inconvenience. Hunter's just having a quick session with Ephraim, so we'll see how he's feeling afterwards. He might want to stay in."

"It's no problem." Then he looked out to where the mountains cut the sky. "You seem a little distant," he mused. "Everything okay?"

"Yes . . ."

He nodded. "I was your submissive for four years, and you never were any good at lying."

I smirked at that. "That transparent, huh?"

"I take it that it has something to do with your new boy."

I sighed. "He might not be staying with us past tomorrow."

He turned to face me. "Still undecided?"

"He can stay if he chooses. He's supposed to decide tomorrow."

"And are you worried that he won't stay? Or that he will?" I glanced sideways at him and he must have found his answer because he smiled and nodded. "Right. And how does Levin feel?"

"Levin wants him to stay too."

He nodded. "Michael enjoyed working with him. Said he was a quick learner. Hunter told him that he liked it here, said you were kind."

I don't know why that didn't exactly sound like a compliment. "Did he say anything else?"

Paul smiled, and looked back out over the mountains. "Remember when I first met Michael and I was so conflicted? I wanted to be loyal to you, but I knew I could have something special with Michael."

"He was a better Dom for you. He could fulfil your needs in ways I couldn't."

He conceded a nod. "Yes, and no. He could give me something permanent. I didn't even know it at the time, but that lost-at-sea feeling wasn't really about finding the right Dom. Not for me. It was finding the man who would be my Dom forever."

I frowned at him. "You never told me that."

"Sometimes only a Dom knows what their submissive needs. Michael didn't *tell* me I needed a permanent commitment. He showed me."

"Permanent commitment," I repeated. "Isn't that what we had? Or what I have with Levin now?"

Paul made a face. "There was always the feeling of a guillotine hanging over my submission to you. Maybe I shouldn't say that . . ."

"Please, continue," I said. "I need to know."

"I love the Sanctus. It is my salvation," he said. "And I mean that. But if Master Colton came here tomorrow and said both Hunter and Levin were to leave, what would you do?"

I shook my head, not wanting to even consider that. "I would object!"

"You would. Yet Master Colton or any of the Grand Masters, Jürg or Valente, could do just that. Not that I think they would, but they *could*. And that's a hard thing for a submissive to ignore. Above everything else, we subs need security, right?"

I tried to process what he was saying. "How does this relate to Hunter?"

"Maybe the boy needs permanence. From what you told me when he first arrived, he's been floated around all his life. Maybe he feels he can't get attached because he'll just be made to leave again." He frowned. "Maybe I've said too much. Or maybe I'm way wrong."

"No." I put my hand on his arm. "Thank you for being honest with me. I appreciate that more than you know." He bowed his head and turned to leave, but I stopped him. "Paul, I was good to you, wasn't I?"

He laughed. "Are you kidding me? Master Sig, you were amazing. I wouldn't be who I am today without what you taught me about myself. And I see how both those boys look at you. I don't think you have anything to worry about."

With a bow of his head, he left me with that, and I let out a long, quiet sigh. I looked back out at the view, my mind trying to process all of what was just said, along with my heart. The mountains held a quiet calm about them, and I tried to breathe some of that in for as long as I could.

"Master," Levin said from behind me. "Hunter and Ephraim are done."

"Thank you, Levin." Together, we walked toward the back door. "Does Hunter wish to go to the sub social? Or are we staying in tonight?"

"He wants to go," Levin said, smiling. Then he whispered, "He seemed happy enough, Master. I hope that's a good sign."

"Me too." I stopped and took his hand. "And you? Are you feeling up to going tonight?"

Levin met my gaze, his eyes filled with certainty and honesty. "Yes, Master. I feel great. Much calmer than before. Our session really helped me."

I cupped his jaw and kissed him softly. "Me too."

He seemed to float for a moment. "Shall I let Paul know we're going?"

I nodded. "Please. Tell him ten minutes."

Levin dashed off to the cottage and I went inside to freshen up and grab my coat, and when I came back down, everyone was waiting for me. I went straight to Hunter and cradled his face, pulling him into my chest. "Are you okay?"

He nodded. "Yes, Sir."

"We can stay for as long as you wish. If you become overwhelmed, we can leave."

"Thank you, Sir."

I looked down at his face, at his beautiful eyes, those goddamn lips that taunted me . . . and took a step back. "Very good."

The cars pulled around to the front, and as we stepped outside, Ephraim clapped his hand to my shoulder. "Let them go in my car," he said, nodding to the three subs. "You and I can ride together in your car."

Well shit. That didn't sound good. Not good at all.

CHAPTER ELEVEN

AS THE CAR left the estate, Ephraim still hadn't spoken. He was watching me though. "Are you enjoying torturing me?" I asked. "Because if this is your idea of edging, it needs some work. Perhaps torture is more your style."

He almost smiled. "You know I can't tell you anything."

I sighed. Petulance really wasn't my style, but I was tired of the games. "Can you tell me if he's ready to make a decision?" I asked. "Or does he need more time?"

"He's ready."

I sighed again. Fuck. I stared out the window. There was no point in trying to gauge a response by Ephraim's expression. He had a world-class poker face. Whereas I was transparent, apparently. "Well, I . . . I just hope he makes the decision that's best for him."

"Whether he decides to go or stay, it will be the right decision for all of you," Ephraim replied. "If he stays and his heart isn't in the right place, then that would be disastrous for all of you."

I nodded. I really wasn't in the mood for his Freudian

approach, but he was right. What he was saying made logical sense. Shame my heart didn't agree. "I know."

"I'd still like to see you all next week," he said. "Regardless of his decision, he needs regular appointments."

That I did agree with. "I know."

"And you and Levin," he added. "I think this week has revealed some emotional imbalance that you could discuss."

I nodded again. "Yes." I couldn't get Paul's words out of my head. "Can I ask your opinion on something? Personal, not professional."

He raised an eyebrow. "Sure."

"Do you think the Sanctus would ever separate a sub from their Dom for no legitimate reason?" I could tell by the confusion in his eyes that my question needed some clarifying. "Let me rephrase that. Do you think it's a valid concern for a sub that one day the Sanctus might just walk in and remove them from their Dom without either party's permission? It's probably crazy, and I've never even given it a thought before now. But I'd never had to. I've never seen the Sanctus as anything other than gospel, and my faith in them has been unwavering. But . . ."

"But?"

"But now I'm not so sure. And maybe it's just because I've been questioning every single thing I've done this week. But if any sub is concerned they might be removed . . ."

His frown deepened. "If a sub is concerned about being removed, then it's a valid concern." I was about to clarify again when he raised his hand. "I know what you're saying, and I think it's a fair question. I trust the Sanctus, and I trust our three Grand Masters. With my life, I do. But there are laws within our dominion that could see them take our subs without question. You saw firsthand how they removed Hunter from Lazzaro. For different and valid reasons, I know. But still, the decision is final and binding within the Sanctus law." Then his gaze shifted, intensified. "It's not recognised by the Italian government." It was then I noticed he was thumbing the ring on his right hand . . .

"What . . . what are you saying?" I asked. "Because I noticed you're wearing the same rings . . . Holy shit, are you and Louella married?"

Ephraim smiled and peered out the window. "If you were to ask Louella what she was to me, she would say first and foremost, she is my submissive. She doesn't just play in the lifestyle; it *is* her lifestyle. And her title of submissive means the most to her, as my title of Dom means to me. The title of wife and husband are . . . incidental."

"Holy fucking shit." I'm sure my expression bordered on comical. "But you wear it on your right hand."

He chuckled. "No one questions it when it's worn on the right hand; what difference does that make anyway? My collar around her neck means more to me than the ring on her finger. It means more to her as well. But that marriage certificate, that one piece of paper, that legally binding document, my friend, means no one but us can decide our fate."

I felt like the world had been ripped out from underneath me. I couldn't even get my head around it. I pointed to the front of the car, to the driver behind the soundproof glass. "Paul mentioned something to me earlier . . . Am I the only one who hasn't thought about that?"

"Of course not. Your faith in the Sanctus is strong, and deservedly so. They are decent people, and they rule their dominion fairly and reasonably," Ephraim said. "But perhaps ask Levin or Hunter if they feel the same. Ask if they fear being taken from you."

And in a moment of clarity, I remembered when Master

Colton had called me because he needed to see me urgently. We hadn't known then that he was about to ask me to take on a new sub, but Levin had paled, his voice whisper quiet, and he asked me if Master Colton would recall him . . .

Oh God.

Levin and I could survive them taking Hunter, as awful as it would be, but what if they took Levin . . . ?

THE CAR PULLED into the grand estate of the Casa di Salvezza, home of the Sanctus Infinitus Redemptio, and my heart was beating a mile a minute, my stomach was in knots, and my mind was swimming in circles. This day was one mindfuck after another.

As we stepped out of the car, I tried to school my features and be the rock-solid foundation my boys needed. I had so much going through my head at that moment, I wasn't sure where to even begin. But they were here for a night of fun, dancing, and laughing with their sub-friends. I wanted Hunter to see he wasn't alone, that he could enjoy the Sanctus life, and hopefully he would have a good time.

"I'll meet you in there," I explained to Ephraim. He nodded and escorted Louella inside, and I took Hunter and Levin around the side of the mansion. The sky was getting dark and no one saw us, no one even cared. We went in through the service doors, through the kitchen.

"It's this way," Levin said, taking Hunter's hand.

"Wait," I said. I put my hands to Hunter's shoulders. "People will be curious about you; you'll be with Levin, which they will deduce means you're here with me. They will be interested in you, but every single person in there understands the gravity of hard limits. If you choose a quiet corner, people will respect that. Don't be afraid. Have some fun. And don't let Levin drink too much soda. The sugar rush will be fun to watch, but the crash isn't so pretty."

Levin smiled and Hunter even managed a smirk. "Yes, Sir."

Then I put my finger to Levin's chin. "Look after him. If he wants to leave, we leave."

"Yes, Master."

"Good boys. Now go have some fun."

Still smiling, Levin dragged him through the hall, and they disappeared through a door that I knew led to the large room where the sub socials were usually held. With a deep breath, I steeled myself and made my way through the main foyer to where the Doms would sit and chat, discussing world politics and economies and the latest toys or newest rope techniques.

I stopped just inside the door, because there in full view of every Dom present, knelt Lazzaro.

Naked except for a painfully small cock-cage, cuffed, and ball-gagged. He also wore a posture collar, which meant he couldn't look down. Oh no, he had to look up and meet the eyes of every Dom who walked in.

When Valente had said Lazzaro would be punished, he wasn't kidding. The humiliation, the degradation was worse than getting whipped or paddled.

I stood in front of him, my feet spread, my hands behind my back, and smiled down at him. Master Colton was soon beside me. "So," I said, "this is the piece of shit who hurt my boy."

"Hmm," Master Colton said. "Good place for him, don't you think?"

"Yes. Deserving of anyone who breaks the hard limit

of a sub. Even more deserving of someone who doesn't care what their hard limits are." I peered down over Lazzaro. "Especially after they'd seen the scars on the boy's back."

I watched as he tried to swallow around the ball-gag in his mouth. Was that fear in his eyes? I certainly fucking hoped so.

"I can have a bull whip brought in if you want?" Master Colton said, ever so casually. He popped an olive in his mouth. "Valente had a new one arrive yesterday."

I sneered at Lazzaro. "He's not fucking worth it."

Ephraim joined us. "Come on, Sig. Let's sit. Want a cigar?"

I wasn't in the mood for it, but I went with him. We were greeted into the circle of other Doms, and we began to chat. A general rule in the Sanctus was that Dominants didn't drink alcohol, so we had soda and lime or tonic spritzers, and conversation soon turned to me.

"I heard along the grapevine," Cecilia said, "that you gained another sub last week . . ."

All eyes drew to me. "Yes. Not permanent . . . not yet anyway," I explained.

"Two subs!" Bernard cried, his smile wide and tinged with a little jealousy. "Oh, the gods favour you, Sig."

"Must have kept you busy all week," Javier added, winking.

"Well, balls deep all week, at least," Moriz said, smirking behind his tonic water.

I rolled my eyes. "Busy, yes. But not how you think. I was given strict instruction not to touch him in a sexual manner."

They all let out a chorus of groans and pained scoffs. "Torturous," Adrien said.

"Why were *you* punished?" Ginevra asked. "Who did you piss off?"

I smiled at that but pointed my chin to Lazzaro, still kneeling by the door. "*That* piece of garbage by the door hurt the boy, and he was released into my care for the week."

They all turned to glare at him. "We were wondering what he did to deserve that," Marius said with a sneer.

But talk soon moved on. I got chatting to Adrien and Ginevra, and I didn't even notice Ephraim was gone until I noticed him having a very quiet, private conversation with Masters Colton and Jürg. I had a sinking feeling it was about Hunter, and when Master Colton's gaze flashed to me, I knew I was right.

And for the strangest second, I had visions of me taking Levin and Hunter and leaving. Running away seemed like a brilliant idea. I could . . . what? Jesus Christ. *Did I really just consider running away?* But then guilt crept in . . . I needed to have faith in the Sanctus. I believed in them. I did. I needed to have faith in their decision. I trusted Master Colton, and I respected him. I needed to believe in him now.

What Ephraim said was true. Whatever the verdict, whatever Hunter decided, it was the right thing for us . . .

It had to be.

"Sig?" A hand tapped my shoulder and I looked up from my seat to see Master Colton. "A word, please."

"Of course," I said, standing. My heart was thumping. Ephraim was no longer in the far corner where he'd been talking to Master Colton. In fact, I couldn't see Ephraim anywhere. Master Colton led me to the same corner, out of earshot to the rest of the room. "Master Colton," I said, trying to play it cool. "Anything the matter?"

He took a moment and he studied me. Then his brow pinched in a way I couldn't recall ever seeing on his face. "As a Dom, and particularly as a Grand Master, I'd like to think I am adept at making decisions. It would seem I've made an error."

"No, Master Colton," I blurted out. Fuck, he was about to take Hunter from me. He was going to remove Hunter, regardless of what the boy wanted. And what about Levin? After my colossal fuck-up this week, had I lost the right to any sub? The control I instilled, mastered, prided myself upon, slipped through my fingers. My stomach fell to my feet, and my heart squeezed to the point of pain. "No. I'll work harder, I'll do better—"

He put his hand up, a signal for silence. Then, with his hand still raised, he held up two fingers. "Two mistakes."

Oh fuck.

It was both of them.

Panic blindsided me. It clawed inside me, desperate to find a way out. I couldn't breathe, I couldn't think. "No. You're not taking Levin. I refuse."

He stared at me. "What?"

"You can't." I was trying to stop the horror rising in my throat. It tasted like bile. Fuck.

"I'm not taking Levin," he said softly. Concern and confusion etched his face. "Sig, what are you talking about?"

"I'll admit, I wasn't prepared for a second sub," I whispered. "But Hunter's not an ordinary sub. He's . . . extraordinary. He's all I could want for a second sub, and you must understand any fault is mine. Not the boy's."

He opened his mouth, tilted his head, then started again. "Sig, what *are* you talking about? The mistake was mine. I thought I was doing the right thing for the boy given what he'd been through, but after speaking with Ephraim, I can see what I'd set out for him—"

"Speaking with Ephraim?"

"Yes. He said the boy was struggling with some of the restrictions I set for him. I thought I was doing the right thing, but evidently—"

The door opened and Ephraim walked in. He had Hunter with him, and Levin too. Hunter saw Lazzaro and tried to take a wide berth, but Ephraim steadied him. Levin looked at all the strange faces in the room, and when his gaze finally landed on me, the abject terror in his eyes broke my heart.

And for the second time in one day, my whole fucking world went careening off its axis.

CHAPTER TWELVE

HUNTER LOOKED SCARED AS HELL. Seriously, the only way to describe the look on his face was terrified. And Levin didn't look too much better.

The whole room stopped and stared, and my heart rate was through the stratosphere.

"Boys, don't be scared," Master Colton said. "Come in, let me see you."

They walked over to us, and Levin met my gaze, a thousand questions in his eyes. Hunter had gone from scared to resigned. No, not even resigned.

Defeated.

He looked like the boy I'd met in this very mansion just six days ago. The light in his eyes was gone, his face was drained of colour, his expression completely blank.

Oh, this poor, sweet boy.

I stepped in between them and put my hand up. "Master Colton, stop."

"Sig, I just want to talk to the boy."

I lowered my hand but met his gaze, unflinching. "If you want me to safe word on his behalf, then I will."

Master Colton stared, someone gasped, and the room crackled with tension.

I let out a breath, surprised it didn't sound as terrified as I felt. Levin was brave enough to do it for him earlier, and now it was my turn. "The boy has a hard limit and you're just about to cross it."

Master Colton blinked. "Pardon?"

"He cannot speak or perform comfortably in front of a crowd," I explained as calmly as I could, side-eyeing every Dom now staring at us. "I would respectfully ask you to please move this to a private room."

Master Colton froze for one second, then he took a step back, I realised, to push on a concealed door. "This way."

My breath left me in a whoosh, and I turned to hold out my hand to Hunter. He took it, and Levin was quick to put his arm around Hunter's shoulder, and together, we walked out of the room. Master Colton and his sub Stefan led us down a hall, and I remembered now . . . there were private play rooms along this hall. He entered a room that was dimly lit, but I could see it was set up like a classroom, for teacher and student fantasy play, no doubt. At least it wasn't a whipping room. I thanked God for small mercies.

I turned to Hunter and put my hand to his face. "Are you okay? I'm sorry about that, Hunter. Master Colton didn't know."

He nodded, though he still trembled. "Thank you, Sir."

I pulled him against me. "You're welcome."

"Hunter," Master Colton said. We turned and I let Hunter go so he could face him. I noticed then that Ephraim was here as well, but I didn't have the opportunity to even acknowledge him before Master Colton spoke again. "I would like to apologise also. I didn't know about any hard limits regarding audiences. I should have known that, so please know that I am sorry."

Hunter gave a nod, though he kept his gaze down. "Thank you, Master Colton."

"I've done wrong by you twice. Three times even," Master Colton said, followed by a sigh. He leaned against a student desk. "I'd like to remedy that right now."

I sucked back a breath. We were supposed to have one more day. Panic clawed at my insides, and I didn't know if I had the intestinal fortitude to hear this . . . Ephraim's hand on my shoulder snapped me out my head, and Levin moved to my other side, clinging onto me. I put my arm around him.

"You've had six days with Sig and Levin," Master Colton said. His tone was kind and he smiled, but I doubted Hunter noticed. "Have you enjoyed that time?"

"Yes, Master Colton."

"Hunter, would you feel more comfortable speaking to me without Sig and Levin in the room?"

Hunter looked up then, glancing to me before turning back to Master Colton. "No, it's fine. I'd prefer them here. Please. I'm okay. It's fine."

Master Colton frowned. "Hunter, if I told you that you were free to speak your mind, free from repercussions, what would you say?"

His bottom lip began to tremble. "Nothing. I . . . I wouldn't say anything."

I put my hand to my mouth. This boy was breaking my heart.

"Sub," Master Colton tried again. "I want you to be safe and happy, and I can't help you if you won't be honest with me."

Then, breaking my heart into a thousand pieces, Hunter slowly went to his knees, as though his soul was too tired to stand any longer, and he put his head down and he sobbed. His voice was broken. "I don't understand, Master. Why did you punish me?"

I stepped forward. "What?"

Master Colton raised his hand to me, his face stricken with worry. "Punish you? Hunter, what do you mean?"

He looked up and tears spilled down his cheeks. "You told Sir he couldn't touch me! You made me his sub, but I wasn't. I had to watch him give his real sub everything I longed for. It's all I ever wanted." He sobbed and could hardly speak. He put his hand to his heart. "Master, you put it in front of me but wouldn't let me have it. Was it punishment? Because I don't know what I did that was so wrong? I don't understand."

Oh God. My heart ached, physically ached. My throat closed over and I wanted to cry. I wanted to scoop up this poor boy and hold him, tell him that he was wanted, worthy, that everything would be okay. Levin cried into my side and I squeezed him tight, but I just couldn't stand one more second of watching Hunter break down. He only had one thread left. I swear, if it snapped, I wasn't sure he'd ever recover.

If the boy needed holding, then I would do it. I went to him and knelt in front of him and wrapped my arms around him while he cried. He clung to me, fisting my shirt, and sobbed. "What did I do wrong, Sir? I'll do better, I promise."

"You did nothing wrong," I whispered. "Nothing at all. It is us who did wrong by you. Lazzaro, Master Colton, me, the Sanctus, all of us. I'm so sorry. You deserve better. Tell me what you want, Hunter. Anything and I'll make it happen."

"Sig," Master Colton said, cautious, wary. "That's not your promise to make."

I stood up and put myself between Master Colton and Hunter. An act of defiance to my old Master, but this was my line in the sand. This boy was my stand. "I'm making it my promise. This boy deserves better, by all of us. Especially you. You're better than this, Master Colton. The Sanctus is better than this. Prove it, prove it to me right now, and prove it to Hunter."

Master Colton stared at me, a dozen emotions flickering through his eyes. I doubted anyone had ever spoken to him like that. I couldn't bring myself to care. Master Colton tilted his head, just a fraction. "You would choose him over me? Over the Sanctus?"

"I don't want to have to choose. You have been exceptionally good to me, Master, and the Sanctus is my home. But I will if I have to. And I will choose Hunter. And Levin. Both of them. Equally." I squared my shoulders and met Master Colton's gaze, unflinching. "Because if I can't defend this boy when he needs it most, I don't deserve him."

Hunter sobbed behind me, and when I turned, I saw that Levin was kneeling with him, holding him protectively, and Hunter clung to him.

Master Colton took a deep breath, and then another, as he no doubt gave his thoughts some time. It was a strange silence, and not a particularly pleasant one. Then he let out a sigh that sounded both pissed off and decided. He took a step closer and, looking around me, turned his attention to the two boys. "Hunter, tell me what you want. Do you want Sig as your Master? Or do you want to return to my care?"

Hunter looked up, his eyes red and face pale. "Sig, please. And Levin. Both of them. Please. Please, I'll do anything."

The relief that flooded through me felt electric and heavy, solid and soul-quenching. I hung my head and almost cried.

This fucking day . . .

Master Colton met my eyes and gave a slight nod before he stepped around me to Hunter. I noticed then Ephraim took a step in as well. Not to crowd Hunter and Levin, I realised. But to perhaps protect them if necessary.

Master Colton put his fingers to Hunter's chin. "You realise what you're asking for, boy," he said. "You will belong to Sig. His property, to do with which he pleases. You will serve him, please him. In accordance with the Sanctus Infinitus Redemptio, you offer to him your submission, you surrender all control, and he gives you everything you need to thrive."

Hunter's reply was a sigh filled with longing and need. A promise. "Yes."

"He will collar you and claim you with his body. It is a binding ceremony, by the laws of the Sanctus," Colton continued. "You've been through this once, Hunter. Albeit, with the wrong Dominant, but you know the rules. You know how the Sanctus operates."

Hunter met his eyes. "Yes."

Master Colton gave a nod. "You are to be taken to the ceremony room and prepared."

Oh God . . .

Hunter closed his eyes, as though a weight was lifted from his shoulders. Serenity settled over his face. "Yes. Please."

Master Colton turned to Stefan. "Fetch a collar for the boy, sub." Stefan gave a nod and disappeared.

I was about to collar and claim Hunter as mine. As ours. Mine and Levin's. Hunter was about to be ours.

My body was aching for this, to finally have him, but the boy had had a helluva day. I put my hand to his hair, then cupped his face and waited until his eyes met mine. "Hunter, today's been a roller coaster, yes?" I asked. He nodded. "You have to be exhausted. If you'd rather wait a day, when you've rested, we can complete this ceremony tomorrow."

Something flashed in his eyes and he whispered, "Please don't deny me. I need this. I need to be yours. I need your collar around my neck, and I need your power over me. I need to belong to you both. I can't take one more day. Please."

My ribs felt too small; my heart too big. His begging, his pleading, his fucking lips that had taunted me . . . Then, as if he knew, he smiled and said the one word that crumbled my resolve.

"I need to call you *Master*."

I couldn't fight it another second. I leaned down and brought his mouth to mine. He opened for me as soon as our lips met, moaning as I gave him my tongue. I devoured him, long and deep. He tasted just as I'd imagined, only better. And we kissed for the longest time, righting everything. The constant flux was now calm and complete. Then he sucked on my tongue and groaned.

Fuck.

I pulled away. His eyes were unfocused, his lips wet and parted. He'd made me hard already. I stood up to my full height, still holding Hunter's chin, making him look up at me. "I won't deny you a single thing, sub."

Stefan came back into the room holding a leather collar, identical to Levin's. A thin but sturdy leather with an O-ring at the front where it fastened. Once clipped together, it couldn't be undone.

Master Colton stood beside me and passed the collar to me. It was a profound moment, and it was fitting that Levin knelt beside Hunter, Master Colton beside me, as Ephraim looked on. The two men I admired most were standing, and the two men I adored the most were kneeling.

"Raise your wrist cuff," I ordered. Hunter kept his head down but raised his hand. I unbuckled the cuff and handed it to Levin, then I lifted Hunter's face. "Look at me."

He did. His gaze was imploring, filled with longing.

I thumbed his bottom lip. "This collar is a binding symbol of your servitude, your submission, to me. You release to me your mind, body, and heart. With this collar, you understand your consent now lies with me—you relinquish your control to me. This collar signifies my responsibility to care for and protect you. I will respect you and your needs, and it will be my duty to keep you safe, provide an environment in which you thrive, and I will learn from you. You will belong to me. You will serve me. And I will honour the gift of submission you give to me. I offer you this collar as a commitment to you." I took a deep breath in. "Hunter Vargo, do you accept this collar?"

"Yes," he answered, teary, choked up, the word whispered like a prayer.

"You understand the removal of your collar is a termination of our agreement?"

He nodded. "Yes."

I smiled, my heart about to burst, and I gently placed the collar around his neck. The soft snap of the clip a final and binding sound. Hunter put his hand to the collar and a tear rolled down his cheek. He sighed as though he could only now finally breathe. I leaned down and kissed him again. "You are mine."

He nodded again. "I am yours."

I stood up to my full height, my two subs kneeling before me. Pride and anticipation exploded inside me. "He's ready." I glanced at Levin, whose lips were curled with the hint of a smile, his eyes glassy. "First sub," I addressed him. "Take him to the ceremony room."

"Yes, Master," Levin said, getting to his feet. He helped Hunter to his.

Colton said, "Stefan will attend you."

I'd almost forgotten Stefan was there. The three subs were quickly out the door, which left me and Master Colton and Ephraim.

"That was beautiful," Ephraim said, his eyes warm. "Are you ready for this?"

"Very ready," I replied, then looked from Master Colton back to Ephraim. "What did you say? To make this happen? It was supposed to be tomorrow."

"The boy needed permanence," Ephraim replied, and he gave me a wink. "He needed your collar, Sig. He needed it more than you needed to give it to him, which was a lot. You two were about to break. Or combust. The boy needs domination. *Your* domination, Sig. He should have had it six days ago." That comment was aimed directly at Master Colton.

Master Colton sighed. "Yes. I can see things were fraught between you. I didn't realise to what extent. I think you and I, Sig, need to sit down and have a chat."

Yeah, he really didn't like me questioning his authority or his ability to make the right decision. I gave him a nod. "Yes, we do."

"But right now, you have a ceremony to perform," he said. "No audience, right?"

"I know it's Sanctus custom to bear three witnesses," I began.

Master Colton shook his head. "A sub's needs come first," he said. "Just one witness. I'll do the honours."

Ephraim put his hand on my shoulder. "I'll be in touch during the week for those appointments," he said. He held up three fingers. "Three appointments?"

I smiled with the realisation that yes, everything I did now and from this day forward would be for three. "Yes, please."

He gave me a grin and walked out, leaving just me and my old Master. I bowed my head when I spoke. "I want you to know, I meant no disrespect earlier."

Master Colton chuckled. "Yes, you did. But you were right." I shot him a look, and he smiled. "Don't look so surprised. You said if you didn't defend the boy when he needed it most, you didn't deserve him. And I knew right then, Sig, you were already that boy's rightful Dom. Because if we don't look after them, we don't deserve them. You reminded me of that tonight." He sighed. "I could have done without the tone or the standoff," he added, and I smiled. "But we learn from our subs, and it looks like I'm learning from you still."

"Thank you, Master Colton," I said, heartfelt and honest. "It means a lot to hear that."

"I'd still like to sit down with you," he said. "And just talk. Next week or the week after. I'll let you get settled into your new life with two subs."

"Thank you."

"And speaking of which, we best not keep him waiting."

THE CEREMONY ROOM was in the dungeon. In actual fact, it was the original dungeon from the very first Sanctus that Master D'Ascenzo had founded hundreds of years ago. It had been remodelled and modernised, of course, but the original stone floor and walls remained. It was small compared to the rest of the mansion. It was the original room where he'd taken the three boys, where they'd bonded and submitted to him. Where the Sanctus was born.

It was fitting that all ceremonies be performed here.

The walls were dark stone, warmly lit. There was other furniture: a St Andrew's cross, a padded bench, a cage, and a wall of whips and cuffs and chains. But at the centre of the room was the crowning piece and atop it the jewel. Two padded wooden blocks protruded from the stone floor, to knee height. Exact replicas of the ones Master D'Ascenzo had made. They were knee rests, shoulder-width apart, and Hunter was kneeling on them. His hands were cuffed and chained above his head leaving his ass at a perfect, deliberate height. He was suspended, unable to move, and ready to be claimed. This ancient tradition was a sacred ceremony. A ritual that binds a Dom and a sub.

For the submissive it was an honour. I should know. I'd knelt on these very blocks for Master Colton.

For the Dominant, it was a privilege, almost like gaining rank. Like when I claimed Levin on these same blocks. A privilege like no other.

But at its most base level, it was the exchanging of gifts. Hunter's gift to me was his submission. In return, he was receiving the domination he craved in a safe, structured, and protected environment. His every wish would be met; his every need, every desire. He'd want for nothing. I would make sure of it.

He was a glorious sight. His pale body stretched on display, my collar around his neck. His thighs were strained, his shoulders too. His cock hung heavy and half-hard. His head hung low; his breathing was even and measured. He was putting himself in that subspace. Getting ready.

Levin and Stefan had secured him, made sure he was safe and comfortable.

I didn't have to double check. I had no doubt they'd done it right.

I stood in front of him and he looked up slowly and smiled. I kissed him again, plundering his mouth with my tongue, and the sounds of chains above us sent shivers down my spine. I pulled away when he was breathless and panting. His cock was fully erect now, and that pleased me.

Very much.

I ran my hand down his neck to his chest. I squeezed his nipple and he bucked. *He likes that.* I pressed my palm down the side of his ribs to his hip and walked around the wooden block. His scarred back was beautiful in this light—in any light—and I placed a kiss between his shoulder blades, down his spine.

I cupped the flesh of his ass and noticed he'd been fitted with a plug. He was here for the taking; he was here for me. My cock twitched and throbbed at the thought.

I walked full circle to stand in front of him. I lightly fingered his collar, then lifted his chin with my pointer finger. His blue eyes were dark and glazed with desire. His lips were pink and plump, perfect for my cock. But not right now. Soon . . .

I clasped my hands behind my back. "Your name?"

"Hunter Vargo."

"You have agreed to give me your submission? You need me to dominate you, Hunter?"

He gasped. "Yes, Sir."

I tightened my hold on his jaw, just a little. That word . . . sir. I still wasn't sure if I loved or hated it. "You're familiar with the rules of the Sanctus?"

"Yes, Sir."

"You know your safe words?"

"Yes, Sir. Yellow to slow, red to stop."

Good boy. I moved in close. "You understand what I'm about to do to you?"

"Yes, Sir."

"Tell me."

"You will claim me. You will fuck me and come inside me. I will be yours."

My belly tightened with anticipation. "You will live with me and Levin as our second sub."

"Yes, Sir."

"You will obey Levin as you would me. He will care for you and tend to you, he will protect you, as I do. If I want him to fuck you or suck you or if I asked you to pleasure him, would you like that?"

He gasped. "Oh yes, Sir."

I glanced at Levin and he met my gaze with pride and lust in his. *Oh yes. We would both take such good care of this boy.*

"Tell me, Hunter," I whispered his name. "Are you ready to sign yourself over to me?"

His pupils dilated. "Yes, Sir."

"When you belong to me, I can remind you of your submission at any time," I murmured against his mouth. "I can put my cock in your mouth any time, any place, and you will suck it, won't you?"

He licked his lips. "Yes, Sir."

"I can fuck you whenever I want," I said and pinched

his nipple. He gasped and pulled on the chains. "I can bring you balance. I can deliver you to that place where you are free. Is that what you want?"

"Oh yes, Sir."

I stepped in so I could whisper against his mouth. "When I'm done with you, when you finally have my come inside you, you won't call me Sir, will you sub?"

He whined. "No, Sir."

"What will you call me?"

"Master."

I took a step back and looked to Levin. He was watching, his hands behind his back, a smile on his face. And Master Colton was in front of the whipping wall, Stefan kneeling beside him. "He's ready," I announced.

Hunter pulled on the chains, and the sound was magical to me. I hadn't even really touched him yet, but he was already squirming in anticipation.

I turned around and took my jacket off, handing it to Levin. Then my shirt, one button at a time, and Hunter broke out in gooseflesh with each sound. I slipped out of my shirt and handed it to Levin. I took Levin's chin between my thumb and forefinger. "Are you ready for me to do this to him, sub?" I whispered against his mouth. "To be first sub, to tend to him, to care for him as I care for you?"

Levin melted into me a little. "Yes, Master."

I kissed him before letting him go. I hadn't exactly been prepared for this ritual. I wasn't wearing my leather pants, but my suit pants would have to suffice. Favourite attire or not, I was ready. I was aching and so fucking hard.

My cock throbbed, knowing what was about to transpire. I was about to claim this boy as mine. As ours. But this was more than that. I was ready to take Hunter into my home, to care for him, to meet his every need.

I stood behind him so he could feel the heat of my body, the warmth of my breath. He pulled on the chains and it sent a rush of warmth through my body. "Are you ready for me?" I whispered into the back of his neck.

He whimpered. "Yes, Sir."

His thighs were spread wide, his ass was too. *So fucking beautiful.* I took hold of the plug and massaged it. "Your ass is ready for me." Slowly, I pulled it out, twisting as I did. Hunter whimpered again, and he drew on his restraints, and the sound of chains clattering sent a shiver down my spine.

I handed the plug to Levin and he gave me a bottle of lube in return. I spread Hunter's ass and examined his open hole. "Mmm," I hummed. "So ready."

I rubbed my thumb around the opening, watching as his skin reacted to my touch. He let out another whimper and the chains jangled again. He was pulling on his arms, trying to push his ass down onto my thumb. He whimpered when I denied him.

"You'll get it when I give it to you," I said, running my hand down the back of his thigh. Then I ran my hands up his back, shoulders, and arms to the leather shackles around his wrists. I leaned my weight on him, stretching his back and pushing my hardened cock against his open hole. "And believe me, you'll get it soon enough."

Still leaning against him, I undid my belt buckle and he froze. It was infinitesimal, but I felt it; his reaction to my belt. I gripped his hips and rubbed his hole over the ridge in my pants. "I will never hurt you," I breathed into the back of his neck. "I will give you a pleasure you've never known."

He relaxed again, the tension leaving his shoulders, so I undid the button on my suit pants, unzipped the fly. Hunter groaned at the sound. I pulled out my cock, hot and heavy, and I pressed it into the crack of his ass cheeks. He whined again.

"Nine inches of pleasure, Hunter," I whispered into his ear, then sucked on the lobe. Taking the bottle of lube, I slicked us both and pressed my cockhead against his hole. "Are you ready to be mine?"

"Yes, Sir," he answered, breathily. "Please."

I pushed inside him. He was hot and tight, and he cried out as I filled him. I gripped his hips and impaled him, driving in until every inch of me was buried inside him. My chest was against his back, my lips at his ear. "Breathe."

He sucked in air and whined on the exhale. He pulled on the restraints and gasped as I thrust in again. "That's it, boy. Take my cock."

The constant sound of chains spurred me on. And so I fucked him. I stood between his spread legs, held onto his hips while his arms were restrained above his head, and fucked him.

His groans got longer, and he moaned like a whore.

My whore.

"You like that, don't you boy?"

He moaned again as I thrust into him. The sounds he made were heavenly.

And then I stopped. I held him so he couldn't move, my length still fully embedded in his ass. It was throbbing inside him; my pulse beat double time with his. With his back to my chest, I whispered in his ear, "I'm going to show you what real pleasure is. How good it can be."

He was trembling, and his breath was coming fast.

"Levin?" I called. He quickly stood beside me. "Would you like to taste him?"

"Oh yes, Master," he breathed his reply.

"Then kneel before him and suck him."

Levin was quick to kneel in front of Hunter. Hunter flinched and gasped, and I knew Levin had taken him in his mouth. I smiled into the back of Hunter's neck. "Oh, he's got a talented mouth, hasn't he?"

Hunter sucked back a sharp breath, his voice hoarse. "Yes, Sir."

"You won't come until I do, understand?" I demanded roughly. I started to thrust slowly again, sliding my cock in and out of him. "No matter how hard he sucks you, or swallows around you, or swirls his talented tongue up your shaft, you mustn't come."

Hunter whined. His whole frame trembled, absorbing the pleasure I allowed him. My cock in his ass, my Levin sucking his cock.

Changing the angle of penetration, I pushed in deeper and deeper. I held his hips, pulling his ass down onto my cock, making him moan, long and low. "Only when I've come inside you will you come down his throat," I rasped into his hair.

He made a strangled sound and pulled hard on his restraints. He was too close, being rocked between us, my cock and Levin's mouth. And even as controlled as I was, I knew I wouldn't last much longer, and neither would Hunter. He was moaning non-stop—such a vocal boy— groaning, panting, slapping, slurping, the chains protesting. The room was filled with sounds of our fucking; this claiming.

"I'm going to come inside you," I breathed heavy in his ear. "Mark you as mine so everyone will know who you belong to."

Hunter grunted and strained. He was at his limit, and I

was ready for this claiming to be complete. I leaned back and pulled his ass hard onto my hips, as deep as I could go. "And you are mine," I grated out, my forehead between his shoulder blades as my cock swelled and lurched. I rammed into him one final time before shooting my precious seed deep inside him.

A loud, strangled scream escaped him. His head fell back, his back arched, and he rocked violently as he came down Levin's throat.

Levin groaned as he drank, sending ripples through the boy between us. And I continued to thrust, slow and deep, prolonging his orgasm. Slick, wet, and hot, there was nothing I loved more than feeling my own come inside my sub. I had filled him, claimed him.

There was no doubt now. He was mine. He was ours. He belonged to me, and to Levin.

We had just become *three*.

I was reluctant to pull out of him, but Hunter was completely spent, boneless. Drained. I quickly did up my pants and Levin offered me my shirt before we both released Hunter from his wrist restraints, and put his feet on the floor, but he swayed with exhaustion. Levin put a robe around him, and knowing Hunter couldn't walk out, I picked him up, bridal style, and gave Master Colton a nod.

"You put on quite a show, Sig," he said. "Forgive me for not walking you out, but my Stefan here has been a very good boy today. I think I'll reward him."

I looked at Stefan. Still kneeling, still in perfect position. "Yes, I think he deserves that."

"I'll be in touch within the week to see how your new submissive is settling in," Master Colton added. Then he smiled. "Though I think he'll be just fine."

Levin had collected my shirt and jacket and Hunter's jeans. He opened the door for me, and before the door was closed behind us, Master Colton already had Stefan spread over the bench, moaning.

CHAPTER THIRTEEN

THE CAR RIDE home was quiet. Hunter was almost asleep on me. Though I held him tight to my side, he still fisted my shirt as though I might disappear. I kissed the top of his head. "You have nothing to worry about, sub. You belong with us now."

Levin smiled, his eyes filled with warmth and affection, for me, for Hunter. He stayed silent though and I knew he'd have questions. We would have a lot to talk about, but that could wait until tomorrow. This day had been long and a horror roller coaster of highs and lows. It was ending on the highest high, though. And I wanted it to stay that way.

I had Paul drop us at the front of the house, and when Levin opened the front door, I helped Hunter inside. He was utterly drained and still clinging to me. I didn't want him to be alone.

"My room," I whispered to Levin.

He blinked back his surprise, then shot up the stairs. When I helped Hunter into my room, the bed was folded back, the lights dimmed. But that was Levin, considerate to the last.

I took off Hunter's robe and laid him down, then stood back, marvelling at the sight of him naked in my bed, wearing my collar. Levin stood at my side, head bowed, hands clasped at his back. I turned to him and cupped his face, lifting upward so I could see his eyes. "You were perfect tonight," I whispered. "You made me very proud."

He smiled serenely and leaned into my palm. "I could say the same about you."

"Did you like watching me claim him?"

His gaze darkened. "Oh yes, Master. Very much."

I chuckled. He was such a sexual thing. "Did you like sucking him?"

His nostrils flared. "I loved it."

I pulled his lips to mine and kissed him. "And you will be rewarded," I murmured. "Tomorrow. Today's been an emotional day. I think a sound night's sleep will do us all the world of good. And tomorrow I'll give you whatever you want."

He preened a little. "Thank you, Master. Shall I go to bed now?"

"Yes. Here in my bed, with me, with us," I nodded to the far side of my bed. "Tonight, both subs sleep with me. I don't want Hunter to wake alone. And I want him to wake up with both of us so he knows to whom he belongs. You're my first sub now," I reminded him. "He will need you, always. As I do."

Levin's eyes shone with pride. "I am honoured, Master."

I tilted his head and kissed him again. "You are perfect. Now get into bed and sleep, and don't worry about your schedules in the morning. Sleep as long as you want. You'll need your energy tomorrow."

He took his clothes off and slid into my bed on the other side of Hunter. I toed off my shoes and stripped as well, marvelling at the sight of two subs in my bed, naked but for the collars around their necks.

My balls drew up, my cock began to fill, but I ignored it. I would have enough of them tomorrow, and all the days after. So I got into bed, and Levin and I sandwiched Hunter. The boy stirred but soon nestled into me. I pulled up the covers and stretched my arm over both of them.

Sleep came quickly, followed by pleasant dreams of contentedness and joy, times two.

I dreamed of leather and chains and plump lips, of pale bodies and tight holes, whispers of thanks and groans of ecstasy . . .

It was so real, so tangible, it woke me. I was hard and aching, precome smeared on my belly. I could roll one of them over and plough into him, or both of them if I wanted, but for now I preferred to watch them sleep.

Hunter faced me, his expression peaceful, beautiful. And Levin spooned him with his arm tight around him, his face pressed to the back of Hunter's head. Their collars matching.

It was perhaps the most beautiful thing I'd ever seen. It made my heart do crazy things.

Levin woke first, possibly feeling my eyes on him. He startled ever so briefly, then smiled and stretched like a cat, only to freeze and reach between them, giving himself a squeeze. "Oh, I'm hard," he mumbled sleepily. "Apparently I like sleeping like this."

I laughed and Hunter stirred, then woke. He jolted a little as well, until he got his bearings. "Did I fall asleep in here? I didn't mean to, I'm sorry."

I put my thumb to his lips. "I brought you in here. I didn't want you to be alone when you woke this morning."

He relaxed immediately, then smiled. "It wasn't a dream?"

"No, beautiful boy. It wasn't."

Levin traced his fingers through Hunter's hair. "Master gave us a sleep-in this morning. And we're in his bed. We're very lucky."

Hunter sighed, his eyes closed, and he smiled. "So very lucky."

God, the both of them were going to be the end of me. "Hunter, Levin has been so good. Do you think he should get one reward or two?"

Hunter's eyes popped open, and when he saw me smiling, he cottoned on. "Two. Definitely two."

"Hmm," I hummed again. Reaching over Hunter, I lifted Levin's chin. "I promised him a reward, but I think he might deserve two as well. And he woke up with a rather large problem . . ." I pulled the blankets back to reveal Levin's erection. But not just his. Hunter's too. Not to mention my own. "Hunter, would you like to taste Levin?"

He nodded and he licked his lips. "Oh, yes."

I got up and stood facing the bed. They both stared at my cock and I smiled at them. "Hunter, lie down on your back, your head here," I patted the mattress in front of me.

He moved eagerly into place while I took the lube from my bedside.

"Levin," I said, pouring lube onto my shaft and smearing, stroking myself. "You will sixty-nine him, fucking his throat while I fuck you. You can both come as many times as you like."

Levin gasped, real low. His cock twitched and precome beaded at his tip. He moved into position; his face at Hunter's crotch, his cock above Hunter's mouth, his ass at the perfect height for me.

I pressed my slicked cock into Levin at the same time Hunter took him into his mouth. Levin mewled and arched, and only when I was in to the hilt did he take Hunter into his mouth.

They sucked and groaned while I fucked Levin's sweet ass. He came first, and Hunter drank greedily, but I didn't stop. I knew my boy. He had a second in him yet. So I drove into him harder and deeper, making him whine. Hunter came with a garbled cry around Levin's cock, and Levin came again just as I reached my peak.

His body milked me dry, and I fucked every last drop into him. When I was done, they collapsed onto the bed, a jumbled tangle of limbs and smiles. I stood there, watching, still marvelling that both these boys were mine.

"I think we need showers and breakfast," I said. "Then we can talk." I noticed Levin was smirking, still high from his double orgasm. "Levin, can you stand?"

He rolled his shoulders and stretched out, his grin widening. "Oh yes, Master."

I chuckled. "Hunter, are you sore from last night?"

"No, Sir—" He froze.

"Sir?"

There was no bite in my tone, but he shot up, scrambled off the bed to kneel at my feet, his head lowered. "Master. I'm very sorry. It was habit, and a mistake I won't make again."

His overreaction was a little alarming, but I was hardly offended. "Call me Master again. Look at me when you say it."

He looked up at me, his eyes wide and imploring. "Master."

"Open your mouth." He did so, obediently. I fisted my

shaft and fed my cock in between his lips, only to give him a taste before I pulled out. "Say it again."

"Master."

I fed him my cock again, and he sucked harder until I pulled out.

"And again."

"Master."

He sucked me again, and I made him repeat my title, over and over until I was certain he'd never forget it. I pulled out of his delectable mouth, already hard again, but I wanted to save this release. "You won't get it wrong now, will you, sub?"

"No, Master."

"That's better." I took his collar and drew him up to his feet. He came willingly, his eyes dark. He really liked that. "Hmm. I think we might need to leash him," I said to Levin. "Shower, clean him, and have him dressed in his sub jeans, leash his collar, and bring him to breakfast."

Levin smiled and slid off the bed. "Yes, Master."

Hunter smirked as he was led away. *Oh yes, he liked that a lot.*

Twenty minutes later, I was showered and dressed, sitting at the head of the table, trying to ignore the pull and draw in my balls and the way my hard cock felt tight and confined in my leather pants. Both subs walked into the dining room, wearing only their faded jeans and leather collars. Levin walked in first, Hunter following dutifully, being led by a thin leather leash.

Christ. I wanted to come already.

Levin handed the end of the leash to me. "Master."

"Thank you, sub," I murmured. "Was he a good boy?"

"Very good, Master."

"Excellent. Take a seat, both of you, and eat all you can. You're going to need all the energy you can get."

They sat and I let the handle of the leash rest on the table near my hand while we ate. And I wondered if Hunter would like to explore puppy play, or if he simply enjoyed being collared and owned. I looked forward to finding out.

When we'd eaten enough and the table was cleared away, I suggested we go into the study. "There are things we need to discuss openly," I told them both. "I'd like us to talk about what happened last night with Master Colton and Ephraim. It was unexpected and we were all thrown into the deep end." I gave a gentle tug on Hunter's leash. "Unexpected, but very welcome."

He smiled. "Thank you, Master."

Master.

God, I loved how he said that word . . .

"Then Hunter will list his soft and hard limits, and when we're all very clear on what he does and doesn't like, we can spend the afternoon in the playroom." I gave the leash another gentle tug. "Unless you're too sore from last night?"

He frowned and licked his lips. A sign of nervousness. "No, Master."

"What are you nervous for?" I asked. "I require your honesty at all times, particularly when it comes to any levels of discomfort, mental or physical."

He looked up at me through his eyelashes. "I don't want you to deny me, Master," he whispered. "I spent all last week being denied. I was shown and promised what you'd do to me, and now . . ."

"And now what, sub?"

"And now you can do whatever you want to me," he replied, the words whispered and hoarse.

Christ. At this rate I was going to have a permanent erection.

I stood, wanting them both to see the bulge in my pants. I took Hunter's leash, just a few inches from where it was clipped to his collar, and drew him up to his feet. Levin stood as well, perfectly in tune with my intentions. I felt almost like a puppeteer, pulling the strings on one to make both move.

I gave Levin a smile, then pulled on Hunter's leash, bringing him a little closer to me. "We'll discuss your limits and your desires before you say I can do anything I want to you," I warned him.

His pupils dilated, his nostrils flared. He really was turned on by dominance. "Yes, Master."

It took every ounce of self-control not to bend him over the dining table and bury myself inside him. I let out an unsteady breath and handed the leash to Levin. "Take him into the study and wait for me."

Levin took the leash without question, and as they walked out, I caught the corner of Hunter's smile. The cheeky brat was loving it.

I collected more soft and hard limit forms and some pens and found both subs sitting obediently on the sofa. I stood in front of Levin. "Stand."

He stood, and I captured his lips for a kiss—giving him just enough tongue to make him melt. Then I took his earlobe between my lips and whispered, loud enough for them both to hear. "I'm proud of you."

"Thank you, Master."

Then I took Hunter's leash. "Stand."

He did, and I held his leash tight and held his jaw and claimed his mouth. He grunted and it almost buckled my knees. I pulled away and gave his leash a little yank, making his body jerk against me. He made a sound that was half moan, half purr. "I'm so happy you're here with us. Both Levin and I wished you'd want to stay, and you've pleased me greatly. I'm honoured to call you mine."

He slow-blinked, floating dreamily in my praise. "Thank you, Master."

"You both may sit." They obeyed, and I unclipped Hunter's leash. "I'll leash you again soon. Right now, I want you free to ask questions, to speak your mind. Remembering, while I encourage curiosity and questions, I expect manners and respectfulness."

"Yes, Master."

I handed them each a form and pen. "Hunter, this is a soft and hard limit form, for things that are sexual in nature. It works the same as before; write a H next to items that are hard limits, an S for soft limits, and a tick for anything you enjoy. I'd like you to add an asterisk next to anything you'd like to try. There's a lot to take in, so please ask if you're not certain or if you need help with anything. And take as much time as you need. There's no rush. We can readdress any limit at any time you choose."

"Yes, Master."

"Levin, I know you only redid your list last week, but you're a first sub now. You have other options," I said, giving a pointed glance to Hunter. "You can add, change, amend, omit anything you'd like. There are three of us now. Your needs will change, as will your demands, and the demands I make of you. I need to know what you're comfortable with."

He gave a nod. "Yes, Master."

"And perhaps when we're done, we can take our lists into the playroom and talk about the furniture and the toys. We need to be very clear with each other. No shame, no uneasiness, no misunderstandings."

So we spent time on our forms, giving Hunter all the time he needed. He was a little faster this time, being more familiar with the process, and he asked for clarification on a few things, which made me happy.

I didn't want him to agree to anything blindly.

But he was so much happier, more settled than he was even yesterday. I noticed him touching his collar every so often, smiling as he did. And I remembered one of the very first things he'd said to me . . . that he needed to be collared. I could only now see just how much courage it would have taken for him to tell me that—this boy who wouldn't ask for anything—and I'd not listened.

Yes, I'd heard what he'd said, but I'd not *listened*. He told me he felt safer being collared, that he couldn't really concentrate when he wasn't. Sure, I'd put a cuff on his wrist, but it was temporary at best, and it wasn't the same.

I could see now what difference it made. And it wasn't just any collar. It was *my* collar. It was my guidance and my acceptance that made him safe and happy. It was my promise to protect him and give him all he needed to be free.

I found myself smiling as I watched Hunter, and then I noticed Levin smiling at me. I grinned at him, so ridiculously happy in that very moment, and Levin laughed. Hunter looked up at him and Levin threw his arm around Hunter's shoulder and helped him with the last of his form. Watching them be happy, helpful, and curious made my heart soar. I could have spent the entire day observing them.

It was so perfect, I wanted that moment to last forever.

But Hunter soon declared he was finished, and we went through each form. Hunter's hard limits were mostly what I expected. Most notably was the definite hard limit on whips, canes, floggers, and that he'd handwritten the word *belt* and put a big H next to it. I gained a tiny insight into his past but thanked him for his honesty and courage for telling me. Levin held his hand, and Hunter gave him a smile.

Then I went through his likes and desires. He'd ticked a whole lot, which surprised me. And not just one tick; quite a few of them had two ticks. Just last week, I'd have thought he wouldn't have ticked anything. Now he'd given the greenlight to restraints, the fuck bench, the cross, the sling. And he'd ticked almost every toy on the list: plugs, blindfolds, gags, Fleshlights, spreader bars, cock rings, harnesses, leads, chains . . . "You've given two ticks to quite a few, I see," I noted out loud.

Hunter blushed but nodded. "I trust you, Master. And Levin. When you said you wouldn't hurt me, I believed you." Then he bit on his bottom lip. "And I see how you treat Levin, and what you did to me last night, and how you cared for me after . . ."

"Hmmm," I moaned just thinking about it. "Master Colton told me you were a sexual boy who craved domination. And I can see how well you respond to the leash."

His cheeks flushed dark red and he licked his lips. "Yes, Master. I like how it feels. It's as though my mind gets quiet, and my body responds without thinking." He smiled, all shy-like. "That sounds crazy."

"No, it doesn't," Levin said. "Makes sense to me. When Master takes me into the playroom and puts the equipment on the trolley and he tells me what he's going to do, nothing else exists."

Hunter nodded. "Yes, like nothing else exists."

God, I knew that feeling well.

"Hunter, we can explore your leash options," I said.

He smiled at that, and we moved onto Levin's list. His was the same as always, though he'd handwritten some notes, which pretty much outlined everything I'd written down to explain and go over. It confirmed to me how ready he was for this responsibility. I held up my form. "Levin, you read my mind. I have no changes or additions to the list I explained last week, though I do have new rules that I've jotted down." I read, out loud, in point form. "Hunter, you are to follow Levin's lead, his instructions, and do as he asks. Your daily schedules will resume when I return to work. There will be no sexual interaction between you without my being present. Though, when we engage in sexual activities, I may ask you to partake with each other. After last night and this morning, I don't expect either of you will have an issue with that?"

Levin grinned. "No issue from me, Master."

"I have no issue with that, Master," Hunter said, a gleam in his eye. I recalled him saying he'd like it.

"Actually," I added. "You both know I like to watch. I'd like to watch you kiss each other right now."

Levin blinked and Hunter smiled, but they turned to face each other. Levin put his hand to Hunter's jaw and brought their lips together. They deepened the kiss immediately, heads tilted, eyes closed. Lips, tongue, hands, moans.

It was hot as hell.

I was beginning to wonder if I'd survive this.

It took me a moment to be able to speak. "You can stop now. Or I'll end up fucking each of you on the sofa right here."

They broke apart, both smiling, their lips wet and plump. They leaned in toward each other a fraction, and I loved it. I just . . . loved it. Hunter squirmed in his seat and Levin laughed. He knew me well enough to see that I was rattled. Then I remembered the forms in my hand. I had to shake my head of the lust fog. "Our lists . . ."

And so we went through the rest of the lists, Levin's and mine, and we talked about what happened last night at the mansion. The focus on the important issues was a welcome distraction from my carnal needs.

"I was scared at first," Hunter said. "When Ephraim came into the party and asked me to come with him. I thought I'd done something wrong . . . But he told me not to worry. And I'd talked to him earlier about how I was worried that Master Colton would take me away from you, and I told him how I loved being here, but I hated that it wasn't permanent."

The boy needs permanence, Ephraim had said.

"He asked me if Master Colton made me choose, what would I say? And of course I said I'd stay, but I wasn't sure you wanted me," Hunter said, frowning. "He said you had to be impartial, but I didn't want to say yes only for you to say no. I was so confused."

"I know," I replied. "And I'm sorry about that."

Hunter smiled. "Then you told Master Colton you'd make a stand for me. You defended me, against him. And that was . . . well, that was amazing."

"I almost died," Levin whispered, his hand to his chest. "Master, I thought my heart was going to stop when you did that. Actually, when you told him you'd safe word, I thought my heart was going to actually stop."

I laughed, remembering. "Mine too. Someone taught me yesterday that sometimes we need to safe word for those we care for."

Levin beamed. "You stood up for him, and I know you would for me too."

"I would, absolutely, yes. Both of you," I replied with a smile. "Without hesitation."

I looked at their collars and was struck with an idea,

inadvertently given to me by Ephraim and Louella. "How would you feel about me giving you both personalised collars. I know Sanctum collars are standard and respected, but it's not uncommon for new collars to be given in place of the Sanctum issued ones."

Levin smiled as though he liked the idea, but Hunter automatically touched his collar and frowned.

"What is it, Hunter?" I asked.

He swallowed hard. "Well, I just . . . I just got it. And I don't care what kind of collar it is, as long as it's yours, Master. And it might be a Sanctus collar but it's *yours*. I wear *your* collar. You could give me string, and I'd cherish it just the same." He shrugged and kept touching his collar. "I mean, thank you. But I just got it and I don't know if I'm ready to take it off yet. Not even for a second."

Levin leaned into him, smiling at me. "Maybe that's something we can come back to. When he's ready."

Hunter shot him a wide-eyed look. "If you want—"

"No. What we do, we do together," Levin told him. "When we're both ready."

I could have burst with pride. I wanted to give these two everything. I wanted to make them happy, I wanted to fulfil their every whim and desire.

Maybe I could surprise them with personalised collars as a Christmas gift or just because they deserved it. Maybe we could take a trip and select them. Maybe have them designed just for us. But as Levin said, only when they were both ready.

I repeated Levin's words. "What we do, we do together." They both looked to me and I couldn't contain it. I was so happy I felt giddy. "I'm just so proud of you both."

Levin gave me a beautiful smile. Hunter beamed and bit his bottom lip. "So," he hedged. "I know subs get rewards, but do Masters get rewards too? For being the very best?"

I laughed. "I have two. You're both the only rewards I'll ever need. Actually, I'm starting to think you both might be more than I can handle." I sighed happily. "But how about we go up to the playroom and make sure."

I stood and clipped Hunter's leash and his demeanour changed again. His smile became serene and he inhaled deeply. I held out the leash for Levin and he took it graciously. "Thank you, Master."

I led the way, and they followed dutifully. The playroom felt different when we entered. More electric, heightened anticipation. My body knew what was about to happen. I was going to have Hunter again. He didn't have to watch anymore. I could do with him as I pleased.

"Hunter," I said. "Do you have any questions about any of the equipment?"

"No, Master."

"Are you sure?"

"I am sure. I trust you, Master. You respect my limits."

"Is there anything you want to try first?"

He hummed, looking around the room. "All of it, Master."

I noticed the corner of Levin's lips quirked into the start of a smile. I met his eyes. "He's eager, isn't he?"

"Yes, Master," Levin answered, his eyes alight with happiness.

"I think it might take the two of us to satisfy him," I added, and Levin swallowed hard. Then I lifted Hunter's chin with his leash. "How hungry are you for it, sub?"

"Very hungry, Master," he breathed. Goose flesh broke out across his chest, and his nipples hardened.

"What do you want, sub?" I asked, still holding his leash taut.

His reply was swift and perfect. "I want you to make me the best submissive I can be. Take me to that place where I'm free."

Fuck.

I let out a low groan, and they both heard it. I jerked his leash, bringing his lips to mine, and I kissed him for all I was worth. Hard, hot, demanding. I could feel his arousal against mine as I took his mouth.

I pulled away as sharply as I took him, leaving his mouth open, his eyes heavy lidded, and he made his first mistake.

He reached for me.

I grabbed his wrist. "You only get what you're given, sub," I warned him. I lifted his arm above his head. "I think we might restrain these." I turned to Levin. "The sling would be best. He can stay in it longer, and we can take turns."

Levin's lips parted; his nostrils flared. His breath hitched. "Yes, Master."

I handed the leash to him. "Get him ready."

He led Hunter to the sling, and I took a moment to collect my wits, tamping down my desire. This was for Hunter and for Levin. Hunter's first time in my playroom as my sub, and Levin's first time as a first sub, his first time topping with me. It was significant for me too, being my first time with two subs in my playroom, but I wanted to show them how much I appreciated them. I wanted Hunter to take us both, one at either end. We would show him who he answered to, who he pleased . . .

Oh, this was going to be perfect.

My cock was hard—had been since I woke up, even

after fucking Levin, it had never fully softened—and when I palmed myself, my balls ached with the need to come.

My body knew.

I watched as Levin finished securing Hunter's legs in the sling. The boy was naked, on his back, both hands cuffed to the chains above his head, both legs bent and spread, restrained at the thigh to the chains at the front. His cock was hard, lying snug toward his stomach, his balls were spread, his ass exposed.

He was so beautiful.

Levin faced me, shirtless, of course, but still wearing his jeans. He was holding the end of Hunter's leash and he offered it to me. "He's ready."

I looked down at Hunter and stroked his hair, his cheek. "How does it feel, sub?"

"Very good, Master."

"What are your safe words?"

"Yellow to slow, red to stop."

"Good boy." I gave his leash a gentle tug and his cock jerked on his belly. "Levin's going to offer you his cock and I want you to suck it."

He licked his lips, his voice breathy. "Yes, Master."

I stepped back and handed the leash back to Levin. "His mouth is yours. Do with it what you want. Keep your jeans on," I said as I reached for his fly. I popped the button and unzipped him, then pulled his erection out and stroked him. "The sub is hungry. Feed him."

I watched as Levin moved to stand at Hunter's face. With one hand holding the leash, he slid his cock into Hunter's eager mouth. Hunter's perfect lips slid around Levin's shaft as he went deep, and Levin groaned.

"That's so hot," I whispered, and my own erection reminded me of my neglect.

I went to Hunter's ass and massaged his inner thighs, pulled on his balls, jerked his cock. The boy moaned like a whore. Like *my* whore, *our* whore, and I loved it. I lubed him and prepped him with no more than a finger. I wanted him to feel my cock, not a toy, not a plug.

Keeping the button on my leather pants done up, I unzipped and freed my cock. I slicked myself with lube and pressed against his hole. Levin pulled out of Hunter's mouth and tugged on the leash, forcing Hunter's head up a little. "Look at him when he enters you."

Oh, hell yes.

Levin was getting *all* the rewards.

I pushed into Hunter in one thrust. Hard, rough, and beautiful. He pulled on his restraints, he tried to arch, to buck, to move, but he was completely tied. He cried out and I held his hips, keeping him impaled on me, and his sounds soon became a groan. "Good boy. Breathe through it." He sucked back a breath and I felt his body begin to relax. "Yeah, just like that."

Then I slowly began to pull back, and I pushed in again. "Levin, feed him more cock," I said. "He needs to know who he belongs to."

Levin put a hand around the back of Hunter's head as he fucked his mouth. The sling moved between us, allowing Hunter's body to take us both in a rhythm of lust and pleasure. And take us, he did. But I could see Levin was getting close; his tempo changed, his grunts became sharper. But I didn't want it to be over yet. So I pulled out, nice and slow, missing the tight warmth immediately.

"Levin, your turn," I ordered. "Bury your cock in his ass."

Levin was quick to comply, gripping Hunter's hips and lining his cock up to his hole, but I stopped him just before he penetrated him. "But you won't come inside him. His ass is mine, for now. The only come he'll know in his ass right now is mine." I pulled Levin's chin up for a kiss. "But I want Hunter to know he answers to you, and I want you to know how tight he is."

Levin's smile died as he pushed inside Hunter. His mouth fell open, his eyes rolled back, and they both moaned. I watched Levin's cock slide in and out—one of my favourite sights—but I knew Levin would never disobey me. He wouldn't come until I told him to.

I went to Hunter's face and kissed him. He opened his mouth wide, granting me all the access I needed, and when I slowed the kiss, he sucked on my tongue. I broke the kiss and gently pulled on his leash. "Do you like him inside you?"

"Yes, Master," he panted. The sling moved with every thrust, and strain creased Levin's brow. He was determined to obey me.

Smiling, I held the base of my cock and tapped Hunter's lips. "Open wide and show me how good you are."

So he did.

And Christ, he was such a talented sub. I could have so easily just fucked his throat until I came, but I would leave that for Levin. I wanted his ass.

I pulled out and gave Hunter's cheek a gentle tap. "Good boy. But you don't get to drink me right now." I gave Levin a nod, and he pulled out too, with a sharp sound of relief. His cock was swollen and flushed, desperate for relief. "Let him drink you."

Levin waited until I was back inside Hunter before he slid back inside Hunter's mouth. Just one long thrust, Levin let his head fall back with a loud cry, his stomach muscles twitched, and Hunter moaned as he drank every drop.

It was so fucking hot.

I drove in harder and fisted Hunter's cock, and he began to grunt and groan with every thrust. His muscles grew tight and he trembled, his cock pulsed. "Levin, it's your turn. Suck his load out of him."

Levin quickly obliged, taking Hunter's erection into his mouth, inside his throat, and I held the boy's hips hard, buried to the hilt. He twitched and cried out, his body strung tight. "Come, Hunter," I ordered.

And he did.

His body clamped around me and he gave a strangled scream as Levin swallowed around him. I wanted to claim this boy again and again. I wanted to come inside him forever so he would know for always who owned him.

My orgasm drew up from the soles of my feet and from my skull down my spine, and I emptied myself inside him.

It was intense and glorious, yet somehow still not enough.

I pulled out, my cock still hard. "Help me untie him," I said, and Levin quickly obliged. We got him to stand; he was smiley and floppy, completely spent. "To the bed." Levin helped me walk him to the bed, and Hunter lay down, half slumping on his side. I took the ramp cushion and put it beside him. "I'm not done with you yet, sub." Kneeling on the bed, I manoeuvred Hunter around like he was a ragdoll. I put the cushion under his hips so he was almost kneeling over it. I bent him over it, pushed his head down, stretched his arms to the mattress above his head, and ploughed back into him.

This was what I wanted. I wanted to fuck him forever. I was certain I wouldn't ever tire of him. And after I put a second load into him, Levin and I showered him. I made them eat lunch and allowed them to nap on the sofa, and after an early dinner, I fucked them both again.

The second day they were to go back to their routines, and at six thirty, when I went downstairs for breakfast, they were on their knees waiting. I'd worried they'd be sore, Hunter especially. But no. He craved it.

He loved the leash and responded to it like a dream. Levin prided himself on teaching Hunter, and I adored watching them together. After another long session on the bench this time, we bathed Hunter and the three of us climbed into my bed.

They cuddled, and when I asked them to kiss each other, they did. It was soft and tender, with their eyes closed and gentle hands holding, caressing. It was sweet, and it was hot as hell.

The next day was much the same. We were learning more about each other, reading small cues, learning our small idiosyncrasies, and helping Hunter adjust to his new life, his new role. He'd never smiled so much, and he laughed freely. It was a beautiful, beautiful sound. He read some chapters of a book and he did some writing skills, he watched some movies—preferring comedies and romances—he helped in the garden and he helped in the kitchen. Just three days in and he was already a different boy. He held his chin a little higher, his shoulders were back. He would touch his collar every so often, and I'd catch him smiling.

It was a magical thing.

Levin was learning his new role too, and Hunter would look to him, his eyes wide and focused, following his every move, his every command. Then he'd look at me with such hunger it took my breath away.

On day four, I had them both wear their new leather boots and used the sewn in O-rings, shackling them both to the pommel horse, and took turns giving them rewards. More fucking, more restraining, more discipline. And that night in my bed, they both kissed me.

I was fairly certain they'd be the death of me, and I wondered if having a heart too full could be fatal.

"I THINK I can tell by the look on your face that the last ten days have been good to you," Master Colton said. He'd come to visit, as he'd said he would. He'd given us some time to settle in, and when he'd called to arrange a meeting, I asked him to bring something with him.

"They've been very good to me," I said. We settled into the patio chairs in the sun by the pool. Levin was giving Hunter a swimming lesson, which was more a lesson in buoyancy and managing breathing techniques, but still fun to watch. Levin was a fabulous teacher, Hunter a wonderful student. Levin laughed again, and I knew Hunter had said something funny. "Hunter has settled in better than expected. Would you believe the boy you gave me a few weeks ago is actually a cheeky brat with a sense of humour? We're beginning to see the real him. Oh, and he craves discipline, and he has a voracious libido."

Master Colton chuckled. "Which would probably explain your smile. And how's Levin handled the transition?"

"Flawlessly. He was born to be a first sub. He leads, he teaches, he corrects, he rebukes any slight missteps," I added with a smile, remembering how Hunter had tried to refuse the ball-gag, so Levin had gagged him with his cock instead. "Which I'm certain Hunter thinks is a reward."

Master Colton laughed. "Reminds me of you when you were my sub."

I snorted. "Which one? I'm certain I've been both."

Another peal of laughter erupted from the pool, this time from Hunter, and I smiled at the sound. Master Colton watched me for a while—I could feel his eyes on me—and when I glanced his way, he looked away to the mountains. "I've been thinking about what you said the other night," he said before meeting my eyes again. "About how we were wrong."

I gave a nod. "I apologise again for how I spoke to you."

"But not for what you said," he noted.

I smiled. "No."

"You were right though." He frowned. "I've told Valente and Jürg that we need a review and an overhaul. Traditions are wonderful, but if we value our traditions more than our subs, then we've failed. And I failed Hunter. Twice. The first time pairing him with that piece of shit Lazzaro; the second time giving him to you and assuming I knew what the boy needed when I didn't. He wasn't adequately prepared or informed. I assumed too much, and that could have been catastrophic. If I'd placed him with any other Dom but you, it probably would have been."

I nodded. "True. He craves discipline and dominance, yes. But he needed kindness too. He didn't know that, and if you'd have asked him a month ago, he would have said he didn't, but I knew. A lot of people in his life have abused his trust. So the week he was here and I wasn't to have him sexually was hard on him, yes. But I think it cemented his trust in me. I promised not to touch him or sway his decision, and as much as he didn't like it, at the end of the day, I kept my promise. He knows now, if I say I won't ever hurt him, he can trust that. And he does. He's a different boy."

"So my decision wasn't a total failure?" he asked.

"Well . . ." I shrugged before giving him a smile. "Hunter will be okay. He started therapy this week, which is fifteen years overdue. But Levin and I go as well. I want Hunter to know there's no shame in it, and I figure given there's three of us now, we could use a sounding board."

"And Christa tells me she met him at the salon," Colton prompted.

"Yes. Hunter mentioned wanting to learn hairdressing, so I made some phone calls. Hunter really liked her and Tanja. It helps that Tanja's a sub in the Sanctus. It's safer and more familiar for him than a non-dominion salon would be. He doesn't need to explain his personal life because she understands."

"Christa said he was sweet and very eager to learn."

I grinned. "That's him. Sweet and eager."

Master Colton eyed me a for moment, then looked to the white rectangular box he'd brought with him. "I hope this is the one you wanted."

I opened the box and smiled at the contents. "Looks right." It was a special-order bulldog harness, and I knew Master Colton would only have to make one phone call and it would be here overnight. It was made of foam and black spandex with an upper layer of mesh padding, sturdy but soft. There were metal O-rings for different clips, and it could be worn different ways, depending on the wearer's needs and comfort levels. "We've been experimenting with Hunter's collar and leash. He loves it. Not into puppy play or roleplaying, just give him a collar and a leash and he's in heaven. He loved the idea of a harness, but the leather straps made him uneasy, and it aggravated his scars. But this . . . ?" I felt the softness and flex of the foam and spandex. "This should be perfect."

Master Colton smiled. "Good."

I put the harness back in the box and turned to the pool. "Boys! We have company."

Two long and lean figures climbed out of the pool, dripping wet and very naked. They collected their towels, and Hunter froze for a second when he saw who it was I was sitting with. Master Colton didn't miss it either.

Levin dried himself a little and wrapped the towel around his waist, and Hunter dried himself, kind of, but carried his towel, his cock hanging gloriously free. "Master Colton," Levin said first, with a slight bow of his head.

Hunter did the same. "Master Colton."

"Levin," Master Colton replied with a smile. "And Hunter, you look well," he said, trying not to smile. "I can see your being here agrees with you."

"Very much, Master," he replied. "I've never been happier."

I held the box. "Hunter, you have a present."

His eyes went wide. "I do?"

"Yes." I nodded to his hand holding the towel. "How about you wrap that towel around your waist."

He made a show of fixing the towel behind him, leaving the front open for as long as possible, until he tied it off at his side. Cheeky brat.

I held the box up. "Open it."

He lifted the lid and took the harness out. "Oh, it's soft," he whispered. Then he shot me a look. "This is for me?"

I nodded. "Yes. If it's not comfortable, we can keep looking." I turned to Levin. "Please take him inside. Dry him properly and perhaps he should wear some jeans."

Levin smiled. "Yes, Master."

They disappeared, and I knew Master Colton was watching me again. I rolled my eyes. "Yes, Hunter's being a brat. I know full well he's acting up because he thinks I'll put the posture collar on him, with an adjoining cockstrap, and make him kneel in the playroom for an hour. Which he adores, mind you. Or maybe I'll shackle him to the cross so Levin and I can take turns fucking him. Which he also adores." I gave him a wink. "I'm running out of training ideas."

Master Colton smirked. "Have you tried spanking?"

I sighed. "I'm hesitant to try impact play," I replied quietly. "I'm allowing him to find his feet and test his boundaries. I'm not going soft on the boy, if that's what you're thinking."

"So which of the aforementioned punishments will you give him for his brazen display of cock?"

"Probably both. I'll have him postured and kneeling for a bit to get him in the right headspace. Then shackle him to the bench or the cross. As I said, he's got one helluva libido. Loves cock, loves my come. Wants it when he wakes up, for breakfast, lunch, and dinner. And dessert. And before he goes to sleep."

Master Colton laughed. "God, he *is* perfect for you."

I chuckled at that, just as Levin and Hunter came back outside. Both wearing their faded jeans and huge smiles. And Hunter was wearing the harness, the big O-ring at his sternum, and I knew he loved it from the dreamy gaze to his eyes.

"Wow," I murmured, taking in how Hunter looked, but also how he held himself. "How does it feel?"

"Oh Master, it feels wonderful." He ran his hands over the straps at his chest. "It's so soft." He turned around so we could see the back and how the straps sat across the tops of his shoulder blades. "Do you like it, Master?"

"Very much," I answered. I knew Master Colton would

have seen nothing but the scars, especially in the daylight. But all I saw was a beautiful boy whose smile outshone the sun. I beckoned him closer with my finger and hooked it through the O-ring at the centre of his chest and pulled him in close. "You're so fucking beautiful," I murmured. Then I kissed him and Hunter responded in kind. It was a quick and dirty kiss; a taste of what was to come.

I let go of his harness and stood, pulling Levin in by his collar and kissed him too, right there in front of Master Colton. I slowed the kiss, sucking on his bottom lip before resting my forehead on his. I cradled his face and sighed. It wasn't quick or dirty with Levin. What we had was more than that.

The boys went back inside, and I sat back down and sighed. "How do you handle three subs?" I asked. "Two is crazy enough, I can't even imagine three, and I don't ever want another, just so you know."

When Master Colton didn't answer, I looked over at him to find him staring at me. "Christ, Sig."

"What?"

"That," he replied, nodding toward where Levin had gone. "You know, since I got here, I've been trying to place what it is that's different about you."

"Different . . . ?"

He nodded. "You're in love with them."

I barked out a laugh, ready to agree, when I realised he wasn't smiling. "Is that wrong?"

He looked genuinely torn. "I don't know . . . It's not wrong. It's just not common, I guess. We hold great affection for our subs, and we're fond of them, of course. But love?" He frowned. I realised he wasn't being critical; he was cautious and curious. "I don't know if I'd call it love. It changes the dynamics, does it not? Does it cloud your dominance? Do you expect less submission and dedication because you're sympathetic to their other needs?"

"What I feel for them doesn't cloud my dominance or change dynamics. It makes me a better Dom." I leaned forward, holding his gaze. "It makes me a better Dom for my boys. I know them, what they need, and how they need it. I'm a soft Dom, and everyone knows that. I know what people say, Master Colton. I'm not stupid. But the hard-core lifestyle, the sadism and masochism isn't for me or my subs. But your subs need that next level. You give them exactly what they need, and they give you textbook submission. That's why you're one of the Grand Masters of the Sanctus, Master Colton. Just because we have different techniques and different needs doesn't mean one is wrong."

He considered this for a moment. "But love?"

"Have you honestly never considered what you do for your subs, what you embody for them, is a kind of love? Come on, I've seen how you look at Stefan. You never looked at me that way."

"Well," he replied with a strange expression on his face. "I'm not sure . . . I . . ." He scrubbed his hand over his face, then he shot a look at me. "Thanks, Sig. Now I have that on my mind."

I chuckled. "Embrace it. It makes the fucking better," I said, and he laughed at that. "It's not a bad thing. Believe me. I love both of my boys. When I was faced with the idea of losing Levin, I realised, a little belatedly but very clearly, that Levin is the love of my life. But Hunter came along, and I realised I can love them both equally."

A quiet gasp carried from behind me, and I turned to see Levin standing there. He'd heard what I just said . . .

His wide eyes went to the ground, and he took a step

back. "Apologies Master," he whispered. "I'll come back. I didn't mean to interrupt—"

I got to my feet. "Levin, stop."

He stopped but kept his head down.

Master Colton stood up and clapped my shoulder. He was grinning. "I'll see myself out, Sig. We'll have coffee next week," he said, walking back into the house.

Levin never looked up, and I had a sinking feeling he didn't take my admission of love as good news.

"Levin, please look at me."

He did, and his eyes were teary. *Oh no, no, no . . .* I took his hand and led him inside but only made it as far as the dining room. I faced him and cupped his jaw. "Levin," I said gently. "I'm sorry you heard me say it like that."

A tear slipped down his cheek just as Hunter walked in. His eyes went wide, and he quickly closed the space between us, his hand on Levin's back, his gaze on me. "What happened? Did Master Colton say something?"

I shook my head. "No, I did. Hunter, perhaps Levin and I could have a moment."

He took a step back, but Levin stopped him. "No, Master, he should stay. No secrets, remember?"

That was true. I had said that.

"What did you say, Master? Why is Levin crying?" Hunter asked, his frown deep, and his eyes were sad.

"Is it true?" Levin asked. "What you said to him?"

I nodded. "Yes."

Levin's eyes welled with fresh tears.

"It doesn't have to change anything between us," I tried. "And I most certainly don't expect anything in return. I will still be your Dom. Your place here remains unchanged for as long as you want it to. Levin, I can apologise for how you found out, but I won't apologise for admitting it, and I won't take it back." I wiped another of his tears away with my thumb. "I do love you, Levin. I've been *in* love with you since day one. You've always been special to me and different to any other sub. It just took the idea of losing you to make me realise what it was. What I feel in here"—I put my hand to my heart—"wasn't expected, but oh my God, it's amazing."

Levin cried some more, putting his hands to his face, and I couldn't help it. I needed to comfort him. So, I pulled him into my arms, and he clung to me and sobbed.

"Master," Hunter said, teary as well. "I don't understand."

"He said he loves me," Levin mumbled into my shirt.

Hunter's eyes went from Levin to me. "Isn't that a good thing? Why are you crying?" he asked Levin, then he looked to me. "Why is he crying? I don't like it."

That was only something Levin could answer. Maybe me admitting my love wasn't a good thing for him. Maybe it confused him and now he was worried about how it would affect our house.

"It's a good thing, Hunter," Levin mumbled. "It's a great thing. I just . . ."

I pulled back and lifted his face so I could see his eyes. "You just what?"

"I just never expected it," he whispered. "I didn't think it was something that happened in our world . . ." He shrugged and got all teary again. "I mean, I'm a submissive and you're my Dom. But you're more than that. You're my entire world, the centre of my universe. I love you too, Sig. I always have."

Sig.

He called me by my name.

I captured his lips in a consuming kiss and he held my

face. His hands weren't by his side or behind his back; they were on my face and in my hair.

It was divine.

As our kiss slowed, Hunter took a step back, but Levin grabbed him by his harness. "Stay right here," Levin said. "He said he loves you too."

Hunter's gaze shot to mine. "Me?"

I pulled him into our hug and kissed him as well. "Yes, you. Hunter, you being here didn't change us," I whispered. "You made us better, stronger."

Levin looked into my eyes, searching, imploring. I don't know what he was looking for, but his smile told me he found it. "Yes, he does."

With a finger to each of their chins, I brought them in for a soft three-way kiss. "You both make me what I am," I admitted. "I am only a great Dom because I have two great subs. I adore you both, I respect you both." I made eye contact with each of them. "I love you both."

Hunter looked a little sad. "What is it, sub?" I asked.

"Well, I . . . I'm not sure I know what love is," he whispered. "I see you two, and I can see the way you are with each other. I can see what love is. But I . . . I'm not sure I know . . . what if I don't . . . what if I'm too messed up?"

Levin put his hand to Hunter's chest, over his heart. "You're not messed up. You just need some patience and maybe two men to show you."

"Hunter," I murmured, running my hand through his hair, holding his face. "You're not messed up or broken. I'm falling in love with you because you're everything we need. You deserve to be loved. I see who you are and what you've been through, and it lets us know how to love you the right way." The truth was, this boy needed to learn how to love himself before he could love anyone else. "Be patient and let us show you how much you're loved before you worry about how you feel. No pressure, just enjoy it."

Hunter nodded, a little teary. "When I'm with you both, I get nervous butterflies, which is kind of crazy," he whispered.

Levin pressed his forehead to the side of Hunter's head. "Does your heart skip a beat?"

Hunter's eyes met mine, and he nodded. "It really does."

Levin pulled him in for a kiss. "We'll teach you what love is. Every day."

I gave Levin a squeeze and pecked Hunter's lips. "We will."

Hunter nodded. "I'd really like that. I feel so . . . blessed that I ended up here. I never knew how good life could be."

Levin pulled him in tight against us and I took a deep breath. "I love you both," I murmured again. It felt strange to say it out loud, but it felt so incredibly right.

"While we're being all open and honest," Hunter said, his lip pulling downward. "Does love change anything? I mean, just so I'm clear and understand, you're both still going to fuck me, right?"

Levin burst out laughing, but he looked to me for an answer. "Absolutely. These collars," I replied, pulling on both O-rings at their throats, "still mean you belong to me. You will serve me, and I will give you both everything you deserve and desire. Just know that now, when I say I will honour you both with my mind, heart, and soul, it's with my whole heart."

Levin sighed happily and snuggled into me, and Hunter sighed dramatically. "Oh, thank God."

I laughed and brought him into our embrace again. I loved this side of him, the true side of him that he only now felt safe to show us snippets of. "And don't think I've forgotten about your blatant cock display in front of Master Colton."

Hunter laughed, and Levin smiled into my neck.

I murmured into Levin's ear, loud enough for Hunter to hear as well. "How about you take this brat upstairs and bury your cock inside him. Leave his harness on. I want to watch you come in his ass for the first time."

Levin groaned and looked up at me with dark eyes. "I love you, Master," he whispered. Then, holding Hunter's harness, he led him upstairs. Hunter gave me a cheeky smile as he was led away. I smiled after them, so happy and content, so in love. I stood there, with a stupid grin on my face, feeling giddy and alive, for a full ten seconds before I snapped out of it. I laughed at myself, then took the stairs two at a time.

EPILOGUE

FIVE YEARS LATER

"ARE YOU READY?" Ephraim asked.

I stood with him in front of our closest friends, in the gardens of the Casa di Salvezza. I wore a tuxedo, tailor made, and tried not to let my emotions get the better of me. I let out a nervous breath. "Very ready."

"Good," Ephraim replied. "Because here they come."

I would have thought they couldn't be more beautiful when they were naked, restrained, suspended . . . but seeing them in suits was a different level of breathtaking.

Levin wore a grey three-piece suit, his shirt was white, his tie silver. His dark hair was short and impeccably neat. He looked sharp and expensive, all class.

Hunter wore a navy-blue suit, a white shirt, no tie. Because oh no, he didn't wear a waistcoat under his jacket as Levin did. Hunter wore his favourite harness. It made me smile. *Still a cheeky brat.* His hair was a little longer now, coiffed up into some artful design he'd perfected years ago.

I loved that their personalities shone through. Levin had completed his studies and was now an official member of the Sanctus's legal team. Hunter had worked hard at his reading and writing, and he'd qualified as a hairdresser, working with Tanja most days and loving every minute. Both of them thrived.

Their smiles as they walked to me shone even brighter.

They stood either side of me, and the three of us faced Ephraim together. A lot had changed at the Sanctus in the last five years. Master Colton had been serious when he'd said he would implement changes for the better. Because Levin, Hunter, and I were about to make our binding ceremony legal.

Ephraim was to officiate the ceremony. He'd become qualified a few years earlier, and I'd told him if I couldn't have him as my best man—because Levin and Hunter and I had decided we were all the best men we'd need—then Ephraim could damn well marry us. Only we wouldn't be signing a marriage certificate. It was a contract, drafted by Levin himself, to bind the three of us together. Not a 'marriage' by law, given there were three of us, but a binding contract to afford us all the legalities of one. Levin had worked out the contractual details, but the commitment ceremony was a wedding to me. In my eyes, and in my heart, Levin and Hunter would be my husbands.

The thing for subs and Doms was that the collars and the collar ceremonies would always mean more than a wedding contract. But like Ephraim had said to me five years ago, something I couldn't get out of my mind, a collar ceremony held no weight in a court of law. And I wanted to be bound to these two boys in every possible way.

When I'd first mentioned it, they hadn't really understood. I'd told them it would provide an added layer of security, and it wasn't that I didn't trust the Sanctus. I knew they wouldn't try and separate us. I thought Levin and Hunter might have longed for another level of permanence, but no, they trusted me to never leave them. I realised it was I who needed the security. *I* needed it. Once I'd explained that and how no ring on my finger would ever replace the collars around their necks, they wholeheartedly agreed.

So here we stood, ready to make it official.

"We are gathered here today," Ephraim began. "To witness the legal joining of these three men. Already bound to each other in accordance with the law of the Sanctus Infinitus Redemptio, they will now be bound by the law of the land on which we stand. What is joined together by heart and soul, let no one, or lawyer, separate."

Both Hunter and Levin squeezed my hands, and Ephraim spoke some more, but I was lost to my boys. Their hands in mine, their shoulders touching mine, my collars underneath their shirts. Nothing else existed but them.

"A marriage doesn't have to be conventional," Ephraim continued. "It needs to be tailored to the needs of those in that marriage."

"I'm all for conventional," Hunter said, a wicked smile to his eyes. "I'm wearing something blue *and* something borrowed. And I have a garter belt attached to my silk stockings and suspenders underneath this suit, so if you'd like to hurry it up . . ."

Everyone laughed, and Hunter leaned into me, smiling all smug and wonderful. He really had come into his own these last few years. With therapy and the proper submission and domination exchange, he was a far cry from the broken boy who had been handed to me. He was funny, flirty, and still overtly, predominantly sexual. I doubted that would change, I hoped that would never change.

"Okay, I won't keep you," Ephraim said with a laugh. "Do you have the ring?"

"We do," Levin said, producing a single silver ring from

his pocket. It was wider than most rings, but they'd decided they would each choose a simple wedding band and they would have them melted down and made it one beautifully hand-crafted ring. It was a perfect solution, a perfect symbol. Two rings, beautiful on their own, but even better combined.

Hunter and Levin stood in front of me. Hunter took my left hand and Levin slipped the band on my ring finger, and it was so profound. The weight of it, the significance. They each wore my collar, a symbol of devotion and commitment, and now I wore theirs. My heart was so full, so very content.

Then they did something I hadn't expected, something we hadn't planned, but they'd obviously concocted between themselves.

They went to their knees in front of me, hands clasped behind their backs, their heads bowed. Levin looked up first. "They can call you my husband or they can call you Doctor Bruckner or Sig." He smiled. "And I might call you Sig if it's warranted . . ."

I gave our audience a smile. "It's true. He does." They chuckled. Louella wiped away a happy tear.

Levin took my hand and kissed my knuckles, my wedding ring. "But you will always be Master to me. You own me in every sense of the word. I belong to you, now and forever. I am honoured and humbled that you would wear our ring."

Then Hunter looked up, his blue eyes glassy and full of love. "You saved me. You both did," he said, giving Levin a teary smile. "You taught me love; what it means to love someone else and what it means to love myself. You showed me how a real Dominant acts and what true submission means. I wear your collar with pride, Master. It grounds me and enables me to fly, and belonging to you *both* completes me."

I kissed Levin first, then Hunter. I was choked up, too overwhelmed with emotion and love to respond. They both stood so we could embrace and kiss and hold each other tight. As we would, always.

Three men, three roles, three hearts, three needs, three desires. Three times the emotion, three times the dedication, three times the fun.

One love.

The End

ABOUT THE AUTHOR

N.R. Walker is an Australian author, who loves her genre of gay romance. She loves writing and spends far too much time doing it, but wouldn't have it any other way.

She is many things: a mother, a wife, a sister, a writer. She has pretty, pretty boys who live in her head, who don't let her sleep at night unless she gives them life with words.

She likes it when they do dirty, dirty things... but likes it even more when they fall in love.

She used to think having people in her head talking to her was weird, until one day she happened across other writers who told her it was normal.

She's been writing ever since...

ALSO BY N.R. WALKER

Blind Faith

Through These Eyes (Blind Faith #2)

Blindside: Mark's Story (Blind Faith #3)

Ten in the Bin

Point of No Return – Turning Point #1

Breaking Point – Turning Point #2

Starting Point – Turning Point #3

Element of Retrofit – Thomas Elkin Series #1

Clarity of Lines – Thomas Elkin Series #2

Sense of Place – Thomas Elkin Series #3

Taxes and TARDIS

Three's Company

Red Dirt Heart

Red Dirt Heart 2

Red Dirt Heart 3

Red Dirt Heart 4

Red Dirt Christmas

Cronin's Key

Cronin's Key II

Cronin's Key III

Cronin's Key IV - Kennard's Story

Exchange of Hearts

Cronin's Key III

Red Dirt Heart

Red Dirt Heart 2

Red Dirt Heart 3

Red Dirt Heart 4

The Weight Of It All

Switched

Point of No Return

Breaking Point

Starting Point

Spencer Cohen Book One

Spencer Cohen Book Two

Spencer Cohen Book Three

Yanni's Story

On Davis Row

Evolved

Elements of Retrofit

Clarity of Lines

Sense of Place

Blind Faith

Through These Eyes

Blindside

Finders Keepers

Free Reads:

Sixty Five Hours

Learning to Feel

His Grandfather's Watch (And The Story of Billy and Hale)

The Twelfth of Never (Blind Faith 3.5)

Twelve Days of Christmas (Sixty Five Hours Christmas)

Best of Both Worlds

Translated Titles:

Fiducia Cieca (Italian translation of Blind Faith)

Attraverso Questi Occhi (Italian translation of Through These Eyes)

Preso alla Sprovvista (Italian translation of Blindside)

Il giorno del Mai (Italian translation of Blind Faith 3.5)

Cuore di Terra Rossa (Italian translation of Red Dirt Heart)

Cuore di Terra Rossa 2 (Italian translation of Red Dirt Heart 2)

Cuore di Terra Rossa 3 (Italian translation of Red Dirt Heart 3)

Cuore di Terra Rossa 4 (Italian translation of Red Dirt Heart 4)

Natale di terra rossa (Red dirt Christmas)

Intervento di Retrofit (Italian translation of Elements of Retrofit)

A Chiare Linee (Italian translation of Clarity of Lines)

Spencer Cohen 1 Serie: Spencer Cohen

Spencer Cohen 2 Serie: Spencer Cohen

Spencer Cohen 3 Serie: Spencer Cohen

Punto di non Ritorno (Italian translation of *Point of No Return*)

Punto di Rottura (Italian translation of *Breaking Point*)

Confiance Aveugle (French translation of *Blind Faith*)

A travers ces yeux: Confiance Aveugle 2 (French translation of *Through These Eyes*)

Aveugle: Confiance Aveugle 3 (French translation of *Blindside*)

À Jamais (French translation of *Blind Faith 3.5*)

Cronin's Key (French translation)

Cronin's Key II (French translation)

Au Coeur de Sutton Station (French translation of *Red Dirt Heart*)

Partir ou rester (French translation of *Red Dirt Heart 2*)

Faire Face (French translation of *Red Dirt Heart 3*)

Trouver sa Place (French translation of *Red Dirt Heart 4*)

Rote Erde (German translation of *Red Dirt Heart*)

Rote Erde 2 (German translation of *Red Dirt Heart 2*)

Sixty Five Hours (Thai translation)

Finders Keepers (Thai translation)

Thank you for Reading

SIR

N.R. WALKER